Sitting at the Wrong Dinner Table

A Novel

Stephen Nauta

Sitting at the Wrong Dinner Table

Published by

www.splatteredinkpress.com

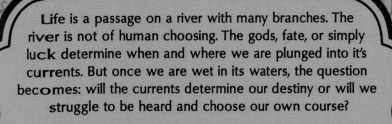

Life is a passage on a river with many branches. The river is not of human choosing. The gods, fate, or simply luck determine when and where we are plunged into it's currents. But once we are wet in its waters, the question becomes: will the currents determine our destiny or will we struggle to be heard and choose our own course?

For the waters hear our cries and might relent. Others see our struggles and may choose to join us. But more important, we hear our own voice and our deepest yearnings become clear to us and move us to fight the currents and choose a course of our own making.

- Stephen Nauta

To Janice Esh, my wife and life partner whose wit, insight, personality, and extensive knowledge of the romantic use of two tracks in rural Michigan so pervade the narrative of this novel that her name should be placed next to mine on the front of this book.

Chapter 1

Fran's Coming Out

Fran stood her ground with the cemetery's caretaker, refusing to change her mind. She insisted on her right to sell the five extra plots, even if it would disrupt the site plan Richard had designed for his internment.

"I don't think you've given this enough thought, Mrs. Vanderhuis. Your husband was very specific and wanted to be buried in this family plot; with his wife and children. Don't you see? He loved you a great deal and wanted to spend eternity with you."

I wouldn't be caught dead in a grave next to him for eternity. "My children aren't interested in being buried here. They have lives of their own in places they find far more meaningful. Besides, he only has one wife and three children. Why did he think we needed an extra grave?"

The caretaker placed his thumbs under the straps of the overalls he wore over a dirty wool sweater, pulling the straps forward in an effort to make it clear he was about to expound on his knowledge. "He told me he had three sons and one daughter."

"No, just three boys. Unless he was referring to Sammy, but she isn't his daughter and I can't imagine he thought she would be buried with him."

He looked up and to the side, squinting one eye. "Did you have a miscarriage when you were young? Sometimes..." He stopped when he saw Fran's face contort in an effort to squeeze her tears back into her tear ducts. He looked away to give her privacy. As he did he saw the small gravestone next to the large headstone. It read, Emily Vanderhuis, 1986, God's Angel.

"Are you feeling alright, Mrs. Vanderhuis? You look a bit pale. Why don't you go sit in your warm car while I get you a bottle of water? It will help you get your thoughts together."

"My thoughts are together and I'm not pale, I'm frustrated you won't tell me how to go about selling the five extra plots."

He placed his hands on both sides of his head, resting them on the wool cap covering his baldness. He shook his head back and forth in slow motion, attempting to rid himself of the aggravation Fran was causing him, so he could think.

After a few seconds of silence, he took her by the arm and guided her toward the car, opening the door on the passenger's side and closing it after she had accommodated herself. He tapped on the window. "I'll be right back, Mrs. Vanderhuis. Just sit tight."

As he rushed toward his office she said, "This isn't necessary. All I want is for you to tell me how I can..." He didn't stick around to hear what she had to say.

Twenty minutes later he returned with no water in hand. She rolled down the window to express her frustration, but was distracted when two cars pulled up behind her. She looked in the side mirror and saw the funeral director step out of the first car. He was a short man. So short that not even the black suit he wore in perpetuity could help slim and lengthen his body. Behind him she spotted Reverend Vermin, her pastor. His tall lean body covered in black slacks and a black shirt with a white clergy collar put him in stark contrast with his cohort. *He's called in the cavalry to deal with the crazy lady.*

They strolled shoulder to shoulder toward the waiting caretaker. "Mutt, Jeff, and farmer Dale," she mumbled. They began to talk about her so she rolled the window up and sat back in the seat, resigned to the fact that what she thought would be an easy errand was about to turn into a full-fledged drama. She turned on the radio, knowing what the men were saying would make her angrier. The church music she was enjoying on her way to the cemetery was soothing, but soothing wasn't what her mood was craving. Fran turned the dial and stumbled onto a classic rock station. She cranked up the volume until all three men turned their gazes toward her, wrinkling their foreheads as they pulled their heads back. The music of Nazareth blared from the old Cadillac's speaker. The words to the song rang out into the cemetery. "Now your messing with a…a son of a bitch…your messing with a son of a bitch."

She turned off the radio, shocked by the lyrics, and decided to be compliant until she could regain her composure.

"You have to do something, Vermin," the caretaker said. "She's talking crazy, saying she wants me to cut the tombstone in half to get her name off of it."

"Was she serious?" the funeral director asked.

"Hell if I know, but she is serious about selling off the other five plots. Says she and the kids don't want to be buried here, next to him. What kind of a woman kicks her husband like that when he is down? I think she's gone loony."

"What do you want us to do?" Reverend Vermin asked.

"I don't know. Do whatever hocus pocus you ministers do in cases like these. I don't care. I just want her off my back," the caretaker said.

The Reverend looked at the funeral director and sighed. "Come on, we'll tag team this one."

The Reverend let himself into the driver's seat, while the funeral home director sat in back. He noticed that even at age 60, Fran was beautiful. Her stunning facial features transcended her wrinkles and enticed him to keep eye contact, even when her shyness caused her to look away. He could also tell she had held on to her figure. She had filled in around the hips, but it complemented her age as it helped her avoid the emaciated look skinny older women can portray.

"Hi Fran. How are you?" the Reverend said.

"I'm fine, Reverend Vermin. He shouldn't have called you. I'm sure you have better things to do than calm down a prospective widow."

"What's all this about, Fran?"

"What are you referring to?"

"For starters, your hair. You've had it cut."

Fran touched the ends of her hair, fluffing them in an attempt to make sure they weren't sticking out in every direction. She wasn't used to having the ends of her hair resting on her shoulders, much less having to worry about it getting unmanageable. Her long braid took effort in the morning, but once it was in, there were no worries. "That shouldn't be big news. Women like to get their hair cut."

"You've had yours long for your entire marriage. Richard liked it long. He believed it was biblical."

"If you haven't noticed, he is dying. He is not in charge of me any longer. Besides, it's still shoulder length. It's not like I buzzed it off like some crazed woman."

"No one is saying you are crazy. It's just that you've been under a lot of pressure as of late and your behavior is...different."

"Different isn't always bad."

"I'm not saying it is. I'm just trying to understand."

"All I'm asking is to sell the five extra plots. Richard only needs one."

"You asked if he could have the tombstone cut in half."

"I wasn't serious. I was just trying to figure out how to get my name off of it."

"You don't want to be buried next to Richard?"

"I've made other plans." She shifted in her seat and looked past him, wishing she was in the driver's seat so she could drive away.

The funeral director interjected, "Richard went to great lengths to plan for your deaths. I know because I helped him.

10

He wanted to be laid to rest next to his family. He made that clear."

"We weren't consulted. And who is the sixth plot for anyway?"

"I thought you had a daughter," Reverend Vermin said.

"No, just three boys. Look, none of us have time for this. All I want is to know how I go about selling the extra plots. Can you get me that information so we can all go home?"

The men exited the car and walked over to the caretaker. "Did you get her to listen to reason?"

"She wants to sell them and she has the right to do so," Reverend Vermin said.

"And go against her husband's wishes?"

"She has the right. You can't force someone to be buried where they don't want to be," the funeral director said. "Besides, she's right. Her boys haven't been around here for years. I don't know what Vanderhuis was thinking. And that sixth plot, who did he have in mind?"

"Who knows?" the caretaker said. "Sometimes people buy an extra just in case. But if you ask me he's a strange one. Always out here checking out his future digs. Who does that shit?"

"Can you tone down your language? You're in the presence of clergy and the dead. Have some respect."

"I'll give you some respect when you get that crazy lady off my back."

"We'll tell her what she wants to hear," Reverend Vermin said. "We'll tell her you will start the process of selling the plots today. It's not like someone is going to buy them tomorrow. I hear her kids are coming into town for the weekend. Maybe they will talk some sense into her."

Mean while Fran was out of the car, leaning against the front fender with her arms crossed, staring out at the grave site. She watched the caretaker's golden retriever circle Richard's tombstone, sniffing as though he had found something of interest. Without warning, he lifted his hind leg toward Richard's name plate and began to pee.

Fran chuckled. It felt fitting to her. She had read somewhere that dog's have the ability to sniff out peoples' character. This one had gotten it right. *Funny,* she thought, *how this old dog could be smarter than I have been for the last forty years.*

"Bruno, knock it off!" the caretaker said.

"Control your dog," the funeral director said. "No respect, just like his owner."

"Piss off, you ambulance chaser."

"Ambulance chasers are attorneys," the funeral director said.

"I know. I hate them too," the caretaker said.

"Now men," Reverend Vermin said. "This is not the time for bickering."

"So get on with it Reverend." The caretaker ushered him toward Fran. "You are wasting my time."

Reverend Vermin looked at the caretaker with wide eyes, but then desisted, shaking his head while smiling. He allowed the caretaker to nudge him toward Fran.

The three men approached Fran, taking short steps to make their advance less threatening. "I'm sorry about the hair comment, Fran," Reverend Vermin said. "It looks nice and you were due a change. My wife always admired your long braid, but shivered at the thought of the amount of work it must have taken to braid it every day. She'd be the first to kick me in the shins for not understanding. And like you said, it's still shoulder length. Even Richard would have to agree it still qualifies as long hair."

The caretaker faked a cough in order to move Reverend Vermin on to the topic at hand.

"We'll make sure the plots go up for sale. You don't have to do anything. It will take a while to find a buyer, so you have some time to change your mind, if you reconsider."

"I won't. My mind is made up."

"Talk to your kids this weekend, Fran. Make sure they agree."

"I'll do that. Thanks for your help." Fran got in the driver's seat. She rolled down her window when Reverend Vermin approached to ask a final question.

"Since when do you drive, Fran? I didn't know you had gotten your driver's license."

"I haven't," she responded. She put the car in drive and pulled away slow enough to absorb the feeling of victory.

Chapter 2

The Therapist

Driving to her therapist's office, Fran wanted to make wrong turns at every intersection; desiring to veer off course to avoid the difficult conversation awaiting her. She might have given in if it hadn't been for the massive size of her husband's Cadillac. Its magnitude propelled it forward with inertia; making quick turns impossible for such an inexperienced driver.

Marcia had announced her intentions for this session at the conclusion of their last appointment. "Why are you stuck cooking in the kitchen? Richard doesn't eat anymore."

Fran was shocked by the question. She didn't consider herself stuck in the kitchen. She was there because she wanted to be.

Marcia sensed Fran was flustered by the question. "It's my job to ask the tough questions. Think about it and we'll talk next week."

Fran turned into the parking lot and steered the car toward her space of choice, pleased it was available. Parking in this spot was one of the rituals she had established over the course of her therapy. It soothed the anxiety she experienced each time she forced herself to undergo this harrowing healing process called psychotherapy. Answering such personal questions seemed aberrant to her. There was a reason she hadn't talked about her life. It was painful and embarrassing. But here she was allowing a total stranger to peruse her heart and soul in hopes of fixing her life.

Getting herself into the office and calm enough to talk in a sensible manner didn't get any easier with each try. A knot had formed in her gut; the same knot she woke up with the morning of every appointment. It tightened as the time neared. By the time she entered the office and sat in her chair; she would feel a twisted mess and wouldn't be able to stop herself from slumping over and looking to her feet.

Per her ritual, Fran chose the stairs over the elevator. The climb to the third floor allowed her to work off her anxious energy. It also allowed her to explain her loss of control over her breath and avoid people thinking she was anxious. She made her usual stop at the bathroom and went through the motions of using the toilet, washing her hands, and checking her makeup. She looked in the mirror and primped over her new hairdo. *How ridiculous could I be? I've been coming here for ten months now and I still need to jump through all these foolish hoops to get myself settled. Why would I need to check my makeup? Marcia doesn't even wear any. She claims she makes up for it by accessorizing with gaudy jewelry which she says takes people's focus off her wrinkles.* She turned on the water, wet her hands, and patted down a few stray hairs. *Maybe I should have stopped at Wal-Mart and picked some up to take attention off the shock of this new hair cut. Then again, why would Marcia care? Her hair always looks a mess; going every which way as if it hadn't been combed in a week.*

She entered the office and Marcia was waiting for her. This threw Fran off balance, since she liked a bit of time to get used to the setting before Marcia came to get her. Fran dragged herself through the door and sat in her designated chair.

"What's wrong with being in the kitchen?" she asked.

Marcia took her seat. "Nothing if you're there by choice and you have someone for whom you are cooking."

"I'm cooking for Richard."

"Richard doesn't eat meals anymore unless they fit through a feeding tube."

"Well, maybe I like to cook. Maybe I am good at it."

"I'm sure there are parts of cooking you like and I'm positive you are good at it. In fact, we may decide that when Richard dies you should be the next Rachel Ray. But for now, you are cooking for a dead man in waiting. Since you've told me you sometimes hate that damn kitchen, it doesn't make sense for you to spend all your time in there."

"I would never say damn. I don't swear."

"I know. I took the liberty to do it for you. I'm thinking you should try the word on for size. It reflects your feelings at times; about the kitchen."

"But I love being in the kitchen."

"Fran, you can do both. You can love and hate something at the same time."

"Next you'll tell me I can do that with a person as well. I might hate Richard and love him at the same time."

"You've been in therapy way too long. You're starting to do my job. In no time you won't need me anymore. I must be the best God damn therapist in the whole state of Michigan. Working myself out of a job, that's what I'm doing."

Fran shifted her weight and crossed her legs. She fussed with the pleats of her skirt. "The kitchen makes me feel safe."

Marcia uncrossed her legs and leaned toward Fran. "Why is that?"

"Richard isn't there. He never was. Even if he wanted a glass of water he would make me or the kids go and get it for him. I'm not sure if in 40 years of marriage Richard ever opened the refrigerator door for himself."

"You are kidding right?"

"No, the kitchen was my space."

"But Richard is confined to his room now. You could have the whole house to yourself."

"I only want the kitchen."

"Why is that?"

"It's hard to explain."

16

"Give it a try."

Fran took a deep breath and exhaled a long sigh, loud enough to let Marcia know she was being pushy. "What I do there is comforting."

"How so?"

"Everything is in order in the kitchen. My cupboards are organized and labeled so everything has a proper place and is always available to me." Fran paused.

"Go on," Marcia said.

"There is a clear and right way to do everything in the kitchen. Take the way I make the coffee. I put in a coffee filter. Then I fill the coffee maker with one third of a cup of..."

"So you feel competent in the kitchen."

"I don't know about that. I just know that in the kitchen everything is predictable if you follow the rules. There is a recipe for everything and if you follow the recipe everything turns out okay."

"So you like the structure of the kitchen. You like that there are clear rules to follow. And you like the fact that if you follow the rules the results are always the same and everybody is happy. Life is predictable in the kitchen." Marcia touched her index finger to her temple. "Does that mean life is unpredictable outside the kitchen?"

"I guess so." Fran looked at her fingernails, but refrained from biting them. She pushed back a cuticle she had missed the night before. She wished she had been brave enough to paint her nails as she had planned. She had bought the polish but left it unopened, unable to defy Richard's rule against women painting their bodies. She was still getting comfortable wearing a tiny bit of blush on her cheeks.

"What's unpredictable outside the kitchen?"

"Everything."

"Everything? Tell me more."

"I don't know. People. I guess people are unpredictable. You never know if they are going to be angry."

"All people?"

"Yes?"

17

"Your sons?   Were they unpredictable?   Did you keep them out of the kitchen?"

"They were unpredictable, but not in a bad way. They were just kids. And no, I didn't keep them out of the kitchen. How else would they find me?   I'm their mother." Fran shook her head in disbelief of Marcia's callous assumption. "Kids need to be able to find their mother. They always wandered into the kitchen when they needed me. They didn't stay long. They would come in and ask me what I was doing. I'd tell them even though I knew they weren't the least bit interested, except to know what was for dinner. Then they would grab a snack and leave. It was almost as if they needed to check to see if I was alright. Once that was established and I had given them a snack, they were good to go. You see there is a recipe for everything in the kitchen."

"So it seems. In fact, it appears there is even a recipe for happiness in the kitchen. But you still haven't told me the identity of these unpredictable people you are hiding from."

"You know who they are."

"They?"

"He, alright! He!" Fran gritted her teeth and shot a momentary glare toward Marcia. "We both know who the unpredictable person is. Why do you make me say it?"

"You haven't said it."

"Richard! I'm afraid of Richard and I like the kitchen because he doesn't come in there. Is that a good enough confession for you?"

"That was a confession?" Marcia placed her elbow on the armrest and leaned one side of her face on her hand.

"I don't know." Fran fidgeted with her wedding ring.

"What are you confessing to?"

Fran looked down at her stocking covered thighs. Despite the pressure her pantyhose put on her skin, she could see the cellulite bubbling her mushy flesh. She rued the days when her skin fit her body the way her pantyhose did; tightly covering her well formed legs. This age thing had crept up on her, leaving her with a puffy layer of flab between her skin and her muscle. She despised her legs.

Nudged by Marcia's steady eye contact, Fran lifted her eyes. She saw Marcia's bony legs covered by the black tights she wore under some form of colorful oversized top. She felt jealous of Marcia's long thin legs. She lifted her eyes a bit further and noticed her bare arms. Marcia suffered from regular hot flashes, so she wore short sleeve tops, even in the cold of winter. She always carried a shawl she used to regulate her comfort, pulling it on and off her shoulders as her body temperature fluctuated. Fran noticed her skinny arms, but as she looked closer she noticed extra skin hanging down from under Marcia's biceps, with the same layer of mushy flab infiltrating her body. *I guess it's just an age thing. Skinny or chubby, old is mushy. It's a fact of life.*

Marcia cleared her throat. "Have you done something wrong?"

"No. I follow the recipes." Fran looked at Marcia. "I always do."

"Does it work?"

"In the kitchen it does."

"Outside the kitchen?"

"Not so good."

"Why is that?"

"I never know what he wants. I mean, now I don't because he can't talk. But even before. I never knew what he wanted from me and I was always making him mad."

"Maybe he should have told you what he wanted."

"He did; kind of."

"What do you mean?"

"He would say one thing, but when I did what he asked it was never good enough."

"You mean he always moved the target."

"Yeah, he always moved the target." Fran nodded to Marcia. She was silent for a moment. Her shoulders drooped. "Why would he do that?"

"You tell me."

19

Fran bent over, as though she had a stomach ache. "It felt like he was always looking for a reason to be angry at me."

"Maybe he was."

"Why would he do that?"

"I'm no better at reading minds than you are, but generally speaking, people use the moving target technique to manipulate and control someone. They want you to be searching to please them and never succeeding. However, that's nothing for you to be confessing. Richard is the one that should be copping a plea."

"You think he is the problem, don't you?"

"I think Richard caused you a lot of pain and that is a huge problem for you. But the root of your problem is you."

"Me?"

"Yes, you. Richard is a bastard. Even worse, he is a self-righteous bastard. That fact is not in question. But you are the one that has put up with him for the last forty years. You are the one who hid in the kitchen and let him manhandle your kids. And after all the pain he caused, you are still taking care of him on his death bed. That is the problem you have to figure out and deal with. The Richard problem is just about over."

Fran looked down at her thighs again. *Jeans. A cute pair of jeans would firm up this mushiness."*

"But I hid because I was afraid of him," Fran said.

Marcia jerked her head at the sound of the phone ringing in the background, but ignored it. "That's true."

"He should be in here, not me."

"Also true. But we both know that was never going to happen."

"It is not fair."

"Life rarely is."

"It is in the kitchen."

"Not in mine. But I don't have a magical kitchen."

"You're making fun of me." Fran looked away. She looked at the painting on Marcia's wall that always got her attention.

It was abstract, but Fran could make out three naked bodies, intertwined in a way that avoided the exposure of genitalia.

"I'm sorry. That wasn't my intent. I was trying to make a transition and I thought a little humor would ease the shift."

"Transition to what?"

"Fran, I think there is a deeper reason why you feel so safe in the kitchen."

"What's that?"

"You know it doesn't work that way. I have a hunch I want to follow."

"You mean we are going to play the guessing game?" Fran said.

"No, you are going to tell me what the kitchen has to do with making others happy."

"I didn't say it did. You did." Fran squirmed.

"No, you didn't. But a reasonable person could infer..."

"Just tell me your hunch and I'll tell you if it is true or not."

"Fine, since we have just a few minutes left in the session I'll break the rules."

"You mean you aren't going to follow the recipe. I can't guarantee the cake will turn out if you don't follow the rules. I won't get mad though. I'll still be happy." Fran smirked while she breathed a sigh of relief. She felt the pressure lift off her.

"Fran, you believe you can fix everything with food. A good meal will cure anything. You think you have a magic kitchen."

"You mean outside the kitchen?"

"Yes. You believe you can quell your husband's anger and sooth your children's pain by cooking the food they love."

"It worked."

"Did it?"

"For awhile."

"Really? So meals were wonderful at the Vanderhuis residence?" Marcia raised one eyebrow toward Fran as a mother does to a child when she wants to say *speak the truth now.*

21

"I didn't say that. Dinners were awful. Richard was always fighting with the kids about one thing or another. They were never eating right. Either too fast or too slow; too much or too little. The stares, the yelling, the threats, the tears; it was overwhelming. Richard sat at the head of the table and had us trapped within his reach. I could see the hidden gleam in his eyes as he orchestrated chaos. That is what he did at the dinner table. He orchestrated chaos so he could squash the hoodlums."

"Now you sound like Karl Marx talking about the tactics dictators used to manipulate the masses."

"Oh no! Don't tell me you are a communist too! It is bad enough I picked a therapist who thinks she might be an atheist; but a communist to boot?" Fran smirked.

"I was making the point that abusers of all sorts use the same tactics to control others."

"No, you were saying I'm married to Saddam Hussein."

"Now you're making fun of me."

"Sorry, I didn't mean to. I was just trying to make a transition."

"I've created a monster; turning the therapist's tactics against her. My you are changing. Although I'm not sure it is for the better."

Fran gazed out the window at the snow that had started to fall. "It never worked did it?"

"What's that?" Marcia asked.

"My magic."

"You tell me."

"No, at least not very well." Fran wiped the tears trickling down her cheek.

"So why did you keep doing it?"

Fran uncrossed and then crossed her legs in the opposite direction in an attempt to buy time. "It was all I had to offer. It was the only thing I knew how to do. I had to believe it worked or I would have been hopeless."

"Everyone needs a magic kitchen at some point in their lives." Marcia said.

"So I can keep it?"

"Do you want to?"

"Maybe for a little while."

"How long?" Marcia said.

"Maybe until the boys come. Did I tell you? They have all agreed to come."

"You did. Have you thought about how you are going to handle that?"

"Yup! I'm going to cook my little heart out in my magical kitchen and feed those boys until the happiness just oozes out of them and we become one big happy family."

"In my experience, oozing boys can be kind of smelly."

"You are awful. The worst part is you are awful on purpose."

"That's my magic." Marcia stretched her neck and raised her head to fake pride.

"Great, leave it to me to find a therapist who is crazy enough to believe she has a bag of magic tricks."

Marcia shook her head and chuckled.

Fran stood up. "I've got to go."

"Not back to your kitchen, I hope."

"As a matter of fact, I've got some shopping to do."

"Something other than groceries, I expect."

"Yes, I've got some clothes shopping to do."

"Good answer."

"In fact, I've got to pick out a couple of cute Rachel Ray outfits. She wouldn't be caught dead in her kitchen wearing these rags."

"Are you going to try short skirts, with black tights?" Marcia spread her arms and exposed her outfit.

"No. I don't think I can pull off your short skirts and leotard look. I was thinking of hiding my fleshy legs with a cute pair of jeans."

"Make sure they are low cut. Not that high wasted granny look. I'm told if you buy the lowest cut, you can let your middle aged belly hang over the top. Young girls tell me this is the new sexy."

"Maybe at 16, but not at sixty. This belly needs to be covered up."

"Then get yourself a loose top that comes down to the waist of the jeans. Just leave a little space to show off the waist. You've got to show a little skin if you are going to be sexy."

"Why would I want to be sexy?"

"Every woman desires to be sexy at any age."

"Speaking of sex, can you explain that painting on your wall?" Fran asked.

"You mean the one with the naked bodies?"

"I count three of them."

"You've been looking at it?"

"Once in a while. When I need a distraction."

"I guess the painting is doing its job."

"And what job would that be?"

"Our lives involve sex. When you come to therapy you have to talk about it. The painting brings up the subject when the time is right."

"So we're going to talk about sex?"

"How about next week?"

"I don't know what you have in mind, but I'm not talking about sex with three people. That would be a discussion to have with your sexually uninhibited clients."

Marcia roared with laughter. It made Fran feel like they were equals; they were just friends. A subtle thought occurred to Fran which was too frightening for her to consider in an outright manner. She pondered the possibility. *Could it be that Marcia approves of me?*

After a short while, Marcia's laughter was muffled by Fran's silent discomfort. Fran could let go of herself for a moment, but her rigidity tended to stifle her natural intuition for fun in short fashion. Marcia considered it a success whenever she broke through the brick wall and released a bit of fun and joy from Fran's vault. If she could just introduce her to the inspiration of the more lighthearted side of life,

Fran could let go of the heaviness that had ruled her for so long. She could choose freedom.

But Marcia realized this was only accomplished in small steps, so she didn't fight Fran's silent walk back into captivity. Instead she gave her permission to choose lockup once again, sending her on her way with the same hope filled words with which she ended every session, "You'll be fine, Fran. You'll figure it out."

Chapter 3

The Magic Kitchen

Fran moved around the kitchen with the grace of a dancer. Her motions were fluid and rhythmical, as though she had choreographed her steps and practiced them for hours on end. She had. For countless hours, she had gone through these motions three times a day for over forty years. Breakfast, lunch, and dinner, not to mention the myriad of requests for beverages and snacks, were her end of the bargain. Having raised three boys and a husband, this added up to more time spent on the worn plank floors of this kitchen than most dancers will ever spend on the tattered floorboards of a dance studio.

The kitchen was her favorite room. It made her feel connected and safe. Even more, she was at her best in this space. She was competent and in control in her kitchen. Richard knew more about most things than she did, but in this room he was a neophyte and she was adept. He could criticize her cooking and refuse to eat it. He could throw it on the floor in disgust. He could yell at her and call her stupid. But when she got back to the kitchen and the swinging doors closed behind her, she found herself in a protective womb. In this bubble, his voice was muffled by the rhythm of the music she danced to in her head.

She continued to live in the kitchen even though the need to retire to her protective womb no longer existed. The boys were grown and long gone. Richard lay in the guest room confined to a hospital bed; unable to speak. She had the whole house to herself. And yet she spent most of her time in the kitchen; making meals that wouldn't get eaten unless one of the families from church suffered a tragedy and needed Saint Francine to bring comfort in the form of a home cooked meal. Her jailor husband had (for all practical purposes) fled the coop and left the doors wide open. But Fran was unable to leave. She continued to dance the Cuisine Waltz to the soothing rhythm of the rituals of the kitchen.

Fran danced throughout the kitchen preparing for the homecoming. She wiped down the cupboards, checking to make sure everything she would need was in them. Tonight the house would be full of people who would eat her cooking. She checked the refrigerator's contents, as if they might have run off while she turned her back. She reached for a serving platter stored on the top shelf of the cupboard. She had placed it there because she hadn't used it much since the boys had left. No need for a big serving platter when there is only two of you left in the house. Her reach fell short. She tried to stand on the tip of her toes as ballet dancers are trained to do, but her calves tired before she could grasp the platter.

She went to the closet and found the small stool Peter had made for her in shop class. "Just the right height for you to reach the top shelf Mother," he had said as he put it on the ground for her to try it out. But she never used it much. She preferred to call one of her towering sons into her sanctuary to reach for her. They would mock her height. She would scold them and remind them she was average in height, living in a house full of giants.

She never thought the boys would agree come. She had used the "he's dying" and that seemed to tug somewhat on their guilt strings. But in the end it was the "do it for me" that sealed the deal. This surprised her, as it had never dawned on her she had that kind of clout.

To tell the truth she didn't care why they were coming. Getting them here was the first step in her master plan to get her boys back. Thanks to Marcia and her magical kitchen analogy, she had no legitimate step two. However, that wasn't going to stop her. What did Marcia know about the power of food? She was probably one of those modern women who couldn't cook and fed their families fast food every day. Besides, Marcia had never tasted her cooking. Maybe she would bring her a taste next session and enlighten her. Her shepherd's pie might not be magical, but it could soften the boys' hearts enough to get the ball rolling. And that is all she was asking for now – to get the ball rolling.

Looking out the window, Fran saw clouds accumulating on the horizon. Concerned, she turned on the small television mounted under the cupboard. This purchase was one of her stealth steps toward making her kitchen self-sufficient.

"Now you will never need to leave your kitchen." Her middle son Peter joked when she told him about the purchase during one of their scheduled phone conversations.

She joined him in his laughter for the appropriate amount of time and with the fitting intensity, so she could hide how shocked she was by his perception of her never leaving the kitchen. She thought no one had noticed.

She found the local news and continued with her preparations for the weekend of feasting; listening for an updated forecast. After several menial news segments and a host of irrelevant commercials that failed to attract even a glance from Fran's eyes, a bright and perky weather girl came on screen. Fran stopped and listened. The girl had bleached blond hair, a deep tan, and was wearing a tight cashmere sweater. Fran guessed cashmere because wool would have led to intolerable itching, seeing she had forgone the traditional turtleneck under the sweater. The young woman's nipples were hardened and protruding through the thin material. *A*

28

turtleneck could have solved this problem, or better yet a decent bra.

The dip in the sweater neckline extended low enough to reveal what no one could deny were well engendered breasts. Her tight short skirt showed off the girl's skinny bottom and her pencil thin fit legs. Fran glanced at her own reflection in the shinny surface of the refrigerator for comparison. The distorted image on the uneven surface made her look wider than she was, causing Fran to fret.

For goodness sakes its noon and only women slaving away in their kitchens are paying attention. And we are in no mood for a visible reminder of what we no longer, or never have, looked like. This girl belongs on the evening news, when men are watching.

Fran experienced a wave of guilt at her harsh judgment of the Barbie weather girl. She heard Richard's harsh opinion permeating her thoughts. The girl was beautiful and sexy and as Marcia had put it, women of all ages want to be sexy and attractive. *Nothing wrong with that.*

The weather girl forecasted winter storms for the next 12 hours throughout the Midwest. Fran accepted this with great reluctance. She took another look at the young woman before turning off the television. *Do I want to be sexy? Do I want to look like that? Maybe when I was younger. I'd die of humiliation if my nipples showed like that. I'm not showing my belly off either. I don't care what Marcia and her young clients say. I really don't want to talk to Marcia about that picture on her wall.*

The piercing sound of the ringing telephone startled her. She ran across the kitchen and picked up the receiver. "Hello, you've reached the Richard Vanderhuis residence. This is Fran." She heard a soft chuckle on the other end of the line.

"I'm sorry. I was trying to reach the Fran Vanderhuis residence. I must have dialed the wrong number."

"Hi Peter, I thought it might be you."

"Let me guess. You thought it was me because I'm the good son and therefore the only one who would bother to call and tell you they would be late."

"That's not true. Well, you are a good son, but I'm expecting John to call as well."

"So when Dad dies Mom, will it still be the Richard Vanderhuis residence?"

"I don't know. I've just answered the phone that way for so long it comes to me as second nature."

"We'll have to work on that Mom. He can't even talk on the phone anymore. If someone is calling, it is you they want."

"Well I'm glad you called and you want to talk to me."

"I can't talk for long. My cell phone is losing its charge. I just wanted to tell you that my flight has been grounded in Chicago because of the storm. They are putting me up in a hotel for the night. I'm scheduled to fly out tomorrow morning."

"I was afraid that might happen. Do you think you'll be able to get out in the morning?"

"They seem pretty confident it will all be over by then. I've got to go Mom. I have to catch this next shuttle. I'm freezing in this place."

"Okay, bye. I'll see you in the morning. You didn't forget your coat, did you?"

"Mom, I've lived in Florida for ten years now. I don't own a coat."

"We'll fix you up with one of your Dad's."

"Yeah, I guess he won't be using them. See you tomorrow Mom."

"Good bye."

Fran felt a mixture of anxious joy after hanging up the phone, attached to the fact Peter would be late. She had wanted everything to be perfect this weekend so she wouldn't have to worry. This was not a good start. John would be stranded in Detroit for the night as well. And Thomas, driving that beat up old Volkswagen bus, the same one he had run away from home in twenty years ago; there was no telling in

30

what kind of mess he would find himself. She hoped he had enough sense to pull into a rest stop and wait it out. A hotel would be out of the question for Thomas. He'd be more apt to pitch a tent along the side of the road in the middle of a blizzard, than stoop to paying good money for a chemically sanitized 12 x 12 cell.

As for joy, Fran had waited twenty years for this homecoming. That is how long it had taken to convince her sons to come home at the same time for a full fledged Vanderhuis reunion. Peter had come home on a yearly visit and had a long established pattern of calling home on Sunday nights after the evening church service. John's visits were interspersed, depending on when he was in the country. She could not recollect the last time he had come home. She found solace in the fact that throughout the years, his calls had become more regular as technology allowed communication with the hinterlands of the world to be more accessible.

Thomas had left home at 18, the day after his high school graduation, and had not come within a 500 mile radius of his birthplace since. He had talked to her over the phone and sent her a letter here and there. He had not spoken a direct word to his father since the day he left. Once she made plans to visit him, but backed out before she bought the ticket. Richard had never discovered her planned escapade, but the fear of his reaction overcame her yearning to see her son.

She tried to forget Peter's comment about her manner of answering the phone. It had bothered her. She wasn't angry at Peter; she was perturbed at herself for persisting in this foolish habit for so long. *Why? Why couldn't I just answer, "Hi, this is Fran." Or even, "Hi, this is Francine Vanderhuis's home."*

Fran returned to her present concern. This would be the first time her sons had come home together and she had good reason to be apprehensive. After all, it wasn't just a coincidence they hadn't been together in 30 years. It was a well choreographed plan. The boys had never meshed well as brothers. They stayed away because they didn't want to be together.

As she did with most of the family's problems, she blamed it on Richard. His parenting style was to divide and conquer. He played the boys against each other so they wouldn't join together against him. As such, they tended to despise each other.

Fran embraced the comfort of her kitchen. She procured the peppers, onion, and celery from the refrigerator and set them next to the cutting board. Fresh produce amazed her with its color variations. At the grocery store she would stand in front of the produce section and breathe in the bright colors of nature. The beautiful colors brought her into a deep spiritual place – a place where you might find God hanging around. For Fran, walking through the produce department was like taking a walk through the woods and soaking up the bits and pieces of God that were all around her. She wondered if God was more present in the produce section than in church on Sunday morning.

With a chopping knife she cut the four sides off each pepper, leaving the core with the seeds to be disposed. Next she sliced the sections into thin strips, after which she would turn the cutting board ninety degrees and slice across the sections, leaving her with symmetrical squares.

To most, chopping vegetables was a nuisance job you pawned off on someone else. When someone offered, "Can I help?" The response was, "No, but thanks for asking." Unless there were vegetables to cut. In that case the answer was, "Sure, why don't you cut up these onions for me?"

But Fran loved the tedious parts of cooking. It was repetitive mindless work at which it was very difficult to fail, since it took very little skill to achieve the same perfect outcome every time. Five strokes with a knife this way, five the other way, over and over again. The calming rhythm drew her into a trance that cleansed her mind of the worries that filled it.

Weighed down by all the unknowns of the impending homecoming of her long lost boys, Fran chopped her worries away. She pretended the boys were arriving. She saw herself greeting them at the front door with an enormous hug. That seemed out of character for her so she downsized the hug to one arm around their waist as she walked them to the door after running out to meet them in the driveway. That image made her seem too anxious so she settled for greeting them at the door with a smile and a subtle wink.

The phone rang and it was John. His plane was grounded in Detroit. He was trying to decide whether to spend the night and take a morning flight, or rent a car and drive through the storm. "It doesn't look very safe, but it's been a long time since I was in the middle of a snow storm. A long drive in the dark through the mesmerizing snow vortex caused by the snow rushing toward my windshield through the tunnel of light caused by the headlights seems appealing. Perhaps it would be a good first peek into the nostalgia that's been growing in me over the past two weeks." He paused. "Yet, a warm hotel room with a tall view of the snow falling over the city is not a bad choice either."

Fran smiled as he talked through his thought process. John had always been one to think out loud. That was how he made his decisions. He needed to hear himself think before he could make up his mind. Richard dismissed it as indecision and despised him for it. Only women had the luxury of indecisiveness.

But Fran loved this about John. She always knew what was going on in his head. He discussed his life with her in this way and over the years, a warm bond had developed between them, which was why John became her favorite son. Ironically, he was Richard's favorite as well. This had led to a long underground battle which, in the end, Richard came to understand he could never win.

"Are you still there Mom?" John asked.

"I'm here."

"I'm going to take advantage of the free stay in the hotel for the night. I'll wake up early for a beautiful drive through what I hope will be the winter wonderland I remember from my childhood."

As evening set in, Fran set the table. The boys had teased her because she always set the table far in advance of meals. In fact, as soon as the dishes were washed from the previous meal, Fran would set for the next. She took great pleasure in every step, even though she set the table the same way for over forty years and could complete the task with her eyes closed.

She felt like an artist. She spread the table cloth, which was akin to stretching the canvas. She laid out the lacy place mats with exact precision so as to establish the symmetry required to create the soothing order essential to Fran's version of beauty. She procured the white china with the floral design and the gold trim around the edge. It took her breath away as she laid each piece in its proper place. She folded the napkins and felt a sense of competence as though she had shaped them each into a unique form.

Fran glanced at her hands as she folded the napkins and was surprised at the wrinkles. Her hands looked like a drought stricken field, shriveling up with thirst for water. Age spots splattered aimlessly over the skin on her hands. She reached up and felt her face, checking to see if the same alterations had taken place there, sighing when she found evidence of lines around her eye, mouth, and forehead. *When did these happen? Time flies.*

The silverware provided the shading that gave the portrait more depth and the placing of the crystal water glasses above each place setting gave her the sense she was walking around a spectacular creation, paint brush in hand, dabbing on the finishing touches. No matter how many times Fran set the table, when she was finished, a deep and satisfying breath left her body and filled the air around her with a sense of awe. She was inspired to believe, once again, that life was beautiful.

Fran worried that Thomas hadn't called. It wasn't that she had expected him to call, since that would have been out of character. He was a free spirit that didn't like to be tied down with the weight of expectations. Not to mention he was without a cell phone. She didn't know this for certain, but felt confident in making the assumption. Thomas thought cell phones were part of the problem with today's society. 'They are a means of keeping track of us and linking us to the same main frame computer so we can be controlled' she could hear him say. The argument that they can be useful when you are driving through a dangerous snow storm wouldn't hold much sway with him. Fran could hear him end the discussion with, 'You worry too much Mom. I'll be fine.'

Fran imagined Thomas in the hospital, bloodied with tubes and wires connected to his nose, chest, and arms. Her hands began to shake. She had learned over time that rubbing them brought more attention to her, so she settled for busying her hands with something. She opened the cupboard with the glass front doors and began to rearrange the dishes the glass doors exposed for viewing. Her boys referred to this as fussing with her hands. When they were near her, she would run her fingers through their hair in an attempt to comb it into submission. Or she would attempt to straighten their shirt collars or pat the wrinkles out of some item of clothing they were wearing. The boys would push her hands off and move away to avoid her dexterous pat down.

The image she had conjured of Thomas in the hospital lingered as though it had a mind of its own, and would stay as long as it saw fit. To outsmart her own mind, she distracted herself with a more pleasant thought. She pictured Thomas sitting on the stool at the kitchen counter. His long thin body bent over as he leaned on his elbows, chin in his hands. His body fidgeted as it had done since conception. His eyes sparkled as he searched for a smart aleck comment with which to bother her. She had never told him, but she loved his irreverent humor. She would shush him and complain that he was awful. But after he left, she would laugh to herself. *My*, she thought. *I've missed hearing him.*

Fran left the kitchen, turning off the light as she walked through the swinging doors. She passed through the dining room; glancing at the dinner table she had finished setting. It was a portrait of a happy family, but it was missing the people meant to sit in the chairs and the laughter needed to fill the air. She would remedy that this weekend.

She was about to turn off the light, but experienced a change of heart. No need to darken such a bright spot in her life. She turned and went to the guest bedroom, where she would take care of her unhappiness. She would follow the hospice workers instructions to the letter. She would do it with a slight smile on her face – a smile that was becoming harder to summon each time she entered his space.

Chapter 4

The Loved Son

John watched Myrna's body move as she busied herself with menial tasks around the kitchen. It never ceased to surprise him how her well proportioned curves elicited such strong erotic thoughts in his mind. She bent over the sink and he focused on the manner in which her firm round butt showed through the thin silk robe covering her naked body. *God, I'm a lucking man. H*is groin tightened. He scooted his bottom down in the chair, leaned back, and placed his hands behind his freshly shaven head.

"I know what you're doing," she said.

"And what is that?" John asked.

"You know I can feel your eyes on me when you look at me like that."

"What, a man can't admire his beautiful wife?"

"Don't get me wrong. I like it that you look at me in that way, but now isn't the time."

"There's a wrong time to admire your lover's sexiness?"

"I was going to say there is a time to keep it to yourself, but that's not true. I want you to tell me every time you think it."

"Sit down, honey," John motioned for Myrna to sit across from him at the table. "Let's just have breakfast the way we do every morning."

Their mornings consisted of a light breakfast, accompanied by dark brewed coffee or tea, and a great deal of lighthearted conversation. It was their most valued time together. After finishing their food, they would make playful eye contact through the steam of the hot cup of coffee they held with both hands. With their eyes they would express how lucky they felt to be together, and how much they looked forward to meeting at this table again at the end of the day.

"This isn't every morning, John," Myrna said. "You are leaving. Can you be a little understanding and cut me some slack?"

The taxi's horn interrupted their conversation and John grabbed his suitcase. Myrna followed him to the door. She kissed him goodbye as tears ran down her cheeks and onto his lips. He felt guilty because he couldn't join in her tears.

"It is always harder for the one who is staying behind," he said.

She pulled away a few inches and looked into his eyes. "That's bullshit, John."

She looked toward the impatient driver, standing outside his car while reaching through the window to blow the horn. She gave him a stare. Throwing his hands into the air he said, "What do you expect from me, lady. I'm trying to make a living here and time is money. Call him on his cell phone if you need to talk."

She looked at John. "Tell me one thing. Do you know you will want to come back to me?"

Aware of her gaze, John sensed this was an answer that mattered a great deal to their future. It was an answer which required precise honesty, because it was being heard with the utmost of scrutiny. A flippant affirmation was not going to carry any weight in these circumstances. His dilemma? He wasn't sure he knew the answer as well as she wanted. So many buried feelings had been surfacing without his consent over the last month, drawing his attention away from Myrna and toward his unresolved past in Michigan. He wasn't sure he had it in him to access the honest answer to what she was asking. He knew the answer, but wasn't confident in his ability to imbed it with enough raw emotion to convey the intensity required by this moment.

But then he saw her tears and her state of mind revealed itself to him with a degree of clarity that shocked him. Like a sponge he absorbed her fear and pain and it filled a vacuum within him which he wasn't aware existed. He wanted her grief to stop and he searched for the means to expand his capacity to absorb her tears; struggling all the while to keep under control, so as not to further grieve this woman he loved.

Overwhelmed by his inability to manage what he was feeling, he pulled her close enough to feel her breath mixing with his. He looked her in the eyes as their lips touched and his tongue found hers. Tears ran down his cheeks and mixed with hers where their lips touched. Their tears bathed this kiss with an honesty that surpassed anything words could communicate.

His tears gave Myrna her answer. They let her know she mattered to him. She had the power to make or break his heart. John trusted her with that information and she would treasure the knowledge until he returned.

The driver laid his hand on the horn and held it there, making it clear he would not let up until John got in the car. With a silence pregnant with joy, he got into the taxi and headed for what was once home. They both knew he would be back. He would not be able to stay away from what he had just experienced. The question was how long would he be gone? For John it was a matter of how long he could tolerate to stay. All his mother had requested was that he stay the weekend. Spending only three days after traveling halfway around the world made little sense, and he did have business contacts he should make. So John left the matter of the return date open.

The plane ride to New York City would have been boring, if it had not been for his good fortune in being seated next to a young American girl. She caught his attention, because she could have passed for one of the attractive Dutch girls that permeated his environment at the Christian high school he had attended in West Michigan. He spent hours during those years admiring these same features on the faces of so many of his female classmates, and spent countless weekends pursuing bodies that could have passed for this young woman's clones.

The major difference was their faces were covered in makeup and their bodies draped with tight shirts and short skirts. This young woman's face was cosmetic free and she was dressed in a loose, flowing tunic intended for comfort and the dulling down of her obvious beauty.

Her presence jumpstarted his growing awareness he was leaving the India to which he had grown so accustomed, and entering his native land in which he had allowed himself to become a foreigner. What he didn't know was by the time he reached his home town of White Lake, he would be in full blown culture shock.

She towered over him as she shoved a backpack in the overhead compartment. She finished and looked down at him. She made eye contact with him and placed her hand on his shoulder, "Don't let me bother you. I'm a bit clumsy in small spaces, but I will try not to hurt you. By the way, my name is Carrie."

"I'm John." He moved over in his seat to make her seating a little easier. Not that she needed the extra space. She couldn't have weighed more than 100 pounds under her flowered tunic and John was a slender man of average height. But the gesture was appropriate for two people who had just met.

Not long after takeoff, Carrie asked John if he was American.

He nodded. "Why?"

"Your physical features shout American, but your style of dress says otherwise."

John was taken off guard by this, since his drift toward his adopted country's style of dress had been so gradual he had failed to notice the difference. He wasn't wearing traditional Indian dress, but he had absorbed a subtle style which identified him with the people with whom he had lived the past ten years. The heavy wool sweaters and jeans had been replaced with light cotton slacks and shirts.

"I guess I've been in country for some time," he said.

"How long is that?"

"Ten years."

"That's a long time."

"I guess. It went by fast."

"I only spent twelve months. I wish it could have been longer. I love it here. But I have to go back and finish my studies. I'll be back though. I know that for sure."

"What are you studying?"

"I'm a seminary student – one year to go. I've been in India for an internship."

"What seminary do you attend?"

"Princeton."

"You're looking at a man with a Master's of Divinity from Calvin Theological Seminary in Grand Rapids, Michigan."

"You've got to be kidding." Her eyes quickened with excitement. "I was supposed to go there. That's my parent's denomination. I can't believe we met on this plane. We have so much in common." She smiled. "Don't you wonder what God has in mind for us over the next ten hours?"

"You think God brought us together?"

"Yes! I think it was a God thing. Yeah God!"

John was annoyed. His eyes glazed as he stared past her, wishing this conversation had never begun. She was like the girls he tolerated in high school and ten hours of high school reruns was not what he needed.

She was undeterred. "How did you come to believe in Jesus?"

"I didn't. For a long time I tried to believe, but the more I tried to convince myself, the less I believed."

"You mean you became an atheist?"

"Some would call me that, but I don't ascribe to the label."

"Would you call yourself an agnostic?"

"At first I did. I felt the need to leave room in my psyche for the possibility that I was wrong; perhaps God might exist. Over the years I've drifted toward more certainty on this whole matter of God, and I've lost my neutrality. I've accepted I don't believe."

"Wow! I'm shocked." Carrie leaned away from John.

"What's so shocking?"

"That a person can turn their back on God after growing up in the church and hearing the gospel for so many years."

"I understand this is shocking to you, but it isn't to me. It makes perfect sense."

"Was your family dysfunctional or something?"

"Aren't all our families dysfunctional?"

"Mine wasn't. We had a very happy life and I had a very happy childhood."

"That's nice. I didn't, but I don't think that makes or breaks my case against God."

Their conversation was interrupted by a middle-aged, petite Indian stewardess who made her way down the aisle with the beverage cart. "Could I get you something to drink?" she asked with the same sprightly smile she had used to make the same offer to the preceding fifty passengers.

"No thanks," Carrie said.

"I'll have a bottle of water and a whiskey on the rocks, please." John said. "And some peanuts or pretzels, whichever is easier."

"Pretzels sound good to me as well," his seat-mate said.

"I can handle that," the stewardess said.

They waited while she made John's drink and rustled up the pretzels and water. John looked out the window as though he was checking on their progress; looking for familiar landmarks that might give him a clue as to what they were flying over. Carrie busied herself by folding down the tray on the back of the seat in front of her. She took care of John's as well. She took the pretzels from the stewardess and set one on her tray and one on John's. Next she was handed the bottle of water and then the drink, which she arranged on John's tray.

John took a deep breath as he sipped his drink. He swished it in his mouth, hesitated, and swallowed. The alcohol burned his throat as it went down. He closed his eyes and exhaled in a long, slow manner. As he did, the vapors of the alcohol filled his head causing him to feel a bit dizzy. After repeating this three times, he experienced the result for which he was looking – a slight buzz that took the edge off his stress. The tricky part was going to be keeping this buzz going for ten hours without overdoing it.

She observed him out of the periphery of her field of vision and then, as though she was a hyperactive child who couldn't control her impulses, she probed, "I hope I'm not driving you to drink with my intense opinions and my persistent questions. My mother always joked that I was going to drive her to the bottle."

John laughed. "Trust me; you have nothing to do with my enjoying this drink so much. You are proving to be a pleasant distraction for me. My reason for treasuring this whiskey has to do with what awaits me in Michigan; not you."

He explained why he was headed back home. She empathized with his father's condition and expressed concern for what this would mean for his mother.

"So when did you lose your faith?" she said.

"You mean the faith I said yes to as a child of six, while being threatened with spending eternity burning in hell?"

"Come on now, it wasn't that bad. You act like your parents brainwashed you."

"I'm saying it was hard for me to know what I believed, because I was being compelled by all these forces that were bigger than I was. What I do know is it didn't work well on me. I tried hard to believe, but I don't think I ever did."

"Then why did you go to seminary?" She raised one eyebrow.

"Believe me, I have asked myself that question over and over. All I can say is I wanted to believe. I wanted the brainwashing to take effect so I could make peace with myself and get on with my life. I wanted seminary to convince me to believe so my father would love me the way I had always wanted." He looked around for the stewardess, wanting another drink.

"Sounds complicated."

"In my experience, faith is a complex phenomenon whose origin in us owes its existence to a host of psychological factors, not the work of a Holy Spirit."

"So it has taken you a long time to work yourself out of your faith?"

"It has taken me a lifetime to figure out how to untie the knot into which religion tied my mind. Religion causes some very deep primitive learning to take place in the tender minds of children. It is then covered with a hardened layer of rationalizing beliefs, which keep the deep learning buried in the unconscious."

"You have done this? You've managed to unbury your so called primitive deep learning and erase it?"

John laughed. "Not at all. I only have one lifetime, so the best I can hope for is to become aware of these demons, and learn to ignore them. And as you can see, I've reacquainted myself with my old friend Johnny Walker in order to tolerate this return to the scene of my childhood encoding. My reprogramming is far from complete." He signaled the stewardess.

"Here I thought I might be causing your need to enjoy that drink."

"That's not at all the case. Besides, I'm talking with a beautiful, charming young woman who reminds me of my past flames."

Taken off guard by the compliment, Carrie became uncomfortable and blushed. The flirtation threw her off her game, and she felt no longer in control of the interaction. She fidgeted in her seat, buying time to find an escape route. She decided to use the restroom.

She undid her seat belt and excused herself. "We girls just can't hold our water like you men." She turned and tripped over her pillow which had fallen off her lap and into the aisle when she stood. She stumbled, then gained her composure as she moved down the aisle.

John watched her departure with a nonchalance meant to mask the slight shame he was feeling over the intensity with which he was observing her. He registered her discomfort, but put it on the back burner of his mind so he could apologize later. He leaned across her empty seat, stretching his neck and turning his head so he could observe her walk the aisle. He watched her slender body move beneath the flowing cotton dress. He imagined her sensual figure moving in the most feminine way; her long slender legs move with the grace of a dancer, brushing up against the soft fabric with each move, revealing their eye-catching form. He sat back and remembered the glimpse he had caught of her small breasts hidden by the fabric of her dress, held in place by the lacy bra he imagined she would be wearing. Sight unseen, her body drew his attention and created an instantaneous excitement inside him. His imagination took him under her clothing where he enjoyed a close-up view; usually afforded only to those paying for a lap dance. He marveled at the intricate beauty of this female figure.

Unbeknownst to her, John's momentary lustful fantasy had turned her awkward thirty-second-escape to the restroom into a sensual ageless waltz. He had managed to transform her half-sixties/half-nun cotton dress into a sexy, low-cut, backless party dress, with a slit up the side of her leg that reached her panty line; only to reveal there were no panties.

John laughed at himself. He hadn't undressed a girl like that in a long time. Nor had he felt his groin warm and swell so quickly since he had left high school; and with it the marvelous excitement of overflowing testosterone. Those days when Misty Johnson shocked him in the front seat of his Dad's Chrysler, by pulling back from his kiss in order to

45

unbutton her sweater and reveal what had to be two gifts from heaven.

Nothing had ever captured his heart and soul as quickly as Misty Johnson's perky breasts. Within seconds of the first button being undone, a rising sense of going out of control overtook his mind and body. By the time the last button was undone and the sweater pulled aside, he was sure he was well on his way to insanity, and about to burst into a thousand little pieces of lustful happiness. Although only minutes had past, it felt like hours before he came down off his euphoric mountain and began to worry about how he was going to clean up the mess he made when Misty pulled the lever on the slot machine and the jackpot had rolled out between his legs. The Chrysler was his Dad's prize possession and sex his Dad's biggest demon. Any evidence the nemesis had been driving his chariot was sure to lead to a self-righteous vengeance.

His reminiscing about Misty Johnson stopped when it dawned on him the young blond woman sitting next to him was a replica of the kind of girl he had always thought he would end up marrying. He wondered what his life would have been like if he had stayed the course and followed his Dad's design for his life. Would he have been happy married to a grown up Misty? Would he have settled into that life and belief system, and convinced himself the irrational was rational? Would her beauty have convinced him to believe? Would he have been able to continue to convince himself, when her beauty faded? Would fathering three children, like his father and mother, have brought out his paternal instincts (and anxieties), causing him to seal the deal with God for the good of the children? Would he make love to a thirty-five-year-old Misty the same passionate way he made love to Myrna?

He saw Myrna's naked body on their bed, lying on her back with her legs crossed to one side, to provide a bit of modesty. He noticed the thickness of her sensual curves, brought about by the natural hormonal changes of a maturing woman. He marveled at her silk, chocolate skin. To this day, it surprised him every time she undressed, expecting it to be the pale white color of skin he grew up around. Her well-shaped, plump breasts caused him to yearn for her, while the few dark hairs that shown from between her crossed legs made him wish he could ask her to spread them. Their bodies fit and danced together well.

God, what is wrong with me today, he thought. *I've got sex on the brain.* But then again, sex had always been an escape for John when stress built in his life. It was a pleasant distraction.

"So, did you become a minister when you finished your degree?" Carrie asked.

John's eyes twitched as he jumped and turned toward her. He hadn't noticed she had returned to her seat. He sat up straight. "I decided to go to the mission field instead."

"Were you excited to go to India?"

"You mean, was I like you; eager to save the world in the name of Christ?"

"Not too many people are as excitable as I am. But you must have been into it, weren't you?"

"I tried to be. I prayed for faith as though my life depended on it. I thought my life would be so much easier, if I could buy into it."

"Your father might have changed, and that would make a difference to you; wouldn't it?"

"Your implication is that my inability to believe is predicated on my father's abusive nature and my distaste for him."

"Parents do have a great deal of power when it comes to shaping their children's beliefs. You yourself called it brainwashing. This could be about your father."

"I will grant you, parents play an enormous role in shaping their children's beliefs. But the way I see it, my father offered me an opening to escape the trap."

"You mean the trap in which you think I'm stuck."

"You said it yourself. Parents have a great deal of power when it comes to forming children's beliefs. If my father is the

47

cause of my disbelief, then perhaps your parents are the cause of your belief. Perhaps the only difference between you and me is your parents used more effective techniques in shaping your beliefs to image theirs. You might have been an atheist if you had been born in my shoes."

"I'm not trapped. I want to be who I am. My faith is my own, not my parent's."

"A great many people convince themselves of this and don't even know they are trapped, until they are set free."

"That is circular thinking, not logical deduction."

"Perhaps, but you started the circle by assuming my father is the reason I am unable to see the truth."

"So why do you think you don't believe?"

"I think it is complicated, but I'll tell you what it has felt like. I feel like it is genetic. It's as if there is a gene that determines belief in God, or should I say determines a person's degree of openness to superstition. Some people have it and some people don't." John sipped his drink. "Take my younger brother Peter. He has had a thirst for my father's religion from the time he was born. He drank up what my father preached and slipped right into preaching it to others. He never missed a beat in his path to become my father."

John turned toward her. "I, on the other hand, was born resisting my father's persuasion. I don't remember choosing to do this. It was just in my nature."

Carrie backed away. "So you think you have better genes than me?"

"I'm offending you and I don't mean to. I don't believe I'm better than you; I just think different."

"I'm not offended."

"I know; and you also weren't uncomfortable when I complimented you on your appearance earlier in the flight."

"Well, I am a bit self-conscious about my body."

"You mean you are uncomfortable with your sexuality."

"Look this isn't a therapy session. It is a simple theological discussion."

"In other words, let's focus on you and not on me."

48

"I didn't say that."

"You didn't have to. But that's fine, I love to expound about myself."

Their conversation was interrupted again by the stewardess delivering dinner. They had both ordered vegetarian meals, which they ate heartily. Having cleaned up his mess and disposed of the leftovers with the stewardess, John pulled down the shade on the window and settled in for a nap. At first, John's cohort was a bit disappointed by his choice, since sleeping seemed to her a waste of time. But sleep tends to be contagious, and she soon followed suit.

She awoke after what seemed like a very long sleep, discovering she had managed to twist and turn her body into what could be construed as a cuddling position with John; as her head lay against his arm and her arm was strewn across his leg. She untangled her body from his; hoping she would not awake him. She wanted to keep her indiscretion a secret. But he was wide awake. In a detached manner, John made it clear he was willing to pretend she hadn't just become a human pretzel with him, but she couldn't contain her embarrassment.

"I'm so sorry. I didn't mean to be so familiar with you."

"Don't fret about it. You were tired."

"Why didn't you stop me!" she said.

"It didn't bother me and you looked like you needed to get comfortable. No harm done."

"God! I'm so embarrassed! I've always been a restless sleeper. My sisters refused to sleep in the same bed with me because I ended up on top of them."

"Well, for a minute I thought you were going to throw your right leg over the top of my lap. I would have drawn the line at that."

She used the back of her hand to wipe at splotch of drool running down the side of her chin. Half way through the second swipe, an embarrassing possibility occurred to her. She glanced over at John's shoulder and grabbed her blanket.

She scrubbed John's sleeve in an attempt to repair not only the condition of his shirt sleeve, but the humiliated state of her mind. "Sorry, I appear to have drooled all over you. I'll get it out. Just give me a few seconds." She spit on the blanket to provide enough moisture to get the stain out of his shirt.

John lifted both hands in the stop position. "It is just a little drool. It's not like you threw up on me or something. It'll dry in a few minutes."

"What's your wife going to think?"

"When I tell her, she'll have a good laugh at your expense, just like the people watching you right now." She spun around to scan the extent of her humiliation, only to find that no one was awake to notice. She turned and punched him in the arm with as much force as she could muster.

"There you go again with your hands all over me."

She laughed and took on the accent of a southern girl. "And y'all thought I was just a proper young lady." She fluttered her eyes in a coquettish manner.

"That's good. Have you done any acting?" He smiled. "You'll need those skills to convince the stewardess we're not the happy couple she has been smiling at the past hour."

"Boundaries! My mother was right. I have to remember my boundaries."

They enjoyed the humor that passed between them. Then their pleasant silence was interrupted by her return to seriousness.

"That is what you think of me, isn't it?"

"What are you referring to?"

"You think I'm a proper young lady, who is confused about her sexuality and hides behind puritanical moral standards, don't you?"

"Are you referring to your sudden departure to the restroom when I admired your physical attractiveness?"

"That and my reaction to my initiation into the mile high club after forcibly sleep-spooning you."

"What matters is what you think. But since you asked, I'll tell you my first impressions of you. I think you haven't yet

50

made peace with your sexuality, so you avoid it at all cost. You pretend it isn't there and that makes you unprepared when it is awakened by someone who responds to it. It is an understandable reaction since your background gave you little insight as to how to integrate this powerful aspect of being a female human being into your everyday life outside of the option of marriage."

"You mean they didn't tell me what to do with my horniness until I get married?"

"Wow! What happened to that proper southern young lady?"

"This is my second personality. I forgot to tell you I am a multiple."

"That's good to know, but back to your question. Our sexuality goes far beyond horniness. I don't buy everything Freud said, but he does make the valid point that our sexuality permeates every aspect of our life, and possibly every human interaction in which we take part."

"You mean I wasn't mistaken to perceive something more than a mere compliment was taking place when you brought up my attractive appearance?"

"You weren't mistaken. However, you did exaggerate it a great deal, which would explain your overreaction. I wasn't, as you put it, horny for you. I was just attracted to your femininity."

"Nothing for me to worry about, huh?"

"There is always something sexual going on when two human beings interact. You are either repelled, attracted, or something in between. The trick is to acknowledge it, and let it happen without getting too wrapped up in wild assumptions. You can't stop your sexuality from expressing itself. You can only manage it, so it is enjoyable and harmless."

"So what is going on between you and the stewardess? Any attraction to older matronly women?"

"I don't kiss and tell. You were asleep for quite a while before you publicly claimed me as your property by sprawling all over me."

"Oh God!" she said as she covered her face with her hands and bent over as if in pain. She bounced back up. "Alright, enough of that. Finish telling me your story."

"I worked with the mission for about five years, developing aid programs in small poor villages. Mission headquarters set goals for me and I kept ignoring them. Then I met Myrna. She was a beautiful Indian woman working as a social worker, establishing schools. She had studied in the United States and spoke English well. We collaborated on a few projects and fell in love. We started living together and that made the decision for me. I resigned."

"So what do you do now? I mean as a career?"

"I am a writer. Novels and short stories; human beings have always been my passion and now I am fortunate enough to tell stories about them."

"Have you published anything?"

"I've had moderate success."

"I'll have to read some of your stories."

"Google me."

"What's your wife like?"

"She is the love of my life. You should come and visit us when you come back to India. You would like each other; especially when I tell her of your pretzeling skills."

"You're going to tell her about that?"

"Why wouldn't I?"

"She won't get angry or jealous?"

"My guess is she'll laugh and ask me if I invited you to visit. I don't think Myrna has many doubts about the fact no one can pretzel me like her."

"Is she a Hindu?"

"No, Myrna grew up in a secular family. Both of her parents were well-educated and out of the mainstream of India's religions. The best way to describe her relationship to religion is to say she is indifferent to it."

52

"I can tell you are attached to her. That's nice."

The pilot announced their arrival and everyone prepared for the landing. The plane docked and the passengers rushed to gather their carry-ons; reaching to open the overhead bins and grab their luggage. The two of them waited for the movement in the line to reach their row, then stood and merged into the lane of human traffic. They walked in silence, except for the customary farewell response to the crew as they exited the plane.

They gathered their luggage from the carousel. John was generous in helping her handle hers; since she had several suitcases and John only had one. They went into separate lines at customs, but joined again on the other side, as though timing was perfect.

"I know. It's a God thing," John said.

She gave him the thumbs up sign. "Yeah God."

As they walked toward the exit doors, she spotted two of her friends who had agreed to pick her up. She turned to John and smiled. "I'll Google you and read some of your books."

"I'd like that."

"There better not be a book about a young sexually repressed seminary student from the Midwest."

John laughed. "You do have a good story. The question is how will it end? I could think of a lot of very interesting paths your life could take."

"I'll let you tell me your ending for my life-story when I return to India and visit you."

"Myrna and I will look forward to your visit."

She felt a twinge of jealousy. John seemed relaxed as though he was saying goodbye to a recent acquaintance with whom he had enjoyed an afternoon of carefree conversation. She felt awkward; as though she had spent the day doing something wrong; like dabbling in an illicit affair with a married stranger. She didn't have time to reframe what she was experiencing, so she let her impulsiveness rule her. She stood on the tip of her toes and kissed John on the lips. It was more of a quick peck than a kiss, but it was enough to elicit the effect she desired; to draw John into her discomfort, so she could hold the upper hand in the final moments of their encounter.

Carrie recaptured her southern accent. "Oh my. I don't know what has come over me. Why John, you might just have saved this young woman from a life of repression." She turned and left for the embraces of her friends.

John's startled state took a while to melt away. He walked past Carrie and her friends at a close distance to hear most of the conversation. It began with questions: "What was that about? Did you just kiss that old guy? Who is he? Did you meet him in India? I thought you were hanging out with nuns? This isn't like you; what happened to you on this trip?" The questions were fired at a pace that didn't allow time for individual responses. Carrie answered them all with two statements. "I had a wonderful time in India. He is just a nice unbeliever I met on the plane and tried to bring back into the fold."

Chapter 5

The Prodigal Son

Thomas gripped the steering wheel with clenched fists, as he made his way through the whiteout conditions. His long thin fingers wrapped around the leather padded steering wheel and his fingernails dug into the palms of his hands. The heavy winds pushed his rusty, 1962 Volkswagen bus around the highway, as though it was a feather being tossed to and fro on a windy beach. The traction of the light rear wheel drive vehicle was inefficient, as it slipped and slid even on the slightest of inclines, going forty-five miles per hour on the open highway. Thomas cranked up the volume on the tape deck which was belting the words of Kansas' song, Slow Ride. He sang along in his head, *Slow ride...take it easy...*

The heating system had always been this vintage car's weakness. With the engine in the rear of the vehicle, pulling hot air forward even while traveling at moderate speeds was an engineering problem solvable only by putting the engine in the front; where it belonged.

As such, this bus personified Thomas's personality. It was an odd duck that refused to bow down to convention, even when convention made sense. It had been the only car he had ever wanted and he couldn't ever see himself without it. In high school, he had bought it from a neighbor who kept it as a souvenir from his stint as a hippie in the early sixties. Upon graduating from high school, he defiantly drove it across the country to Arcada, California where he would attend Humbolt State University. Twenty years later he found himself still elated to be driving it cross country once again, even though he was headed back to the disaster she had helped him escape.

Thomas leaned his shoulder into the door to brace himself for the blast from the semi-truck that sped by him. He chuckled with an odd sense of pride. *Only an old bus like mine could be out-run by a fully loaded semi truck during a snow storm.* He worried when he spotted the mile marker, as he couldn't remember anything that had transpired over the last fifty miles. It was the experience people have when they arrive at a destination and don't recall getting there, leaving them wondering if they had been driving in their sleep. He vowed to drink more coffee and smoke less pot.

In order to allow blood to flow to his freezing hands, he adjusted his grip on the steering wheel. His body trembled under the layers of winter clothing he had added as the trip went on. He couldn't tell whether the shaking was due to the cold that had seeped into his body or the caffeine that had accumulated in his system after forty-eight hours of drinking and driving.

Julie was asleep under a bundle of blankets in the passenger seat. She was a twenty-four year old grad student he had agreed to bring on the trip, after she responded to his complaints about the long drive to Michigan; offering to tag along. He had tried to dissuade her, but she was persistent and insisted she loved adventure.

Julie was a reoccurring drama in his life since he had become a professor at his alma mater, Humboldt State University. Pretty grad students would pursue the detached, but intriguing professor, seeking to entrap their rejecting father figure and make him love them. Becoming aware of the futility of their ill advised plan, they moved on after graduation. Thomas was aware of the cycle, but comfortable in letting it play out. It worked for him, providing a revolving and adoring audience which never tired of their exhausting role as unappreciated cheerleaders.

He was intrigued by how much Julie physically resembled Sammy. Julie was short and fleshy with marvelous sexy curves. She had beautiful blue eyes and long, bleached blond hair. It was thick and curly, just like Sammy's. Everything about her was small and yet her personality was large. It dawned on him how much all his girlfriends reflected Sammy. He hated to admit this. He liked to think of himself as a liberated guy. By liberated he meant free – free from his past. And yet here he was; forty years old, serially dating different versions of his high school sweetheart.

Again, Thomas adjusted his grip on the steering wheel. This time he adjusted the rest of his body as well, wiggling his counter body parts in opposite directions to experience the strain of stretching, so he could enjoy the release. His head brushed the bus's ceiling as he stretched his neck and shoulders.

There was a stirring in the passenger seat, but he was disappointed when Julie turned over and kept sleeping. He was hungry for conversation to distract his mind from his wayward thoughts. Driving toward his childhood home was eliciting a depressing urge to reminisce, which is why he had fought his mother about participating in this homecoming in the first place.

He found his stash of pot and began to prepare a joint, while steering with his knees. Julie reached over to take it from his hands.

"Oh sure, now you wake up."

"Fuck off, Thomas! If you wanted me to wake up, you should have asked me."

"It's not like I didn't try. You sleep like a bear in hibernation."

"Only when it is ten below zero and the God damn heat in the car you are traveling cross country in doesn't work worth a damn. Jesus Christ Thomas, you could have at least tried to fix it, or brought along a plug in heater or something like that.

We aren't going to Florida; we are on our way to fucking, freezing Michigan."

"I warned you about that when you begged me to come."

"You also whined for the last three weeks about coming on this trip all alone. What is a girl supposed to do when the grown man she is supposed to love cries like a baby?"

"I don't know, you tell me."

"She fixes it. That is what women who have agreed to mother chronically screwed up older men do when they hear them whine."

"So what is this about you loving me?"

"Don't flatter yourself, Thomas. Or should I say don't pee your pants. It was just a figure of speech. My spin on the gerbil's wheel with you is almost over. I graduate in three months, and then I'll join the list of confused young women who have survived you."

"You got accepted to USC's doctoral program?"

"I did."

"Why didn't you tell me?"

"Oh, I don't know. Because I know you don't give a damn."

"You are supposed to talk to me about these kinds of things. We could have celebrated."

"We're just roommates Thomas; and not very good ones."

"Since when have we been just roommates?"

"Since you haven't wanted to sleep with me, you fucker. That is what you are when you live together and never screw each other's brains out – roommates."

"Now wait a minute. If I haven't wanted to sleep with you, how can I be a fucker?"

"Cute. You know what my friends call you?"

"Go ahead. Hit me."

"Julie's gay boy; you know like Sex in the City where Carrie has that cute little gay friend she hangs around with all the time." Julie sat up and pulled her stack of blankets up to her chin.

"And I suppose you encourage the nickname?"

"I'm neutral. Sometimes I think it would be an easy out. If you were gay I could make sense of the past year and a half."

"Suit yourself. If it works for you, I don't mind."

"How fucking grandiose of you, Sir Thomas! Sacrificing your reputation to sooth the broken heart of the girl you have rejected for eighteen months."

"You don't travel very well do you?"

"Not when I'm being driven by an asshole." Julie reached over and gave Thomas the finger. Thomas opened his mouth and attempted to bite it.

"I haven't seen this bitchy side of you before."

"You haven't been trapped with me in a God damned rusted out freezing old van named Puff the Magic Dragon for twenty four hours before."

"It's a bus, not a van."

"Fine, a fucking freezing bus. What's the difference? No, don't tell me. That's a lecture I can do without. Give me a minute to take a few more drags of this reefer and I'm sure I'll be more pleasant."

Julie inhaled and held it in. After her third drag she said, "What's up with this van, excuse me, bus of yours?"

"It's my dream vehicle. It was my neighbor's party van. I convinced him to sell it to me for $300.00 after his wife mysteriously found out he was sneaking out to smoke pot in it."

"And how did she find out?"

"Let's just say I arranged for the rumor to come to her by way of one of my girlfriends."

"You are an awful person."

"I was in high school. Everyone does a little conniving in their adolescent years. It doesn't mean they have bad character."

"That's true if they outgrow it." She raised an eyebrow. "You haven't."

"When is that pot going to kick in? I'm getting tired of your kicking me in the ass."

"Why is it painted like this?"

"What do you mean, like this?"

"Psychedelic. All these mixed up colors make it look like it belongs in the 1960's."

"I was a sixties fan in high school. I always said I was born a decade too late. I painted it myself."

"I can tell." Julie leaned back in the seat and relaxed. "So why do you call it Puff?"

"You ever heard the song Puff the Magic Dragon by Peter, Paul, and Mary?"

"Hasn't everyone?"

"Someone told me it was a story about smoking pot. As you can surmise from the joint you stole from me, I liked smoking pot. So after I finished painting it into a masterpiece, I christened it Puff the Magic Dragon."

"That explains things." She handed him the joint and laid her head back.

Julie did become more pleasant after a few more drags; she fell asleep. Thomas pulled into a rest stop to nap before the sun rose. Since the morning sunlight was his built in alarm clock, he didn't worry about oversleeping. What he failed to take into account was there wasn't much of a sunrise in the middle of a blizzard in the Midwest. Five hours later, he awoke to frost on Puff's windows and his toes and fingers falling off from frostbite. Turning the key, he was relieved when Puff managed to grown its way to a start.

He ran into the rest stop and warmed himself while he used the bathroom, but shook with a preparatory shiver as he stepped back out into the blistering wind. He woke Julie so she could use the bathroom, too. Having scraped the frost off the windows, he sat in the bus and waited for her.

Dundee, his aging golden retriever, pushed his way between the front seats and laid his head on his master's lap. His age showed in the grey hairs that had begun to push their way through his golden fur coat.

"Hey old boy," Thomas said. "I forgot you were back there. You shouldn't be so good. People forget about you when you are too good."

Dundee whined.

"Meet me at the side door, old friend, and I'll let you out. Don't be shocked by the cold."

Thomas opened the door and Dundee sniffed the air. When the cold hit his nose, he did an about face.

"Suit yourself, old boy, but it is a long ride to Michigan. I don't want to find any presents in the back of the bus when we get there."

Dundee shuffled to the back of the bus, spun in a circle, and dropped his body down into a ball; falling into a deep hibernation.

It took Julie a while to return, since she was taking her time trying to warm up in preparation for the discomfort of the rest of the day. She knew he would be angry about losing half an hour of traveling time, but she didn't care. She felt awful and a makeshift warm bath was what she needed. She returned to the bus and found him finishing a conversation on her cell phone. Thomas didn't believe in owning one. He didn't want to be tied down to technology. He had insisted she leave hers at home, but there wasn't a chance in hell she was going to let that happen, so he gave in. He agreed it might be helpful in case of an emergency.

"So you decided to call your mother and let her know we're alive and we'll be late."

"You mean, I'll be late. She doesn't know about you yet."

"Well don't worry. I'll be out of your way as soon as I can catch a ride to Detroit. God, I swear. I've landed back in high school with another idiot boyfriend."

"A few hours ago I was a fucker and an asshole. Now I'm only an idiot. Your Prozac must have kicked in."

"So what did your mother say?"

"I don't know."

"What do you mean you don't know?"

"That wasn't my mother. It was a friend."

"That's all I get? My God, it wasn't a dream. This damn dragon is a time machine, and I'm begging my high school boyfriend to talk to me with answers that go beyond yah and nah."

"I thought I wasn't your boyfriend. I thought I was your gay boy."

"Gay boys talk to their girlfriends. Besides, shit happens in dreams."

"There has been a change of plans." Thomas buckled his seatbelt and helped Julie do the same. Julie thanked him by touching his arm as he pressed the buckle halves together.

"You changed your mind and we're headed to Florida."

"Why Florida?"

"It is a dream! Good shit happens in dreams, too. I'm freezing and Florida sounds great."

"Well, in this dream we're taking a slight detour. Don't worry, just a quick jaunt south of Chicago to pick up my friend."

"Does this friend have a name?"

"Sammy."

"And you know this friend from...?"

"High school. We went to high school together."

"Does he have a decent car we could borrow for the rest of the trip?"

"No. Sammy commutes to Chicago on the train."

"Well, just so you know; I'm not giving up my seat. He'll have to sit on the cold floor."

"Fine."

"So why are you bringing him home with you?"

"Good friend of the whole family."

"I see." Julie settled in for another nap.

The half hour detour turned into several hours since Thomas had no idea how to get to Sammy's house. It took four calls to Sammy to get the directions straightened out. When Thomas spotted 10070 on the front of the small row house, he breathed a sigh of relief and pulled into the driveway. The sudden halt woke Julie, but he shushed her when she asked if they were there yet, telling her to wait in the bus. She protested she was cold, but he assured her it would only be a couple of minutes.

Several minutes later, Thomas came out carrying a pink suitcase.

"Sammy's a gay boy, too? I've got two of you now?" Julie said.

Thomas ignored her and went back inside. He emerged from the garage with a beach chair, which he set up in the back of the bus. On his third return trip, Julie spotted an attractive version of herself, perhaps fifteen years older, walking three steps ahead of him. She wore tight fitting jeans that showed off her well-shaped ass; tall black boots with high heels and pointy toes; a fitted ski jacket and a matching wool cap. The woman walked around the front of the bus and was about to open the passenger door, when she made eye contact with Julie. Recovering, she saw the open side door and got in.

Thomas took his seat behind the wheel and waited for Sammy to settle into the lawn chair; avoiding Julie's penetrating stare. He could avoid eye contact, but he could not avoid the reality of the stream of angry energy coming his way. He backed Puff out of the driveway, placed it in first gear, and drove as though nothing out of the ordinary had happened.

It was Sammy who broke the twisted silence. "Hi, I'm Sammy."

"So I heard. I'm Julie," she said, looking straight ahead.

"I get the distinct impression you didn't know about me?"

"Well, I did learn several hours ago we were picking up an old high school friend named Sammy. He did forget to mention Sammy was a girl."

"Sorry. If it is any consolation, I just learned about you when I tried to climb into the front seat."

"I could tell from your expression. I like your bitch shoes." Julie looked down at Sammy's pointed boots.

"Thanks. A girl needs a few weapons if she is going to hang out with the Vanderhuis boys."

"I get that. Sexy weapons."

"I take it you and Thomas are involved?" Sammy said.

"We were involved, but I'm graduating in two months and I'm evolving. As for Thomas, I'm sure he'll find my replacement among the next class of graduate students."

"Congratulations."

"For graduating or for evolving?"

"Both are worthy of the compliment."

"Thanks. I'm sorry for the attitude. It has been a long couple of days on a trip that was a mistake in the first place."

"Let me guess. He acted like he needed you to come with him. You made the mistake of letting your maternal instincts take over and got excited about the idea. He then forgot he begged you to come and acted like it was your idea, treating you like you were burdening him."

"Wow!" Julie said.

"Are you wondering why I agreed to come?"

"No. I'm wondering why he wanted you to come. You have his number. How does he think you're going to be of any help?"

"I've been expecting the call from the moment he told me he was going to his mother's. In high school, I ran interference for Thomas with his family. They love me. He wants me around because I make it easier for him to be with his family."

"You mean he is afraid to go home without you?" She looked at Thomas and chuckled.

"He won't admit that, but between you and me; yes, he is terrified."

Thomas squeezed the steering wheel and tapped his thumbs, wishing he could drown out the women's conversation.

Sammy jumped in her lawn chair, startled by Dundee's nose pressing up from under her bottom. "There you are," she said. He came around to her side and she grabbed his head with both hands. She put her nose up to his and he began to lick her lips. She laughed. "I was hoping I would get to see you."

"I see you know him and his bad habit," Julie said.

"We go way back, don't we Dundee. You're still a crotch sniffer aren't you? Always will be. Alright, that's enough of that. No more kisses." She told him to sit and he laid his head on the arm of her chair where he kept his eyes focused on her.

Julie reached over and pressed her hand on Thomas' thumbs.

"So why did you agree to jump on the Puff Express?" Julie asked.

"The honest answer is I've recently divorced, I have no kids, and I'm bored with my job. In other words, I have no life and a train to nowhere is better than being nowhere. The more honest truth is I've been jumping on and off the Puff Express for so long I don't know how to stop. No matter how many different trains I take, sooner or later I end up back on this one. It is dysfunctional, I know. But it is my dysfunctional."

"Well, you know what they say."

"What's that?"

"The best we can hope for is to know our dysfunction. Overcoming it is meant to be fuel for our dreams."

"That's comforting. You are his type, aren't you?" Sammy said.

"You mean your type. I can see we've all been younger versions of you."

"He's brilliant, isn't he? He has found the secret to the fountain of youth. All you have to do to stay young and immature is keep dating younger versions of your high school sweetheart. Are you staying with the family?"

"No, I only agreed to accompany him on the trip. I have friends in Detroit I've been meaning to visit. Besides, Thomas hasn't even told them I'm riding with him, so they'll be caught in an awkward situation. Now that there are two of us, I can't imagine how he will explain this threesome."

"It should be interesting. It always is. They know I'm coming. I called and talked to his mom to make sure it was okay. I figured he wouldn't. I would have broken the ice for you, but I didn't know you were part of the package. But don't worry; they'll handle it just fine. They expect these kinds of shenanigans from him."

"I'll just stay out of the way until I can make arrangements for a rental car."

Thomas reached over to the center of the dash board and turned on the radio. He turned the dial and found a classic rock station. He turned up the volume and leaned his head back.

Julie stared at him while she reached over and pushed the off button. "We're talking. Do you mind?" She lifted her left foot and tucked it under her bottom, rotating her body so she made eye contact with Sammy. "So you'll go back with him?"

"That was the plan, but I won't be following through with it. I'm flying home, even if I have to sell my body to get the money for the air fare."

"Looks to me like you could get a pretty good price." Sammy scanned her up and down.

"Thanks. He does like us pretty, doesn't he?"

"Pretty, but not gorgeous; fit, but not skinny; blond, but bleached, not natural. Maybe he has a secret cloning lab someplace."

"So tell me more about Thomas and you," Julie said, turning in her seat.

"Well, we dated our sophomore, junior, and senior years."

"Ahh, true high school sweethearts."

"In an odd sort of way, that was true. But it wasn't your typical high school romance. He wasn't like other boys I had known, who wanted a five minute love affair and a quick romp in the hay. He was somewhat uninterested in sex. He liked my body. I knew that from the day I spotted him watching me take a shower, and from the fact that he liked to draw my naked body every chance he could get. But when it came to having sex, or even interacting romantically in any way, Thomas just wasn't all that moved."

"Were you frustrated?"

"On the one hand I was, because it made me feel like something was missing. But on the other hand it was quite convenient. I was just a teenager and not all that interested in sex yet. A little hand holding and making out would have been nice, but at least I didn't need to put up with the constant groping other girls were having to deal with. He was interesting to me, and for the most part, that was enough. I think of myself as his almost platonic girlfriend."

"Well I'm not a teenager and he frustrates the hell out of me. I'm too old to be a platonic anything. Did you think he was gay?"

"No! Well I mean I asked myself that question sometimes, but I knew how he reacted when I forced the issue, and I could tell the desire was there by the way touching my body affected him."

Thomas fidgeted in his seat. Listening to his two former girlfriends talking about him without defending himself went against his nature. Every time there was an opportunity to state his case, he nodded his head as though he agreed. But in his head he shouted, *No, that's not fair.*

But he understood he had fucked up and this was his penance. More important, he understood Sammy was more effective than he at getting him out of the messes he created. He was sure to dig the hole deeper. Sammy knew how to fill it in and smooth it over. She had been doing it for him since high school.

They had met when he invited her to party with some friends to celebrate the christening of Puff. She had agreed and he was pleased she fit in so well with the boys. The party went all night. He awoke and started to walk home, after discovering Puff's battery was dead.

He had walked two blocks when he heard his name being called in the distance. He dismissed it as paranoia, which he tended to experience on a daily basis, whether or not he was doing something wrong. It was part of the cluster of symptoms that resulted from living his life in constant opposition to the world; you always assumed you were breaking some kind of rule and were about to get nailed for it.

He heard it again; louder. He turned around to a blurred image of what he guessed was Sammy, running to catch up with him. He stopped and waited for her. When she was steps away, he turned and resumed his walk home. She quickstepped her way alongside him, intertwined her arm through his, leaned her head against his shoulder, and matched his pace.

"I'm going to walk with you," she said.

"Aren't you going to ask if I mind?"

"No. It would be polite of me, but that would give you the choice of rejecting my offer, and that would break my heart. Why would I want to give you that option?"

"I don't know. It is just what most people do."

"That's true, but then you and me; we're not like most people, are we?"

"Where would you get that notion?"

"I've been watching you for a long time, Thomas Vanderhuis. I've been watching you since Mrs. Parker parked our asses next to each other, after you managed to irritate everyone else in the second grade. No one would sit next to you. She had been sparing me the torment, since I was a shy girl. But after exhausting all her options, she made you my responsibility."

"I've got to get to church by eleven."

"Thomas Vanderhuis is a choir boy?"

"Not by choice."

"I get it. Thomas Vanderhuis chooses his battles. I thought you were one of those people who fought every dragon that showed up, regardless of the collateral damage."

"Could you stop calling me by my full name?"

"Why would I? You are the star of the show. You need to be shown some deference. After all, you wouldn't want me calling you Tommy, would you? That wouldn't reflect the nature of my admiration."

"Thomas is what I like people to call me."

"But we are going to be special friends. Special friends make certain allowances for each other."

"Whatever."

"So here is what I'm going to do. I'm going to walk home with you and go to church on your arm. Afterwards you can invite me to have dinner with the Vanderhuis family."

"You can't go to church looking like that."

"You have a shower at your house right? I'll take a shower and you can lend me one of your sweatshirts. I'll be good to go."

"I don't know."

"Come on! You can score some points with your Dad. You can tell him you are working on converting this lost soul. We'll make up a story to make me look like I need to be saved. Doesn't your church have some kind of alter call or something where people come forward to be prayed for or saved? I could put on a good act and make myself look pathetic. I know how to make myself cry."

"You do look like a lost soul."

"Come on. It will be fun."

"You are a devious girl. I didn't know that about you. I like it."

"Trust me, I'm lost and waiting to be found."

"I'm not looking to find anyone."

"I'm not giving you a choice."

Sammy reached up and shook Thomas' ponytail. "I like your hair. It makes you look like a bad boy. That's sexy."

"Thanks."

"Do you ever wear it down?"

"Only at night. I look too much like a girl."

"I'm going to braid it for you some time. I think it would look good on you."

"What, now you are my hairdresser?"

"I'm going to be a lot of things to you, Thomas Vanderhuis."

They reached the house and scavenged the kitchen for breakfast food. Having finished the milk and cookies, Thomas got her a towel and showed her his parents' bathroom. He turned on the water and made sure she had soap and shampoo. Before he left, Sammy called him over to her. She snuggled in, reached her hand up behind his head, and pulled it toward her face. She kissed him on the lips and whispered. "Thanks, I've already had more fun than I could have imagined."

He smiled. "I'll come find you when I'm done." Under his breath he thanked God his family was off to Sunday school.

He finished his shower and got dressed. He set out a couple of options for t-shirts and sweatshirts, and checked on Sammy.

He was surprised to find the door to the bathroom open a slit, offering an invitation to take a peek. He pushed it open until he could see the shower door. He was stunned when he saw Sammy's naked silhouette through the foggy glass. She was a short girl with a well proportioned muscular body. He hadn't paid attention to her looks and had assumed she owned a round unremarkable figure. What he had failed to notice was under her baggy clothes she had developed beautiful, large breasts that altered the appearance of the rest of her body.

Sammy's well shaped breasts transformed what Thomas had expected to be an unremarkable round shape, into a mature, sensual figure that captured his attention. Every curve in her body pulled him toward her, creating desire that far surpassed anything he had felt while dealing with the paper version. In the many hours he had spend looking at pictures of naked girls in Playboy magazines, he had never imagined looking at the real thing would be so much more exciting.

He watched Sammy shift behind the glass, mesmerized by even the slightest movement. He watched her run her hands through her hair to help the water rinse the shampoo out of her long curly hair. He gazed as she stepped back to let the water run over her breasts. He imagined her hands were his, as she cupped her breasts in her hands and pushed them upwards into the stream of water, as though she was offering them to the gods. She turned to rinse her back side, and he thought he was going to burst when she ran her hand over her muscular buttocks and thighs. She turned to face the shower once again, spread her legs to allow the water to run between them, placing her hand over her vagina to employ a subtle rubbing movement to help rinse the prized spot.

He stared at her until he began to experience the creepy feelings that come with peeping on an unsuspecting naked girl. He gathered himself and caught his breath.

"Everything okay in there?" he said.

"Just fine. I'll be out in a few minutes. I'll come find you when I'm done."

He wandered back to the family room and sat in front of the television. Sammy's naked body was engraved on his brain.

She entered the family room and startled him with a soft "hi." She had wrapped her hair in a small towel. This would have reminded him of his mother had it not been for the fact Sammy had wrapped the rest of her body in a towel as well, which is something his mother would never do. Afraid he was going to stare; he dismissed her to his bedroom, telling her he had laid out a couple of sweatshirts from which she could choose. As she turned to leave the room, he called out, "By the way, I put out a pair of my cleanest underwear. Thought you might want a fresh pair. I didn't think you would mind, seeing you were so good at being one of the boys last night."

She turned and flashed him a devious smile that outdid the one he was wearing on his face. She reached down and pulled her towel above her waist, as little girls pull up their skirts in order to show off their fancy panties. In doing so she revealed a pair of baggy granny underwear she had borrowed from his mother's drawer. They were three sizes too big and she had them hiked up more than six inches above her belly button. She cooed, "I thought you might like these better." She twirled several times, contorting her face into awkward expressions meant to mock the looks models make while

71

walking the runway. She then threw the towel at his face and skipped out of the room laughing as she raised her hands in victory.

"I can't believe you put on my mother's underwear. Are you some kind of weirdo pervert?" he yelled.

"That would be your fantasy come true, wouldn't it? To meet a real pervert and turn her into your girlfriend."

"I hate to ruin your outfit, but you can't wear those. My parents would kill me if they found out you went through my mother's drawers. You need to put them back where you found them." As the words left his mouth, he cringed; realizing he sounded like a prude.

"Thomas Vanderhuis, I had no idea you had this choir boy side to your personality. Here I thought I was attracted to a bad boy. Maybe I'm not so screwed up in my taste in men after all."

"Just put them away. We have to leave if we are going to make it on time."

"I forgot. We're going to church. Why didn't you remind me?"

"Why should I?"

There was a moment of silence which brought relief to Thomas because he felt he might have gotten the last word. His small bubble burst when she stuck her head through the doorway and in a flirtatious voice said, "Because, I don't wear underwear to church."

Thomas shook his head and came out of his nostalgic trance. He saw a sign advertising shops in Michigan City and was pleased at the good time they were making. He smiled as he resumed his penance.

"God, I am so glad I got to meet you." Julie said. "This trip has become worth the agony. The last two years of my life are making sense. I've been trying to figure out what is wrong with me so I could fix it and get this man to love me, or at least fuck me. It was driving me crazy."

"It should be required you have an established therapist if you are going to date him," Sammy said.

"Therapist? Who needs a therapist? A few minutes with you is all I require."

"The day after graduation, he left me. Packed his stuff, jumped into Puff, and was gone."

"Didn't even say goodbye?"

"He drove to my house and told me he was leaving early for college. I had known he was going to Humboldt State in the fall. He had discovered it in his junior year, and determined it was where his hippie soul needed to be. It was all he could talk about. The red wood forests, the Pacific Ocean, the free spirited atmosphere. You would have thought he was going to heaven."

"You didn't want to go with him?"

"I did, but I didn't want to be stuck out in California depending on him. Besides, he didn't want me to come. He said we needed to go our different paths and see how it felt. My path was Northwestern, in Chicago. I had always loved that city."

"What was your major?"

"I'm a social worker."

"What did he tell you when he left?"

"He couldn't take living with his family a day longer and he was going to California for the summer to live in Puff. He would find odd jobs to make money to help him get by, without using his savings. He assured me he would keep in touch, kissed me, and drove off. He escaped to California on the back of his magic dragon."

"Did he keep in touch?"

"Yes. He wrote me two or three times a week. The one thing I have been able to count on is Thomas staying in touch with me. Through college, graduate school, other lovers, marriage, divorce; whether I wanted him to or not."

Thomas looked at the dash board and wished for a fast forward button.

"God," Julie said. "I hope that doesn't mean I won't be able to get rid of him in a few months."

"Don't worry. History says otherwise. Fate has assigned that role to me. I am and always will be his lady in waiting."

"How depressing. I'm sorry for you."

"Thanks, but you needn't burden yourself with sympathy for me. I'm a firm believer we make our own fate. Consciously or unconsciously we choose what happens to us," Sammy said.

"And you are choosing him? Why?"

"Truth be told, I don't know and I don't want to spend the time, energy, and money to figure it out in therapy. I'm not sure having the answer to that question would change anything."

"Well, could you move in with him and save the female population of HSU the grief?"

"Ladies in waiting don't get the job. Waiting is their fate."

"Don't get me wrong Sammy, I like you. But this is weird."

"From an outside point of view, I guess this is true. But from my point of view, it is just the way it has always been. It is my story and I need to see it through to the end. We all have our stories to live out. At least mine is never dull or ordinary."

"Please, God! Give me ordinary or dull. I don't need complicated drama."

"Then why did you choose it?"

"I didn't know it was going to be this way."

"Thomas Vanderhuis' reputation is quite well entrenched all over HSU. You would have to be deaf to not have heard about it."

"I don't know. I'm a romantic. I thought it would be different with me. I thought he would be different with me than he was with all the others."

"You thought you could bedazzle him and be the one lady in waiting to get chosen. Now that would be an exciting life story. It would make you a better woman than me and the many others that went before you."

74

"It's not that way."

"Alright then, I'll guess again. It would make up for the love your father never gave you after leaving your mother."

"That is what I wanted. But I guess we don't get to write our own endings."

"It is not about him, Julie. He is who he is. It is about you. You chose your story and now you're choosing the ending. You've made the choice to stop waiting."

"You could move to HSU and start a recovery program for all the ladies in waiting."

"I lived in Arcada for a few years after Northwestern. I went there to get my MSW. I was accepted at Northwestern, but Thomas suggested I come live with him so we could work on our masters together. I did, and it was good for a while."

"Why didn't you stay?"

"I did. Thomas left to work on his PHD at UCLA. He didn't ask me to come with him, and I'm not the type to beg. He packed up his stuff and drove away in the dragon, yet again. I found a job in Chicago and moved back."

Sammy shivered. "God, it's freezing in here. Is there no heat at all in this thing?"

Julie offered her a blanket from the stack under which she was snuggled.

"Thank you," Sammy said as she grabbed it and curled up under it.

"You must hate Puff," Julie said.

Thomas leaned back, rolled his eyes, and stared at the pattern of dots on the roof of the bus. He made a fist and pressed it into the fabric of the roof.

"I've had a lot of fun in this old bus. I could never hate it. Besides, Puff is responsible for our meeting."

"What do you mean?"

"It was sitting out in the back of his neighbor's house rusting away. Thomas wanted to buy it from him, but he refused to sell it. My mom was good friends with his wife, so Thomas started hanging out with me. He let it slip that the guy used it as a hideout to smoke pot. I told my mom and she..."

"Told his wife," Julie finished her sentence. "You're that girlfriend. He told me."

"I'm the one. He thanked me by inviting me to a party to celebrate her christening. The rest is history."

"Weren't you angry he used you?"

"No, I was interested in him. So I used the opportunity to get in with him."

Julie looked at Thomas for the first time since picking up Sammy. His shoulders were slumped and his lips drooped. She shook her head in disgust.

"I've seen the nudes he has painted of you. They are beautiful," Julie said.

"I always have been beautiful in Thomas' eyes. He started painting them in high school. I was taking a shower at his parents' house and I left the door open as a teaser. He took the bait, stood in the doorway, and watched me for five minutes. He insisted on painting me the very next afternoon and again everyday for a month. Each time he painted me, I would let him convince me to take off one more item of clothing."

"Wasn't that odd for you?"

"It felt good at the time. I think it was how we had safe sex. It satisfied Thomas' desire for my body and it made me feel wanted."

"What happened to them?"

"He kept the ones he liked the best. He gave my favorite to me as a wedding present. Said he thought my husband would enjoy it. It was the one he painted of me the day before he left for UCLA. I was laying on the couch looking out the window with a deep sadness in my eyes and a single tear running down my cheek. Needless to say it created quite a stir at the wedding. My husband never trusted him after that. I told my husband I got rid of it, but I stored it in my friend's basement. After the divorce I hung it in my bedroom. It makes a good impression when it comes to dating."

76

Thomas grinned, while turning to make sure Julie wasn't noticing.

"He hasn't sold any of the paintings he has done of you."

"I'm planning on inheriting them when he goes to an early death. I'll make a fortune."

"He wanted to paint me, but I couldn't bring myself to do it. I'm a bit prudish. But make no mistake; I'm a hell of a lay under the cover of darkness."

"You're going to have a tough time selling your body for the ticket home, if you can't even pose for Thomas." Sammy smirked.

"Didn't I tell you, Sammy? I'm taking you along as my billboard girl."

"My nude on a billboard on a Detroit freeway? You might have to set up shop and stay."

"He is a talented artist," Julie said. "It is what attracted me to him. He had an exhibit in the local gallery during my first month at HSU. I went to see it every day until it closed. His work is so shocking and yet tender in some ways."

"Just as he is with his women. As he honed his skills in college, he discovered his art was a safe way to play out his need to shock. It provided him with a larger audience, and God knows Thomas needs an audience."

"It has provided him a way to never have to grow up. He can remain an adolescent/child in a grown man's body."

"Who can hold on to the bus he bought in high school, which he still calls Puff the Magic Dragon, and drive it to pick up his high school sweetheart, who he still has wrapped around his pinky, so she can help him deal with mommy and daddy?"

"And masturbate himself by painting her still beautiful body." Julie laughed.

"Ouch! That was shocking and mean." Sammy laughed with her.

Sammy looked at Thomas who was about to say something. She cleared her throat, reached around him, and placed her pointer finger on the tip of his long bony nose, protruding from his elongated thin face. She held it there until he desisted, noticing how rough his skin had become under his unshaven face. *He is still ruggedly handsome,* she thought.

"What the fuck," he mumbled. "I suppose I deserve this abuse."

"Yes you do!" they both said.

He slumped in the seat.

"We were starting to talk nicely about him and I'm not done being angry at him. He is our captive audience." Julie looked to Sammy for validation.

"You have every right."

"So this is what you do for him. You run interference for him, not only with his family, but with his girlfriends. Or should I say ex-girlfriends. You charm them into forgetting what an asshole he was."

"I'm afraid it's my gift and my calling. How did you meet him?"

"I found out he was a professor at Humboldt and transferred into his class two weeks into the semester. In order to do this, I had to get his permission. I made an appointment. When I got there I was so nervous I couldn't speak a word. I about fainted when he told me we should talk about it over lunch."

Thomas drove in silence, listening as the two women bonded through their solidarity as victims of Thomas Vanderhuis, and emerged best of friends. It was his penance. He was to listen to these two women analyze his faults in great detail.

The snowstorm had subsided and the plow trucks were hard at work clearing the roads. By the time they hit the Michigan border, driving was almost clear sailing. By the time they passed the Saugatuck exit his penance was complete, and he was allowed to join in the conversation. They passed Holland twenty minutes later and all three of them laughed at how silly they must look driving this ridiculous bus in the middle of winter, freezing to death. All the while Sammy sat in a beach chair as though she was looking forward to a warm day in the sun at Grand Haven State Park. They waved a passing goodbye to Muskegon, heading into the last twenty minute stretch to White Lake. Sullenness came over Thomas as he realized his true penance was just beginning.

Chapter 6

The Good Son

Peter slumped in his chair when the announcement came over the airport intercom informing the passengers all flights were cancelled. His long legs extended across the aisle, almost tripping a young mother with her baby in her arms.

"Sorry," he said as he recoiled his body and folded it back into his chair.

The woman glared and moved on.

He was aware of the threat of a blizzard since yesterday, but he had hoped to be able to get in and out of Chicago's O'Hare before it hit and land in Grand Rapids before everything was shut down.

He told himself Midwesterners were used to this kind of weather. They were experts at keeping things moving, even in high wind and snow conditions. If they let a little wind and snow stop them, they would be locked down half of the winter months. To increase his odds, he placed himself on the church's prayer chain so his parishioners could keep his plight before God, who was tougher than Midwesterners when it came to managing blizzards. Resigned to the fact his prayer wasn't answered as he would have preferred, Peter made his way toward the airline's ticket counter. He breathed a sigh of dismay when he saw the long line that had formed. He looked up and said, "Can't I get one break, God?" He looked down. "I know. Patience is a virtue." He looked back up. "Didn't we agree I had learned enough patience for one lifetime?"

Peter reached the front of the long line where he was informed he had been booked on a morning flight leaving at 10:00. He asked about renting a car and driving. "The state troopers have shut down all the major expressways. Besides," the ticket woman said. "You don't look like you are used to driving in weather like this. Are you from Florida?"

"How did you know?" Peter asked.

"You're sporting the kind of tan you can only have if you spend winters in the tropics."

"I grew up in Michigan. I'm headed home for a family reunion. I don't expect it will be pleasant and this weather isn't going to help."

"Well, that's too bad. Here's a voucher for the Holiday Inn. You can catch the shuttle through those double doors. Get a good night's sleep. There is nothing better than sleeping through an Illinois snowstorm."

Peter lowered his gaze as he reached out to take the voucher. The young woman handed it to him with her right hand, covering her exposed cleavage with her left. Clearing her throat in a corrective fashion, she made her gesture obvious enough to convey her discomfort with the apparent focus of Peter's vision. He yanked his head up while shaking it sideways, as though he was coming out of a trance. Humiliated he began to apologize, but the young woman took her hand off her bosom to give him the universal stop sign. This sudden move drew his vision back to her breasts. This time he self-corrected with a whiplash-inducing jerking back of his head.

He was about to explain his malfunctioning radar, when the women cut him off. "You've had a rough day sir. Quit while you are ahead. Enjoy your night at the Holiday Inn." She nodded to the next customer. "I can help you over here sir."

Like a rebuked puppy, Peter obeyed. He stepped aside, grabbed his carryon suitcase, and headed for the double doors. He wished she would have let him explain. He didn't like to leave misunderstandings unresolved. This is the way it had been for Peter with women. He could understand it when he was young and uncomfortable around women; in his adolescent years. But he was a grown man and married at that; having sex on a regular, or at least semi-regular basis. He could stare at his wife naked; that is whenever she let down her guard and flashed him a peek while getting dressed or undressed.

In high school Sammy, Thomas' girlfriend, chided him for having roving drop-eyes. She would catch him staring at her breasts when she spoke to him. Taking hold of his chin, she lifted his head saying, "Make eye contact, Peter. It is impolite to ogle a girl's breasts, especially when she is your brother's girlfriend." Over time she developed a subtle signal for those occasions. She would raise her left hand to her collar bone and tap her index finger pointing upwards, while clearing her throat in a corrective manner.

He explained to Sammy he wasn't looking at her breasts. He was shy and couldn't look girls in the eye. He looked down and being as tall as he was, the view just happened to be down short girl's blouses. She laughed at his explanation. She reached out and placed her hand on his cheek to keep his eyes on hers. "I know that's true most of the time. But it doesn't matter to a girl. It is ogling her breasts no matter why you are doing it. Don't you know every girl believes guys have tit radar? When you get nervous, look at the stars or something."

He tried to plead his case, but she cut him off. "It is not worth trying to explain yourself, Peter. That will only make it worse. No girl is going to buy it. Besides, you can't tell me you don't enjoy the mountain view."

"Why don't girls just cover up?"

"That will help your case. Blame the victim. Like a little fabric is going to stop boys from seeing what they want to see.

You need a girlfriend, Peter. Why don't you ask Maryann out? I heard a rumor she likes you."

Peter entered his hotel room and panicked. When he was with his wife, he didn't mind them. But when he was by himself, feelings of disgust and loneliness overcame him. He saw hotel rooms as seedy places, where lonely people tried to find comfort in senseless, morally flawed ways.

He called his mother. She was expecting his call and wasn't surprised when he told her he would be spending the night in Chicago. She had been following the news and heard O'Hare had been shut down. She updated him on his brothers' plights. John was stuck in Detroit and Thomas, well she hadn't heard from Thomas since he left Arcada. But Sammy had called to make sure it was alright if she came with Thomas for the weekend. She said she would be spending most of the time at her mother's, but they both knew it wasn't going to play out that way. Thomas had called her on the spur of the moment and invited her to come along for the ride. Peter noted this was of no surprise, since Thomas had always insisted Sammy be with him when he was near the family. His mother agreed. They chatted about the cold weather and the plans for the upcoming weekend.

Peter hung up the phone. The news of Sammy's addition to the guest list gave him hope the weekend would provide at least some pleasant reminiscing. He called Sandy to see how she was managing with the kids.

"Hi, honey."

"Hi Peter. Where are you? I heard O'Hare was shut down. Did you make it out in time?"

"I'm stuck in the Holiday Inn next to O'Hare. Everything is shut down until tomorrow. I'm booked on a flight to Grand Rapids at 10:00 tomorrow morning."

"Are you freezing? It looks like a lot of snow." Sandy looked into the bathroom mirror, smiled with her teeth clenched, and looked for food between her teeth. She found a speck and dug it out with a plastic toothpick she stored next to the sink for such occasions.

"There's a lot of it and its still coming down fast. For the most part I managed to stay out of it. I made a quick dash for the shuttle and another one from the shuttle to the hotel. I slipped on a patch of ice when I tried to stop at the door of the hotel and almost broke my neck. But I'm in the hotel room now, and I've cranked up the heat."

"Does it make you want to go out and play in it?" She pressed her lips together as if she was going to kiss the mirror but instead she pressed the cylinder of lip balm on them and ran it back and forth twice on each lip.

"It does. It makes me want to build a snow man and throw a few snowballs; for old times' sake." Peter fell backwards onto the bed. He kicked off his shoes and sprawled out.

"Maybe you can get your brothers to help you build a snowman – bonding time."

"A good old fashion snowball fight might be more in order. Sammy might get the gang to build a snowman."

"Sammy?" Sandy raised one eyebrow.

"You know, Sammy; Thomas' on again, off again girlfriend from high school."

"Oh, that Sammy. She's going to be there?"

"Thomas invited her. I guess it was a last minute thing; a la Thomas." Peter fidgeted as he lay on the bed, running his hands through his short graying hair, making sure it was still neat.

"I thought this was a Vanderhuis boys' only weekend?" Sandy walked over to the full length mirror on the back of the bathroom door. She surveyed her figure from head to toe, turning sideways in order to see if her waistline had widened. She shrugged her shoulders, satisfied there had been no catastrophic expansion in her mid section. She turned facing the mirror and leaned in to get a close up view of her face. Most of her skin blemishes were camouflaged by the light tan she maintained on her face. Her bright blue eyes sparkled, drawing attention away from her naturally blond hair which

84

turned under as it met her shoulders. She extended her lower lip and took a quick breath, blowing a few stray bangs out of her eyes.

"It was, but you know Thomas. No one expects him to follow the rules, because everyone knows he won't do it. Besides, Sammy was always like one of the boys."

"Well, I don't know Thomas all that well. However, I do remember seeing a couple of pictures of Sammy and she didn't look like one of the boys."

"That's true. It sounds like you're feeling a little left out?"

"Let's just say I'm tired and leave it at that. How are you feeling about the weekend?" Sandy left the bathroom and took a seat in the chair next to the dresser, curling up with her feet tucked under her bottom.

"I'm gearing up for it. Sammy's appearance on the scene provides a sigh of relief. She always brings out the best in the Vanderhuis boys."

"Is that so? Maybe I should take the next flight up there and take a few pointers from her. I've got a few Vanderhuis boys that could use some managing. Especially the young one I just managed to put to bed."

"How's Robbie? Is he giving you fits?"

"Actually, he has been quite good. He thinks he is supposed to take your place while you are gone. He has been bossing everyone around all day long as though he is in charge. Margie had to put him in his place several times. Richie just avoids him."

"That's funny. Why don't you tell him he has to preach for me this Sunday? He'll get a kick out of that."

"He might just do a better job than Brother Barnabas."

"Brother Barnabas?"

"It's what people are calling Bernie. Get it? Your assistant pastor, your sidekick, Paul/Barnabas? I swear! You are the last one to pick up on the behind the scenes stuff at church."

"How did you hear about this?"

"Your secretary told me. She also told me the verdict is out. Barnabas is a sleeper, a snoozer, a dozer..."

"Enough already! I get the drift. I don't even want to know that kind of stuff."

"Chill out Petie. It is all in fun. Besides, it will just make people more grateful when you're back in the pulpit next Sunday."

"You're a conniver."

"Just trying to make the most out of the cards I've been dealt. Think you boys will go to church on Sunday?"

"I am. And I'm sure Mom will go with me. I don't know about the two lost boys. John will probably go to make Mom happy. I doubt Thomas will be caught dead in the White Lake Reformed Baptist Church."

"What about Sammy? Can't she get him to go?"

"She is a wild card. She used to go to church with us; mostly because Thomas begged her to keep him company."

"Heard anything about your father's condition?"

"Nothing has changed, as far as I know. Mom never gives many details. I can't help but think it is coming to an end; with Mom's urgency to get us all up there at the same time."

"Maybe you can get some answers when you get there; if not from your mother, then from the hospice nurses."

"I suppose." Peter sat up and put his legs over the side of the bed. He looked down at his size 13 feet.

"You don't sound too motivated."

"You know me. I don't want to know more than I have to know. It will happen when it is supposed to happen."

"Ah, yes. St. Peter's interpretation of the Doctrine of God's Providence – 'Que sera, sera.' In English, 'it's all in God's hands, don't sweat it." Sandy brought her feet out from under her bottom and examined her toenails. She had colored them pink the night before.

"What is wrong with that?"

"Nothing, unless you use it to avoid the hard stuff."

"Hard stuff?"

"Your father, your mother, your brothers, me..." She grabbed the polish from the night stand and touched up a spot she had chipped.

86

"Don't start in on me with that. I do what I have to do."

"I don't care what you do with them, but I expect a bit more than 'I do what I have to do,' when it comes to me. I'm a high maintenance girl. I expect your undivided attention, intimacy, romance, and a well oiled sex machine."

Peter got up and walked into the bathroom. He looked into the mirror and noticed a few grey hairs peeping through his dishwater blond hair. He leaned over to get a better view and tried to pluck them. He noticed a blossoming pimple on his chin and squeezed it. *I thought these were supposed to go away after puberty.*

"Brother, I'd better get off the phone before this conversation deteriorates any further," Peter said.

"I kind of liked where it was going."

"Next thing I know, you'll be asking to have phone sex with me."

"Phone sex? I don't know what all that entails, but I like the sound of it. Will you teach me? Wait a minute. How do you know about phone sex?"

"I guess I do pay attention to some things that are going on around me."

'Who is having phone sex? I want names."

"There are no names because no one is having phone sex."

"Ah, you're going to pull the confidentiality card on me, aren't you? What's the use of being married to a minister, if he can't talk and give you the skinny on people?" Sandy walked over to the closet and searched for what she would wear tomorrow.

"Go to bed, woman. Nobody's having phone sex at our church. You are wearing me out."

"Down, you mean I'm wearing you down, so you'll give me the names." She picked out a pair of slacks and a light cotton sweater, laying them out on the bed to see how they looked together.

"Good night, Millie Hendricks."

"Oh that was low. Millie Hendricks! You're calling me out as a Millie Hendricks? The prayer chain gossip queen?"

"I call it like I see it."

"No phone sex for you, mister." She decided to go with the outfit and laid them carefully on a chair.

"I never asked for phone sex. That was your idea."

"My idea! I still don't even know what it is. Maybe I'll give Sammy a call. I bet she and Thomas have phone sex all the time. She could clue this innocent minister's wife in on the whole craze my husband has gotten himself caught up in."

Peter walked over to the toilet and unzipped his pants. He tilted forward and leaned against the wall with his left hand. He squeezed the phone between his left shoulder and his cheek so he could continue talking. He began to pee.

"You know, if the congregation could hear you behind closed doors, they would be shocked at how their prim and proper minister's wife behaves."

"Only you will ever know, Petie. Only you will ever know. In the daytime, I'm the minister's matronly wife, but at night I'm his play kitten."

"Good night, Sandy."

"Are you peeing while you are talking to me? Because if you are that's disgusting."

"Good night, Sandy."

"Good night, darling...Hey, wait a minute. What about the phone sex? I'm wearing that red pushup bra from Victoria's Secret; the one that makes me look like I actually have a chest."

Sandy waited for a response, cupping both her small breasts in her hands and propping them up until they resembled some of the famous Hollywood bosoms. When the response didn't come, she uncoiled her legs and leaned forward in her chair. "You remember. It makes me look like your friend Sammy."

Peter sat down on the toilet and leaned forward, placing his elbows on his knees.

"You don't look anything like Sammy. You are blond and she is a brunette."

"She dyes her hair blond; probably so she can look like a Vanderhuis."

"You are tall and thin. She is short. You dress more elegantly."

"She dresses sexy; tight jeans and fitted low-cut tops; shows off those breasts."

"I like the way you dress."

"How did you end up with me?"

"What do you mean?"

"Everyone knows you like big breasts. How did you end up with this flat-chested wife?"

"You are being silly, Sandy. I'm going to bed."

Sandy got out of her chair and went over to the dresser to look in the mirror.

"Let's get back to the phone sex. Do you want me to tell you what my pushup bra looks like?"

He hung up without responding because he knew Sandy could go on with this banter forever. He would have played along, if he hadn't been so sure she was joking. That was what Sandy liked best about sex – teasing him. When it came to having sex, she wasn't very interested. He had thought she was when they were dating. This misunderstanding was due to the fact that while courting, all they could do was joke about sex, since they believed in abstinence until marriage. Once they were married, Peter assumed they would have sex as much as they joked about it during courtship, but that didn't materialize. In fact, they started to joke less about it, because it made the not having much sex more obvious.

In all honesty, he thought Sandy was just not very sexual. She liked to cuddle and hold hands and under the right circumstances was even open to an occasional open mouth kiss. But when it came to intercourse, she was shy with her body and complained of physical pain. When they did have sex, she seemed relieved it was over. She had yet to admit to having an orgasm. This frustrated Peter, so he had stepped back from her and pretended he shared her lack of interest.

The painful humiliation of being an inadequate lover was too difficult to endure, for what ended up being sex with a body – a body you weren't even allowed to see.

Peter jumped into the warm shower to wash off the airport sludge. Being trapped in a small space with a couple hundred people for three hours made Peter feel filthy. Walking through the airports, touching doors and railings that had been touched by thousands of others, added to the disgust. He believed flying wasn't healthy and tried to avoid it. He flew back home once or twice a year. When they had first moved to Florida, the whole family would come, driving the fifteen hundred miles in the minivan. But as the kids grew older, Sandy became more vocal in her discomfort visiting his parents. He began to do the trek alone; by air.

Peter finished his shower and hurried to get under the covers so as not to let any of the heat his body had absorbed from the shower escape before he could trap it in his skin with the warm blankets. When he got settled under the covers, he realized he had failed to pick up the remote for the television set. This meant he would have to unwrap himself from the covers and let cold air into his warm cocoon, while he reached for the remote on the dresser, just a few feet from the bottom of the bed.

Peter pushed back the heavy covers and crawled to the foot of the bed. He thought he could reach it if he stretched, but he feared falling off the end of the bed. This would mean his feet would touch the floor, although in the hotel room this would be of little consequence, since the room temperature was set at 68 degrees. Peter stretched and managed to get the tips of his fingers on it and drag it forward until he could grab it. As he lifted it in his hand, lost his balance, and tumbled forward onto the floor, dropping the remote in the process. He scrambled to recover it and rushed back to the bed.

Settled back into the warmth of his bed, Peter turned on the television and watched the evening news. Bored, He scrolled through the channels until he reached the adult pay per view. He read the titles and was again shocked by his strong erotic reaction to the names of these movies. Housewives Gone Wild, College Girls Bare It All, Slow And Slippery, Mandy Gets Rear Ended.

This was a very specific ritual in which Peter engaged when he was alone in a hotel room. He began by scrolling through the titles until he found something that peaked his interest. The blatant invitations toward seduction these titles offered excited him in a way that out flanked the rare invitations his wife offered. Having settled on a title, he took two Kleenex and placed them on the pillow. He began to watch the movie, telling himself he would only take a peek. As the body parts became more exposed and the sex became more prominent, his excitement grew. He told himself he would quit after a few more minutes, and in the moment, was able to convince himself it was true. But a few more minutes, gave way to a few more, and then a few more until it all ended in the predictable manner it had in the past. He came, his semen flowing into the Kleenex stashed on his pillow.

Afterwards, Peter lay still, enjoying the afterglow of his self-induced orgasm. His mind returned to reality and his erotic feelings faded into the background, forcing him to review his escapade under the scrutiny of his judgmental reasoning. He begrudged himself the pleasure of such manufactured reality and felt the shame of having fallen prey to his weakness one more time. The passion he experienced as erotic pleasure was replaced with an intense shame – leading to a prolonged session of self-loathing.

The voice in his head was brutal. *You are disgusting! You betrayed Sandy. How many times are you going to promise to stop and then do it again? You are weak, ugly, and unattractive! You can't even get your wife to make love to you and why would she? You are repulsive! All you can do is sit back and fantasize about other men's wives, other men's girlfriends, and other men's daughters.*

He withstood the punishment of his self-induced verbal assault for what seemed like an eternity, until he found relief in a desperate state of repentance. Alternating between apologizing and pleading, Peter convinced the voice in his head to relent in exchange for a promise to never engage in such self-indulgent promiscuity again. He then slumped to the bathroom where he disposed of the evidence by flushing it down the toilet. As penance he showered in cold water to wash away the remnants of twisted desire and returned to his bed, where he hoped such craziness would not possess him ever again, let alone before morning came.

Peter woke early and headed for the airport. He called his mother to tell her his arrival time and she informed him their neighbor, with whom she had made arrangements to pick him up, had other plans this morning.

"When are you going to learn how to drive, Mother? With Dad in this state you need to think about getting your license."

"Even if I did drive, I wouldn't be able to do it in this kind of weather."

"I know, but my point is you need to think about taking some driving lessons so you can get around on your own. You have a perfectly good car sitting in the garage."

"I know! We've talked about this before. Now is not the time. We have to figure out how to get you home from the airport."

"Now is never the time for you, Mother. Maybe we'll teach you this weekend. It will give us something to do together."

"Me? In the car with you three hooligans laughing at me while I try to learn how to drive? I don't think so."

"Come on! It would be fun and you would get a head start on your lessons."

"We'll see what the weather does. If you haven't learned how to drive after sixty years, a blizzard is not the time to change your mind."

"The weather is going to clear up."

"So how are we going to get you home from Grand Rapids?"

"I'll rent a car."

"You can't do that. It is too expensive and you won't need one once you get here. Besides, your brother John rented one in Detroit and is driving here now."

"Why did he do that?"

"He got caught in the storm and decided to see the Michigan winter wonderland from the ground instead of the air."

"Sounds like John."

"Anyhow, I don't want you to rent a car because I don't want a yard full of cars. The whole world will be wondering if your father passed away."

"Maybe I should rent a suburban and park it in front of Thomas' bus. Dad always hated that eye sore parked in front of the house."

"Oh, your Father was always looking for ammunition with which to hurt him. People will be happy to see that he came home to see his father."

"I suppose."

"Hey, John will be passing through Grand Rapids in a few hours on his way here. He'll be driving right past the airport on 96. I'll call and tell him to pick you up."

"Mother, you know he likes to drive alone. He gets into those trances."

"Well he shouldn't be doing that when he is driving. I'll give him a call and let you know. I'll leave a message on your cell phone. I'm sure it will be alright."

"Do what you want. I've got to go. They are boarding my plane."

"I'll take care of it, Peter. See you in a little while."

"I'm looking forward to it."

"Are you? Really?"

"Yes. I haven't seen you and Dad for a while now and I miss you."

"But what about your brothers? Are you looking forward to seeing them?"

"It will be good for us. It is about time we got together. This is a good idea you've come up with Mother. I've got to go."

Peter arrived in Grand Rapids hoping John had agreed to pick him up. They had been the closest of the three; a union forged under duress in order to survive the onslaught of their brother, Thomas. Peter thought it would be an easy way to break the ice and give them an opportunity to make a plan to deal with Thomas. Peter checked his messages and found one from his mother confirming John would be happy to give him a ride. When he reached the baggage claim area, he saw John waiting for him. They stopped short of each other by several feet and scanned each other up and down, so as to evaluate how the other had changed.

"Hi Peter! You look good."

"So do you John. It has been a long time."

"I see you haven't gotten any shorter."

"You were expecting to grow taller than me?"

"Wishful thinking I guess. I forgot I was the shortest of the three of us," John said.

"Not that you're short. What are you, 5'8"?"

"Hey, 5'9" and still growing."

"Finally going to break that six foot barrier?"

"I might have been shorter than you and Thomas, but I made up for it with brawn and athleticism."

They walked toward the exit doors, their self-assured manly gaits matching step for step.

Peter looked at John while they walked. "What happened to your brawn? You look skinny as a rail. And your hair, why did you shave it off? You look like a monk."

"A vegetarian diet suits me well. As for the hair, you had the short, neat hair cut. Thomas took the long and messy look. All that's left is the clean shaven look."

"You're going to freeze your noggin off in this weather," Peter said.

"I'll have to buy a cap won't I?" John rubbed his head. "I see you've managed to stave off the preacher's girth."

"Sandy makes sure of that. She doesn't want me looking like Dad."

"I think that fear has kept us all fit and trim.

They reached the car and Peter threw his suitcase in the back seat, and then opened the passenger door. He looked across the roof of the car at John, who was waiting for Peter, so they could enter the car at the same time.

"So are you ready for this?" John asked.

"As ready as anyone can be," Peter replied.

They ducked, got in, closed the doors, and drove off.

Chapter 7

Fran's Plan

John and Peter drove from the airport to White Lake, tracing their old stomping grounds. They drove through Grand Rapids with little to note, since they had never spent much time there. Muskegon was a different matter. They had attended the Christian schools from kindergarten through high school, so there were meaningful sights to see. At Peter's suggestion, they left the expressway and found their old schools. The elementary/junior high school was identical, but the high school had now become a charter school. Peter knew the high school had been moved to a new location, which was central to the district and away from the failing neighborhood which was being overtaken by blight. The school building remained unchanged, except for the new sign.

They parked the car and surveyed the school premises in silence.

"This place has memories." John looked to Peter to see if the sight of the school was affecting him in the same way it was unnerving him.

"Yeah, goofy teachers, friends, enemies, sports..."

"Those dreadful chapel services we had to endure."

"They weren't that bad." Peter said.

"Come on Peter. We were bored out of our minds and you know it."

"I guess Mr. Westra's Bible puppets were pretty corny."

"At least the puppets were entertaining. What about Reverend Ricks? Remember him?"

"He managed to put the kids on Ritalin to sleep." Peter said.

"Even when they forgot to take it."

They laughed with relief that they were no longer trapped in this world.

"I didn't know you had enemies in high school," John said.

"Sometimes it felt like everyone was my enemy back then," Peter said.

"I didn't mean to be your enemy."

"That doesn't mean you weren't."

John nodded and left the subject alone.

They drove toward home on the back roads. Neither stated their intent out loud, but both longed to visit the place that would wash away the turmoil the sight of the high school had brought about - Duck Lake Channel. As much as high school brought back memories that polluted their state of mind with tormenting emotions, the channel would fill their consciousness with a playful exuberance that would drive out the melancholy of real life.

Duck Lake Channel was a quarter mile creek that served as an overflow outlet for Duck Lake into Lake Michigan. It was the perfect recreation area, with multiple venues to enjoy the water. On colder days, you could find shelter in the warmer waters of Duck Lake. On the occasional hot days, when Lake Michigan waters became tolerable to human skin, the beautiful sandy beach of the Great Lake provided an ample playground for young and old. The creek connecting the two diverse lakes was the most treasured spot of all. Adults planted their beach chairs in the refreshing waters while they sunbathed. Children played in the calf deep waters, running and falling at will, with no fear of scraping their knees and elbows. And teenagers frolicked in the water with footballs and Frisbees by day, and made out in the shallow waters when the sun had set, the moon taking the edge off the cover of darkness.

Duck Lake Channel had been a consistent sanctuary for the Vanderhuis boys from the time they could walk. This was where they played by running up the enormous sand dunes that cushioned the shore line and splashing in the shallow water. They built sand castles with tunnel systems that interconnected, buried each other in the sand, and threw muddy sand balls at unsuspecting friends. There was fishing for bluegills, specs, and perch, and later in their lives, scoping out the pretty girls in skimpy bikinis.

They felt safe in this place, as it allowed their minds to put distance between the tension at home and the carefree atmosphere of the beach. It was the only place in their world where the boys felt like they belonged together; like they were brothers.

Peter and John cruised down Lakeshore drive, through the trees that in the summer provided a protective canopy for those who traveled the route. They came to the curve at the top of the hill overlooking the park and were swept away by the beauty of the frozen beach, pushing up against the iced sand dunes. The waves crashed into the ice, spraying the air with drops of water that sparkled like crystals in the sunlight, building the icebergs that lined the shore. They got out of the car and made their way through the snow toward the beach. Running on the frozen sand, they chucked a few pieces of ice at each other. John challenged Peter to a race up the dune, then both cried uncle one quarter of the way up the hill.

"How did we manage to do this all day when we were kids?" John gasped for air and bent over.

"Age," Peter took a deep breath, "has crept up on us. I haven't been this out of breath in a long time."

"Sex." John gasped again.

"Sex?"

"It's the only time I breathe this hard anymore."

"Ahh."

They left the beach in high spirits, renewed by the reminder that not all of their childhood was pain. They had, for many hours during the summer, been a family – a single parent family, since their father had set foot on the beach only once – but still a family. A happy family.

Turning into the driveway they spotted their mother beaming out of her kitchen window. Fran met them at the front door. She hugged until the awkwardness was unbearable and the boys disentangled themselves and moved into the house.

As expected, the house was immaculate with everything in its proper place. The white carpeting and the white furniture that had kept them out of the formal living room was still there, menacing as ever. It was their father's showroom and only special guests were allowed.

"Why don't you take your stuff up and get yourselves settled," Fran said. "Then you can meet me in the kitchen for a bite to eat, nothing too special, just something to hold you over until supper."

"That would be great Mother," Peter said.

The boys, now men, walked up the stairs to the space which had been so familiar. They had both been there since leaving home, but never at the same time. The other's presence added to the reality the room triggered in them.

They went to their respective beds without questioning the legitimacy of the rights of ownership established in their childhood. Dropping their suitcases on the floor, they fell onto their beds. Not a thing had been changed since they had left. The posters on the walls, the collections they had once treasured: matchbox cars, GI Joes, stamps, coins, and Thomas' swords. Nothing had been moved; cleaned for sure, but not moved or tossed. It was a museum of sorts, preserving the evidence of a time twenty years ago, when three boys lived between these four walls.

Peter's space was neat and ordered; as was his life. Thomas' corner was messy and disorganized. It had been cleaned, but not organized; keeping it comfortable for his return. John's area was sparse, reflecting his inherent desire to keep life simple. Nothing much on the walls with a small bed stand to contain what he once thought was essential – a journal and a pen.

They headed to the kitchen and found Fran preparing lunch.

"There you are. Are you settled in for the weekend?"

"You could say that. We threw down our bags, tossed everything onto the floor, and messed up the beds. We're good to go Mom – just like high school."

"John, you're such a kidder."

"What do you mean kidding? We're getting into this trip back to the future. Peter and I were contemplating tearing holes in our jeans. You know, Mom, in the knees and in the butt."

"That used to drive your Dad crazy. He never did figure out how you wore through your jeans so fast. I used to tell him you were rough-housing, like three normal boys."

"Did he buy that?" Peter asked.

"No, he never saw you playing rough."

"So what did he settle on for an answer to the mystery?" Peter said.

"I believe he decided Levis wasn't keeping their commitment to high quality; mixing polyester with the cotton to save money. He told me to buy another brand."

"Let me guess," John said. "He went on to rant and rave about the state of American manufacturing. Or was it the foolish practice of importing cheap goods from foreign countries, who knew nothing about manufacturing quality goods?"

"Oh yes – both! And it went on for days."

"So how is Dad?" Peter asked.

"He's not good." Fran offered the boys a small bite of cheese. John refused, so Peter devoured his and John's.

"Whose car is in the driveway?" John asked.

"It belongs to Jane, the Hospice nurse. She is taking care of your father."

"How long is she here for?" John asked.

"A couple of hours. She's getting ready to leave. One of them comes at least once a day to look in on your father."

"So the end is near?" Peter asked.

"That's what they tell me. They also told me he would be gone weeks ago, and he is still here. He is a fighter and wants to hang on to life."

"So he isn't conscious?" Peter asked.

"He hasn't opened his eyes in a month. The nurses say he is in a deep coma, but there is no way of knowing for sure if he is aware of what is going on. They tell me to act normal around him – to touch him and talk to him as though he's aware – just in case."

John surveyed the small changes his mother had made to her kitchen. The small radio attached to the underside of the counter, next to the new flat screen television caught his eye. He wondered if she still listened to the old gospel music that drove his father crazy because it wasn't the traditional singing of the Psalms.

"Do they expect him to wake up before he dies – is it possible? Peter said.

"The nurses say anything is possible, but they don't expect he will regain consciousness. You can go and see him, Peter. The nurse won't mind. You can ask her whatever you want. They're all very nice."

"I know."

"I forgot you are a minister and used to all of this death and dying stuff." Fran approached the boys with a knife and apple in hand. She held them out in front of her. John nodded and Fran cut him a large slice. She cut Peter a piece but he waved her off, so she ate it herself.

"I wouldn't say, 'used to it.' Besides, it is different when it's your father."

101

"I know." Fran swallowed. "I was just talking about the mechanics of dying in Hospice care. Of course it is different when the person dying is your father."

"So is he all hooked up to wires and stuff?"

"He is on oxygen and has an IV. There is also a special port in his chest where they can administer the medicine. He isn't too frightening to look at, but he is pale. He is down to one hundred pounds, so there isn't much left of him. What am I saying? You can hardly recognize him with his girth gone. He's quite scary to look at, so be prepared."

"Thanks for being honest. I'll go say hi."

"Introduce yourself to Jane. She is the nurse in charge of his care. She'll tell you anything you want to know."

"Except time of death, I surmise."

"She's not a fortune teller."

Peter left to see his father. John sat down on a stool and watched Fran walk around the kitchen rearranging things that were not out of place.

"Something is different about you, Mom."

"I see you're ready to join the conversation again, now that I'm done talking about your father's condition."

"I did get a little distracted, didn't I?"

"Trying to avoid the subject?" Fran tilted her head toward him.

"I didn't think so, but back to you. You look different."

"You think so?"

"I do."

"That's a good thing, I hope? I've lost a few of the pounds I put on over the years. I could stand to lose a few more."

"You seem happy."

Fran squinted while her jaw dropped. "I've always been happy, John."

"That's not how I remember you. You never smiled, except when you forced yourself to do so for our sake. You trudged around the kitchen as though it was a burden. You didn't talk, much less joke like you are doing now. Look at you. You have a little hitch in your step. If I didn't know better, I'd say you are developing a bit of a swagger."

"That's silly, John. I've always been a cheerful person. If my walking has changed, it is because I've lost a few pounds worrying about your father. Besides, how could I be happier now? Your father is on his death bed, for God's sake." Fran walked across the kitchen, trying to avoid any evidence of a hitch in her step.

"The weight loss suits you, Mom, but that isn't it. You've got a bounce in your step; a lightness about you. You're more confident. As for Dad's impending death, I expect it to bring as much relief as it does grief."

"John, I can't believe you are talking that way about your father's death. You sound like your brother Thomas, with all that anger."

"Mom, we are all angry at Dad. The biggest difference between Thomas and the rest of us is he is honest about it."

"You think Peter is angry at your father?" She looked at John.

"Mom, Dad denied him his approval all of these years, even though he followed him like a puppy dog. Of course Peter is angry at him."

"You're angry at your father?"

"I've always been angry at Dad. I just handle my anger in a different way than Thomas. I try not to create so much collateral damage. Why do you think I stayed away from home?"

"I don't know. I thought you wanted to get away from me." She looked away from John and chopped carrots.

"Get away from you? I would have taken you with me, if I could. Gotten you away from Dad. I was never trying to get away from you, Mom. If anything I felt guilty leaving you to deal with him on your own. I was staying away from Dad."

Tears ran down Fran's cheeks. She lifted the bottom of her apron to her cheeks and wiped away her tears, hoping John wouldn't notice. "I was fine."

103

"No you weren't Mom. None of us were. Maybe we will be, someday, when this is over. But none of us is fine."

Fran looked at her son and saw he had tears running down his cheeks. At first she felt ashamed for him, and had the urge to look away and pretend she hadn't seen them. But she held steady, confounded by the fact her son made no attempt to hide his tears. He did look away to lessen the intensity, but he let the tears remain.

His vulnerability moved her. She moved closer to her son, looking him in the eyes. Taking the hem of her apron, which she was still holding in her hands, she wiped away his tears, mixing his with hers. She put her arms around his neck and hugged him. When his body relaxed in her arms, she placed her hands on both of his cheeks, looked into his eyes and said, "I hope you know how much I love you."

John was surprised how his mom's words and actions affected him – making him shrink in size, until he felt like a young boy, yearning for her to pick him up and envelope him in a hug that would last all day and send him off into a deep sleep at the end of it.

John broke free of the hug and leaned back.

"I meant it as a compliment, Mom."

"What's that?"

"The swagger in your step, the lightness in your attitude, your laughing, it all suits you."

"Thank you, John."

"Wow, there it is again! The new you!"

"What are you talking about?"

"Since when do you accept compliments with a simple 'thank you'? Where is the string of rationalizations denying there could be anything good about you? What is going on with you?"

"That would be Marcia's doing."

"Marcia?"

"My therapist, Marcia."

"You have a therapist? My God, Mom! Who is this woman standing before me and what has she done to my sweet, pathetic mother." John leaned toward her. "How did you get a therapist? Dad hates therapists. He always said they were the devil's right hand; coddling people as they walked them straight toward the doors of hell."

"That is what he said about them, isn't it? Trust me; he would think that about Marcia. I think I picked her because I knew your father would hate her. I wanted to prove it wasn't his decision anymore. It's mine."

"Yes, but he isn't even dead yet."

"I got tired of waiting. I've waited on that man all my life. I don't have much life left, so I can't let him steal any more of what little I have left."

"For a minute, I thought I was talking to Thomas."

"Thomas isn't all wrong about your father."

"I never said he was wrong. To the contrary, he is right on most counts."

"He is my son. I have to believe he got some of what he is from me."

"You mean to say Thomas was acting out your rage?"

"Yes. I think I made him do my job for me. That's why he hates me so much." She wiped her hands on a towel and tossed it onto her shoulder.

"Thomas doesn't hate you; at least, not anymore than he hates everybody else."

"Now you are being kind. He has always put me in the same category as his father; and rightly so. I stood by his father and let him do his thing. Thomas has every right to hate me, and so do you and Peter."

"You are not being fair to yourself, Mom. You were in this with us. You were just as afraid of Dad as we were."

"That might be true. But I was the mother and I should have protected you. And for that, I'm sorry." Fran looked at the floor.

"I've never held that against you, Mom."

"That's kind of you, but perhaps you shouldn't let me off the hook so easily."

"Well I do let you off the hook, and I forgive you."

Fran opened the refrigerator and put away the extra vegetables. She had worked up a sweat in this conversation and the cold air from the refrigerator felt good on her face. She took a deep breath and closed the door, keeping her back to John.

"Sweet and pathetic? Is that how you saw me all of those years?"

"Forget I said that. I was joking."

"Marcia says there's a grain of truth to most jokes. It's alright, John. I won't break. I was sweet and pathetic. It is the price I've paid all these years for your generous forgiveness. You exonerated me by accepting me as sweet and pathetic; unable to take care of myself and my children. That isn't a flattering portrait. It might be accurate, but it isn't becoming. Not that I blame you in any way for coming to that conclusion."

"So what's this all about, Mom?"

"What do you mean by this?"

"This homecoming you've managed to pull together?"

Fran turned to face John.

"I want my family back. I sat by and watched while your father drove you away. At the time I thought I had no choice. I thought you hated me as much as you hated your father. I now realize that isn't true. I am my own person and I want a chance to show you I'm a good mother."

"That is a tall order. Do you have a plan?"

"Sort of."

"Sort of?"

"Marcia says families change in small impetuses and they do so in response to each other. She said you don't need a detailed plan with a set outcome. That would feel like manipulation and would backfire. She says I need to find one thing I can do different this weekend – one thing that will catch you boys off guard and require you to respond in a different manner toward me than you have in the past."

"And?"

106

"And that will jumpstart our relationship in a different direction." Fran looked at her son. It's like dancing. If you follow the rules and do all the same steps, nothing ever changes in the dance. If you sit down with your partner and try to change the whole dance routine, your partner is going to flip out and refuse to budge. However, if you start doing one different step without telling him, he doesn't have a choice. He can't keep doing the same thing. He has to adjust his step in order to match yours. Once he reacts and changes that small step to respond to your purposeful mistake, you have an opportunity to alter another step in order to adjust to his misstep. In the process, you end up doing a dance that is unlike any you've ever done before." Fran shuffled her feet, as if she were dancing. "Does that make sense?"

"My, my! Sweet and pathetic she is no longer. Meet the new and improved, sweet and assertive Fran Vanderhuis."

"You're mocking me."

"Not at all; I'm encouraging you. I like you this way. I am a bit shocked, but I like it."

"Shocked?"

"To hear you talk like this about yourself and your family. Mom, my biggest worry in coming here was how we were going to take care of you after Dad died."

"You were planning on visiting nursing homes where you could dump me?" Fran grinned.

"No, but Mom, I remember you as incompetent without Dad. How was I to know you were transforming yourself into a modern day super woman?"

"That's right – sweet and pathetic. Did you think I would just lie down and die when your father passed away?"

"You can't hold it against me I assumed you would be at a loss with him gone. He managed everything for you. You don't even drive, Mom."

"I understand why you would make that assumption. But I'm working on changing, and there is more in me than I ever thought possible. Life with your father just sucked it out of me, but that is done. I'm starting over."

107

"I'm thrilled for you, Mom."

"Thanks."

John stood up and walked over to the window to see if anyone was out and about.

"So what is it that you are going to do different in your dance with us?"

"Hell if I know."

"Hell!" John turned and looked at his mother. "You're going to start swearing? That's the brilliant plan you and your crackerjack therapist cooked up?" He raised an eyebrow.

"No, that's just a bad habit of Marcia's that has rubbed off on me."

"Your therapist swears?"

"She says it helps her be more expressive when she needs to make a strong point."

"I'm sure there are other ways to be more expressive."

"I don't know, but I kind of like it. The first time she used bad language she was responding to an opinion of your father's I had shared with her. She said, 'That's a crock of shit.' At first I was offended. I told her it was wrong to swear. She said the Ten Commandments only refer to using God's name in vain; not saying poop. Not that I haven't heard her use the Lord's name in vain, mind you. So I thought about it and she was right. It was a crock of shit."

"Let's get back on track. What is it you are going to do different?" John walked over to the counter and fussed with the food.

"I'm going to have to surprise you and myself with that one."

"Mom!" He turned to look at her, but she countered in the opposite direction.

"What can I tell you, John. Therapists don't work like that. They don't give you all the answers. They just give you the general direction and make you fill in the blanks. After you've done that, they won't even evaluate your choice. They make you critique it yourself. They give you the old 'How did that work for you?' routine."

"I hope it doesn't involve cooking."

"What's wrong with my cooking?" Fran wrung her hands together.

"Nothing is wrong with your cooking. You are a great cook."

"So why did you say my solution should not involve cooking?"

"Because, Mom, cooking is what you have always done to try and make things better."

"You know about my magic kitchen?"

"Magic Kitchen?"

"Marcia says I think I have a magic kitchen and I can fix what ails my family by cooking good food for them."

"We all know about your magic kitchen, Mom. The problem is the only magic it has is to make you feel better; not us. The only thing it does for us is make us gain weight."

"Oh come on now, John. You can't say my cookies didn't improve your mood when you were brooding. They always put a smile on your face."

"Brooding? I never brooded!" John backed up to the counter, placed his palms on it, lifted, and sat his bottom down, letting his legs hang over the edge."

"That's just not true. You were forever brooding about your life in high school, in junior high, and as a matter fact in grade school as well. I think you came out of the womb brooding."

"Define brooding for me."

"Moping around when things don't go the way you want."

"Oh, that. Myrna says I still do a good bit of that."

"How is Myrna, these days? I'm anxious to meet her, John."

"She is doing fine and you will meet her when the time is right. But you have to stop changing the subject. Tell me what it is you think you are going to do different?"

"Relax, John. It will all work out in the end. I'll think of something. Marcia says I should trust my instincts. I will know when the time is right."

"Look, Mom. I'm sorry I have stayed away so long. It's not because I don't love you. I'm sorry you haven't met my wife and I will do my best to correct that when this is all over."

"I would like that."

"You know, Mom, I do believe it suites you well."

"Not this again."

"You are talkative, funny, opinionated, and feisty. You're kind of a pill, an easy one to swallow, yet still a pill."

"I feel like I have always been this way. It got pushed down and locked away when I married your father."

"Well, I'm glad you found yourself."

Peter came into the kitchen trailing the hospice nurse. Jane gave a short report along with a few instructions, and Fran took them in as though she had heard it before.

"Hi, I'm Jane." She shook John's hand. "Do you have any questions?"

"Mom seems to have it all under control," John said.

"She does. She has been wonderful with your father," Jane said. "But this weekend is about saying goodbye to your father and I can help you get through it, if you like."

John winked at his mother. "I don't know. I prefer to see this weekend as a time to say 'hello' to my mother."

Jane moved toward the door. "I'll be back in the morning. I'm on all weekend so I'm sure we'll have time to talk further, John."

Peter gave a puzzled look to his mother and brother. "What was that all about?"

"What was what all about?" John asked.

"The nod-off you gave the hospice nurse and the private party you and Mom have been having during my absence."

Peter joined John sitting on the counter.

"I don't know if I like you two sitting up there. It makes you even taller than me."

"I wasn't rude, was I? I just haven't got myself together enough to have questions about dad. Besides, we have the whole weekend," John said.

110

"If dad lasts that long. He looks terrible, Mom. There is only a quarter of him left."

"He is hard to look at, isn't he? It has been scary to see death happen in slow motion. It's like something is consuming him from the inside and his skin is collapsing on his bones. I can understand why you would be shocked."

"I wish he could talk."

"You do?" John asked.

"Don't you? I mean it is hard to say goodbye without a response from him."

"I was looking forward to the silence. I've been trying to get a word in edgewise with Dad for the last forty years. I believe I might have found my opening."

"Except you won't know if he is listening," Peter said.

"I'm willing to settle for the opportunity to state my case. His listening is the frosting on the cake that I stopped expecting a long time ago."

"Jane said anything is possible. She said dying people have defied science before and come back to lucidity for one last time before they died," Peter said.

"And what is it you think he would say?" John asked.

"I would hope he would want to make peace with his family before he went on to meet his Maker."

"A deathbed confession! Wouldn't that be something? It would have to be a long awakening. People would form a line that would stretch all the way out into the street. His confession to Thomas alone would take hours."

"What about his confession to you, John? How long would that take?" Fran asked.

"It doesn't matter. Dad's life is over. I have made peace with Dad on my own; without his help. Besides, do you really think Dad would be any different if he woke up before his death? Do you think Dr. Vanderhuis would end his self-conceived pristine life with a confession? I highly doubt it. And if he did wake up, I wouldn't bother going in to listen. Why would I give him one more chance to work me over?"

Peter raised his eyebrows. "I thought you made peace with Dad on your own?"

"I didn't say I reconciled our relationship. I said I made peace with him from two thousand miles away. I was hoping to maintain that peace by keeping the distance between us."

"You sound like Thomas," Peter said.

"Speaking of Thomas, where is he? I need him to get here and do his job."

"His job?" Peter asked.

John smiled at Fran and said, "I need Thomas to get here and take this burden off my back. I need him to be angry for me. He is the angry one. We use his anger so we don't have to go there ourselves. I need him to get here and take this monkey off my back."

Fran raised her eyes at John, making the connection he was offering her in his clandestine way. He was joining in her confession to having used Thomas to express her anger. Her face softened and her shoulders dropped, and she leaned closer to him.

Chapter 8

The Sniffing Dog

Fran set out two types of cheese, crackers, and hummus.

"Is this hummus?" John asked, knowing full well it was. "Since when do you make hummus?"

Fran frowned at John in an attempt to short circuit his plan to harass her about the magic of her cooking. He carried on undeterred. "Something different on your menu. What a surprise. You are usually so predictable with your menu."

Fran smirked. "I saw Rachel Ray making it and thought you might like it; seeing you are used to exotic cooking from the east. I didn't want you to get bored with our Dutch cuisine."

He laughed. "You mean meat and mashed potatoes?"

"What's up with you two? You've been together less than an hour and already you have secrets." Peter shook his head.

They heard a car and walked toward the kitchen window so they could see the driveway. Peter and John pushed against each other in a playful attempt to get the better view. Fran warned them not to be too obvious, lest Thomas feel like he was being spied on.

"Isn't that what we are doing? Spying on him?" Peter said.

"You and John might be spying. I'm trying to find out who I'm going to be meeting at the door so I can be prepared. You never know who your brother is going to bring with him and it is best to be prepared, lest you open the door and meet them with a dropped jaw," Fran said. "Well there is Sammy. She looks good as always," Fran said.

John chided Peter by bumping him in the arm with his elbow. Peter pushed him away and ignored him.

"Who is the other girl?" Fran said. "Didn't I tell you? There is no predicting who your brother will bring with him."

"Remember when he brought home that Jehovah Witness guy?" Peter said. "He met him canvassing the neighborhood and invited him to dinner so he could discuss theology with Dad."

"Your father got so mad at that poor man," Fran said. "Remember how he pushed him out of the house?"

"What about the Hari Krishna monk he befriended at the mall and brought home with him?" John said. "For three days they hung out in the front yard and did that chanting and dancing thing."

"I don't know how your Dad put up with it for that long," Fran said.

They waited as Thomas motioned the third guest to get out of the car.

"They look awful!" John said.

"Wouldn't you, if you had ridden in that contraption for hours in the dead of winter?" Fran said.

Dundee stuck his head out of the bus and took a reluctant sniff of the cold air.

"He brought a dog? Oh, it is a good thing your Dad's unconscious. He would have a fit if he saw this coming. Who brings an uninvited dog two thousand miles in the dead of winter, to stay at someone else's house? I hope he is house trained," Fran said.

"Thomas does, Mother. He does whatever he wants. And don't bet on the dog being trained. An untrained master can't be expected to train his dog," Peter said.

Dundee slumped out of the bus and he attempted to climb the snow bank bordering the driveway. When his old body

114

failed him, he squatted with one foot on the snow bank and relieved himself.

"Now Dad would love that yellow landmark on his pristine driveway," John said. "Who has been plowing the driveway, Mom? It's as de-iced as it was when Dad used to make us do it."

"You remember Archie from church?"

"You mean the Archie Dad referred to as the half-wit?" John asked.

"You shouldn't repeat your father's insensitive remarks; but yes, that Archie. Your father recruited him to replace you when you left for college. It took him a while, but he trained him to do it."

"Imagine that Peter. We were replaced by a half-wit."

"He does a nice job and he has never missed a day. And, he doesn't complain, like the previous snow throwers did," Fran said.

"You're not going to up and adopt him now, are you Mom?" John said.

"Oh no! Here it comes! The dog is circling. Once, twice, and...the third time is the charm!" Peter narrated the dog's movement. "And there you have it, ladies and gentlemen. The dog has done the unthinkable and relieved himself right on top of the pitcher's mound."

John joined him. "Call a time out, Mr. Umpire. Bring out the grounds crew and tell them to bring the largest shovel they've got. It's a big one."

Fran walked toward the front door. "You two are awful. I was hoping you had grown up a bit, but I can see this environment has caused you to regress. This weekend might be a bit tougher than I thought. You better clean up that dog's mess, John. If not, Peter might get his wish. Something like that might give your father reason enough to come back from the dead."

"Talk about awful, Mother! Since when have you become so callous about Dad's dying?" Peter followed her toward the door.

Fran opened it and waved the crowd in. Sammy led the way, running the last few steps in order to embrace Fran with an engulfing hug. Fran, who slipped back into her old discomfort, dangled between Sammy's arms as though she didn't know what to do with her arms. Eventually she managed to free her elbows enough to wrap her arms around Sammy's torso and patted her with both hands, while they rested in the small of Sammy's back.

Sammy ran to Peter, embracing him the same way. Peter reacted as his mother had. He decided against patting her on the back, because he couldn't free his arms and didn't want to pat her on the ass.

John raised his arms before Sammy wrapped hers around him and returned the embrace.

Julie stepped into the entryway and stood wringing her hands, both to warm them and to quell the anxiousness the uncomfortable situation was creating for her. Sammy had left her hanging, since she thought Thomas was walking with Julie. Dundee had held Thomas up and Julie was deliberating between introducing herself and waiting for Sammy to finish. Not knowing how she should be introduced, she opted to wait.

When Sammy made it through the reception line, she turned and noticed her misstep.

"Did everybody meet Julie?" she asked.

Julie raised her hand and offered a princess wave with a forced smile.

"I see everybody has met Julie." Thomas burst in, bumping into Julie and almost knocking her over.

Fran walked over and shook Julie's hand; veering her eyes toward Thomas to scold him. "We weren't expecting you, so I didn't know how to welcome you. I hope the rest of the weekend is more comfortable than your introduction to us."

"Oh, I won't be staying long. I just caught a ride with Thomas. I'm renting a car and driving to Detroit to visit some friends."

"It was nice of you to keep Thomas company. It must have been a dreadful ride in that tin death trap."

116

"Vintage, Eddie! It is a vintage car." Since middle school, Thomas had referred to his mother as Eddie. He named her after Edith, Archie Bunker's dingbat wife on the sitcom All In The Family. Fran took offense so he had settled on Eddie.

"It wasn't all that bad. I slept under blankets most of the way."

"Well we are glad you are here for however long you choose to stay."

"Thanks, Mrs. Vanderhuis."

"Call me Fran, dear."

"Thank you Fran."

Dundee made his appearance by heading straight through the door toward Fran. Sammy noticed the direction the dog's scent track was leading him and spoke too late. "Fran watch out for…"

Dundee's snout slid between Fran's legs and rested in her crotch. "Oh, dear me."

Sammy pulled the dog from his comfortable niche. "I was going to say, watch out for Dundee. He has this thing about sniffing crotches. His head has been nudging me from under the lawn chair all the way from Chicago."

"Thomas! You made her ride here on a lawn chair; without a seatbelt?" Fran said.

"I thought it might warm her up Eddie; make her think of the beach in the summer."

"Mother hasn't had anyone show that kind interest in her since…" John stopped mid-sentence by the jolt of Dundee's snout between his own legs.

Peter roared. "I guess the dog doesn't discriminate by sexual preference." He stopped laughing as he squeezed his legs together, noticing the dog moving his way. He lifted his open hand in front of the dog's face. "No! Bad dog! No!"

The others laughed and Sammy told Thomas to leash the beast. He ignored her. "He believes in freedom of expression; even for animals," Sammy said.

"So what's the dog's name?" John asked.

"His name is Ralph, but I'm calling him Dundee."

117

"We got him when I lived in Arcada and I named him Ralph. Thomas never liked the name, so he keeps giving him surnames. Dundee is his present calling," Sammy said.

"Why Dundee?" John asked.

"It's from the movie Crocodile Dundee. You remember; the crocodile man goes to a party and sees what he suspects is a man dressed up like a woman. So he walks over to her and puts his hand between her legs. The woman asks him what he is doing and he responds he is just checking. You know, checking to see if she is a man or a woman," Thomas said. "In his old age, Ralph developed this habit of sniffing crotches. So I call him Dundee."

Peter relaxed his stance, since the dog had desisted. "You should think about retraining him. It is a nuisance."

"He is too old to be retrained. Besides, he's been a good dog. If he wants to take a sniff, he has earned the right," Thomas said.

"Tell that to the Dog Whisperer," Peter replied.

"I'm starved!" Sammy stated in blunt fashion as she moved toward the kitchen. The group followed.

Fran ran ahead of the group, "I've got plenty of snacks to tide you over until dinner."

They gathered around the kitchen counter and filled their plates. The girls and John sat on the stools, while the boys stood between them. Fran joined the group on and off, while she fussed with the food. They chatted about superficial things, as people do when they are buying time to adjust to each other.

Dundee followed Peter around trying to finish the job he had been denied. Peter responded with a periodic stare, letting Dundee know this was going to be a competition he couldn't win. Peter wasn't about to be beaten by Thomas' dog, but he had not been made aware of Dundee's pension for persistence. Once Dundee set his mind on something, he was doggedly importunate.

Without even the slightest attempt to be coy, Dundee edged closer to Peter. He would stop when Peter glared at him,

118

but the moment Peter looked away, Dundee was on the move again, scooting along on his belly as though he was a commando dodging enemy fire. He reached the legs of Peter's chair and touched his nose to one of the legs, while resting his head on the ground. He waited with his eyes pushed back into their sockets, so he could look straight up and keep an eye on his prey; like a crocodile waiting in the waters below; stalking even the slightest move.

It was Julie who reached over and touched Peter's arm to get his attention. "You might as well stand up and give him what he wants. Trust me; he will stalk you until you let him get a good sniff. Then he leaves you alone. Well there is that time of the month, when things change and he becomes even more persistent. But you don't have to worry about that."

"I gave in around Michigan City and he hasn't bothered me since," Sammy confessed.

"Come on Peter! Get it over with," Thomas said. "Stand up and give him what he wants."

"I'm not letting this dog stick his nose between my legs, even if it kills me. Someone has to teach him some manners."

"Good luck with that," Thomas laughed. "Everyone has to act right. I can see you haven't changed."

Sammy broke the tension. "There is nothing wrong with having high expectations."

"Except they suck the life out of everyone around you and make you the most boring..."

Sammy's threatening glare stopped Thomas mid-sentence.

John looked at Julie and wondered what her status was in this unique family saga. He knew there must be an interesting story. "So Julie, how was the ride in the bus?"

"You mean Puff?"

"He still calls it that?" John asked.

"He does. Loyalty isn't a bad character trait," Julie argued in an attempt to keep herself on Thomas' side in this plethora of conflicting family dynamics. She was angry with him, but he was the only lifeline she had in this situation. She needed to stay somewhat attached to him until she could leave on the next life boat.

"Loyalty is a good thing," John granted her, not wanting to push her to betray her allegiance.

"To answer your question, it was quite an adventure. I found myself wishing I could steal Dundee's fur coat on more than one occasion."

The rest of the group turned their eyes toward her. Curiosity was killing them and she was going to have to explain her presence on the scene. She looked to Thomas for help, but was not surprised he made no attempt to rescue her. Instead, he sat back to observe how she would play her cards. Sammy tried to distract the mob by changing the subject, but found Fran's menu had no chance of competing for the attention of this gang when it came to the mystery of Thomas' new friend, who happened to be a girl.

"It was a long trip, but Thomas did all of the driving. I caught up on my sleep. My biggest concern was Puff would break down and leave us stranded. Thomas assured me she could make the trip."

"And you believed him?" John asked.

"What can I say? I'm gullible when it comes to men."

"You drove straight through?" Peter inquired.

"We stopped a couple of times. I don't know for how long, because I slept through most of it. As long as I get an occasional potty break, I'm good to go. I did offer to drive, but I got the impression Thomas has an exclusive relationship with Puff."

"You would be correct in assuming this. No one we know of has ever driven her except for Thomas."

"I drove it once," Sammy said. "It broke down and Thomas and some of his friends had to push it to the garage. I got to steer."

"Did it have any heat at all?" John said to Julie.

"Thomas said there was some warm air coming out of some place, but I couldn't feel it."

"So you aren't staying with us?" Fran asked. "You are more than welcome to stay as long as you like. We'll find a nice spot for you to sleep and there is plenty of food. You could give Sammy and me a hand in managing these three boys." Fran hoped no one had noticed how her tone dropped off, when she realized she might have made a mistake in bringing up Sammy. After all, she didn't know the status of their feelings for Thomas and each other.

"Thanks, but I made a commitment to visit my friend in Detroit. As appealing as it might be to spend the weekend watching Thomas squirm, I need to go."

The change in her tone of voice, accompanied by the rolling of her eyes, gave away the secret of her hostility toward Thomas. She didn't want to get into her relationship with him, because she didn't want to display the intense anger she felt. She had already let herself vent in Sammy's presence, and although that turned out to be a helpful voyage into self-disclosure, the Vanderhuis family was a different matter. Sammy liked Thomas and could empathize with her without squashing Thomas in the process. The group seemed ready to join the lynching.

"So how did you meet?" John asked.

The group looked at Thomas. He spread his arms, holding his palms up and gave the floor back to Julie. Julie pleaded for relief with her eyes, while threatening bodily harm if he didn't provide it. He spun his hand in small circles, signaling for her to get on with it. She took a deep breath and gathered herself. She wanted to be at her best as she spun answers to their questions that would disclose personal information, while preserving her sense of dignity. As for Thomas' dignity, she had lost all concern for his sense of self-respect and could care less if he was embarrassed in front of his family. The problem was their fates were bound together and in order to keep herself above reproach, she would have to bring him with her. She had been the co-author of this insipid love story and thus, equally responsible for any dysfunction directing it.

"Oh for God's sake!" Sammy said. "Stop torturing your guest. If you want to know what her relationship is with Thomas, then ask him."

"Right, like Thomas is going to tell us anything." Peter leaned back in his chair.

"It would be the polite way to start off the conversation and if he did happen to answer, Julie would be enlightened as well." Sammy put her hand on Julie's shoulder.

"Spoken by a person with hands on experience, Sammy," John said. "We've survived our curiosity about Sammy's relationship with Thomas for twenty-five years."

"I see the smart one has grown a pair and turned into a smart ass," Sammy said.

John raised his hands above his head and bowed toward Sammy acknowledging her superiority. "I should have known better than to challenge the Queen of Verbal Fencing."

Sammy slid down on her stool to kick John under the counter, punting Fran's foot as she flung her foot in his direction. Fran winced while John shoved himself away from the counter.

"Are you alright, Fran? I'm so sorry. I meant to kick your son for mocking me." Sammy said. "John, go get her some ice. I hit her pretty hard."

"Why me? I'm not the one that just tried to drop kick Mom into the next county. You're the Karate Girl. You should clean up your own mess."

"I'm fine. There is no need for ice or anything else," Fran said. "Sammy dear, I must say, you are out of practice. I don't think I remember you ever missing your intended target before. You seem to have developed a need for glasses for those eyes you've always had on your knees." she looked at Julie. "You should have seen her when she was young, Julie. She could take any one of these boy's legs out at the ankles under the dinner table without anyone noticing until they saw the poor boy wince in pain."

She paused. "My husband, Richard, would see the boys squirming in pain as they pushed themselves back from the

122

table, and without a clue he would say, 'Where do you think you are going, young man. Dinner isn't over until we've had our devotions. Pull your chair back up to the dinner table and wipe that stupid look off your face.' The boys were afraid of her. I think she did a better job than their father at keeping them in line."

The group laughed. Peter's attention was drawn to her muscular legs, wrapped tightly in her jeans. He looked to Julie's and compared them, concluding they were equally well-shaped. He pictured Sammy's legs naked and spread apart, but stopped himself mid-image. Instead he riled them even further. "She was like one of those Irish dancers, whose legs bend every which way at the knees, while their upper body stays still as stone." Peter stood to imitate an Irish dancer, flicking his feet off to the side in quick sudden movements, almost falling over in the process.

"We should have called her the River Dance Assassin," Thomas said.

"Well, Fran, I wasn't always as accurate as you are crediting me. You remember the time I went after Peter and took out Richard instead?"

"How could I forget?"

"He didn't know what hit him," Thomas said. "He sat there stunned. Then he pushed himself back from the table and excused himself, all the time looking at Mom for an explanation for this assault by his favorite daughter."

"You think he knew it was me?"

"It was pretty obvious where the blow came from," Fran said. "Peter jumped back like he was expecting it to hit him. The only option was you."

"We never did thank you." Thomas said.

"Thanked me for what? Placing a hit on your father for you?" Sammy shifted in her seat. "You are right. Not only did you not thank me, you never paid me the fee we had agreed on."

"I was referring to the fact that you got us out of those dreadful devotions. He never came back to finish his dinner.

For the first and only time in the Vanderhuis history, we didn't have devotions. We got up from the table and left when we were done."

"I was worried about him. He was limping pretty badly when he left the table," Fran said.

"You were afraid he would come back and take off Sammy's head," Thomas said.

"Oh, he wouldn't do that. Maybe if it was one of you boys, but not Sammy."

"I wouldn't have blamed him. I walloped him a good one. I did notice I lost my place of honor, next to him at the dinner table after that incident."

"That was my doing. I thought it best not to risk any further errant kicks."

"Did he ever say anything to you about it, Fran?"

"He never mentioned it and I wasn't about to broach the subject. I brought him the ice and left. He did make me sit you next to him again, after a few days."

"I wonder what he thought," Sammy said.

The laughter subsided and the mood turned somber as the fear they had all felt at the moment of the actual occurrence set in. It was funny in retrospect. But at the time, the humor of the situation was kept at bay by the fear of what might erupt. This was the first time any of them had thought of the assault as funny.

"Maybe you can ask him that when he wakes up for one last chat," Peter said.

Sammy looked around the room for an explanation to Peter's odd remark.

"Peter thinks Dad is going to wake up long enough to make amends with us," John said

"There's a nightmare I didn't know I had to worry about," Thomas said. "Is that possible?"

"Which part - the waking up or the making amends?" John asked.

"The only plausible question is the part about waking up. The making amends is Peter's wishful thinking," Thomas said.

"That old stubborn bastard would rather die and go to hell, than admit he was wrong about anything." He dipped a cracker in the hummus and put it in his mouth. "This stuff is good, Eddie." He picked up the dish and grabbed a handful of crackers.

A quiet filled the room and matured into dead silence. The group, except for Julie, who watched it unfold with the intensity she reserved for Broadway plays, turned their heads in chorus and looked toward the bedroom door where Richard was laying. The look on their faces one of fearful expectation; as though they had done something wrong and were waiting to see what the consequence would be when what was in that room came out. Even Thomas looked as though he fit into this family – a choir boy, going along with what the choir director had demanded. Sammy might as well have been born into the fold; she coordinated so well with the rest of them. They held that pose until Fran broke the spell.

"Thank God you are back, Thomas. Right John?" she nodded toward John signifying he should take her lead and help her bring the group out of their frozen state.

John shook his head to clear the fog. "That's right. I'm glad you are here to take back your job, Thomas."

"My job?"

Peter jumped in. "John and Mother have decided the reason they didn't get angry at Dad is because you did it for them. Your rage was grand enough to work for all of us."

John and Fran looked down in shame. It had felt so insightful when they discussed it together, but the contempt in which Peter made it public suggested they were weak and conniving.

"I'm the family's hit man. I like that. Sorry it didn't work for you, Peter. But then, I think you had your own placebo."

"Dare I ask what would that be?"

"You had your head stuck up his ass. Every time you'd kiss it, he would come to a sudden stop and it would slide right up there. They say the smell of shit turns anger away."

Sammy stepped in to take over. "Then I think you should take a short walk down the hallway, Thomas, stick your head in the toilet and sniff some, because you are going over the line."

"Or find that dog of yours and sniff his old mangy butt." Peter grinned.

Surprised at Peter's willingness to fight back in such a childish way, Sammy tightened her jaw, tilted her head, and stared him down.

"He's back." John shook his head from side to side. "And in rare form! You do your job so well, Thomas. That's what I call loyalty, family loyalty. I don't know why anyone would say you don't love this family. Only a deep and loyal love could motivate you to keep this family working the same way it always has. Oh, I know, you camouflage it as a desire to destroy us, but it is the preservation of this family that is behind your anger."

"I think I'm the one with the degree in social work," Sammy said. "I'd appreciate it if you would leave the family system's analysis to me. Such thought requires an unbiased perspective and that would be me, not you John."

"You, unbiased?" The sarcasm dripped off John's lips.

"John, you know I've always loved you all equally. That has been my role in keeping this family together." Sammy dipped her finger in the cheese, brought it to her bright red lipstick covered lips, and licked it off.

"You misspoke, a bit, my dear. I'm sure you meant to include the word enabling in your job description."

"Thomas, I think you had better kick into a rage now. John's getting a bit hostile and it doesn't suit him," Peter said.

"Could I borrow your phone book?" Julie said. "I need to rent a car."

"Now look at what you have done," Fran scolded. "You've frightened off our guest."

"You mean Thomas' guest. We still haven't heard the nature of their relationship," John pressed. "Our lives are all a little boring compared to Thomas', so we would appreciate a bit of vicarious thrill."

"Don't fret about me, Fran." Julie ignored John. "Thomas frightened me off long before we stepped through your front door." She turned to John. "I'm afraid there is not much thrill to talk about, just boring repetitive patterns of reoccurring mistakes. Is that enough, or do you need to know the intimate details of our torrid sex encounters that only happened in my imagination?"

"I wouldn't mind hearing about those..."

John was interrupted by his mother. "That is more than enough information for this family's inordinate curiosity."

"I don't know, Julie. I think you should stay," Peter spoke up. "Sammy could use your help managing the testosterone in this family. You seem to have the chutzpa required to be her right hand woman."

"You really are welcome to stay," Fran said. "You can have supper with us, spend the night, and head out in the morning. You've been riding in a car for so long. You should get a good night's sleep before you get back on the road, especially Michigan's icy roads. Have you driven in these conditions before?"

"Not for a long time. I suppose you are right, Fran. I'll stay the night. But I will take that phone book so I can make arrangements for tomorrow morning."

"That's great. You can sleep in the basement with Sammy. She always says she is going to stay at her Mother's house, but it gets late and we give her an excuse to stay with us." Fran looked at Sammy who was laughing because she knew it was true.

"I think you're supposed to ask me before you offer up my bedroom, Mom," Sammy winked.

"It's settled, then. I'll get you the phone book. Boys, get the girl's things out of the bus and put them in the extra room. Supper will be in a few hours, at six o'clock to be precise. Oh, and Thomas, I hope your brought me some of your oregano. I was hoping to make some of those brownies you liked so much."

Everyone's eyebrows rose as they heard Fran's request, including Dundee's, whose age had taught him to conserve his energy for important matters.

Chapter 9

Shepherd's Pie

Fran suggested the boys take the girls outside to build a snowman while she cooked supper. "For old times' sake," she said.

The boys and girls agreed and started searching for warm clothing with which to bundle up. Thomas was the last to emerge from the basement, having put in the extra time to locate the Carhart jacket they had all vied for when they were younger. Richard had bought it to wear when he worked outside, but since he never did much work outside, the boys and Sammy had taken to fighting over it whenever they played in the snow. Thomas burst into the kitchen holding it up with both hands as if it was a trophy he had won.

"Look what I found," Thomas said.

Sammy pounced on him like a hungry lioness attacking her prey. "Give me that," she growled as she yanked on the sleeve.

Thomas laughed and pulled on the other arm, spinning Sammy toward him. "Let go of it you greedy dog."

Fran let them wrestle for a short while, and then took the coat and gave it to Julie. "Here you go dear," she said. "You should wear this. I can tell you aren't used to being out in the cold snow."

"That's not fair!" Thomas said.

"She is your guest," Fran said.

"Fine. I guess I owe her that much. As long as greedy dog here doesn't get it." He pointed at Sammy.

As they headed for the door Fran imposed the same rule she had always insisted when they were young. "I don't want to see any snowballs being thrown. You can take out someone's eye with a thing like that."

The boys all groaned in unison as they always had. John said, "How are we supposed to have any fun when we can't throw a few snowballs?"

Fran laughed. "Like my telling you not to throw any snowballs ever stopped you, John. Maybe you can get the better of your two brothers now that Peter has lost his bulk and become gaunt, like Thomas. That is if you stop acting wimpy so Sammy can have a chance."

"Hey, I used to beat him fair and square. I'll have none of this questioning my reputation as the third best snowball fighter in this family," Sammy said.

"I take it this means girls are included in this barbaric winter tradition?" Julie said.

"Come on, Julie. It will be fun. I'm sure Peter will be willing to roll over for you as well." Thomas grinned.

"We'll see." Peter raised his fists and flexed his biceps.

The girls wore down and came inside to warm up, while the boys ran off chasing each other around the neighborhood. Sammy and Julie came into the kitchen.

"We took them out Fran," Sammy said as they high fived.

"You two look like best friends. I'm surprised. It must have been quite a ride from Chicago in that bus?" Fran said.

"Not as bad as I thought it was going to be when I discovered her sitting in my seat," Sammy smiled, took hold of Julie's hand, and leaned her head on Julie's shoulder. Julie leaned in as well allowing their blond curls to mix together.

"Thomas didn't tell you about each other?"

They both shook their heads to reinforce the "no" that came out of their mouths.

130

"I don't know how that son of mine gets away with the things he does. You would think someone would have strung him up by now."

"Well, it turned out fine. We bashed him for the first three hours of the ride and he took his penance well. In the process we discovered we have a lot in common," Sammy said.

"Yeah, we have both loved your unlovable, lovable son." Julie flashed a plastic smile.

Fran looked at Sammy to see if she agreed with the past tense Julie had used. Sammy gave no signs Fran could read. Julie smiled at her own wit and Fran and Sammy humored her with mirroring smiles.

They offered assistance, but Fran refused. "Just sit down and keep me company. It would be nice to have some girl talk while I put on the finishing touches."

They sat on the stools. "Feel free to put us to work," Sammy said. "By the way, I love your haircut. It looks good on you." Sammy turned to Julie. "She used to have hair down to the middle of her back. She would braid it into a beautiful French braid every day."

"It must be a relief not to have to deal with it," Julie said.

Fran reached back and lifted her hair off of her neck. She fanned herself with the pot holder in her other hand. "It is a lot easier in the morning, but I have to worry about it during the day. My hot flashes are more uncomfortable because my hair sticks to the back of my neck and to my face when I get sweaty. You'd think I would be done with this after ten years."

"I'm glad I haven't had to deal with that yet," Sammy said.

"I should hope not," Fran said. "You haven't had your babies yet."

"No, I haven't and time is running out." Sammy looked down.

"Well, your hair looks great," Julie said. "I like the grey. It is almost white. Looks distinguished."

"Thanks," Fran said. "The boys haven't even noticed."

"Thomas doesn't even notice when I get my bikini wax," Julie said.

131

"Bikini wax?" Fran's ears perked up. "What do you wax in a bikini?"

Julie was about to explain, but Sammy waved her off.

"Oh." Fran formed prayer hands and slid them between her thighs as she leaned forward. "I get it." She turned toward the oven but changed her mind and made an about face. "You girls do that?"

The girls turned toward each other, smiled, and then said, "Yes."

"Oh God!" Fran cringed and pressed her knees together. "That must hurt."

"Yeah," said Julie, "but it's worth it."

"Wh... no, don't answer that. I don't want to know."

They all burst out in laughter.

Fran opened the oven to check on the shepherd's pie and was pleased to find the mashed potatoes were turning crispy brown. "Perfect!"

"That smells delicious," Julie commented. "What is it?"

"We're having shepherd's pie. It's one of my favorites," Sammy said.

Fran grinned at the sound of the compliment. "How did you know?"

"I could tell by the smell. I could never forget the smell of your shepherd's pie."

"What is it?" Julie asked.

"It's incredible! She makes a pie crust and fills it with vegetables, and meat. I'm guessing that it is chicken today. Sometimes it's beef. My favorite is lamb."

"You are in luck, Sammy. I made all three. I wasn't sure which one was everybody's favorite, so I decided to make them all. It might be overkill, but it makes for great leftovers."

"Are you kidding me? Those boys can each eat one by themselves. Jules hasn't had a decent meal in four days. And me, well I could be stuffed and it wouldn't stop me from gorging on your shepherd's pie." Sammy patted her stomach. "Anyhow, Julie, once she's got the meat and vegetable in the crust, she covers them with gravy. Best of all are the mashed

132

potatoes she puts on top. They turn crispy brown. Don't let the boys steal your crispy brown part. It's to die for. And trust me, the Vanderhuis boys won't steal your money, but they won't hesitate to swipe the crispy brown topping off your piece of shepherd's pie."

Fran laughed at Sammy's excitement and was pleased she had decided to start the weekend with her shepherd's pie. She had forgotten the boys' ritual of trying to lift each other's crispy brown topping. "They did manage to swipe yours quite often, didn't they?"

"They were vultures. That is what your knife is for, Julie. Keep it in your left hand, raised to the level of your chin," Sammy demonstrated her technique. "This is the perfect position to stab their grimy little hands when they reach over with their forks to pick it off your plate. I could have gone into fencing after all the knife fighting I've done in this household protecting my crispy brown mashed potato topping."

Julie imitated Sammy's knife fighting pantomime. Fran enjoyed their laughter.

"Thomas said you were a great cook, Fran. He said it was worth fighting for. It was one of the things he told me in order to get me to come with him on this trip," Julie said.

Fran got quiet, and then used her apron to wipe tears from her eyes. "There were good times, weren't there Sammy? I know it was awful for the boys, with Richard being so mean. But there were some good times, too, weren't there?"

"There were good times, Fran."

"Sometimes I think I'm fooling myself when I think it wasn't always bad. But you remember it too, don't you?"

"I do Fran. I remember laughing a lot when Richard wasn't around. It is why I was always over here. There was more laughter in this house than in mine."

"The boys don't remember. That's why they don't like to come here. They think it was always awful. I don't think they remember me ever loving them."

"They remember your shepherd's pie." Sammy reached over and touched Fran's forearm.

133

"I suppose, but that isn't much consolation."

"The bad memories get seared in our minds in a way that the good memories don't. We remember them in a more powerful way. But the good memories are there, Fran, and they will remember them sooner or later. Our minds have a way of preserving those good memories until we are ready to be done with the painful ones."

"I hope it is sooner, rather than later. I miss them."

"Isn't that what this weekend is about?"

"I suppose, but we've got to get past the bad times first."

"They will."

"Thank you, Sammy."

"For what?"

"For remembering the good times."

"My good times were at this house, Fran – all of them. And he wasn't my father, so the bad times weren't as bad for me. I had distance from him. But I didn't have distance from you. I loved you."

"I know. I tried to love you back, but things were so hard for me back then. I was in a fog and I couldn't find my way. I knew what I wanted, but I didn't know how to get there."

"You can see it now."

"I hope it isn't too late."

"It never is."

All three women wiped their tears. Even Julie was enveloped in the moment through the tears she shed into the community cup. The timer went off, ending the moment.

"Sammy, could you get the bowl of cottage cheese out of the fridge and put it on the table? Oh, and grab the applesauce while you're at it. Julie, grab a couple of bottles of wine. They're in the pantry. You can't miss them when you walk in."

"My kind of woman and my kind of pantry!" Julie said.

"Wine at a Vanderhuis family dinner." Sammy looked at Fran. "When did this come about?"

"Oh, it's no big deal." Fran patted down the front of her apron. "My family used to have wine with dinner. It was such a treat for them. I've decided to take back some of my traditions."

"The boys will be pleased," Sammy said.

"I don't know about Peter. He doesn't like to go against his father."

"We'll get him past that. It is about time he lightens up. The wine will lighten us all up. Maybe it will help us remember the good times."

Fran turned toward the kitchen but changed her mind. "Sammy," she said.

"Yes?"

"Did Richard ever mention anything to you about being buried in our family plot?"

"Not that I recall. Why?"

"Well." Fran paused. "Richard bought an extra burial plot and I'm trying to figure out who he had in mind."

"You thought he wanted me to be buried with your family?"

"I don't know what else to make of it. He was fond of you."

"Is that what you call it?

"What would you call it?"

"Weird, but I can go with fond."

"But he never mentioned it to you?"

"God no. I would have remembered something like that. I would have entertained Thomas with it for hours on end. I can hear him laughing already."

They chuckled.

"What's so funny?" Julie returned from the pantry.

"Richard's funeral plans," Sammy said.

Julie raised her eyebrows. "Where's the cork screw?"

Fran pointed toward the drawer in the china cabinet as she continued to chuckle, shaking her head.

Chapter 10

The Dinner Table

The boys came in from the cold and moved toward the table, rubbing their bodies in an attempt to create warmth through friction. They talked trash about who had won the snowball fight, until they arrived at the table. Without prompting, they took their customary places at the table. Peter and Sammy sat across from each other next to the head of the table where Richard sat. Thomas and John did the same at the other end of the table, bookending Fran who sat opposite Richard's place at the other end of the table. Fran set a place for Julie between Sammy and Thomas.

Julie poured the wine. Thomas nudged her. "Did you bring that wine?" Without letting her answer he went on, "Does Mother know you are pouring that and where the hell did you get these wine glasses?"

Julie told him to relax and lower his voice. Sammy explained Fran was experimenting with some of her parent's traditions, which she had given up when she married Richard.

"Grandma and Grampa drank wine at dinner? Why didn't I ever see that?" Thomas asked loud enough to make sure Julie would know he wouldn't be managed by her or anybody else.

136

John rolled his eyes and motioned toward Richard's place at the table. Thomas rolled his head backwards in what could best be described as a reverse nod – allowing disdain to accompany his message to John that he understood his silent answer. "I'm all for digging up old traditions," Thomas said as he raised his glass announcing he had just made a toast.

Fran took her place. They all looked toward the empty place at the head of the table, as they had done so many times in the past; expecting those familiar words, "bow your heads."

When the words didn't come they continued to sit in silence staring at the empty chair. The oddness of the situation disturbed Julie and she spoke up, startling the others out of their psychotic stupor. "Am I missing something here, or is this a little weird. Don't get me wrong, I can get into unconventional, but whatever you all are waiting to come from that empty chair, isn't going to happen."

They all looked at Fran for an explanation. When none was forthcoming, John spoke up, "Mom, you seemed to have set an extra place setting. What exactly did you have in mind?"

Fran covered her face with her hands. "Oh my! I'm not sure. I...I guess it was out of habit. He sat there for so long and nobody else has ever sat there. I guess I didn't want to give away his place without his permission. I'll take care of it."

She rushed to stand up, but John put his hand on her arm and guided her back down into her chair. "Just leave it Mom. It will be fine. Saying goodbye is harder than one would expect. It won't hurt us to have one last meal with Dad sitting at the head of the table. Maybe it will even be a good thing, you know, a healing goodbye ritual."

"Don't the Native American Indians have an empty chair ritual when a loved one dies?" Sammy asked.

"They do," Thomas answered. "They have a meal with an empty chair for the dead person, and spend some time talking about how much that person meant to them."

"The key word," Julie noted, "is dead."

"We can borrow from the tradition and make it our own." John argued.

"Does that mean we can nix the sharing how much he meant to us part?" Thomas asked.

"I'm sure you could come up with at least one thing to appreciate about your father." Sammy attempted to coax him to a more tenable position.

"I guess I could appreciate the fact he breathed well. I know this because I spent my childhood hoping he would stop breathing."

"Well then, you are finally going to get your heart's desire." Peter threw his napkin into his lap and patted it down.

The group agreed to reframe Fran's subconscious slip into a healing ritual. Peter offered to pray in his father's stead and uttered those familiar words, "Let's bow our heads." He prayed with a rigid eloquence that reminded Fran of his father, except there were moments when a tender tone softened the prayer as Peter addressed more personal matters of concern. Richard stayed away from the personal; preferring a more global agenda. She noticed Peter prayed on behalf of those seated at the table. He tried to put himself in their shoes and pray for their desires. Richard, on the other hand, prayed about them; asking God to make them who he wanted them to be. This distinction pleased her as it reinforced the notion Peter was not just Richard's child.

When the prayer was complete, the business of getting everyone served took over the agenda. It all happened in silence and that silence continued after the serving transitioned to eating. As the quiet meal progressed, it became obvious the present arrangement wasn't working. The empty chair had the effect of placing a pair of invisible eyes at the head of the table, which had an oppressive impact on the family's ability to interact. The carefree exchanges that had been developing throughout the afternoon had been suppressed, replaced by discomfort and distrust. All involved knew what had happened, but could not, or perhaps would

138

not, speak up and confront the situation, since none of them was sure how to come up with an antidote. Even Julie, who had experienced none of the past history dominating this table, couldn't bring herself to challenge the force that emerged from that empty chair.

"Do you think dying will really kill him?" Thomas broke the spell. No one answered. "I was hoping it would end it all, but I'm starting to wonder if it will. He is in our heads more than we care to admit. Putting two thousand miles between me and him didn't get him out of my head. Why would I expect dying to be any more effective?"

Julie shrugged her shoulders. She didn't feel it was her place to interfere in a sensitive matter like this, with a family in which she was a complete outsider. John cleared his throat as though he was going to address Thomas' question, but kept on eating. Peter never raised his eyes from his plate, shaking his head at the inappropriate nature of the question, dismissing it as another episode of Thomas' irreverence – meant to be an end in itself. Sammy looked at Fran.

Fran rescued the son she had left hanging in the wind at the mercy of the storm for so many years. "I've wondered the same thing myself, Thomas." She spoke a few decibels louder than a whisper, as if she was afraid of being heard beyond the confines of the table, or perhaps even at the other end of the table. All eyes turned toward her. "He hasn't been able to speak for a month, but I keep hearing his voice everywhere and I keep behaving as though he is still watching my every move. Marcia says it will get better with time, but only if I talk about what it was like living with him. She said even if he is dead, you have to confront his voice in your head so you can force him to leave and so you can think for yourself."

"Who the hell is Marcia?" Thomas voiced the group's curiosity. Not only was it surprising to the boys that Fran would have a friend, it was shocking that she would have a friend she would talk to about the happenings in their father's house. Privacy was a pet peeve for Richard and he always warned everyone about airing family laundry in public.

"Marcia is my therapist."

"Well I'll be damned and sent straight to hell right along with you Eddie." Thomas slammed his hand down on the table, shaking the place settings as if an earthquake was taking place. "Since when have you had a therapist?" Thomas roared as though he wanted to draw the gods' attention to this incredible act of defiance.

"I've been seeing her for the last six months."

"And you've been talking to her about Dad?" Thomas asked.

"I think that would be the point of my going to see her and spending $100.00 an hour to have her help me figure out my life."

"Does Dad know about this?" Peter asked.

"Does it matter?" she asked, pointing to the empty chair.

"So what is she saying about Dad?" John asked.

"I suppose she is a Christian therapist and she is siding with him," Thomas said, "telling you to stand by his side and be subservient to your husband who is the head of the household."

"Thomas, I'm surprised. You were listening to those sermons from the back pew."

"My childhood ear plugs weren't as effective as the ones I've grown in adulthood."

"Hear! Hear!" Julie tilted her wine glass, and then took a big gulp.

"Don't mind her. She can be a lush sometimes," Thomas said.

Julie lifted her glass with a raised pinky and then, imitating the tone of a drunken hussy – said, "A giiirl'sss gotta dooo, whaat aaah giiirls gotta d..do, when ssshess living w…wit aaah deaf..ff d…dope."

The group's laugh lowered the tension that had been rising steadily since Thomas had begun interrogating Fran. However, the thermometer began rising again as Thomas repeated his question. The mercury skyrocketed when Fran answered.

"I think Marcia is an atheist. But that's none of my business. She is helping me understand my life in a different way and that has been helpful."

Thomas stood up. He towered over the group as his face muscles tightened and his glare intensified. "Is Dad's bed on wheels? I'd like to get him out here so he can get a load of this shit."

He made his way toward the bedroom when Sammy called him back. "Thomas, your Mom is being serious."

"And you think I'm not? I think the old man should hear what's becoming of his family. I'd like him to know his spell is being challenged."

"You mean you want to see him suffer?" Fran asked.

"I would prefer to think of it as suffering a bit of humility. Come to think about it, humility would cause Dad to suffer. It always did. But then again, I'm not above revenge."

"Which is why you spent your life trying to humiliate him?" Peter said.

"You're doing it again, Peter. You've got to pull your head out of Dad's ass if you are going to make any sense," Thomas said.

"Now let me see...you want to humiliate Dad on his death bed, since you haven't been able to do so while he was alive. I think you could use some time on Marcia's couch. She would probably charge you $200 an hour and she would deserve it." Peter responded.

"Let's get back to eating," Sammy took a large bite of the casserole and groaned out loud with pleasure.

Thomas reached over to Julie's plate with his fork. He began to lift a piece of the crispy brown topping off her plate. Julie spotted him, reached for her knife, and stabbed him.

"What the fuck, Julie."

Julie looked at Sammy who smiled with approval.

"I should have never let you two meet." He licked his wound.

"Is that what she is suggesting, Mom?" John took a sip of his wine.

"What are you talking about, John?"

"Marcia – is asking you to bring us all in for a family session?"

"Would that be so awful?"

"I'm sure it wouldn't be pleasant, as we can see from tonight's dinner party."

"She hasn't suggested it. She thinks we can figure it out on our own – or at least try to."

"Alright Mother, what's this really about?" Peter set down his fork and sat up in his chair.

"What are you referring to when you say this?"

"You know what I'm referring to. This homecoming you've worked so hard to arrange – getting us all here for a weekend together before Dad dies. What are you trying to accomplish?"

Fran hesitated and John answered for her. "She wants her sons back. Mom feels she has lost us and she wants us back. She thinks we are angry at her for not protecting us from Dad."

"Now there is a revelation worth paying $100 an hour to discover," Thomas said.

The bottom half of Sammy's leg jetted out in a sweeping motion catching Thomas just below the knee, while she maintained her upper body motionless. Julie was brushed aside by the airflow caused by Sammy's high velocity foot as it swept past her legs. Thomas squirmed in pain, "Jesus Christ, Sammy! I can't believe you can still do that at your age, with your arthritis and all. What are you doing, taking karate lessons or something?"

"Could you teach me to do that?" Julie said. "It could come in handy." She tried to imitate Sammy, but hooked Peter on her way around and almost fell off her chair in the process. Peter grimaced with pain.

"Sorry about that, Peter. I think I need a few lessons."

"That would be a good idea." He crossed his legs and rubbed his knee.

"So what's your plan, Eddie?" Thomas said. "You've got us all here, what's next? I mean, other than feeding us until we can't move and therefore leave."

"Why do I have to have a plan? Why does everybody always want a plan? Can't we just sit together and enjoy a meal?" She stirred the cottage cheese on her plate and took a bite.

John answered for her again, "Mom's therapist told her to start small – to just think of one thing she could change to get the ball rolling."

"And what is it you are going to change, Eddie?" Thomas asked.

This time Peter answered for her. "I think she has already more than accomplished that. She has been breaking the mold ever since she started organizing this homecoming party. She has been talking, giving her opinions, cracking jokes, and laughing; not to mention swearing. Where is it going to end?"

"She's cut her hair," Sammy waved her hands like a choir director. "Doesn't it look nice?"

"Yah, it looks great," Thomas put his arm on Sammy's shoulder and pushed her aside. "What's it going to be, Eddie?"

"Marcia did say that if you focus on doing one thing different, things would snowball and you would end up behaving in a lot of unusual ways. It alters your mind set and opens your mind to the whole idea of change. Before you know it, you and everybody around you are doing things another way and liking it."

Julie retrieved another bottle of wine. She handed it to John, along with the corkscrew and he opened it. She walked around the table and topped off everyone's glass, and then she filled hers to the brim.

"Alright, if we are going to be taking advice from this Marcia person, I've got to know more about her. Where's your computer, Eddie? I'm going to Google her," Thomas said.

"There is a laptop in the roll top desk." Fran pointed toward the hallway.

"You own a computer?" Thomas asked.

Fran nodded.

"Is it hooked up to the internet?" Thomas was prepared to be aghast.

"How else would I keep up with the times?"

"Keep up with the times? Since when does Richard Vanderhuis' wife care about keeping up with the times? I suppose the next thing you are going to confess to us is that you are addicted to Facebook."

"I prefer My Space. I would like to sign you all up as my friends, if you would like."

"I hope you haven't stumbled onto MatchMaker.com and hooked up with some kind of pervert," Peter said.

"No, but I do find the chat rooms interesting."

"If Dad's bed doesn't have wheels, I'm going to the hardware store to get some. I need to see him experience this conversation," Thomas said.

"You mean you need to see him suffer?" Fran said.

"Marcia didn't convince you to get a psychology degree, did she? Because you are starting to sound a bit like one," Thomas said.

"I can understand why you would want to see him suffer, Thomas. A part of me wants that too," Fran said.

"Eddie, I'm trying to be nice here and avoid Bruce Lee's avenger feet." Thomas glared at Sammy.

"I'm not asking you to be nice. I've put no preconditions on any of you coming here. I expect this weekend to be messy and uncomfortable. I want us all to say what we think and feel, even if it is painful to me."

"There's that snowball again; gathering change. What if it is painful to us?" Thomas gulped his wine.

"I was hoping it would be worth it to you and your brothers."

"What's the payoff, Eddie? Why would we want to go through it?"

"Getting your family back. That's the payoff."

144

"Why would I want my family back? I ran away because I didn't like them. We can't change that fact."

"We can rewrite our story."

"You mean lie to ourselves? That wouldn't be a change. We've been pretending to be a happy family for as long as I can remember."

"I'm talking about admitting the truth of what happened to all of us back then and listening to each other's versions. I'm talking about accepting responsibility for what we did to each other."

"What makes you think we would ever agree on what happened?" Thomas said.

"I don't need you to agree with me. But I am hoping you can understand me."

"I'll have to think about that. It sounds like semantics to me."

"Don't you think we can break the spell, Thomas? That is what you said your father had put us under. Do you think we can break it and get him out of our heads?" Fran folded her hands in her lap and leaned forward.

"I don't know, Eddie.

"Fair enough; you don't need to know, in order to try."

"I do. I don't open a can of worms unless I'm sure I can stomach it," Thomas said.

"Can't you just put the lid back on, if you find you can't stomach it?"

"I'm afraid my lid doesn't work that way. It never has."

Sammy gave Fran a subtle nod of approval, which Fran relished in silence. Sammy also reached her foot over to Thomas and rubbed it against his calf. He didn't acknowledge it, but he didn't move away from it either. Sammy sensed the conversation needed to be lightened, so she began to go through the pleasantries families go through when they get together; the catching up. The stress of the initial meeting had been so high they had foregone the ritual altogether. She began by asking Peter about his kids.

145

Peter smiled as he talked about their personalities and lives. He told funny stories about the things they had said or done. Everyone could tell, by the warm way he told the stories, he was attached to them. She went on to ask about his wife and his church. She was warmed when his eyes dropped down to her bosom as they had done so many times in the past. Per their long established ritual from their teenager years, she tapped her finger near her clavicle, pointing up to her eyes, where she met him with a smile. Peter responded with the same downward look of shame that resulted in a second corrective finger tapping.

Peter found the interaction with Sammy a bit comical, as he knew she would take it all in fun. It was when he was met with the same corrective tapping on Julie's neckline that he went into full blown humiliation. *Did Sammy warn her and tell her what to do when it happened? They couldn't possibly have talked...But how else would she know what the signal was? She must think I'm a louse. Sammy and I have history and an understanding. Julie doesn't know me from Adam and here I am ogling her breasts – my own brother's girlfriend's breasts. It really wasn't an ogling. I only glanced at them. But, I'm not sure how long I stared at them before she gave me the finger. What if I starred at them for two minutes? Sometimes I lose track of time when I'm ogling breasts. When I looked at her, she didn't smile at me like Sammy. She raised her eyebrows. What if she complains to Thomas? He would have a field day with this. My secret would be exposed. What if I'm already exposed? What if Sammy talked to Thomas about it and he is holding on to it as ammunition for the right moment. What if all three of them talked about it together, on the trip from Chicago? Did Mom notice? Am I blubbering like an idiot right now, while talking about whatever it was I'm talking about – oh yes, my job.*

The merry-go-round thinking was about to make him insane, when Sammy rescued him from his floundering and transitioned the conversation toward John. "It sounds like you love your work at the church, Peter. I always knew you

146

would be a sensitive minister. Now John, what is it you are doing these days? I know you are no longer with the mission."

John explained he was helping Myrna in her work and writing short novels.

"Why short novels?"

"I think novels should have something to say and should say it in a succinct manner. I've never been able to tolerate those long novels that describe every irrelevant detail."

"I always felt the same way about sermons," Thomas shifted in his seat. "If you can't say it in five minutes, it isn't worth saying."

"Same concept," John said.

"So what are these novels about?" Peter asked.

"They describe people's unique journeys to find meaning in life."

"I downloaded one of your novels," Thomas said. "It was quite inspiring."

"Wow!" Sammy gave John a nod of admiration. "You've won over one of the toughest critics out there – your toughest critic, I'm sure. You must be quite a writer."

"My income doesn't reflect it, but I would like to think I can tell a useful tale."

"That would change if you stop letting people download them for next to nothing," Thomas said.

"My goal is to get my stories read, not to make money."

"Those goals aren't mutually exclusive. One leads to the other. The more you charge, the more people think it is worth reading."

"So is your art selling well?" John asked. "You've done some interesting things the last few years. It's good you've moved on from your obsession with painting Sammy's nude body."

"Hey, what's wrong with my body?"

"Nothing Sammy; but even your beautiful body can get tiring if it is the subject of every painting. After a while the paintings start to end up inside firemen's lockers."

"I wouldn't mind being a pinup in a cute fireman's locker," Julie said. "That could be a status symbol. But I'm drunk, so what do I know."

John ignored her and went on. "I've enjoyed some of the spiritual themes you've been painting. They're intriguing."

"You mean the anti-religious bent my art has taken?"

"That's a different way to put it, but yes. You've been asking some interesting questions and making some bold statements. Has it helped or hurt your sales?"

"It is hard to tell. In this economy art isn't selling well no matter the subject. But then again, I paint so it can be seen, not to make money."

"Hasn't your art always been anti-religious?" Peter asked.

"So John," Sammy said. "You're married. Tell us about Myrna."

Before John could respond, Thomas got out of his chair. "I can't take this empty chair thing any longer. It is just plain weird; and if it is weird to me then it must be really fucked up, because I'm into weird."

"I'll take away the place setting," Fran started to get up.

"No, Eddie. I've got a better idea." Thomas walked over to the chair and pulled it out. He took the plate and put a healthy serving of the shepherd's pie on it; topping it off with a large spoonful of cottage cheese. He whistled. "Dundee, come here! Come on old boy, you'll like this." He had to repeat himself three times before Dundee was motivated enough to get up on all fours and make his way to the table. When he got there, Thomas motioned for him to jump into the chair. Dundee looked at him.

Julie gave Thomas a disapproving look. "Thomas, I don't think that is a good idea. Not everybody loves dogs and he'll make a mess."

"Dundee here will be on his best behavior. He won't bother Sammy and John. He'll love Mom's shepherd's pie and I'll clean up any mess he makes."

"Like you cleaned up the mess he left in the driveway this afternoon," Peter said.

Thomas looked at Peter and Sammy, scanning their faces for any signs of disapproval. They backed away from the table communicating they were washing their hands of the situation. Sammy said, "Make sure he uses a napkin to wipe his drool. I'm a bit queasy when I dine with the canine persuasion."

"Dundee's good at this. He dines in the chair next to Thomas at home. He's a little loud is all," Julie reassured her.

"You put up with this every night?" Peter asked.

"You can't imagine how many romantic meals I've had with my lover here and his mutt." Julie circled the rim of her crystal wine glass with her finger.

"So finally Julie answers the question. She is his lover." The silly smile on John's face gave away the fact he was buzzed from the wine.

"Slow down on the wine there, big brother," Thomas warned. "Getting drunk at Dad's table on the first night back, might not be your best course of action."

"It appears this is not Dad's table anymore." John attempted to deflect the unwarranted attention. "Unless I've had so much to drink my vision is distorted, which is quite possible since I quit drinking four years ago. I believe this is Dundee's table now. The table seems to have gone to the dogs."

"Which is why I feel more comfortable already," Thomas said. "Don't you?"

"He isn't going to go after my food, when he is done with his, is he?" Peter asked.

"He might ask you to share if you don't give him seconds," Thomas warned. "But at least he won't ask you to serve up your soul, like the previous occupant of that chair."

"Quite frankly, it's disrespectful to Dad. He is not even dead yet and you are replacing him with a dog no less," Peter said. "I know you had your issues with Dad. We all did. But why don't you just grow up and get over yourself?"

"I have issues with Dad," Thomas glared at Peter. "Not had, but have – and getting over Dad is what I'm trying to do.

149

Believe it or not, it is what I've been trying to do for the last twenty years; quite unsuccessfully I might add, not that the effort hasn't been valiant. And if by growing up you mean settling for becoming a clone of Dad's, then no thank you. I don't know what growing up is, but your version doesn't interest me."

"How is replacing Dad with a dog helping you grow up or get over Dad?" Peter said.

Sammy wanted to intervene, but she knew this was a fight that needed to take place. She saw the desire to fight in Peter's eyes and wondered if she had been wrong all these years in her attempts to protect him. Had she been protecting a boy who didn't want to be protected? What if her mothering had only prolonged the agony, instead of minimizing it as she had intended. Perhaps they could have had this fight when they were younger and the stakes weren't so high. When the weapons they would have used would have been less sophisticated and the injuries they would have sustained would have been youthful ones that healed faster.

"It's facing the truth, Peter! That is what grownups do. They stop hanging on to comforting lies and they face the painful truth. The dog is an improvement. The dog makes you feel welcome at this table. The dog loves you, even when you screw up. In fact, when you screw up with the dog, he doesn't have to forgive you because he never blames you in the first place. The dog always loves you. The dog always makes you feel like you belong."

"So what is this painful truth you are trying to accept?" Peter said.

"Dundee is more of a father to me than Dad ever was. That's why I want him in the chair. He deserves that place more than Dad."

"That's ridiculous," Peter turned his head and waved Thomas off as irrelevant. "Poor Thomas, he didn't have a perfect father and the world owes him now."

"Peter, why do you feel the need to defend your father?" Fran asked as she picked up the shepherd's pie and passed it.

150

"What, you are on Thomas' side now, Mother?" Putting his palms on the table, he leaned forward. "Perhaps I wouldn't feel the need to defend Dad if you did your job and defended him yourself."

"You think it is my job to defend your father?" Fran's inflection rose at the tail end of her sentence.

"You are his wife. Yes, you should defend him. You never have Mother. You've never defended him to Thomas. You've just sat there and tolerated his bashing Dad." Peter was shocked at his strong response toward his mother. More than anything, he couldn't believe she didn't fall apart when he confronted her, which is what had kept all the brothers from holding her accountable in the past. What surprised him most was he was the one daring to cross over the invisible line in the sand that made his mother off limits due to fragility. He had expected it to be Thomas. He was the angry one. "Dad defended you. We didn't dare talk bad about you around him."

"What if I felt the same as Thomas did about your father?" Fran took her napkin from her lap and placed it on her plate. "What if the truth was I agreed with Thomas, but didn't have the courage to say it myself, so I put it on his shoulders? Peter, my sin wasn't that I didn't defend your father. My sin was I didn't call him on anything, no matter how wrong he was. So please don't ask me to judge Thomas for doing my job for me. He might have done it in a hurtful and ineffective way, but that happens when you ask a boy to do a woman's job."

"I'm sick and tired of everybody blaming Dad for everything." Peter stood up and paced. "Look, I get it. Dad had a few flaws. I wished he would have done some things different. But that doesn't make him all bad. He was a good man in many ways. He did a lot of good in this community. He tried his best with us. What more can you ask of a man?"

"I understand how you feel, Peter. And you are right; you can't ask a man to do more than his best. But you don't pretend the pain his shortcomings caused wasn't real. I'm not saying your father was all bad, but I'm not going to sit here and make believe he didn't hurt a lot of people; including you. I tried that and it didn't work."

"Well, I won't tolerate it!" Peter started to leave the room.

"What won't you tolerate, Peter? Other's views of the truth?" Fran's heart broke as she saw how her statement cut through to Peter's core and burst a boil that had been festering for years.

Peter did a slow about face. His face flushed with redness.

"I'm sorry, Peter, I didn't mean to hurt you," Fran lifted the hair off of her neck and wiped her forehead with the napkin she retrieved from her plate.

"Well, you did, Mother. You insinuated I'm like him; I'm intolerant. I'm not."

"We're all like him in some ways. Better, but still like him. You can't be around a strong willed person like your father for twenty years and not absorb him into your bones. Even if you swear you will not let him influence you." Fran glanced over at Thomas. "It happens. It is contagious. It takes on different shapes and forms, but in the end we are all replicas of sorts."

"So what do you want from me, Mother?" Peter asked.

"What I want from all of you is to listen to each other with an open mind. You lived in the same house. You saw the same things. I have to believe deep inside each of you there is a recording of the past which tells the same story. You may have chosen to interpret that recording in different ways, in order to make sense of it from your perspective, but the recording is the same. It speaks the truth. What I want from us is to listen to each other's versions without defending our own, in hopes we can discover the original recording. We need each other. We are the only ones who were there. We need each other to figure out what happened to us. Without each other, we are stuck with our own corrupt versions. And worst of all, we lose each other – the only people who can understand what we went through."

A deep silence ensued. The silence that comes when people are digesting a truth they are trying to resist, even though they know it has validity.

152

"I am sorry I hurt you Peter. But I have spent my entire married life trying not to hurt anyone, and look at what it has gotten me. What I've come to understand is hurting each other is a necessary part of loving each other. In order to love someone, you have to tell them the truth, at least your version of the truth. That unrefined version of the truth might hurt them, but that hurt will lead to a discussion that will refine your truth and bring you closer to each other. We've never done that in this family which is why we are so comfortable living thousands of miles away from each other, where no one can contradict our story."

"Mom," the discussion drew John out of his pleasant alcohol induced buzz. "We weren't allowed our own versions of the truth. Dad insisted we hold his."

"That was true back then, but he isn't here anymore. That congenial crotch-sniffing dog has taken his place." Fran smirked, pleased with her wit.

"Mother! He's not dead yet," Peter said.

"I'm sorry, but I thought we needed comedic relief from my lecture. I wasn't implying anything about your father when I called the dog a crotch-sniffer. That just slipped in there. It must be that Dundee touched me in a place I haven't..."

"No, Mom!" John put his foot down. "We're not going to have that conversation. We didn't witness that, nor do we care to."

"Speak for yourself, big brother. Was he, Mom?" Thomas asked.

"Was he what?"

"A crotch-sniffer? The old man? Was he a crotch-sniffer?"

Fran was about to answer, but John cut her off. "You are two peas in a pod. I didn't know that. I thought Thomas was adopted. But now I can see where he gets his irreverence – his maternal genes. I'm all for letting the genie out of the bottle, but this needs to stay in the bottle."

The family laughed. Sammy caught Fran's attention and gave her a nod. Fran was pleased with herself, and for the first time since giving birth, she felt like a good mother. It was

153

then she noticed her hand wrapped around John's under the table. He had offered it to her as a gesture of support. She had grabbed it in an attempt to keep her balance. Now that she had survived the storm, she let go and patted it, communicating she was fine now and grateful for the balance he offered.

The family got back to eating and everyone raved about the shepherd's pie. Julie noted Dundee had cleaned his plate spotless. Fran tried to dismiss the compliments, as the limelight made her uncomfortable. Not that she didn't enjoy every minute of it, when her shame allowed her the luxury.

Peter addressed Dundee. He placed his untouched glass of wine next to Dundee's plate and said, "Don't forget your wine, old boy." Dundee leaned over the glass and with great precision, so as not to spill a drop, began to lap up the wine. He stopped every few seconds to do several dry laps, to clear his palate before he continued. "I see, Mr. Dundee. I take it you've done this before."

"Thomas thinks it will help keep his cholesterol levels down." Using her fork, Julie drew circles in the gravy left on her plate.

The boys helped themselves to seconds, including Dundee. The women tried to refrain from overeating, which meant they gave themselves permission to pick at the boys food instead; spotting what they liked best and helping themselves. Julie was hesitant so Sammy got her over the shyness when she stole a piece of Peter's lamb and put it on Julie's plate. She caught the drift. Thomas moved his plate closer to her. "Help yourself. Sammy has always claimed the right, so you might as well have the same privilege."

"What? It tastes better coming from someone else's plate," Sammy said.

"Remember the time you helped yourself to Dad's meat?" Peter said.

"God that was awful! I was so used to helping myself; I just reached over and stabbed one of his pieces of steak. You remember how he used to cut them into perfect squares and take his time relishing each one of them. They looked so good. By the time I realized what I had done, it was in my mouth. Not off my fork, mind you; just in my mouth. I saw the look he gave me and was so afraid I took it out of my mouth and put it back on his plate – fork and all."

"He reached down and picked up your fork with the slobbered piece of meat still on it," Peter said.

"I know. For a minute I thought he was going to eat it. But he reached over and put it on my plate."

"Did you eat it?" Julie asked.

"Are you kidding me?"

"She remembered she had homework to do and left the table, leaving her stolen meat behind," Fran joined the storytelling. "Thomas grabbed the fork and ate it with pleasure."

"Always making a statement," Peter said.

"When are we going to see what's in Dad's box?" Thomas said.

No one answered.

"Come on now, you can't tell me you aren't dying to see what Dad's been stashing in that damn secret box he has been flaunting at us for all these years?" Thomas said.

The others gazed toward Richard's chair. Dundee had given up getting thirds or a second glass of wine, slumping off the chair and back to the corner he had claimed as his spot. His departure erased the humor that had softened Richard's inherent presence at the head of the table. Even Julie, who had never met the man, had her gaze set in that direction, following the strong lead of the crowd.

"So are you waiting for your Dad's ghost to appear?" Julie tried to break the trance.

"He's not even dead!" Peter protested.

"I know," Julie defended herself. "I was speaking metaphorically."

155

"I understand, Julie. I didn't mean that comment for you. I was addressing my remark to Thomas, who can't seem to wait until the body is cold to ransack my father's privacy."

Thomas' jaw dropped as he looked around the table for support. "You can't tell me you aren't curious to see what the hell Dad's been hiding in that box? You know damn well you want to know what's in there. The fact he isn't dead yet might be distasteful, but what the hell, I might want to talk to him about it before he dies. Besides, I've waited twenty years."

"I don't want to know what's in that box. If Dad wanted us to know, he would have told us. A man deserves some measure of privacy," Peter said.

"You want to bury it with him without ever opening it?" Thomas asked.

"Yes! There is a good chance it is his private journal. I wouldn't want my children to know my every private thought," Peter said.

"You've got your head so far up Dad's ass you are starting to forget where he ends and you begin. Pretty soon you'll be sucking his brain into yours," Thomas said.

"I know I'm just a guest, but if you are going to talk about this in front of me, I need a few details so I can follow the train of thought," Julie said.

"My father kept a box on his night stand. It's a wooden box his father built. It's the size of a shoe box. He made it clear we were never to look inside," John said.

Julie looked at Fran, "Do you know what's in it?"

"No." Fran shook her head.

"So what? You didn't know where he hid the key?" Julie asked.

"There is no key," John said. "It wasn't locked."

"Did your father ever look in it?" Julie asked wide-eyed.

"We assumed he did, but we never saw him open it. Did you?" John looked at Fran.

"Never in my presence. Once in a while I would walk in on him looking in it, but he put it away until I left again."

"I don't get it?" Julie said.

"What don't you get, dear?" Fran asked.

"I have lived with this one for two years," Julie pointed at Thomas, "and have had no privacy whatsoever. My underwear drawer might as well be his. If I kept a diary, I can assure you he would find a way to discover the password and read it. He would paint my most private sexual fantasies and sell it to the highest bidder. How could your father have kept an unlocked box with his greatest secrets in this house, in plain sight, without anyone getting into it? That is unfathomable to me."

"Yes, but you don't see the ghost sitting in that chair, do you?" John led her eyes back to the empty chair at the head of the table. "You weren't here when that chair emanated a threatening presence that paralyzed this family with just the promise of anger."

"What do you think is in there, John?" Thomas asked.

"I'm not sure there is anything in it," he replied.

The group gave him a collective "Huh?"

"I'm not sure this was ever about what was inside the box. I think it was just a game Dad played to relish the power he had over us," John continued. "Think about it, the thrill of exercising that kind of control over this entire household. The delight of daring anyone who lives under his roof to open an unlocked box which he filled with curiosity inducing wonder, and have them all exercise unwarranted self-control at your request. That thrilled Dad. It wasn't about what was in the box. It was about exercising power and control."

"Like rape isn't about sex. It is about having the power to control the victim and do as you like to her?" Julie asked.

"Yes, it was the same twisted motivation," John answered.

"That's horrible," Fran spoke up. "I don't think your father would think like that. You make him sound like a barbaric dictator or something worse."

"That would be another analogy that illustrates the same twisted motivation."

"I can't accept that," Fran said.

"Mom, there was something wrong with Dad. He wasn't normal. He didn't think like the rest of us. He was twisted. If you don't accept this about him, you will never understand him; you won't get him," John said.

"I don't think I have to go to that extreme to understand your father. I don't have to turn him into a monster. There has to be a better explanation."

"You mean a more palatable explanation, Mom. You want an explanation of Dad's behavior that isn't quite so embarrassing to you," John said.

"How is this about me, now?" Fran asked.

"Face it, Mom. You married the guy and had three children with him. You followed his every command. What does that say about you if he is who I say he is?"

Silence ensued. "You are in a quandary, mother. We all are," John said. "If we admit he was a sick monster, then we are either his victims or his offspring. I'm not sure about you, but I don't care to be either. On the other hand, if we deny he was a malicious human being, our only option is to believe him. You know what that means. It means we have to agree to blame ourselves for his outrageous behavior, just like he did. This requires we admit there is something wrong with us. We are the monster children he had to manage."

John stopped and made eye contact to see if his audience was following him. "Don't you see? Dad set it up so we couldn't win; which is why we felt powerless. We didn't look in the box because he had us convinced the truth couldn't set us free, no matter what it turned out to be."

"What does the truth have to do with the box?" Fran asked.

"The box contained the truth and he owned the box. Thus he owned the truth. The box was a symbol of his power over us. It was a small but powerful representation of how much power he wielded in this family."

"Like a thermometer that measured his power. He could look at it any time and know he was still in control?" Fran asked.

"Exactly," John said.

"I think you've been writing too many of those short novels," Peter argued. "You are reading too much into this box. It is just his personal diary."

"I can't believe you don't want to read his personal diary," Thomas said. "Don't you want to know what he thought – how he rationalized the things that he did? How he felt about each of us? I'd kill for that information."

"I know what he thought and how he felt. He told us. Besides, that isn't what you want to know. You want to know if there is any dirt on him in that box so you can destroy his reputation. Like Mom said, you want to hurt him."

"I want to know why the hell he hated my ass the way he did," Thomas yelled.

"I can tell you," Peter said. "He didn't hate you. He hated the way you behaved – the disrespect, the constant challenges, the way you looked at him. If he hated you at all, it was because you hated him and everything he stood for."

"He was the father, I was the child. Kids don't draw first blood. Parents do that. I mean, it's not like I came out of the womb hating him."

"What do you think, Mom?" John shifted in his chair toward her. "What do you think is in the box?"

"To be honest with you, I never thought about it much. It was his box and that was that. If he didn't want me to know what was in it, then so be it. Everyone needs their own space. Lord knows I needed mine. He didn't go in my kitchen and I didn't go in his box. But now that I hear you boys talking about it, I wonder why I didn't question it more. He was kind of weird about things after he looked in it."

"So, what is your guess, Eddie?" Thomas asked.

"Maybe he had some of those naked girl magazines in there."

"Why would you think that, Mom?" John looked her in the eyes.

"A couple of times...after he was done looking at the box...him...you know..." Fran signaled with her hands in an attempt to illicit her answer from the boys, as if she was playing charades and couldn't say the answer herself.

"He what? Spit it out, Eddie."

"He...you know...he had a..." she started to motion toward her groin, but changed her mind mid gesture. Instead she reached her hand over the table and pointed downwards toward Thomas' groin.

"Mom, what the hell are you doing pointing at my penis? What's that got to do with anything?" Thomas was frustrated.

"His..." she shook her pointer finger again toward Thomas' groin, as though she was avoiding something disgusting.

The rest of the table laughed as they became aware of the answer to the charade. But the disconcerting effect of having his mother pointing toward his groin put Thomas on a slower curve. It was the tone of the other's laughter that gave him the clue he needed to figure it out. It had that naughty quality to it that signifies the laughter is sexual in nature. "Oh my God! The fucker had a boner?" Thomas noticed her puzzled look. "An erection Eddie; a boner is an erection."

The family leaned back in their chairs and laughed. Even Fran was able to get out a couple of chuckles in the midst of her stifling embarrassment. The focus of the laughter turned toward Fran who attempted to stop her entire body from blushing. When she was successful, the group started laughing again which in turn, jumpstarted her laughing, which prompted the blushing all over again. She was caught in a self-sustaining cycle of comedic shame. The family remained amused as they waited for her to gain hold of herself, so she could answer the question. Just when they thought she was able to speak, she would burst out laughing and the cycle would start all over again.

After a half dozen cycles, Fran gathered herself. "You call it a boner?" The group rolled their eyes out of frustration, as they would be forced to wait another ten minutes for their answer. But the childlike manner in which Fran delivered her question and her ensuing girlish laughter, created an amusement that made the wait bearable, if not downright enjoyable.

Fran tried to get out of verbalizing her answer, but the family insisted she answer. It was a test she needed to pass in order to be accepted into this familial fraternity. In the end, out of a desire to belong, she acquiesced, "Yes, he had a boner," she giggled. "I mean, he had an erection."

Julie retrieved yet another bottle of wine. This time she opened it herself and passed it around the table after reaching over and refilling Dundee's glass.

Relieved, the group moved on. Julie became the interrogator. "What did you think was in the box, Sammy?"

Sammy was a bit startled to be put on the spot. She had been enjoying the spectator role for a change. "Um...I don't know. In all honesty, I didn't even know the box existed. This is the first I've heard about it. I can't believe you never said anything, Thomas. All these years I've missed the excitement of the Vanderhuis' unsolved mystery."

"We didn't talk about it." Thomas seemed amazed at the revelation those words carried with them. "We didn't even talk to each other about it. It was not allowed."

"Since when has that stopped you?" Peter didn't bother waiting for an answer and turned his look away from Thomas.

"You'd be surprised how much I kept inside. I held my tongue about a lot of things."

"You weren't very obvious about it," Peter countered.

"Well now...I wouldn't have wanted to give Dad what he wanted." Thomas said.

"And what was that?" Peter asked.

"Fear. The bastard wanted to see it in our eyes. I'll be damned if I was going to give him that pleasure."

"I'm surprised you didn't paint the box," Julie noted. "Seems like rich material for a provocative work of art."

"He did." Peter looked at Thomas with a predictable sense of disrespect. "It was called the Ark of the Covenant."

"That's the box?" Julie sounded surprised. "The little box with the big naked birds protecting it?" She paused. "What's with the title?"

Peter, the resident theologian, said, "In the Old Testament the people of Israel had an ark they carried with them as they traveled toward the Promised Land." Peter added the necessary details a non-churched person would need to get the full gist of the explanation. He assumed Julie had little exposure to the biblical stories that had been the canvas on which his family's history had been played out. He also assumed Julie hadn't had to memorize the detailed descriptions and dimensions of the portable temple and its contents, as he and his brothers did in Sunday school. Thus his long explanation of the title to Thomas' painting, the Ark of the Covenant, droned on as he enjoyed not only the process of teaching Julie, but the feeling of satisfaction he had about being able to remember so many of the details after twenty-five years.

The family had learned to tolerate Peter's pedantic style, but Julie didn't have the patience. "What was in the box?"

Peter glared at her, annoyed at her precociousness. "The presence of God."

"So what does that have to do with your father's box?" Julie asked.

"Here is the connection," Peter picked up on Julie's hints about his droning on and got to the point. "No one was allowed to look in the box except the high priest."

"And what happened if someone snuck a peek?"

"A couple of priests tried it."

"And?" Julie rushed him. She was a bit intrigued.

"God fried their asses with a lightning bolt." Thomas jumped in to finish the explanation.

"Ahh..."The light went on in Julie's head. "The Ark of the Covenant and your Dad's box; you don't touch and you don't look, lest you get struck down by your father's fury. Got it! Thanks Peter. You all are a complicated bunch. You have to be a theologian to participate in your conversations."

Julie turned toward Thomas "Back to the box," The group thought she was just curious. They didn't realize she was trying to understand the last two years of her life – the ones spent living with a product of this intriguing family. "What do you think is in it, Thomas?"

"Dad was weird about the box. I assumed there was something kinky in it."

"Why kinky?" Peter asked.

"Dad was weird about a lot of things, but he was especially weird about sex. Don't look! Don't touch! Don't talk about it. Sammy, remember the time he lectured us because we were holding hands while we walked up to the house in our bathing suits? He went on about how you shouldn't hold each other's hands when you weren't wearing any clothes."

"I thought you had your bathing suits on?" Julie said.

"We did, but to Dad a bikini was being naked," Thomas said.

"Give her the context, Thomas. Sammy's string bikini didn't leave much for the imagination," Peter was uncomfortable because of the way the statement came out of his mouth with such certainty.

"How did he put up with your nude paintings of her?" Julie asked.

"I don't know if he knew about the paintings. Did he, Eddie?"

"He knew alright. I was with him when he saw them. He looked away and walked out of the room. I don't think he liked the way it made him feel to see Sammy that way. He never spoke of them to me; acted like they didn't exist. Your father could do that when he wanted. Some things would get stuck in his craw and he would obsess about them. Other things he let go, pretending they didn't happen. I could never figure out his rhyme or reason. But sex was one he put out of his brain."

"Anyhow," Thomas continued, "Dad went on about if you grab her hand, pretty soon you'll be wanting to touch something else. The same old slippery slope argument he applied to all his ethical arguments."

"God, I was so embarrassed!" Sammy said.

"Not as embarrassed as the old man. He couldn't wait to finish and get the hell out of there."

"So the box!" Julie said. "What do you think was in the box?"

"Jesus Christ, Julie. This isn't a soap opera. It is our lives," Thomas took another gulp of his wine.

"Stop being so dramatic, Thomas," Sammy said. "Get on with it."

"Fine, Dad was weird about sex so the box must have something sexual in it. That was my logic. I mean sex doesn't just go away. Everybody has to do something with it. I'm assuming you weren't his little whore by night, Eddie, so I figured he kept her in the box."

"Whore by night!" Sammy said. "How do you forgive this son of yours, Fran?"

Fran waved her off, not wanting her sex life with Richard to become the next topic.

"I figured there was kiddy porn or pictures of naked men," Thomas said.

"Oh for God's sake!" Peter stood up and began to pace in circles.

"What made you think that? Did he do something to you?" Julie looked at Thomas and then at Sammy. When they shook their heads, Julie moved on to check with John and then to Peter. Turning back to Thomas, "So then why would you assume that?"

"I told you! He was weird. What could be weirder than kiddy porn? Gay porn!"

"You think gay porn is more perverted than child pornography?" Julie asked.

"No, but I'm positive Dad did. Nothing was worse than being gay."

Fran decided to conclude the dinner. "Well, we're not going to come to any conclusions on this matter of your father's box tonight, so I suggest we move on." She began to gather the dishes. The women joined her effort, while the boys began to leave. Sammy and Julie cleared their throats sending a clear signal the men were to join the cleanup effort. With chagrin, they complied.

There was a steady trail between the dining room and the kitchen, while everything was cleared from the table. It took good care not to get hit by the swinging doors that led to the kitchen.

"Wasn't Dad going to put some glass in those doors so you could see oncoming traffic?" Peter asked.

"He never got around to it," Fran explained without looking up from the dishes she was rinsing and handing to Sammy. "Once you boys left, the need seemed to be so minimal. I'll find a carpenter. I'd hate for my grandkids to get hurt."

The boys looked at Peter since he was the only father in the litter.

"Thomas, you need to get me that oregano you brought for the brownies. I'll mix up a bunch for a snack for tonight. I thought we'd play a game."

The group looked at Thomas.

"Are you going to tell her?" Peter demanded in a pressed whisper.

"She has to know, doesn't she?" Thomas said. "How could she not? That therapist of hers would have figured it out and told her, I'm sure."

"Then why would she be asking for it?" Sammy asked.

"I don't know," Thomas mumbled. "Maybe she is fucking with me? You know, screwing with my head."

"Right," Peter said. "That sounds like mother. You've got to tell her."

"Maybe tomorrow, but tonight; tonight a batch of pot laced brownies and a game of Yahtzee is what this homecoming party needs." He ran upstairs and came bounding down with a small plastic bag. He entered the kitchen and gave it to Fran. "Eddie, would you mind making an extra batch. I'd like to look up some of my old friends and give them a few for old time's sake."

"You think they are still around, after all these years?" Fran asked.

"I don't know. I'll find out. I'll visit my old stomping grounds to see if I can find them."

"What kind of friends are they? Why would you expect them to be hanging out at the same place they did in high school?" Fran asked.

"It is a long story, Eddie. Maybe tomorrow I'll tell you."

Sammy stuck her head in the kitchen, "Fran, where is the Yahtzee game?"

"Goodness, it has been so long. Did you try the hallway closet where it used to be?"

"It's not there."

"Try the closet in your room. I probably moved it down there."

Peter declined to play the game and went to spend time with his father. He managed to catch the hospice nurse on her way out and got a progress report. The nurse was kind, but there wasn't much to report, except slow movement through the dying process.

Peter turned his head to the side and shielded his eyes with one hand as he observed the plastic tubes that brought nourishment, oxygen, and medicine into Richard's emaciated body. Monitors informed him there were still signs of life. His father was unable to communicate, and as far as anyone could tell, unaware of what was happening around him. He was waiting to die from a slow growing brain tumor which his faith required he accept as an act of God. Accepting anyone's choice for his life went against his nature, even if the one doing the choosing was God. But in this case he had no choice but to accept the fate decided for him.

While he was with his father, he decided to call Sandy.

"I'm so glad you called, Peter. Your timing is perfect. I'm ready to have that phone sex you promised. You'll have to tell me what to do, since you are the expert."

"I'm not an expert at phone sex, Sandy. I've never done it before."

"Oh good, we can be virgins all over again. How about if..."

"I'm in my father's bedroom, Sandy. He is on his death bed. I hardly think it is appropriate for us to have phone sex in front of him."

"He is unconscious and won't hear a thing."

"Now you are starting to sound like Thomas."

"Oh dear, I'd better stop then. I wouldn't want to be like that slut brother of yours. How have you and Thomas been getting along?"

"He's in the kitchen right now giving Mother the oregano for his brownies."

"Oregano?"

"Code word for pot, in this family."

"Dear God, does she know what she is doing?"

"We don't know. Mother has changed a lot in the past six months and we're not sure where she is coming from. Thomas thinks she might be messing with his mind, but I doubt it. Not that it matters to him, as long as he gets his brownies."

"You sound bitter, Peter. Remember the plan. Relax, loosen up, don't make it personal. Respond, don't react."

Peter saw the dust ruffle on the bed move. He bent over, lifted it, and found himself staring down Dundee's snout.

"Imagine that," he said.

"What are you talking about?"

"Dundee, Thomas' dog has taken a liking to Dad. He has made himself a cave under his bed. It looks like he is on death watch."

"I've heard of dogs doing such things. Thomas won't like it."

"It's ironic, but fitting."

"Don't rub it in. Let it come out in due course."

"That's no fun."

In the dining room, the others ate brownies and played Yahtzee. The game started out competitive, but as the night wore on and the pot worked its way into their systems, the

167

game mellowed to the point where losing was as good as winning. Each roll of the dice led to a howl that could have awakened the dead.

The laughter broke Peter's heart. It reminded him of the price he had paid for choosing his father. He was an outsider in his own home; even more now that his father no longer sat at the head of the table. He yearned to go and join them, but he knew he wouldn't be welcomed. Well he would be welcomed, because people high on pot aren't very discriminate about the company they keep. But he wouldn't be able to be one of them. So even if they did welcome him, he would feel like a misfit – like the party pooper he was in this family. Even his Mom would fit in and no longer keep him company on the sidelines.

Peter went to bed. The rest of the family played late into the night.

Chapter 11

Religion
To Each His Own

The sun shown into the upstairs dormer and woke Thomas. It was a rare treat to wake up to a sunny snow covered Michigan morning and his brothers had risen to take advantage of it. He washed his face and brushed his teeth, but when he looked in the mirror, it wasn't enough. He found a towel and headed for the shower.

The shower walls were wet, so he assumed his brothers used it. He was surprised they hadn't awakened him. He had slept so well in his old bedroom, fully stocked with memories that triggered a long list of emotions, both good and bad. When it came to his past, Thomas' emotions melted into one category – "Do Not Disturb."

He turned the nozzle to make the water as hot as he could tolerate and then turned it a little further. This was Thomas' recipe for life. Find your level of tolerance. Then push it one step further. Living just over the edge can be a peaceful lifestyle, if it distracts you from the trauma of the boring and mundane. Thomas strove to live there.

He finished his shower and dried his semi-scalded body. He looked through his bag for a clean sweater, but discovered he hadn't paid much attention to what he had packed and found nothing warm enough to suit his fancy. The warm clothes he had brought were dirty from the long drive to Michigan.

He turned to his brothers' side of the room. He would have preferred to borrow clothes from John. Not only was John more open to sharing clothes, his taste was closer to Thomas', preferring the casual look of jeans and sweatshirts over Peters formal look of dress slacks and button down shirt. Of course, Thomas wore his jeans and tops two sizes too small in order to get that sixties rock star look Mick Jagger perfected. His tall thin body allowed him to pull off this emaciated look.

But all of this was irrelevant since John had lived in another country for fifteen years and his taste in clothes had adjusted. Everything Thomas had seen him wear so far was cotton. Peter had also moved away to a different climate, but Thomas was sure Peter would have kept his warm sweaters from his high school years tucked away somewhere for this very occasion. Besides, a part of him wanted to pilfer from Peter to perturb him.

He found a wool sweater on Peter's dresser and pulled it over his wet, uncombed hair. He'd forgotten to tie it back into a ponytail and had to fuss to keep it out of his eyes. The wool penetrated the long sleeve t-shirt he had put on to avoid this discomfort and he remembered why he had never worn wool. In Arcada he had discovered Smart Wool and fell in love with it because it kept him warm without scratching his sensitive skin. Upon occasion technology brought about something Thomas thought was worthwhile. He ransacked Peter's suitcase, finding a grade of wool that looked less prickly and switched the sweaters out.

Thomas went down the stairs and found his mother busy in the kitchen with breakfast. He greeted her with a 'good morning' that communicated 'where's my coffee' more than it did 'I'm pleased to see you.' The cup was in his hands before he could make the request in a more direct way, so he took it and asked about everybody's whereabouts. She explained the girls had yet to stir and the boys were enjoying their morning coffee in the living room.

Fran waved him toward the living room, as she had much to do in the kitchen. He obeyed, since her command read his mind's desire. He wandered through the dining room and sauntered into the living room where a strange sight accosted him. The furniture had been rearranged to provide an open space in front of the picture window that looked out on the front yard. Peter sat in one of the displaced chairs, off to the side of the open space. He was reading his Bible, which sat on a pillow resting on his lap. His legs and arms were crossed in the opposite direction, leading him to appear centered in prayerful meditation.

In the center of the open space John was upside down in a headstand, appearing relaxed. His body was still, forming a straight line that reached for the ceiling with his pointed toes. His shirt dropped down around his neck, revealing a thin, toned chest and abdomen. It was the look of someone who performed steady exercise and a healthy, moderate diet. Thomas wondered how long John had been in this position and how long he intended to keep it. He made his way over to the chair next to Peter and took a seat.

"Better watch out. Too much of that could cause permanent brain damage," Thomas said.

Peter broke his prayerful pose and elbowed Thomas. "Leave him alone. You will break his train of thought."

Keeping his eyes on John, Thomas replied in the same loud voice, "I was talking to you," after which he tilted his head as a way of pointing to the Bible on Peter's lap.

Peter rolled his eyes and went back to reading his Bible. Thomas entertained himself watching John's slow and methodical movements. He came into the downward facing dog pose. He wondered why humans would want to imitate dogs, as though dogs held secrets unavailable to humans. He recognized the position from Julie's occasional venture into yoga. Somehow, it had made more sense to him when Julie performed this canine pose, due to the fact her ass was much more flattering than John's when displayed in this intriguing position.

John moved through his poses in what appeared to be a form of dance. Thomas marveled at how John was to be able to hold himself in these awkward positions for extended periods. Just watching the dance-like movements brought Thomas into a relaxed state of mind and made him yearn for a joint. As a finale John came to a sitting position, where his legs were crossed at the ankles and his spine was stretched straight, lifting his head high on his neck. His hands rested on the inside of his knees and were opened, with his palms facing upward. He held that position for five minutes with his eyes closed, breathing so slow that at times Thomas wondered if he had passed over into the land of the dead.

John stood up and began to roll up his mat. The girls bounded through the door, coffee in hand, only to be silenced by the aura that filled the room. Sammy made her way over to the couch, greeting Thomas and Peter in a subdued manner. Julie took note of John.

"Yoga! I hope you aren't finished. I'd love to join you."

"I've always got time for more yoga," John replied.

"Great! I'll get my mat."

John unrolled his mat and moved it to the side to make room for Julie's. She was back in seconds, mat in hand. She spread it out next to John's. "You all don't mind, do you?" she asked the group.

"No, go right ahead," they responded in choral fashion.

Thomas moved over to the couch next to Sammy. "This will be great entertainment. I can watch Julie's ass and you can see if John's meets your fancy."

Sammy rolled her eyes and pushed him off the couch so he would go back to his chair. "Leave me out of your nonsense."

"Wow! Your morning mood hasn't changed, has it? I thought age might have mellowed your bad morning chemistry."

"You haven't changed either, Thomas. Do us all a favor and grow up." She looked at his sweater. "Isn't that Peter's sweater? He used to wear it all the time, back in high school."

Thomas tried to ignore her so she would move on, but Peter's attention was drawn to the sweater. "I thought it looked familiar. Where did you get it from?"

"I grabbed it from a suitcase."

"Why are you dressing yourself out of my suitcase?"

"I forgot to pack enough warm clothes. I didn't think you would mind."

"I might not have, if you would have asked."

"Peter, could I borrow one of your high school sweaters you have preserved for posterity?" Thomas asked. "Who does that anyway?"

"Who does what?"

"Who keeps their high school clothes in museum condition?"

"I get it. We've shifted the focus on to me, so we can leave your obsessive pilfering unresolved."

Sammy reached over and undid the top button of Peter's shirt. He didn't resist so she proceeded to undo the buttons on his cuffs and roll them up. He interrupted her as she finished the second cuff.

"Am I not dressed to your liking?" he asked.

"Sorry, I just thought you needed to lighten up a bit." She removed her hands from his space. "You were looking so serious."

John and Julie began to move through the different poses, while Sammy and Thomas watched in silence. Peter read from his Bible, pausing at each verse to study its meaning, closing his eyes to ponder a thought or offer up a short prayer. John invited Sammy to take his place on the mat, but Sammy declined.

"Didn't you mention doing yoga at the dinner table?" John asked.

"That was ammunition to get Thomas off my back. I've only tried it once and I wasn't very good at it."

John pushed the issue and she declined again. John insisted, arguing it would give her a better outlook. Thomas commented on how great of an idea that was; her being in such a poor mood. Sammy capitulated. She warned she wasn't very flexible to lessen the expectations, and made her way to the mat. John followed her and was patient as he explained the poses and waited for her to follow his instructions.

"Isn't yoga wonderful," Julie proclaimed as they rolled up the mats and walked toward the couch. "I wish I could do it every morning."

"I don't know about that, but it was very relaxing," Sammy looked at John. "Can I join you tomorrow? That is if you are yogiing tomorrow, or whatever it is you call it."

"I am. Myrna and I start every day this way."

"Lucky you!" Julie smiled at Sammy. "It almost makes me want to stay. You are a good teacher, John."

"Why don't you, Julie?" John asked.

"You mean, stay?"

"Well, that too. But I was referring to your desire to do yoga every morning."

"Oh, I don't know. Things get in the way." She kicked Thomas' leg as a means of pointing out her major road block.

"You mean you don't do yoga because of Thomas, or you aren't staying because of him?" John asked.

"I meant the yoga part. But now that you mention it, he also has something to do with the not staying."

"Hey, I can't be the cause of all your problems. I'll accept responsibility for you not wanting to stay, but the yoga, that's on you."

"You heard him. He and Myrna do it together every morning. I'm just saying it would be easier if you showed some interest in something other than...never mind."

"She is referring to my spiritual routine," he pulled a joint out of his pocket. "Anyone care to join me?" He put the joint up to his nose and took a deep breath, inhaling the smell of the pot. "It is the only kind of deep breathing I need."

"I'm not sure smoking pot qualifies as a spiritual activity," Peter said.

174

"Tell that to the Native American Indians and the court that ruled smoking Peyote should be allowed under the freedom of religion act," Thomas said.

"I don't rely on the liberal courts to tell me what is spiritual and what is not. Besides, they don't just smoke Peyote. They smoke it as a part of a religious ceremony."

"There you go again, Peter, always insisting your way is superior to all others."

"I didn't say that."

"You didn't have to."

"Well you have to admit praying and doing yoga are different than smoking pot."

"Just admit it, Peter. You are as despising of our pagan brother for doing yoga as you are of my pot smoking. In the end, your Christian way is the only way."

"I didn't say that."

"You don't have to, Peter. You and your religion are as predictable as the sun rising and setting every day. The whole point of the Christian religion or any religion for that matter, is to establish its truth as the best, and if possible, the only truth."

"You might as well tell me. Why is it we would want to own the truth?" Peter disentangled his legs.

"There are a lot of reasons, but the heart of the matter is you want to feel special."

"And you are above wanting to feel special?"

"To the contrary, I admit I'm fucked up. Most of what I do is driven by my desire to feel significant, in order to compensate for being fucked up. My painting, my never ending search for the perfect woman – sorry Julie – sorry Sammy – my smart-ass cockiness, my anger at Dad, that god damn piece of shit I call Puff. Need I go on? The difference is I acknowledge my motives. I don't hide my need to feel special under the blanket of spiritual awakening. You want to feel superior to the rest of the world? Be my guest. Join the club. All I ask is that you be honest and drop the self-righteous bullshit."

"Where do you get this from?" Peter said.

"Your hero, Dad. He used his religion to hide his insatiable need to control his little part of the universe in an attempt to feel an ounce of significance. I know you believed his religious fervency. But I saw right through it. It wasn't piety, which is what he wanted us to believe. He wasn't trying to serve God. He was trying to serve his own self-interest. He was trying to be the big man in town and the only way for him to do that was to pretend he was God's right hand man. Religion is a great cover for avoiding the humility of what ails us."

"What are you talking about? Religion heals what ails us." Peter pounded the arm of his chair.

Sammy, Julie, and John sat still, mesmerized by the prize fighters.

"If that were true, I'd be sitting in the front pew every Sunday morning. But it's a myth. It didn't cure Dad. It made him worse. It gave him a platform on which to play out his pathologies on everyone around him. It didn't make him a better person, it made him worse."

"Let me guess. You know this because you are smarter than the rest of us. You are better than Dad and you see through him."

"Quite the contrary, Peter, although that is what Father would have wanted us to believe. I was the bad one because I was proud and arrogant and couldn't tolerate his righteousness. The truth is, I didn't see through Dad. I saw myself in him, which is why I tried so hard not to be like him. I understand Dad, because I'm like him."

"I suppose you think you have done better than him?"

"I've tried. Believe me I've tried."

"Have you succeeded?" Peter asked.

"The most I can say is I've been more honest than him. I don't pretend to be righteous. I'm as mean an asshole as Dad, but at least I'm an honest son of a bitch." He looked at Sammy and Julie because the confession was meant for them. Neither of them was moved by it.

"So how do you want me to see this family portrait we are acting out in this living room?" Peter asked.

"That's simple. We are all trying to cope with the same fucked up world. To do so, we need to find some way to get high enough to tolerate it. John has decided yoga is how he wants to get high and cope. It focuses his attention inwards; off the stress of world. This allows him to get through the day without being so overwhelmed."

Thomas turned to Peter. "You get your high from losing yourself in idealistic thinking or something like that. I don't understand it myself, but praying and reading the Bible gets you high. I would recommend you consider converting to Pentecostalism. Those folks don't need pot. They get jacked up on the rock music they play in their church services. It is like an Aerosmith concert." Thomas looked around to see if his humor was taking effect. It wasn't, but he was undeterred. "If I could afford to go to an Aerosmith concert a couple of times a week, I wouldn't need pot. But, since dropping out and becoming an Aerosmith groupie isn't in the cards, I smoke pot. It makes me a better person. Ask Julie. She'll give testimony I'm a better person after I inhale this mystery incense."

"I'd hate to know you without the pot," Peter shook his head.

"I'd like to know you without religion. I'd also like you to smoke a joint with me to see if it helped us get along. I'm sure I'd like you better and I'd bet my life savings you would find me more tolerable. Hell, I think Dad and I could have gotten along if he would have joined me for a reefer, instead of dragging me to church every Sunday in hopes the Holy Spirit would turn me into the son he always wanted."

"You're suggesting your pot is better than my religion. I thought..."

"I didn't say I had overcome my heritage. I am an evangelist of the Gospel of Pot. No one can help wanting others to agree with them. You don't want to go to church alone. Self-righteousness is more intoxicating in a crowd, where others can validate you. Why would I want to smoke pot by myself? You would prefer preaching to the choir in a full house, I prefer a congregation of potheads over smoking alone."

"What do you think, John?" Julie turned and looked at John in a soft adoring way.

John hesitated, but when Julie persisted with eagerness he answered, "I think we all do the best we can. Peter finds comfort in religion. I find my center in the practice of yoga. My little brother here likes the way pot makes him feel – to each his own."

"Forever, the peacemaker." Thomas sighed and shook his head.

"Don't get me wrong. I'm tempted to believe my way is better than Peter's or Thomas'-and it is for me. I've tried them all and yoga fits my needs at this time. I'd like to think yoga is more than just a coping method and the clarity of mind I derive from it comes from a connection to some transcendent reality, only available when we reach an altered level of consciousness."

John stretched his legs and continued. "That would be, as Thomas would say, a wonderful aphrodisiac. But the truth is, the clarity of mind yoga brings is nothing more than a product of the relaxed state of mind I derive from the ancient techniques. It helps me face reality in a more effective way because I'm less anxious. The less anxious I am, the more clearly I see."

"An honest salesman! That's a rare commodity." Thomas tried to sound impressed; but the cynicism in his tone betrayed him.

"I prefer to think I'm not the evangelist you and Dad hoped I would be," John said.

"Dad and I? Since when have I hoped you would be an evangelist?" Thomas asked.

"You've always tried to convince this family to think your way, Thomas. You've been promoting your opinions over Dad's as far back as I can remember. Face it Thomas, you were always relentless in your attempt to convert us." John said.

"It runs in the family," Thomas grinned. "Wasn't Dad's grandfather a snake oil salesman"

Peter, the family historian, corrected him. "That's what Grandpa called him. The truth is grandma's father was a preacher up north. He was a charismatic healer and Grandpa accused him of being a snake handler and therefore a snake oil salesman."

"There you have it. It is in our blood," Thomas said.

"I don't care to convince either of you to practice yoga, much less to stop going to church or smoking pot. It is enough for me you are trying to find your way. I hope you succeed, just as I hope I do. Who knows; maybe someday I'll change my mind and start going to church with you, Peter, or smoking pot in the mountains by Arcada with Thomas. I've said 'never' before and found myself eating my words. Certainty is not part of my vocabulary anymore."

"So why are you writing all these books?"

"Self-reflection, Thomas."

"But they are for sale," Thomas noted.

"In case others find them helpful."

"Then why not give them away?" Thomas said.

"A man has to make a living, or at least cover the cost of his self-indulgence. Besides, if I was giving them away, you would accuse me of spreading propaganda. That is what free opinions are, am I right? It is impossible to win with you, Thomas."

"Aha! So you do want to win the argument!"

"You win." John fell to his knees, raised his hands over his head and bowed to Thomas.

"That's my aim in life – intellectual annihilation!" Thomas said.

"So we will share your joint?" Peter widened his eyes in disbelief.

"On that note, anyone care to join me in my search to become a better man?" Thomas waved the joint between his fingers as he headed for the front door. "It is much less effort than yoga or devotions."

The group waved him off and dispersed.

Chapter 12

Coffee Time

John headed for the kitchen to check on Fran's progress with breakfast. The smell of bacon filled his nostrils with a nostalgia that brought instant comfort to his entire body. Fran spotted him and motioned for him to sample a piece. He dismissed her offer with a polite wave and settled in one of the stools off to the side of Fran's working area. She grabbed a fork out of the drawer and brought a bit of the eggs over for him to taste. He acquiesced.

Noting his reluctance she asked, "You don't like eggs anymore?"

"I've become a vegetarian over the last few years. It isn't that I don't like eggs and meat, I've just decided it is healthier to avoid them."

"Oh dear," Fran's eyes bulged and her hands began to fidget as she felt pressed to think of some alternative foods to satisfy John's palette, "that could complicate my menu for the weekend."

"Not to worry, Mom. Being here has revived my taste for meat and I'll be fine as long as I pace myself. Besides, I see those delicious pancakes on the griddle over there and they're making my mouth water. I haven't had a pancake with maple syrup for a long time."

"I was wondering why you were picking out the meat last night. I should have known."

"Now you are a mind reader? I should have told you, and I would have, if it was that important. Just do what you have planned and I'll fend for myself. It's not a religious thing. A little meat isn't going to hurt me." This was a bit of a lie, since his morning bowels had reflected his change in diet. But he figured it would pass soon. Besides, he didn't want to make a big deal out of his vegetarianism. In this crowd, it would cause him a lot of grief.

"No, no. I'll figure out at least one meatless meal. Sammy might have some ideas. She lives in Chicago and people in big cities are exposed to these kinds of things."

"Suit yourself, but it isn't necessary. You might get a lot of unwarranted feedback from your other two sons. They love their meat."

"Well, Peter, maybe. But the girls will be fine with it, I'm sure. I would be surprised if Thomas hasn't been a vegetarian at some point in his life. It is very California-ish, you know."

"I'm sure he has been a lot of things," John said.

John sat in the kitchen, enjoying the harsh taste of the strong brew of coffee his mother had set next to him. She wasn't drinking coffee. "No coffee, Mother? Is that by doctor's orders?"

"Oh, no. Well, I suppose he might think it was a good idea. But then again, these days they say coffee is good for you. Something about anti...anti..."

"Antioxidants, Mom."

"Yes, that's the word I'm looking for; antioxidants."

"So why the abstinence?"

"I wouldn't call it abstinence; just a lack of interest. Your father loved his coffee strong. He kept asking for it to be stronger and stronger. At some point, my coffee became so strong; I didn't enjoy drinking it any longer. So I stopped."

"Don't you miss it? I mean you could stop brewing it so strong, now that he...um..."

"Isn't drinking anymore? I surmised you were looking for a nice way to refer to your father's slow walk toward death."

"It is a bit awkward to talk about him as dead, but it feels like he is."

"Trust me, he is not. You would know this if you had gone into his room to see him." She paused. "What's this about, John? I would have expected it from Thomas. In fact, I'd be surprised if he went in there at all, unless it is to ransack that box of your Dad's. But your avoidance surprises me."

"You realize the box issue isn't over yet. Thomas isn't going to let up on this until he knows what's in there."

"We'll see. Maybe we should know what is in there. Maybe solving the mystery would help us all move on."

"You mean break the so called spell Thomas says he has on us?"

"That isn't that farfetched. It does seem like he has a spell on us. Just look at yourself. You can't go in there and see him. Are you afraid?" Fran sat down on the stool next to Him.

"I'm not afraid, but I would rather think of this weekend as being about us and not him."

"But it is about him. It is about saying goodbye to him so we can get to the, us part. Don't you want to say goodbye to him?"

Fran let the silence stand and waited for John to settle on a response. She had learned this technique from Marcia, who loved long silences. The more uncomfortable Fran was with the silence, the quieter Marcia became, until Fran couldn't stand it and was forced to blurt out an answer. It was always more honest than Fran had intended it to be.

"I'm afraid." John paused. "I'm afraid of what will happen to me when I go in there to see him. How do you say goodbye to someone you hoped you would never see again?" John paused again, breathing deeply to fend off tears. "I don't know what to say. I don't even know what to feel. I can't go in there without a plan."

"Why do you need a plan?"

"I have never dealt with Dad without a plan. Even if I was just greeting him when he got home from work, I had to make a plan. I had to think about what I would say if he was in a good mood. Then I had to think about what I would say if he was in a bad mood. I had to think about what answers I would give him if he asked me any questions. You know how he interrogated us as though he was a detective trying to get to the bottom of a mystery which was never solved. I had to scan my day to remember if I had done anything to make him mad, just in case he knew about it and confronted me. I was forever making plans for my encounters with Dad."

Fran bit her lip to help with the silence strategy that was working so well.

"So... so I could stay one step ahead of him and not get hurt," John said.

"It sounds exhausting."

"It was exhausting. It is exhausting, and he is in a comatose state, incapable of saying anything, much less interrogating me."

"He hurt you."

"He did, but I don't even know if the hurt was the worst of it."

"What do you mean?" Fran asked.

"When he hurt me, it was a relief of sorts."

"I don't understand."

"I don't know if I do either, which makes me worry I'm a bit crazy." John shifted on the stool. "The worst was waiting for him and making my plans. It was like torture when I knew I was going to have to deal with him. My head would go in circles trying to think up ways to fend him off. I couldn't stop my mind from panicking. It only stopped when he yelled at me. That was my relief."

John took a deep breath and sipped his coffee. "You see, after he was done yelling, I knew I would have a reprieve. I knew he was done for a while, as if it was out of his system and there would be a safe waiting period before it all built up again."

184

"You weren't just worrying about yourself were you?" Fran asked.

"What do you mean?"

"Marcia thinks you were my protector. You tried to run interference for me and you paid a price for that loyalty."

"I don't know about that." John checked his watch.

"What time is it?" Fran asked.

"I don't know. I was just distracting myself."

"I'm sorry, John."

"You seem to be saying that an awful lot this weekend, Mom."

"I don't think I've even begun."

"It wasn't your fault. You didn't do this."

"Yes, it was. I did my part. I was the mother and I should have been running interference for you; not the other way around. I'm sorry I didn't protect you." Fran's tears made her confession slip deeper into John's consciousness.

"What is it you are afraid will happen when you go into your father's room?"

"I'm afraid I won't have a plan and I'll be forced to wing it."

"Why don't you just make a plan? I'll help you."

"It isn't that easy, Mom. I've pictured this in my head and it is different than any situation I've ever been in with him. That's why I don't have a clue how to prepare for it."

"What makes this so different from your other encounters with him?'

John thought and Fran waited in silence. "He's going to be vulnerable. He'll be this wasted away, pathetic figure that no longer resembles the monster he is in my head."

John took in a deep breath. "I'm afraid I'll feel sorry for him. How can I feel sorry for a monster? I can't feel sorry for him and still be angry at him. You saw the look on Julie's face last night when we were all afraid of the empty chair. It was a look that said, 'What's wrong with you people. How can you be afraid of an empty chair?' I'm afraid I'll look at him and think the same thing. I'll look at the harmless, vulnerable figure laying in that bed and wonder, 'What's wrong with me? How could I be afraid of this pathetic little man? How could I falsely accuse him of being a monster?' I can't afford that, Mom. My psyche can't take that kind of a blow. I can't, I won't rearrange my story to let him have the last word."

John cringed and slumped, bending over his hands folded in his lap.

"You weren't crazy, John. We weren't crazy. It happened the way you remember it. That is why this family needs to be together this weekend. We were there. We witnessed it. We suffered it. And even if no one else believes us, we can believe each other. We can understand why we've done the things we've done. We know why we are afraid of the empty chair. We understand why we didn't open that box your Dad kept in plain sight."

"That may well be true," John paused. "But what about forgiveness, Mom?"

"What about it?"

"If I can't feel sorry for him, how can I forgive him?"

"You think forgiving someone requires feeling sorry for him?"

"Maybe feeling sorry for someone is the wrong term. Maybe what I'm trying to say is that forgiveness seems to require some kind of empathy and understanding. That requires a certain amount of feeling sorry for the person who wronged you. When I first met Myrna, we would have long, drawn out fights. She drew them out; I moped around, part of that sulking you talked about earlier. She would engage me to explain herself, but I shut her out. After a while she would say to me, 'If you want to be mad at me, then there is nothing I can do to stop you. Let me know when you are ready to be done.' She was right. I did want to be angry with her, because I wasn't done. I knew if I listened to her, she would explain herself and I would understand. Once I understood, I would want to forgive her."

"So what are you saying? You're not ready to stop being angry at your father?"

"I'm saying I don't want to understand Dad. I don't want to see him in a vulnerable state, without all the arrogance that made him the monster he was to me. I don't want to know that underneath that egotistical exterior, lies an insecure little boy who all his life was afraid he wasn't good enough. I know if I tried, I would be able to unravel his story and come to an understanding of why he did what he did to us. If he was someone else's dad, I could do it. But he was mine and he did it to me. He did it to you, to Peter, and to Thomas. Yes, I'm not done being angry with him."

Fran gave John's tears space, wiping them away with her apron. "I believe you answered your own question."

"I guess I did. The problem is I'm getting tired of being angry. It is exhausting and it gets in the way of everything I do. I used to think it didn't, but I know it does. Even my relationship with Myrna is affected by this anger. I have to fight myself to forgive her for small insignificant things she does. They make me angrier than they should. I think it is because I have a pool of anger for Dad inside of me that gets dumped out on anyone who crosses me. And this weekend, wow. I've lost the composure I have worked so hard to establish since leaving high school. I'm right back where I was when I left – raw."

"Maybe it will get easier after he leaves," Fran said.

"Is that what you're hedging your bets on?"

"I don't know, John. I don't have a plan for forgiveness yet." Fran walked over to the cupboard, grabbed a cup and brought it over to the table. "I just figured out how to be angry. Marcia and I haven't addressed forgiving him. She and I have been too busy being mad."

"You and her?"

"Sometimes I think Marcia is angrier at your father than I am."

"I'm not sure it is supposed to work that way."

"That wouldn't surprise me. Marcia doesn't do many things the way they are supposed to be done. But it has been good for me. I think she is modeling anger for me; showing me

187

how to feel the way a normal person would feel when they have been treated the way I was treated. I tell her stories about your father and I am shocked when I hear how irate she is at him. It wouldn't have dawned on me to be that angry. But I see her response and I say to myself, 'why wouldn't I be angry at him?' She gives me permission to join her."

"What do you think she would say about my predicament?"

"You mean our predicament?" Fran poured coffee into her cup. "I don't know what she would say, but here is what I think. I'm guessing forgiveness comes when anger has run its course. You know anger has run its course when you are sick and tired of being angry all the time. I'm not there yet, but I can feel it coming. This anger thing makes sense and feels good, but it is exhausting. I'm not about to spend the rest of my life swimming in it. It's just too toxic. Either Marcia finds me a way out, or I'm back to my old self."

"Do you think it will be easier when he dies, Mom?'

"God, I hope so. You know what happens to me when I see him shriveled up in that bed?"

"Tell me."

"I see contentment on his face, as though he is on his way to heaven. Marcia wanted me to tell him how angry I am at him. I tried, but that look made me angrier. At first it made me angrier at him. But after a while I started to get angry at myself."

"Why, Mom?"

"Because my anger didn't make a bit of difference to him and I felt like a fool for thinking it would. He just laid there with that bound for glory look on his face. He never flinched. I know what you are going to say, 'he is unconscious,' right? But deep in my heart, I know it wouldn't have mattered. Even if he was conscious, it wouldn't have bothered him – at least it wouldn't have bothered him enough. He would have explained it all away as he did with everything. And even if, by some miracle, he accepted responsibility for what he did, he would find a way to minimize it and blame me for being angry at him."

"We have to face it, Mom, don't we?"

"What's that, John?'

"Dad is going to leave us holding the bag and there is nothing we can do about it."

Fran went to the refrigerator and retrieved the cream.

"What do you think is in the bag?" she asked.

"Poison."

"It's suffocating us," Fran said.

"Didn't someone say that about anger?"

"What's that?" Fran asked.

"I remember reading where someone said anger is like drinking poison and expecting someone else to die."

"Sounds like something Marcia would say. I'll have to use that to impress her the next time I see her." Fran acted out her next visit with Marcia. "Guess what I learned this weekend, Marcia. I've been drinking poison and expecting Richard to die. She'll love that."

"Will we ever find a way to beat him, Mom?"

"I don't know, but maybe there is a way to just quit playing the game." She poured cream into her coffee until the dark brew became the color of chocolate milk.

"I think that technique would be called forgiveness," John said.

"Not ready for that one yet," they chimed in together.

Fran raised her cup to her lips, savoring the rich smell of the coffee as it filled her nostrils. She took a slow sip. When she was done she smiled at John. "I forgot how good this tastes."

John wrapped his hands around Fran's cup, engulfing her small hands in his. "Nothing better than drinking coffee with someone you love."

They paused.

"I felt sorry for him in the beginning," Fran said.

"For who, Dad?" John removed his hands from hers.

"Yes." Fran ran her finger around the rim of the cup. "He had a harsh upbringing."

"How do you know?"

"He used to confide in me."

"What did he say?"

"Your grandpa Vanderhuis was a closet alcoholic who managed to maintain a high reputation in the community. Everybody loved him, but they didn't know what he was like behind closed doors. Your dad said his face would alter the minute he walked in the front door, as though he had just finished performing an eight hour play and was relieved to get out of the costume that squeezed his body into a shape that wasn't his profile."

"Did he beat them?" John leaned forward.

"Yes. He would pick a fight with your grandma and then come after your dad. I guess he said awful things and beat him bad."

"What did Dad do?"

"Take it, I guess; so he wouldn't go after his mom. He felt bad for your grandma."

"How do you know?"

"He told me he used to sit outside the kitchen and listen to her cry. I asked him why he didn't go and talk to her, but he never responded. I got the feeling he was angry at her."

"Angry, why?" John shook his head and took a drink of his coffee.

"I don't know. Maybe he thought it was her fault."

"That doesn't make any sense."

"Doesn't it?"

John looked away.

"Did you ever hear me cry?"

"It was a long time ago, Mom." John waved her off.

"Are you angry at me?"

"Of course not."

"I would understand if you were."

"That's Thomas' job." John laughed

Fran sighed.

190

Chapter 13

Parting Advice

The group wandered into the kitchen, following the scent of bacon, eggs, and pancakes. They gathered around the kitchen counter that jutted out from the wall, allowing it to serve as an island. Fran planned to eat at the table, but made the decision to go potluck style when she saw how the island drew them into a closely knit circle.

"Let's eat in here this morning. Why don't you all go get your place settings from the table and bring them in here," Fran said.

The group moved through the swinging doors and returned with plates in hands, silverware tucked under their plates, forming a line in front of the stove. Fran served them. When she was done, she made herself a small plate which she ate by the stove. Sammy offered to make room for her at the Island, but she waved her off. She was content to watch her children gathered around the island they had used to eat an occasional snack when they were young, joining her in her inner sanctum. She listened to the sounds of their sporadic chatter and the rattling of their silverware on their plates and she was pleased with herself – pleased with the way her homecoming was working out.

After breakfast, Thomas got ready to take Julie to the airport so she could rent a car for her trip to Detroit. Fran reiterated her invitation for Julie to spend the weekend, but desisted after Julie insisted on taking leave. Julie said her goodbyes and headed for the door. Fran called her back and told her she should leave through the garage. "I'll tell Thomas to take you in Richard's car. It will be nice and warm."

Thomas heard from the other room. "What, and ditch Puff? That wouldn't be right."

"I'll tell you what is not right; making her ride two thousand miles in that jalopy."

"It's a vintage car, Eddie."

"It's a jalopy with no heat." She handed him the keys to the Cadillac. "I won't take no for an answer."

"Dad would never allow me to drive his precious automobile."

"Let's just say it is mine now."

Thomas took the keys from Fran and they made their way into the garage. As soon as the door shut, the rest of the crew ran to the front window to watch them leave. They pushed and shoved, like young siblings, to get the best viewing spot.

"What's with all the interest in Julie's departure?" Fran asked.

"You kidding me, Mom? Thomas driving Dad's Cadillac? We just want to see his face when the wheels fall off," John said.

"I think I see your dad's ghost chasing him. See, right over there," Sammy pointed and the boys laughed. Fran chuckled.

Thomas took Julie to the airport on the scenic route. First they drove past Art's Auto Shop to see what had become of old Art. He had worked for Art in high school and used his shop and expertise to rehabilitate Puff. Thomas reiterated bits of his conversation with Art when he first asked him for a job.

"You go to church, boy?" Thomas mimicked Art's gruff voice.

"Twice on Sundays, Wednesday evening for prayer meeting, and Saturday is youth group." He chirped in a high pitched adolescent tone.

"You some kind of religious fanatic?"

"No, why do you ask?"

"I didn't think anyone could take that much church and stay sane."

Thomas laughed. He looked at Julie and could tell from her blank stare she wasn't amused. He tried a few more lines and exaggerated the gruff voice and the screechy tone.

"What kind of car do you want to fix up?"

"It's a Volkswagen bus."

"That's a hippie car. You some kind of hippie, boy?"

"No, I just like the car."

"You smoke any of that funny weed?"

"Never touch the stuff."

"I can understand you wanting to have a beer every once in a while. I keep a few in the fridge here myself. Just in case one of these cars is giving me fits. It helps me think better. But that weed stuff is another matter."

Thomas chuckled as he pulled into Art's parking lot. He took a deep breath. As he exhaled his body deflated into the car seat and relaxed. He surveyed his surroundings and nodded his head.

"It seems this Art meant a great deal to you." Julie broke the silence.

"This place was my sanctuary. It was the only place I felt at peace growing up. Art is a good old bastard. We had a beer together the day I left for Arcada."

Thomas got out of the car and headed for the shop. There was exhaust coming from the hole in one of the large garage doors. Thomas made some noise and a young man noticed him. He rolled himself out from under a truck in the first stall and greeted Thomas. He was a younger version of Art. When Thomas introduced himself, the young man said he was aware of Thomas' history with the place. He introduced himself as Art Junior. Unbeknownst to Thomas, Art had an estranged son who was also a mechanic. When Art died, Junior came home to take care of his mother and the business.

Julie offered Thomas sympathy as they drove off, but he dismissed it as unnecessary. "Why do you always do that?" Julie asked.

"Do what?"

"Push me away when I try to be close to you?"

"Is that what you were trying to do? Be close to me? I could have sworn you were trying to feel sorry for me."

Julie raised both hands toward the sky and looked through the sun roof, rolling her eyes and shaking her head from side to side so as to plead for understanding from God concerning her incomprehensible boyfriend. "I can't win." she said, "That is what people do to get close; it is called empathy."

"Yeah, people say I don't have much of that."

"That's not true. You have it, you just don't like to use it, much less receive it. I see it in your paintings."

"What's that?"

"Empathy! It's written all over your paintings."

"Name one."

"Your paintings of Sammy."

"What about them?"

"The eyes you give her. They portray a sadness most people miss in her normal presentation. But you understand it. You paint it every time."

Thomas changed the subject with his silence. They drove around White Lake and made their way toward Lake Michigan. He pointed out the country club and the yacht club. They hadn't changed much. They stopped at Duck Lake Channel and Thomas reminisced about the many hours he had spent here as a kid. Julie was anxious to move on, but gave him this moment he needed. She pictured in her mind what it would look like in warmer weather and understood why Thomas was drawn to California's beaches.

"My father came here once," Thomas said.

"I take it he wasn't a beach kind of man?"

"No, and he didn't like Eddie bringing us down here all the time either. But it didn't stop her from putting us all on the trolley, carting all of our shit, for a day at the beach." Thomas looked out the passenger window and watched the waves crashing on the iceberg shoreline, tapping his thumbs on the steering wheel.

"There is something good she did for you."

"Chalk one up for the dingbat mom."

Julie shook her head but kept silent.

"He came down to find us, dressed in a three piece suit. Didn't even take his shoes and socks off. He looked like a freaking black man in China. Eddie was shocked when she saw him. I could tell it upset her; invading her space that way."

"What did you boys do?" She turned toward Thomas.

"We asked him to play. Can you fucking believe it? We thought he came down to play with us. We thought he was going to build a sand castle with us or something."

"What's wrong with expecting that from your father?" Julie leaned her seat back and rested her feet up on the dashboard.

"Nothing if your father isn't Dr. Richard Vanderhuis. He doesn't play children's games. I can't believe I let myself think...What an asshole. That was the last time I ever let myself expect anything from him."

"Why did he come down here?"

"He needed to talk to my mother about something."

Julie remained quiet.

"This is where you are supposed to use empathy to make me feel better, love," Thomas said.

"Jesus Christ, Thomas." Julie took down her feet and sat up in her seat. "I can't win with you. Just drive me to the fucking airport, will you?"

"But..."

"Drive me to the fucking airport." She pointed forward.

He turned the key and drove ahead.

The back roads to Muskegon were beautiful. A tree canopy covered Lakeshore Drive. Snow clung to the tree branches and bright rays of sunshine streamed through the gaps, lighting the branches as if they were made of crystal. Upon occasion, the wind dislodged snow from a branch and it drifted to the ground, dazzling like fairy dust in the beams of sunlight peaking through the trees. Julie commented on how beautiful winter could be. Thomas assured her that her admiration only held true when you were viewing it from inside a heated car. She lamented they hadn't had a chance to take a hike in the woods. He knew they wouldn't have, even if they had found the time, since his distaste for cold weather was so strong.

As they approached Muskegon, the winter wonderland gave way to the muddy reality of winter in the city. The sanding and salting of the streets caused winter in the city to lose its mesmerizing effect. Without the picturesque sightseeing, the silence made less sense. Not one for beating around the bush, Julie began the conversation where she wanted it to end up. "You should give your family a chance."

"What brought this on?" He searched for time to recover from his startle affect.

"Oh I don't know. Perhaps it was the last fifteen hours I spent observing you with your family, coupled with the unhappiness I've observed in your life, while living with you for the last two years."

"You were observing? I thought you were participating."

"I was, but I can multi-task. I'm a woman. Studies show we can do that better than men."

"So what makes you say I should give them a chance?"

"It has been twenty years and it might just be they have changed or are at least looking to change. They aren't the same people you left, and neither are you. I'm just suggesting you take off your adolescent glasses, so you can see things are different now. You might even find things weren't what you thought they were back then."

"Maybe, but I'm comfortable with my adolescent glasses. I know what to expect and that allows me to believe I can manage things."

"I do have to credit you for being honest, Thomas. What is it you need to manage?"

196

"A lot of pain has gone down in this family. Stirring the pot could cause awful reactions."

"You don't know that. Besides, it might cause some good reactions to take place."

"I don't know. We all have our roles to play in this gig and I don't like change."

"They're nice people; hurting like you. Unlike you, they've managed to be nice about it."

"Even Peter? You think he is nice?"

"Yes, if you would stop baiting him to brawl with you. I think he's nice. More than that, I think he wants to have a relationship with you, if you would let him."

"Why would you say that?"

"Why else would he keep brawling with you, even though you beat him up every time?"

"I don't know, but that is irrelevant. This is not about them, it is about him."

"About your father; you're talking about your father?"

"Yes. I need my father to stay the monster he was. In fact, I need more evidence he was a monster – proof, you might say."

"Because?"

Thomas paused. "I think I'm afraid I might have misjudged my father. It has been so long since it all happened. My memories aren't as clear and vivid as they were. They are becoming murky. I don't want to forget."

Thomas spotted an airplane taking off in the distance and pointed it out to Julie.

"Why not? Why would you want to hold on to all of that negative energy?"

"I'm afraid if I forget, he'll get the last word."

"Would that be all that bad?"

"Yes, it would. He would alter the story and make me out to be a liar. You see, I need him to be the monster, so that I don't become one. If he wasn't all that bad, then I was. That was what he was always holding on to. He wasn't the problem, I was. He only treated me the way he did, because I

197

deserved it. You heard Peter, his resident echo. Dad didn't hate me, he hated my attitude. That's pure bullshit – Vanderhuis bullshit. I can't let that stand. I won't let him sacrifice me to save his reputation. What was wrong with my attitude? Not a God damn thing. It was the only honest attitude in that whole miserable house. I was the only one with enough guts to take on the old man and beat him at his own game."

"Did you win?"

"Not yet; but I didn't lose either. I didn't give up like the rest of them."

"Maybe they didn't give up. Maybe they just chose to fight him in a different way."

"They chose to fight me; that's what they did. They refused to back me up. Even now, they won't fight."

"Your mother is fighting back. She's making a lot of changes."

"It's too little, too late. Now that he is dead, she gets the balls."

"John has found his way around your father and I'm sure if you knew him better, you would find that Peter is probably the minister of a very different church than your father would have chosen for him."

"Whose side are you on?"

"I hope everyone's."

"You're supposed to say, 'Yours, I'm on your side.' That's the correct answer, Julie."

"Everyone's side includes yours."

"I don't need one more person telling me it's my fault."

"I'm not saying it's your fault. I believe you. I felt the power your father's empty chair had on your family. But I wasn't there when it happened. They were, and they were as terrified as you. They, more than anyone, know you are telling the truth and if you would let them breath a bit, they might tell you what you need to hear; that they know it wasn't you, it was him. I know they know. Give them the chance to tell you."

"What if it was me?"

"They weren't afraid of you. Well, I guess they are afraid of you and with some good reason. But it was the empty chair that brought terror into their eyes; not you."

"I need it to be him."

Thomas drove to the entrance to the airport and made the turn.

"It will be. Give them a chance to tell you what only they can tell you. You need eye witnesses and they are all you have," Julie said.

"They won't open the box."

Julie put her arm around him while he drove to the front entrance and stopped the car. "Is that what you think is in the box? Evidence that your father was a monster?"

"It is my last hope." Thomas leaned toward her.

"They are your last hope; and they will open the box. What is in there, I don't know. But they will open the box in their own time."

He offered to park the car and accompany her to the car rental desk, but Julie declined, saying he should get back to his family. She opened the door, but changed her mind and closed it again.

"One more thing."

"What's that?'

"Look at Sammy, Thomas. Pay close attention to her."

"What are you talking about?"

"You two have unfinished business."

"Unfinished business? What kind of unfinished business?"

"That sadness you paint in her eyes?" Julie paused. "Some of that sadness is about you."

"I can't be the cause of that one, too."

"I'm not saying you are the cause. In fact, you might be the answer, but you've never allowed yourself to become what she needs you to be for her."

"You are telling me to go back to my ex-girlfriend. I must have really hurt you."

"I am your ex-girlfriend and I survived you. I'll get over you, but I don't think Sammy ever will, unless you let her finish what she started with you in high school."

"We've tried that. It doesn't work."

"All I'm saying is maybe you should try again. Give it one more serious try, without your adolescent glasses so you can both move in or move on for good. She is a wonderful person and she makes you a better person."

"You don't think I make her a better person?"

"It doesn't matter what I think. What matters is what she thinks."

Julie started to open the door again, but Thomas interrupted her. "The sex thing, Julie; it wasn't about you, it was me. You're a wonderful lover; I'm just not a very good..."

"You don't need to tell me the rest, Thomas. Save it for Sammy. It was enough for me to hear those words from you. Thank you for the truth. At some level I knew it, but I needed some evidence." She leaned over and kissed him on the cheek. She turned and got out of the car. He watched the familiar sway of her hips in her tight jeans. The high heels lengthened her legs. The heavy bag strung over her shoulder cause her to accentuate her stride, exaggerating the sway. She disappeared through the doors.

He yearned for her.

Chapter 14

A Crush Rekindled

On the home front, the family dispersed in different directions. Fran went to the grocery store to pick up the ingredients for a vegetarian recipe she found in one of the magazines she subscribed to since Richard had been confined to his bed. She had remembered seeing it and browsed the magazines until she found it. She wasn't sure the local Shoprite would have the ingredients, so she had enlisted her friend Lynn to venture to the Meijer store in Muskegon. Lynn had been teaching her to drive and a practice run to Muskegon would be a good thing.

John found Sammy and Peter in the living room. "Where's Mom?"

"She's off with Lynn shopping," Peter said.

"Why didn't she ask one of us to take her?" John asked.

"I don't know." Peter shrugged his shoulders. "You know how Mom is – always secretive about the strangest things. She's like a CIA agent that hasn't realized she is not under cover and there's no reason to be covert. Why does she do that?"

"I have no idea. I'm off for a hike in the woods." John didn't invite Sammy and Peter to join him. They weren't offended since they knew about his penchant for long walks in the woods alone. Besides, neither of them could tolerate the woods in the middle of winter.

Instead, Sammy invited Peter to join her for a walk in the neighborhood. She wanted to visit her mother and would enjoy Peter's company. They hadn't had the time or the privacy to get reacquainted. She yearned for the discrete intimacy they had shared in high school and wondered if the connection was dissolved, or just dormant. Peter agreed, so they left Fran a note disclosing their whereabouts and a general idea of when they would be back.

Within the first block, their old rhythm was awakened. Peter relaxed as though he was in the company of a trusted friend and the distance between them dissolved to the point where they were walking arm to arm, brushing against each other as they took each step. It was a safe alternative to holding hands which would have been even more inappropriate now than it would have been back then.

They chatted about old times: the conversations they had, the jokes they had played on each other, the advice she had given him on girls (both good and bad), the times she had cried on his shoulder, and the occasional times he had let his eyes moisten in her presence.

"How is your mother?" Peter asked.

"She's doing alright." Sammy sighed. "She has some hip problems and I think dementia is creeping in."

"She still drinking too much?"

"Some things never change."

"You always handled that so well."

"Yeah, right." Sammy scoffed. "I did a great job of pretending it wasn't so."

"Don't be so hard on yourself."

They lost themselves in the moment and the walk took on a surreal quality. Peter garnished the courage to ask her the question to which he had longed to know the answer since their days together in high school.

"So..." he paused.

"So? You were going to ask?"

202

"So would you have dated me in high school if it weren't for Thomas?"

She was taken aback by the directness of the question. It transformed the surreal quality of the moment into an intense reality. Her silence led him to offer her an out, both for her and his benefit. "I'm sorry. You don't have to answer. It was unfair of me ask you. It's just... I've always wondered where we stood; if you liked me or if you just pitied me."

"It's not an unfair question, Peter. The truth is we did have something together. I never knew what it was we were doing, so I guess I decided to ignore the question and just enjoy us. But you deserve an answer. My silence when you asked the question wasn't an attempt to avoid answering. It was an attempt to stall so I could think about the answer. I have the feeling the answer is important to you and me, so I want it to come out right."

"How much time do you need?"

Sammy laughed, wondering if he was aware of the childish impatience he emoted. She took a moment to treasure the raw authenticity he always displayed with her and the trust he placed in her. "Alright, here goes my honest attempt to answer your question." She paused. "Peter, I couldn't date you."

He dropped his shoulders, moving away from her.

"Don't be upset Peter. It's not what you think. It wasn't because I wasn't attracted to you or because you were a nerd or something like that. The reason I couldn't date you was because you saw me and I was afraid of that. I needed someone who would keep his distance."

"You'll have to explain that to this middle-aged minister. We don't get the social work jargon."

"You asked me about my mother earlier."

"Yes, was I not supposed to?"

"Peter, there was a reason I practically lived at your house. When I met Thomas I wanted a new family. Mine was broken and I wanted a new one."

"And you chose ours? What were you thinking?" Peter shook his head and snickered.

"Ironic, isn't it. I don't know if your family was more or less dysfunctional, but somehow I fit better into yours than mine. I think your family needed a girl, and that gave me an important role to play in your family." She paused. "My point is I felt more at home at your dinner table than at mine, so I had your parents adopt me without knowing."

"So what does this have to do with me seeing you?"

"I'm getting to that, Peter. Do you know you are the only one in the family who knew about my mother? All these years and you are the only one who knows she is an alcoholic."

"I didn't know she was an alcoholic. I had my suspicions, but all I knew was she drank too much."

Sammy stopped walking and turned toward Peter. "For God's sake, Peter. How did you ever land a wife? It's almost impossible to give you a compliment without you fumbling it. Lie, Peter, lie! Say you knew and take credit for it."

"Sorry."

"And don't apologize so much. Girls don't like a wimp."

"Forever my personal Ann Landers."

Sammy smiled, took hold of his arm, and they walked on.

"Sorry, it just comes to me when I'm with you." They laughed. "My point is my family was screwed up, really screwed up. I needed someone who wouldn't see that. All I wanted was an opportunity to get away from it without anyone noticing. I was ashamed of my family and I needed it to stay a secret. If I had dated you, you would have noticed. That is the kind of guy you are. But Thomas, he was perfect for me. He never noticed. He never asked. Do you know he has never said a word about my mother's drinking? You wouldn't have been able to do that for me. You would have cared too much. You would have brought it up and made me give away my secret. I couldn't have handled that back then. It is hard enough to handle now."

"I thought women wanted to be noticed?"

"Most women do, which is why your wife is a lucky woman. I'm not most women. I'm a woman with deep and painful secrets I need to keep locked up."

"That's sad."

"It is, but I survived my secrets and that makes me happy. I found a new family that agreed not to notice my secrets, if I agreed to keep theirs locked up with mine."

"You know, most men don't want an ordinary woman," Peter said.

"Are you saying I'm an extraordinary woman?"

"I'm saying you were never ordinary to me. I would have dated you in a second. But you are right. I would have insisted on knowing."

"Is Sandy extraordinary?"

"She is. You trained me well in the art of picking women."

"Well good. I didn't know if it would ever happen after all the disastrous dates I tried to send you out on in high school."

"They never worked because I wanted to date you. But then you knew that, didn't you?"

She looked up and leaned into his arm. "Peter, the whole family knew. The whole neighborhood knew. The whole county..."

"Alright! Enough! I get the point. It was obvious." He bumped her with his hip.

"I'm afraid so. But I treasured your adoration with all my heart."

"You want to know my secret?" Peter slowed their pace.

"You only have one? You always did have an affinity for the boring."

"Do you want to know or not?" He stopped and turned toward her.

"I am dying to know." She leaned into him and he wrapped his arms around her. She looked up and stared into his eyes with the eagerness of a teenage girl being asked to go steady.

"In my head, you are my first girlfriend. That's how I think of you. It helps me feel like I wasn't such a dork in high school."

"I'm touched. You have my permission to keep telling that lie."

"Well, I didn't tell anyone that. I just...well there were a couple of times when I did..."

"Peter, it doesn't matter. You have my permission to think of me that way. I'll add you to my list of the men with whom I've loved and failed."

Sammy moved away and resumed walking. A few steps down the road, she rammed Peter with her shoulder, thrusting him into the snow drift on the side of the road. Peter could have kept his balance, but he faked a dramatic fall so he could get up and chase her down to return the favor. He caught her and attempted to push her across the road and into a mound of snow, but loosened his body so she would have a chance to defend herself. She did more than defend herself, she thrust him one more time into the snow and leaped with glee, hands above her head; imitating Rocky Balboa on the top of the stairs on his way to victory.

"You are such a wimp!" she trashed talked. "You shouldn't be such a wimp. Girls don't like men who are wimps."

"I don't know about that, Ann Landers. Sandy loves it when I let her win."

"You saying you let me win, boy?" she continued with her Rocky Balboa impersonation. "That ain't nice to lie like that about a girl. Lying like that will get you beat up and thrown in the trash."

She offered him her hand to help lift him out of the snow drift. "I won fair and square. You have your little lies and I have mine, deal?" She started to shake his hand, which she still held in hers.

"Agreed." He raised his other hand and squashed a handful of snow into her face.

"You dirty rat!" She chased him down the road with snow in both hands. "You have gotten better at this, haven't you?"

Chapter 15

The Brownie Mission

John returned from his walk in the woods inspired by the beauty of his old stomping grounds. He was hoping everyone would be gone so he could continue to enjoy the soothing exhilaration his walk through the forest had brought about in his head. Aloneness is something John had learned to treasure in the last few years, yearning for more of it than this environment permitted. He wanted to sit in a chair in the living room and look out the front window, enjoying a cup of tea. He would light the fireplace and let it warm him.

To his dismay, Thomas was sitting in the chair he had in mind, holding a plate of brownies still covered with tin foil.

"Good, you're home. I've been waiting for you."

"You were waiting... for me?" John lifted his eye brows.

"Yeah, I want you to go with me to deliver these brownies to my old friends. I could use some company."

"And where is it you expect to track down these old friends? And why would you want me to come along, since I've never met your pothead friends?"

"Don't go disparaging people you don't know. They will be there."

"And why me?"

"Why not you? You are my brother."

"How long is this going to take?" John buttoned his coat.

207

"We'll be back in time for supper."

Thomas insisted on taking Puff, even though Richard's Cadillac was still warm from his trip to the airport. He reasoned his friends would recognize Puff and his friends were poor and a Cadillac might come across rather snooty.

"Are we taking Dundee?" John asked.

"Not this time. Where is that mutt? I haven't seen him all day."

Thomas drove to Muskegon through the back roads and John didn't argue. He enjoyed the back roads. They held history for John; history consisted of all the two-tracks he had driven girls down in order to find private places to try and undress them. He was surprised how many of the two-tracks were still there, and even more amazed he remembered which girls he had driven down each of them. Thomas had his friends, and he had his.

They drove through downtown Muskegon and made their way to Seaway Drive. Thomas took a left on Sherman and drove a few more blocks. John began to recognize the neighborhood.

"Hey, isn't this where the Mission used to be. Dad made us come here on Sundays, after church. We helped him put on a church service for the homeless. Then we served that god-awful food to them for lunch."

"This would be that neighborhood," Thomas rubbed his unshaven chin.

"You're bringing me to the Mission? You hated this place. You threw a fit every time we came here. Dad used to say to you, 'You're going to end up living in this place at the rate you're going.' How would you know anybody around here?"

"You'll see." Thomas went past the mission and after several turns, parked in front of an empty lot sandwiched between two abandoned factories. He grabbed the brownies, holding onto them as if they were a security blanket, and got out.

"I'm not getting out in this neighborhood. I can see why you didn't want to bring Dad's Caddy."

Thomas didn't respond and after stalling, John followed his lead, even though it was against his better judgment.

They made their way through the empty field as if they were looking for someone with whom to play. Five men hovered over a small fire. They looked at Thomas and he returned the gaze, but they made no move to welcome them so Thomas and John kept walking. They wandered the field for ten minutes before they were startled by a voice calling out. They turned and saw a grungy middle aged black man, about ten yards behind them. He stopped, bending over to catch his breath, motioning for them to come to him.

When they reached him, he looked up and between his gasps for air said, "I gotta quit smoking them damn cigarettes. They's eatin' up my damn lungs. You two wouldn't happen to have one to spare, would you?"

The boys shook their heads and the man said, "Yeah, I figured as much." He paused for a couple of breaths and then asked, "That your bus over there?" he pointed toward Puff.

"Yeah, she's mine," Thomas replied.

"She's a beauty." He looked at the plate Thomas was holding. "Those be brownies you're holding there?" Thomas uncovered them to show he was right. "They spiked with weed?" John looked at Thomas, wondering if he knew what he was doing. Thomas held out the plate so the man could pick one. The man surveyed his choices, picking the biggest one. He took a bite and savored it. He shook his head in disbelief. "Well I'll be goddamned. I told them assholes it was you, but they didn't believe me. I saw that bus and I knew God was looking to make my day."

He motioned for them to follow him. He led them to the group around the fire. It seemed to have grown in numbers since they had first passed. Thomas nudged John, and looking toward the crowd surrounding the fire said, "My congregations a bit larger than Dad's isn't it? And I didn't have to threaten to lock them out in the cold and not feed them to get them here." He put his arm around John's shoulders and smiled satisfied. "I done stole Dad's sheep without his even knowing it."

"Yeah, by getting them high." John looked around, trying to comprehend what he was witnessing.

"What? It's biblical. There is a verse somewhere which says to give the weary and down trodden a little wine to sooth the pain."

"You can make the Bible say anything, if you want it bad enough."

"Well, why isn't what I want it to say just as valid as what Dad wanted it to say? Would you rather go to his party or mine?"

"It's obvious these fellows would rather be at yours."

As they approached the fire the man yelled, "I told ya'll what that psychedelic bus meant. I told you it would be him. I told you he would be carrying the brown weed." The man motioned for them to snuggle up to the fire with the rest. He introduced himself as Ray.

"Do I know you?" Thomas asked.

"You don't know me, but I know someone who was your friend a long time ago. The way he told it, you was a legend in this neighborhood. His name was Roger Jones."

"Roger Jones, I remember him," Thomas said. He looked at John "I told you..."

The group gave Thomas a stern stare down which was meant to shut him up. After it had accomplished its purpose, one of them spoke up, "The man is telling the legend. You don't interrupt the man when he is telling the legend." The man nodded at Ray to tell on.

"The legend says a preacher's boy used to come to this very field every Sunday afternoon, just before the sun went down. He came to the same place, at the same time, every single Sunday afternoon. He traveled in a junkyard bus, painted in a crazy way, with some ungodly colors all mixed up. The boy's daddy was a preacher over there at the mission. Tried to get everyone to come and listen to what God had to say. But the preacher's boy wasn't like that when he came to this field. Unlike his daddy, he didn't come bearing the word of God. In fact, the preacher's boy didn't have much of anything to say. Instead he came bearing a big plate of brownies, loaded down with some mighty fine weed. The men took to calling it brown grass cookies. He came, shared his brown grass cookies with whoever was here, then sat back and enjoyed the spiritual effects of the brown grass cookies around a fire just like this one. He would stick around for an hour or so, and then he would get up, go to his bus, and drive off; never asking anyone for a single thing."

"That's the legend! Yes! That's the legend!" the men chimed in when he was finished.

"Roger Jones told me the preacher's boy stopped coming when his daddy sent him off to college. But Roger believed he would come back. He knew that for sure. I believed him. I done told these faithless sons of bitches you was coming back, but they didn't believe me. I have to admit, I was just about to give up on Roger's legend, but as soon as I saw that crazy bus of yours parked over there, I knew Roger was right all along. Then there you were, brown grass cookies and all. Not as strong as Roger told it or as handsome. But that doesn't matter because you brought the brown grass cookies."

"Amen!" the group yelled out. Ray motioned for Thomas to pass out the brownies. With a smile that smirked with pride, Thomas served them. As he stood and watched the men consume his gift, his only regret was he hadn't brought a few bottles of wine to help the men wash them down. That would have made for true communion. He wondered why he hadn't thought of that when he was younger, as it would have enhanced the legend.

They sat around the fire and listened to the stories the men told about their lives on homeless lane. Even the saddest of the stories seemed funny the way the men would tell it. When it was time for them to head for the mission for the evening meal, they left one by one, each offering some token of thanksgiving. Ray was the last to leave, staying back to ask one question that was puzzling him. He came closer and leaning in toward Thomas he asked, "So why did you come on the wrong day?" He saw Thomas' puzzled look. "The legend says you came on Sunday afternoon. It's Saturday."

Dumbfounded, Thomas shrugged his shoulders and said, "I don't know. I guess sometimes things just change."

Ray walked away shaking his head with a bewildered sense of pleasure.

Thomas and John headed back to the bus.

"I didn't know about this side of you," John reached up and put his hand on Thomas' shoulder.

"What side is that?"

"The nice guy." John nodded his head.

"We all have our soft spots." Thomas put his hand over his heart. "You aren't going to tell Eddie, are you?" Thomas grabbed John's shoulder and turned him until they were facing each other.

"I think she should know."

"What, that she's been smuggling dope to the Muskegon homeless population?"

"No, I think she needs to know she has reason to be proud of her youngest son."

It was almost time for dinner, so Thomas and John didn't have the luxury of wandering the back roads home. They did have time for a conversation John was eager to have.

"So, what is it with you and these women?" John looked straight ahead.

"You have to be more specific with me, big brother. I'm kind of dense when it comes to these conversations."

"These conversations?"

"Well it's obvious you're about to ask me about some personal stuff. These women you are asking about can attest to the fact I don't do the personal stuff very well. They would say I have great clarity of mind when I'm in the abstract, but when my inner workings are the subject matter; a dense fog enters my brain."

"Julie intimated you and she never had much sex. Sammy has said the same in the past. You've always had this reputation for being a ladies' man. I'm trying to put the two together."

"Ah... the long awaited talk concerning my sexual orientation."

"Who said anything about your sexual orientation?" John looked over at Thomas to judge his seriousness. Then he put his left foot up on the dash and stared out the passenger window.

"You didn't have to. It has always been an unasked question in this family. I'm sure it was generated by Father's homophobic fears. I'm not sure why, since it was obvious Sammy was my girlfriend. But, never-the-less, it has always been floating out there."

"Why didn't you just answer it, and get it over with?"

"You sound sure I'm not gay."

"That would be my assumption."

"You would be correct. I don't have a gay bone in my body as far as I know. Now according to Dad, my bones dangle in an effeminate way some times. If they do, it has nothing to do with my wanting to attract men."

"I never did understand why Dad insisted you walked like a sissy."

"He had his reasons to perpetuate the lie. He had a reason for everything he said and did. I've always assumed he hated me so much he wanted to offend me in the worst possible way. Accusing me of being a fag would qualify as such in Dad's simpleton mind."

Thomas pressed the center of the steering wheel. "God damn it Puff. Why didn't you tell me your horn was broke? Why the fuck are these assholes going so slow?"

"Take it easy, Thomas. We're not in a hurry," John said.

Thomas banged his fist on the horn, but Puff remained silent. "Fuck this," he said. He downshifted and turned into the oncoming traffic lane. He stepped on the gas and Puff's engine screamed as it worked as hard as it could to gain speed. As he passed the older couple enjoying a slow safe ride, Thomas reached up and flipped them off. John grabbed his arm and yanked it down.

"There is no need to be stupid about this, Thomas," John said.

Thomas was about to respond, but was distracted by the blazing horn of an oncoming truck. He yanked the steering wheel to the right, barely in time to avoid colliding with the angry truck driver who continued to sound his horn until well past them.

"Jesus fucking Christ, John. You almost got us killed."

"I almost got us killed?" John asked with his mouth wide open with disbelief.

"Sorry, I might have had something to do with it, but that couple could have sped it up a bit. They've got an eight fucking cylinder engine in that damn Oldsmobile."

"Just forget about them," John said. "So why didn't you just tell him you were straight?"

"It's complicated, as everything was with Dad. By this I mean Dad set it up so I couldn't win."

"How is that?" John didn't remove his eyes from Thomas face.

"If I told him the truth, he would have taken it as a personal victory. He would have seen it as evidence I agreed with him, or I was somehow on his side in this matter. If I lied and told him I was gay in order to hurt him, he would have used it to rail against me and prop up his self-righteousness. I thought about telling him I wasn't, while invoking the claim it wouldn't have mattered if I was – that I would be proud to be a gay man. But that would have led to an unending battle I didn't want. So, I settled for a non-answer. That way he could invoke neither his pride nor his indignation. It left him flapping in the wind for a way to deal with me."

"You always did know how to throw him off his stride. Wasn't it exhausting; always thinking so much about everything you said and did?"

214

"It was just in my nature to do battle. I don't like to admit it, but a part of me came from him. We are genetically alike, I think, and that made for an even match. You, Peter, and Mom just didn't have it in you. I think I exhausted you all, more than I exhausted myself." Thomas smiled.

"That makes sense, but why the complaints from the women?"

"You mean, if I'm not gay, why am I not fucking the women in my life?"

"Your proclivity for straight talk is always shocking to me."

"That's because our family's inclination toward the indirect is well ingrained."

"Well, straight talk me on this one." John looked around for a blanket. He found one in the lawn chair, yanked it toward him, and snuggled himself up under it.

"My sexual prowess has been a myth I didn't care to dispel. Truth is, you were the ladies man of the family. Your affinity for the two tracks wasn't rumor, it was reality. Truth about me is I'm not good at it. I tried hard with Sammy, but I don't know; it just never worked very well. It was uncomfortable. That's why I preferred painting her nude. I thought it might be different with others, but it hasn't been. My failures led to decreased desire. Either that, or an unwillingness to keep failing."

"Maybe it is hard for you to switch from making war to making love. Maybe being good at one hampers your ability to do the other?" John looked at Thomas.

"Thomas the warrior and John the lover!"

"So what makes you a poor lover; premature ejaculation?" John looked straight ahead.

"You mean do I have a happy trigger?"

"Is that what you call it?"

"It sounds less devastating than premature ejaculation."

"I suppose."

"No, the problem isn't a happy trigger. In fact, quite the opposite is often true – there is no trigger. The problem is I'm just clumsy about the whole process. I get anxious and I become a bumbling fool. That doesn't do much for the women, and feeling like a bumbling geek doesn't turn me on. It makes me feel like Peter."

"Have you..."

"I think I've reached my limit in the personal arena." Thomas shifted his body and leaned against the door. "That's enough brotherly bonding to last me a lifetime."

He turned on the radio and dialed it up to WLAV. Surprised it was still on the air with classic Rock and Roll, he turned up the volume and let the music take them away from the intimacy developing between them. John acquiesced, joining his brother in slapping out the beat of the music on the dash board, as they slammed their heads forward to the beat of the base drum.

Chapter 16

Secrets Revealed

They drove in the driveway and all the lights were on, signaling everyone was home and waiting for them. They entered through the garage and peeked in the kitchen to check on the status of dinner. To their surprise, they found their mother talking (or at least attempting to talk) Spanish to someone on the phone, while Sammy listened.

"What's up with Eddie talking Spanish?" Thomas asked.

"She's developed a relationship with your father's Dominican friends. They keep calling her wanting an update on his condition," Sammy said. "Your mom said your father used to talk to them regularly, but when he wasn't able to do so they talked to her instead."

"Who are they?" John asked.

"She doesn't know for sure. As you can see there is a language barrier. She said there's a man and a woman, and a whole lot of kids, cars without mufflers, and Spanish music in the background. She thinks the man was your father's chauffeur, because he keeps talking about your father's truck."

"I thought Dad's people down there lived up in the mountains," John said. "Why all the noise?"

Sammy shrugged her shoulders. "Your mom doesn't know much about what he did down there."

"That's odd." Thomas turned to John. "Do you know what he did down there?"

"At first he went on mission trips with other doctors, but then there was a falling-out with the sponsoring mission."

"Sounds like Dad," Thomas said.

"After that he went out on his own and set up a permanent clinic in some mountain region. He used to call it Jarabacoa, or something like that. I believe he provided free medical care to the people there."

"Did he speak Spanish?" Sammy asked.

"Some, but I don't know how well." John looked at Thomas. "Do you remember him listening to those tapes and repeating all those Spanish words? You used to mock him and he would get so mad."

"May yamo Ricardo, grasias," Thomas said.

"Si, si," John said.

They laughed.

"How often did he go?" Sammy asked.

"When we were young only a couple of times a year," John said. "But after we left I think he was going three or four times a year for weeks at a time."

"Where did he live?" Thomas asked.

"A shack I presume." John shrugged his shoulders. "I never saw pictures."

"Did anyone ever go with him?" Sammy asked.

"Not that I recall." John scratched his head. "Mom wanted nothing to do with it. I think Peter was supposed to go with him, but I don't think it ever happened."

"Why didn't you go?" Sammy asked.

"Two weeks with Dad alone on an island," John said. "Not my idea of a fun time."

"Weird, if you ask me," Thomas walked out of the room and John followed. "Our father, Dr. Livingston, I presume."

"I wonder how he survived." John said.

"Dinner is about five minutes away," Sammy yelled after them.

"It smells good. What are we having?" John yelled back.

"I think we're having your mother's pot roast. You just can't tell these days. She is changing everything up. Cherry pie for desert, though. That I know for sure."

As they walked up the stairs to their room, John said, "Who would have thought we would be talking about Mom as an agent of change?"

"Changing your cooking habits hardly qualifies you as an agent of change."

"Open your eyes, Thomas. She is not just changing the way she cooks. She is changing the way she lives, she's changing the way she looks, and she is trying to change the way she mothers."

"I suppose you are going to tell me it takes two to change a relationship."

"I don't have to. You already said it."

Dinner was infused with a subdued mood. Julie's absence might have contributed some to the downcast atmosphere, since her outsider's dispassionate curiosity wasn't there for the group to satisfy. A group without an audience is less interested in performing. It also could have been due to the fact everyone was quite tired from all the activity they had engaged in throughout the day. They had carried on like a pack of eighteen-year-olds and at forty, that takes its toll. But then, it is hard to restrain yourself when you are in the midst of full blown regression; and that is what it felt like to them. They had entered a time warp and they were responding to their familiar environment with the age appropriateness of the age they were when they left.

Dundee wasted no time taking his place of honor at the table. Peter warmed to the old boy. He reached over and patted him on the head, asking him if he was hungry. He told

Dundee the menu, expecting him to get excited at the news he was having beef for supper.

"You're excited, aren't you, old boy? You dogs love beef."

Dundee kept looking down at the empty plate.

"Don't you worry; Uncle Peter will make sure you get your fair share."

"He grows on you, doesn't he?" Thomas said.

"I guess he does. Unlike his father, he blends in with the crowd. Soon you feel like he has always been here."

"I think he wants you to pour him some wine," Thomas said. "By the way, where the hell have you been all day. I've been looking for you." Thomas rubbed the dog's head.

"Mom, don't you have some cheap stuff we can give him?" Peter asked.

"You mean Morgan David?" Thomas said. "Wasn't that the name of the God awful wine we used to buy for a couple of bucks?"

"I don't remember," John ran his hand over his prickly head. *I've got to shave,* he thought.

"Now they have something called Two Buck Chuck. It's pretty good for the price," Fran joined in, "or so I'm told." She changed the subject and inquired of Sammy how her visit with her mother had gone. She received the usual generic answer and accepted it without a follow-up question. Peter caught Sammy's eyes and they smiled at each other.

The conversation stalled as the group focused on eating. The pot roast was tender and moist. Lighter gravy had replaced the thick and creamy one they were used to, but the potatoes and vegetables were soft and tasty as they remembered them.

"What's that flavor?" John asked.

Fran shrugged her shoulders.

"Is it Thyme? It tastes like Thyme to me."

"Oh, that's right. I started using Thyme. I also have been adding a bit of wine to add some zest."

"It's an improvement," John said.

The others nodded in agreement, moaning with pleasure.

They finished dinner and began to clear the table. Thomas disappeared after his first trip to the kitchen, not returning for a second run like the rest. No one said anything, perhaps because they were used to Thomas' inclination toward opportune detours. They wiped off the table and Fran suggested they play Yahtzee again.

"It was so much fun last night," she pleaded.

"We don't have brownies, Mom. It won't be the same," John said.

"I could whip us up a batch if you get your brother to give me some more oregano."

"No thanks, Mom. I think I can speak for the group when I say we have had enough brownies for now," John said.

"I bet Thomas would take issue with that. He loves my brownies. Speaking of Thomas, where is he?"

Sammy, feeling like his keeper now that Julie was gone, answered, "I don't know where he snuck off to. I'm sure he'll join us with some grand entrance any time now."

"Mom," John spoke in a slow deep tone. "Do you know about Thomas' oregano?"

"What do you mean, do I know? What's there to know? Oregano is oregano. It seems a bit strange to put it in brownies, but it tastes fine. I don't know that it tastes better to me, but Thomas likes it when I put it in them, and you all seemed to like them a lot last night. You finished off a whole batch. Come to think of it, even your father used to like them. He always wanted to make sure I saved him a couple for his evening snack. Sometimes he would ask for one in his lunch. He didn't have much of a sweet tooth, but he took a liking to those brownies."

John looked at the others. Sammy waved him off. Peter waved him on.

"Peter, you never liked them, did you?" Fran continued. "I didn't notice until last night, when you didn't touch one. That caused me to realize you never have eaten them."

"Do you want to tell her, or should I?" Peter looked at John.

Knowing it would be more palatable coming from him, John proceeded with the revelation. "Mom, it's not oregano."

"What are you talking about? Of course it's oregano. Thomas told me..." she stopped dead in her tracks as she heard herself vouching for Thomas' honesty. She crossed her arms and put both hands on her own shoulders. The others looked away.

Sammy came to her rescue. "It's alright Fran. Every mother wants to believe her child. It's only natural to want to believe what they tell you. How were you to know...?"

"What; what is it that I need to know?" She uncrossed her arms. "If it is not oregano, then what is it?"

Their silence gave her the answer. "Oh my God! It is marihuana, isn't it? I once read people do that, but it never dawned on me that...I've been making druggy brownies, haven't I? And serving them to my children! No wonder you wouldn't eat them Peter. And making them for Thomas' friends! Who knows how many children my brownies have corrupted? What if their parents find out? What if the police find out?" Fran stood up and paced back and forth between the door to the kitchen and the table.

"It's not that big of a deal, Fran," Sammy said. "It was a long time ago and..."

"A long time ago? Just yesterday I made him a batch and he took it to his friends. You helped him, John?"

"Well, I didn't have much choi..."

"And what about your father?"

"What about him?"

"I fed them to your father. No wonder he liked them so much. And he took them to work! He could have lost his license for doing drugs while doctoring. He used to say those brownies smoothed out his day. They made the long afternoons easier to tolerate. And here I thought it was my magic kitchen." Fran fell into her chair.

"Magic kitchen?" Sammy and Peter looked at each other and then at John.

"That's a long story," John deferred his explanation for a later time. "It is not a big deal, Mom. Nothing bad happened and I'm sure his patients liked him better on the brownies."

Fran pondered her horrifying acts, while the others waited for her to gain her composure. "He was nicer after he ate them. Maybe that's why I didn't bother to think twice about what Thomas was up to."

"I think we all felt better, Mom," John said and the others nodded their heads in agreement.

Fran chuckled. Her chuckle was a relief to the group and they joined her. Within seconds they were all lost in hysterical laughter, unable to stop themselves even if they wanted. They tried, but then one of them would break into a chuckle and it would start all over again. They did manage to calm down enough for John to introduce round two and complete his effort to communicate to his mother the extent of her career as a drug pusher. "That's not all Mom."

"What do you mean?" Fran asked, still laughing.

"You know I went with Thomas to deliver the brownies to his friends this afternoon?"

"Yes," Fran urged him to go on, still chuckling.

"His friends aren't who you think."

"What do you mean; they aren't who I think they are?" She stopped laughing.

"He drove me to the mission."

"What mission; the mission in Muskegon your father used to preach at?" Fran asked.

"That would be the one. We drove past it to an empty field. We took the brownies and started walking around. It wasn't long before someone recognized Puff and came looking."

"Looking for what?"

John looked at Fran as though she should know the answer to her question. "The brownies, Mom. Thomas has been a missionary in his own right all these years; delivering pot laced brownies to the same homeless people Dad was trying to bring into the fold. He referred to it as stealing Dad's sheep right out from under his nose. It appears he was quite the legend back then. In fact, the legend of his weekly drug deliveries has been told enough over the past twenty years that this new generation of homeless men recognized him when we drove up; looking for the comfort he was known to offer."

"Twenty years after the fact? Unbelievable!" Peter reached up and ruffled his hair. Catching himself, he patted it down, trying to tidy it back up.

"I've been providing Dad's homeless people with drugs and didn't even know it. I'm the pusher to the displaced. Wait until I have to confess this to Marcia. I better schedule a double session. It will take her the first hour to stop laughing at my naiveté. She will spend the second hour bragging me up as a promising entrepreneur or something like that, in order to rescue my sunken self-esteem. How could I not have known? I should have known."

"Mom, it was quite a nice spectacle I observed. You shouldn't be disappointed with Thomas," John said.

"What do you mean?"

"In his own way, Thomas tried to minister to these men in the best way he could. They did appreciate him, and in an odd sort of way, I was proud of him. I hadn't seen that side of Thomas before."

"What side is that?" Peter asked. "The criminal side?"

"The compassionate side," John answered. "He wasn't being self-serving in this. It may have started out as a way to get back at Dad. But in the end, I think he was caring for these guys in his own way."

"By giving them marihuana?" Fran asked.

"Face it, Mom. It's how Thomas takes care of himself, isn't it? He believes in the stuff. Why wouldn't it be the central piece of his missionary zeal?" John said.

"I'll have to think about this. Don't anyone tell him I know. I want to think about it before I talk to him."

Thomas entered the room, causing a silence so he knew they had been discussing him.

"What did I do now?" he asked. "Whatever it is, I'm sure I did it. So tell me and I'll confess and you can forgive me."

"What you did is of no consequence, at least, in light of what you are doing right now. What are you doing with Dad's box?" Peter said.

Thomas' head twitched, as though he had forgotten what he had in his hands. "Oh, yeah, I decided it was time to get this over with and see what Dad's got hidden in this damn thing."

He placed it in the middle of the table. The family pushed themselves back from the table as though there was a snake in the box.

"What do you mean you decided?" Peter said. "You don't get to decide this, or anything else that involves this family. We decide things together, and the last time we talked about this, it was clear you didn't have enough support to have your way."

"I don't know about that. It seems to me we just talked about it. We didn't make a decision. Why are you so afraid of opening this thing? You think you'll lose your precious idol?"

"I already explained it to you. It's a matter of Dad's privacy."

"Fuck Dad's privacy! We need to know what's in this thing or this family will never be able to move on. He can't hide behind the Fifth Amendment. I'm sure I could get any level headed judge to sign off on a warrant, if that is what it will take to satisfy you."

"Why don't you just take a vote?" Sammy asked.

"Sounds like a great idea to me," Peter agreed, thinking his mother and John were sure to vote in his favor.

"I'll agree to that," Thomas said. "Does Sammy get a vote?"

They all looked at Sammy. She pushed herself away from the table to disqualify herself from the invitation. "Thanks guys, but no thanks. I love you all and am touched you consider me to be a part of your family. But he wasn't my

225

father and I don't think I should participate in this decision. My vote would only be about satisfying my curiosity and this is about a lot more than curiosity. I choose to abstain."

The boys protested and an argument ensued. At the height of the argument's intensity, when a decision needed to be made by one of the parties to back down or move to all out rage, a stern voice broke through the bedlam and stopped it dead in its tracks.

"There will be no vote!"

The group came out of its stunned daze and located the voice which had just spoken with such authority. "There will be no such vote in this family." Fran paused and let the silence continue to stem the anarchy that had filled the air. "This is not your choice, it's mine. I'm the parent and I'm your father's wife. It falls to me to decide what to do with his things." She scooted forward in her chair.

The boys and Sammy waited. They wanted to ask her about her decision, but they didn't want to rush her. They were forced to predict what she might do, in order to prepare themselves for victory or defeat. But they had no idea what to expect. They had never detected this tone in her voice before, leaving them with no past experience with which to predict what her next step might be. Their best guess was she would postpone her decision and the thought of this was unbearable to all parties.

Looking at Peter in an attempt to preempt what he was sure to experience as a betrayal, Fran said, "Thomas, give the box to your brother John so he can open it."

Sammy wondered where this woman had been hiding all these years. It wasn't just that she made a decision; it was that she carried it out with the Wisdom of Solomon. To begin with, she preceded the rendering of her decision by showing respect and compassion for the one who would be offended by it. She then nullified any smugness the apparent victor's arrogance might produce, by deeming him unworthy to carry out the decision. She honored the level headed one, putting him in charge of unveiling the truth, without his being tainted by having to win the right through an outright brawl, making his right to open the box an honor given him because of his character, and not part of the spoils of war.

Thomas followed Fran's directions and handed the box to John. John looked at his mother to assure himself this was what she wanted.

"Go ahead, John," Fran said. "It's alright. This family needs to know whatever truth is in this box. We can't be a family until we know."

"But what if it destroys us?" Peter protested.

"You mean him, Peter, don't you? What if it destroys him?" Fran paused. "Then so be it. We'll all survive his downfall. We are not him, Peter. What he did or didn't do is on him, not us. I know he made it seem like we were all attached to him at the hip, and our fates were intertwined with his. But they are not. We will survive if what is in this box destroys his reputation. What I'm not sure of is if this family can survive without knowing the truth. The silence is killing us."

Fran gave John the nod and he opened the old wooden box. He looked inside and then looked up. There was no reaction on his face for the family to gauge. He looked down again and this time reached inside. "I think it's just photographs."

"Photographs of what?" they all asked in unison.

"I don't know. They are bundled and bound with rubber bands. There are notes on each pack with dates on them. I think it must be his version of a photo album." John lifted them out onto the table. Sammy began to place them in chronological order, using the dates on the packs. "There, that's the last of them. Oh, wait. There is an envelope on the bottom. He picked it up and brought it out of the box. It is addressed to you, Mom. See, he wrote Fran on the envelope."

John handed Fran the envelope, but she waved it off. They all looked at the stacks of photos Sammy had arranged. There were thirty stacks in all, each containing about ten photographs. "I guess he meant for us to look in his box," John said.

"Why would you say that?" Peter asked.

"There's the letter to Mom."

"That only means he expected her to look inside. It doesn't mean he meant for all of us to have a family gathering over it."

"I'm sure it's a monument to himself," Thomas said. "A monument to his mission work – so the world can see how godly and humble he was."

"Shall we look at them?" Sammy asked, volunteering to be the one to take them out of their stacks and arrange them to be viewed.

"Start with the last year," Fran said.

Sammy laid them on the table, starting from the last and working her way back through the thirty years. She started at the bottom right hand corner of the dinner table and worked her way toward the top left corner; making rows as she went. The group sat in silence and watched her work; taking an occasional peek, but not stopping long enough to be able to make any serious conclusions about the subject matter of the pictures. Sammy reached the top left corner of the table and set down the last photo. She moved them around, adjusting the spacing between them so they were symmetrical, filling the entire space like a giant collage.

Fran started at the end with the most recent pictures; the end of the tale, if there was a tale Richard meant to tell. John and Thomas began at the other end, where the picture story commenced. Peter came to the middle of the table and looked at the pictures in no particular order. Sammy bounced around looking over everyone's shoulders; placing her hands on their backs in an attempt to offer comfort if it was needed. Fran and Peter were silent.

"They appear to be pictures of the same family," John said. "She seems to be the main character." He pointed at a beautiful woman who appeared in the photographs at different stages of development.

"She's in most of the pictures," Thomas said.

"It appears she had three children. You see, she is pregnant here and again over here," John moved around Peter to get to the other picture of the pregnant woman. "There is no picture of her being pregnant the third time, but that little one is definitely from the same brew."

"God, I'm glad I didn't get pregnant," Sammy said. "Look at what it does to your body. In the beginning she is a beautiful, sexy girl. You see?" Sammy pointed to the pictures of the young girl at the start of the tale. She then pointed toward the pictures where Fran was looking on and said, "Look at her now. She's a different woman."

"Maybe that's why Dad stopped going," Thomas said, causing the group to give him a look meant to shame him. "I'm just trying to figure out what the deal is with Dad and this woman."

They shifted ends as Fran worked her way toward the beginning and Thomas and John found themselves examining the photos at the end of the tale. Sammy continued to look in a scattered fashion. She paused and without taking her eyes away from the search asked, "Does anyone see the father? She is everywhere, but I don't see the father."

Peter pointed to a photo of a man who appeared to be the same age as the woman. "This guy could be the father."

The group surrounded him to look. "I don't think so. He is only in a few pictures and he is never with her," John said.

"Maybe that's their culture," Peter said. "Maybe they don't take pictures together like our families."

"He seems more like a brother to me. Look, they have the same eyes. I think this is him next to her when she was young," Thomas said. "They look a great deal like each other. He's got to be her brother."

"Good call, Thomas," Sammy responded. "Definitely not lovers, these two." She picked up two of the pictures and showed them to the group side by side. "They could be identical twins. They're definitely brother and sister."

"Then where is the father?" John asked.

"She could be a single mother," Fran joined the investigation. "Lord knows it is common enough in this country. There is no need to presume it would be any different

229

over there. Maybe your father just took an interest in helping the poor girl out."

"A little," Thomas chuckled. "He is in every picture. Here he is with her. He's got his arm around her shoulders. And over here he is with the two little ones playing on his lap. The third one, who looks the oldest, is hanging over his shoulders. Since when does Dad let kids play on his lap? Look over here. He's got his arm around her again. And here! He has his hand on her lap. Do you ever remember Dad being affectionate like that?"

"It's a cultural thing," Peter said. "The Latin culture is very touchy/feely. Trust me; I've lived around it for a long time in Florida. They will put their arms around a total stranger."

The group stared at him in an attempt to stop the broken record from repeating itself. Sammy stepped back from the table with the look of a detective who had figured out the mystery and was not ready to be the one to break the news to the unsuspecting clients.

"Look at these kids. Look at their mother's hair, and then look at theirs. She has heavy dark hair and the kids all have fine hair," Thomas said.

John chimed in, "Her hair is jet black. This one is practically blond."

Fran stepped back and joined Sammy in the background. Sammy embraced Fran and let her cry on her shoulder. The boys kept investigating.

"Look at the color of her skin. She's a dark chocolate. The kids are...lighter is all I can say," John said.

"That guy is definitely not the father. Those two couldn't have cooked up this brew. They are too alike to get kids that look like these three," Thomas said.

"Oh, who cares," Peter argued. "It is obvious we aren't going to get any answers from these pictures. I don't know what Dad was thinking, leaving these behind without any explanation." He looked at Thomas. "Of course, we weren't supposed to see them in the first place."

"So much for a private diary," John said. "Pictures without words, instead of word pictures."

The boys kept rummaging through the pictures.

Peter turned around and looked at Fran, then Sammy. He shook his head. "This can't be. There has to be a different explanation.

"Peter," Sammy said. "I'm sure..."

"I can't do this." Peter threw the photographs in his hand onto the table and walked toward the stairs.

"Sore loser," Thomas yelled after him.

Peter waved him off and kept walking.

John held up a picture of the three kids, with the woman and Richard standing behind them. Thomas joined him for a closer look.

"Son of a bitch!" Thomas' eyes appeared to pop out of their sockets. "Son of a fucking bitch! That conniving bastard!" He looked at John, "We're not alone, big brother. We're not alone on this planet."

John caught on and joined Thomas in his thunderstruck state. "We have three half siblings. Dad had another family. That was what he was doing down there, growing another family."

"To replace the one he had, because we weren't to his liking," Thomas said.

The two continued to delve into the pictures. Their new discovery gave them a whole new perspective of the mysterious tale. It was Sammy who distracted them by clearing her throat a half dozen times. John was stunned into silence when he spotted his mother crying on Sammy's shoulder.

"Mom," John said, moving toward her. "I'm sorry, Mom. This must be awful for you."

He went to relieve Sammy, but when she let go, Fran covered her face and ran past John. She picked up the envelope on her way out of the room. John was about to follow her, but Sammy took hold of his arm.

"She needs to be alone for this one."

231

"But..."

"She needs to be alone, John. Give her some space to deal with this."

John desisted. Sammy hugged him. John cried on her shoulder.

Thomas ransacked the photos, devouring the information he had so yearned to possess, in hopes it would set him free.

Peter left the house.

Chapter 17

Late Night Response

The next few hours were dominated by a silence that muffled John's emotions. He took the seat in front of the living room window, staring into the dark night. He was aware of his emotions, but unable to feel them. They were floating out there, waiting for him, but he couldn't draw them in. Exhausted, he gave up and accepted the numbness.

Sammy retired to her room in the basement and Thomas joined her. She checked on Fran several times before falling asleep. Peter returned after midnight, waking John. He hoped Peter would by-pass the living room and head straight for bed. Peter did.

John sat in the chair and tried to go back to sleep. He was almost there at 2:30 in the morning, when a presence in the room startled him back to an awakened state. He turned and saw his mother. She placed something on the floor and made her way toward him. He pulled over another chair and placed it next to his. He moved the ottoman over so they could share it. Fran sat down next to her eldest son and rested her feet next to his on the ottoman. They sat beside each other and stared into the dark winter night. Snow had begun to fall, big fluffy flakes that took forever to float to the ground. John placed his arm on the arm rest between them, with his palm facing up. Fran put hers on top of his and their hands clasped.

Half an hour passed before Fran spoke. "I can't do this anymore."

"I know this is difficult for you, Mom."

"I'm sure it is difficult for all of us."

"I don't know about Thomas. He seemed pretty satisfied with the treasure in the box."

"What about you John? How are you taking it?"

"For now I'm just shocked. I look at those peoples' pictures all over our dinner table and...I don't know what to make of it. I can't fathom Dad would do something like that – a whole secret life with marriage, children, and a home."

"I guess we didn't make him feel special enough."

"He thought of himself as a king. How do you validate that? I'm sure they complied, seeing all he had to offer."

"I wonder if he was happy there; with them? Or did they fail him too?" Fran stared out the window off into the distance.

"Everybody failed Dad, Mom. It was his gig and failure was everybody else's role to play. Think about it: us, the ministers he fired, the members of the congregation, the politicians, and other doctors. He thrived on other's failure. He sought it out so he could capitalize on it and shine in their downfall."

"I know, John. But I can't help but wonder if it was different there? I wonder if he turned over a new leaf in this new life."

"I doubt that, Mom. But we could go visit them and see, if you like."

They shared a chuckle. "You'd go with me?" She turned, pulled her knees toward John, tucking her feet under her bottom, and looked at him.

"If that's what you needed, Mom, I would be happy to accompany you."

"Something is wrong with that."

"It would be weird, wouldn't it?"

"Quite odd, to say the least."

"What did he say in the letter?"

"It appears your father wants me to take care of his other family. He didn't want to put them in the Will. My guess is because that would be too public. He wants me to support them financially; without making a fuss."

"That's it, huh? One last small favor?"

"You can read it if you like. It's laying on my nightstand."

"Maybe later."

"You know what shocks me most?"

"What's that?"

"That he would take it for granted I would do it. Can you believe his nerve? He didn't even try to convince me to do it. It is as though he was sure he wouldn't have to. He just flat out says I'm to take care of them. Not even an explanation or an apology of any sort."

"What makes that so shocking to you, Mom?"

"What was I to him? I'll tell you. Nothing. I didn't exist; at least not as a human being with feelings and needs of my own. I didn't matter. I was just a person he expected to do his bidding without question. I was like his arm or his foot – an appendage meant to carry out his desires as they came to his mind. That's all I was to him. Our whole lives together, I was nothing but an appendage to his body. How can someone treat another person like that? Especially someone they claim to love?"

Fran would have cried, but her tear ducts were empty and too tired to produce any more.

"I'm sorry Mom. I'm sorry you had to live that way."

Fran grabbed a Kleenex and blew her nose. "Did Sammy tell you about the extra grave plot your father bought?"

"She said he bought 6. I figured the 6th one was for the baby."

"No. The baby was buried between your father's and my plot."

"Maybe he thought you would try again and have another baby after the miscarriage."

"I doubt it. Things got cold between us after that."

"Then perhaps you were right and he thought Sammy would join us in death."

"Or," Fran paused, "he bought it for his mistress."

"Mom, even he wasn't that cruel of an asshole."

"Your brother Thomas would beg to differ."

"I'm sure he would, but he is invested in portraying Dad to be demoniacal."

Fran gazed out the window at the falling snow.

"You know what makes me the angriest? What makes me feel rage?" She paused. "When I read it, without even considering any other options, I was ready to do it. I read it and started to make plans to take care of them. What kind of person am I? Who just agrees on the spot to take care of her husband's mistress and kids, just because her husband tells her she should? I'll tell you who does that; a non person; a person who has given up her soul to please her bastard husband without even putting up a fight."

"Mom, don't beat yourself up like this."

"John, I need to beat myself up right now. Not because I deserve it, but because I need to face the truth. This isn't punishment, this is facing reality, and in this case, reality hurts; which is why I have put it off for so long. I can't keep avoiding the truth, John. Too many people got hurt so I wouldn't have to feel my legitimate pain. I am what I am, John."

"And what is that, Mom?"

"I am pathetic and weak."

"But..."

"Don't rescue me John! Don't tell me your father did this to me. I already know the part he played. I've already spent that anger. Now it is time for me to face my real rage. Now it is time for me to be angry at myself for being stupid enough to let him turn me into this pitiable shell of a woman I've become. I played my part. I let him do it to me. I had choices. Maybe they weren't very good ones, but I had choices. I took the easy road. I listened to my fear and took the easy road, at the expense of my children, I might add."

"But Mom, he didn't let you..."

"Don't tell me I didn't have a choice, John. That would only mean your father was right about me. I was an empty shell needing to be filled by him; a weak and foolish woman who needed him to make my choices for me. I don't want to be a victim. Victims are weak and stupid."

"Not always. Sometimes they are smart and kind people, who get sucked in by someone who takes advantage of their kindness. Kindness makes a person vulnerable to some degree. You can't blame yourself for being kind, nor can you blame yourself for being a victim."

"But being a victim doesn't feel good."

"I know it doesn't."

"I can't win. He has done it to me again." Fran sat up and moved to the edge of her chair, looking out of the window and watching the snow fall.

"I don't know what to say, Mom."

Silence was her answer for a long while. "It is not your job to know what to say to your broken-hearted mother. You are the child. I am the adult. Children don't comfort their parents, even when they become adults. It's supposed to be the other way around."

Fran reached for a Kleenex and blew her nose. "I wasn't always like this, John. Before I met your father I was happy and confident. I had dreams for my life. Good dreams; exciting dreams. At least that's how I remember myself. Maybe it was an illusion."

"You are getting stronger, Mom."

"I hope so. I'm trying, which is why I'm not going to do this anymore. I was going to say I couldn't do this, but that's not true. I'm going to choose not to do this anymore."

"Do what?"

"Take care of your father. I won't do it. I'm leaving, John. I've called Jane, the hospice nurse, and told her. She will come first thing in the morning and help you work out a plan. He'll be fine until then. You can put him in a nursing home or hire someone to stay with him full time. I don't care. She will give you your options."

"Are you sure, Mom?"

"I've never been more sure of anything in my life. For the past six months I have forced myself to take care of him; washing his body, cleaning up after he messes himself. Every minute of it was disgusting to me. I had to force myself to touch his body, but I did it. I did it, even though it sent chills through my body that made me want to throw up. The sight of my hands touching his body is just too much for me."

Fran shivered. John looked on with a puzzled expression. He was unable to comprehend what his mother was going through. Fran muttered, "But I did it. I did it anyway. I touched him even though I didn't want to. I made him feel good. I took care of him..."

John interrupted her chant and asked, "Is this about sex, Mom? Is that what we're talking about here? Because..."

Fran was shocked and wanted to move toward the door so she could escape the insightful eyes of her son, which were making her uncomfortable because he was becoming aware of a part of her she had yet to process. Marcia had tried to get her to talk about her sex life with Richard, but Fran kept putting it off. Now it had snuck up on her and she needed time, time to think, time to talk to Marcia, and time to get herself together.

"It is about taking care of your father and that's it John! But I don't want to talk about it anymore. I'm suffocating and I need to get away from this house. I just need you to promise me you will figure this out with your brothers tomorrow. Will you?"

"I promise, Mom. But are you sure?"

Fran nodded.

"Where will you go?"

"I don't know. I'll go to a hotel or something for the night. I'll call one of my friends tomorrow and make better arrangements."

"Do you need me to drive you?"

238

"I'll be fine. I drove all the way to Muskegon with Lynn this morning."

"But you don't have a driver's license yet. What if they stop you?"

"I'll give them no reason to stop me. If they do, I'll tell them I forgot it at home. What are they going to do to an old lady like me? Arrest me? I know those young officers' mothers; not to mention all their dirty little secrets. They would be afraid I would tell on them."

"Now we know where Thomas gets his readiness to break the rules."

Fran smiled a bit. "I am his mother. I'll call Lynn in the morning. She'll be happy to have me stay with her. She is a lonely old girl." She paused for a moment and then her tone changed. "I'm sorry to be dumping this on you."

"You mean him, Mom? Dumping him on me?"

"I suppose that would be more accurate."

"It is alright. We'll figure it out. Maybe now I can make my way in there to see him."

"Oh, don't get spooked by Dundee. He's taken up a spot under your father's bed and has imposed himself as his guardian. He's been growling at the nurses."

"Thomas will love that. How will I get a hold of you?"

"My cell phone number is on my dresser, too."

"I didn't know you had a cell phone."

"Jane made me get it in case of emergencies. You know, in case I'm gone when they are here and something happens. I don't tell anybody about it because I don't want them calling me on it. I can't ever figure out how it works, so it makes me nervous. But you can call if you need. I promise to answer."

"Can you promise to be alright, Mom?"

"That I can promise you, John. I will be alright with time. You will, too." She turned and grabbed the handle of the suitcase she had put down when she entered the room. She turned and exited. John heard the garage door open. He waited for his mom to back the Cadillac out of the driveway, getting past Puff and his rental car. He watched her drive away and wished this would all just end.

He sat back in his chair and stared at the falling snow in hopes it would hypnotize him and relieve him of his overburdened state of mind. He meant to go check on his father but the snow did its job and he fell asleep in the chair.

Chapter 18

The Children Take Over

He awoke at 7:00 with a hand touching his shoulder. He looked up and saw it was Jane.

"You must be John," she said. "Sorry to disturb you. Your mother called me last night and told me what was happening. I thought I should get over here early. I have a key, so I let myself in. I hope you don't mind."

"Mind? I'm relieved." John rubbed his eyes.

"It is a lot your mother put on your shoulders. I hope you are okay with this."

"I'm fine. I fell asleep and didn't check on him though. I hope he is okay." John checked to make sure he looked halfway decent after his restless night.

"I'm sure he is fine, but I'll go in and make certain. Give me an hour or so and then I'll talk to you." She started to walk out of the room. "Don't be too hard on your mother. These times can be overwhelming to caretakers."

"Hard on her?" John did a double take. "The woman is a saint. No one in this household will hold this against her. Trust me. They'll give her a standing ovation. She should have walked away a long time ago."

"I didn't know. She was so concerned and devoted to him."

"Like I said; the woman is a saint, but she bears her cross in silence."

Jane left the room. John went to the kitchen to make coffee. He was surprised it was already brewed. There was a note on the counter saying breakfast was in the refrigerator. John opened the refrigerator and found a breakfast casserole front and center. The second shelf held lunch, a tray of sandwich meats, cheeses, and other sandwich garnishments. He shook his head at his Mom's efficacy. *Forever the caretaker.* He took out the breakfast casserole and followed the instructions; setting the oven temperature and placing it in the oven once it reached the correct temperature.

He poured a cup of coffee and headed for the bathroom to freshen up before he met with Jane. He didn't know what to expect, but Jane seemed both tender and competent, which were the character traits he was looking for under these circumstances. He brushed his teeth, splashed a little warm water on his face, and headed downstairs, making as little noise as possible so as not to wake Peter. He entered the living room and found Sammy sitting in his chair.

"You look awful," she said. "The evidence tells me you spent the night in this chair."

"The evidence never lies."

"I got up early, hoping to catch you before you did your yoga. Am I early enough?"

"Plenty early, but I'm not sure we'll be doing yoga today."

"Why not?"

John motioned for Sammy to scoot over and make room for him. This, despite the fact the chair Fran had pulled up was still next to the chair she was sitting in. Sammy didn't question it and he lowered himself into the chair with her. They squirmed around a bit until their hips found a comfortable position.

"It is a good thing we are both skinny," John said.

"Why thank you John. I'm not used to compliments from you."

"No? I'm surprised. I thought I always made it clear I admired you."

"In high school, all the admiring I remember you doing was carried out on lonely two tracks. I don't recall being on a two track with you."

"I suppose you're right. That was the extent of my admiration those days. But I did admire you, Sammy, and I meant to tell you."

"That's nice of you to say, John."

John snuggled a little closer, shivering from the cold he felt sneaking under his clothing. "I hope you don't mind. I've been cold all night and I could use some sisterly snuggling."

"Have your way with me, please. Your brothers always have. By the way, where is your mother? It's an odd day in this house when your mother isn't awake before the rest of us."

"She is gone."

"What do you mean, she is gone?" Sammy pulled away from him and turned to face him.

"She left last night. She told me she was done taking care of Dad and she left."

Sammy sat up and asked a hundred questions in rapid fire, which John attempted to answer. A wide-eyed look stayed plastered to her face as she tried to accept what had happened.

Jane returned with a note pad in hand and took a seat next to them. She looked at Sammy with a question mark and refused to start the conversation until John introduced her.

"Oh, I'm sorry, this is Sammy. Sammy, this is Jane."

"Nice to meet you," Sammy said, offering a formal hand shake.

Jane accepted the hand, "Nice to meet you as well. You are?"

"It is okay. Sammy's the family's only daughter." John rubbed the top of Sammy's head. Sammy tilted her head and accepted the affirmation.

Jane looked suspicious. "I'm surprised. Fran never said she had a daughter."

"We adopted her. Trust me, she's our sister and I want her to be a part of this discussion. Fran would want it that way as well." John squeezed Sammy's hand and she returned the gesture.

"I'm sorry. I don't mean to be a stickler, but the HIPPA rules are very strict so I wanted to be safe rather than sorry." Jane went on to explain there were two options for Richard's care. He could stay in the home and the family could hire home health care nurses to fill in the gaps in care that Fran had been providing, or they could place him in the Hospice Home located in Muskegon, where he could finish out his life. There was a third option, which was for the children to provide the care, but she discouraged this. In her experience, children didn't fare well filling that role in their parent's death process.

They asked her opinion and Jane told them she didn't expect Richard would live much longer. Signs of death had been increasing each day and she felt he would be lucky to last another week. She made it clear this was an educated guess. Death took its own course with each individual and it was always possible he would bounce back and lengthen the process. But in light of her educated guess, it was her opinion that as long as someone was in the house most of the time or at least available to the nursing staff if needed, the option of remaining in the home made the most sense. "No sense putting him through the stress of a move to a strange place at this stage of the game." She had checked with the hospice home and they did have a bed available if that was the family's wishes. John asked about the cost and Jane assured him insurance would cover either option.

John thanked her for her candor and explained they would discuss the matter when the rest of the family was awake. Jane offered to get a nurse to fill in for the day and John agreed.

John and Sammy talked a short while and went their separate ways to get dressed for what they sensed would be a long day. When they finished, they met in the kitchen to check on breakfast. The smell was robust and they breathed it in with pleasure.

"Your mother is quite something. She runs away from home in the middle of the night, but has the courtesy to cook her family a breakfast most people reserve for holidays."

"There's more. I saw lunch in there, and I'm sure supper is hidden behind that."

Peter and Thomas dragged themselves into the kitchen, drawn there by the smell of eggs, sausage, and bacon that had permeated the house. They asked about Fran's whereabouts, as though she was a fixture in this kitchen which left an inescapable void when she wasn't present. John told them to grab some breakfast and he would tell them about it. Curious, they slapped some casserole on their plates and gathered around the island. Sammy poured coffee. John told them the story.

"I don't know what to say," Peter said. "I didn't see this coming. That's not like Mom. She never does anything so dramatic. I knew she was upset last night, but to get up and walk out on Dad when he is about to die? I had no idea."

"Well, as far as I'm concerned, it is about time the old lady ditched him." Thomas said. "I didn't think she had it in her, but I guess this change she has been talking about is real. God damn! I wish I was a writer. I'd turn this family into a best seller. What am I thinking? You are a writer, John." He reached over and slapped John on the back of his shoulder. "This could be your big hit that takes you off the internet and puts you on the shelves at Barnes and Noble."

John ignored him and clued them in on the fact they had a decision to make. He explained Sammy and he had talked with Jane and outlined the three options for them.

"Smart nurse," Thomas retorted. "There is no way in hell I'm going anywhere near that old man's excrements. Jesus,

245

the thought of touching him at all gives me the creeps." Thomas shivered in an attempt to rid himself of the unwanted feelings he was experiencing in his body.

"That is understandable, since you haven't even been in the room to see him," Peter threw his fork down on his plate in disgust. "Oh, wait. I stand corrected. You did sneak in there to steal his box."

"Why are you harping on me? I haven't seen John cross that threshold either. You aren't crucifying him. I am staying for the funeral. Don't I get points for that in your moral calculator?"

"I think we might as well have him stay here with the help of the nurses," John said.

They nodded in agreement. Sammy was surprised Thomas agreed to stay.

"You can get the time off from the university?" she asked.

"They'll find someone to fill in for me."

"It's settled, then. I'll tell Jane to hire the nurses," John said.

"What are we going to do about Mom?" Peter asked.

"Let's give her the day to be by herself," John suggested. "I'll call her later this afternoon and fill her in on what is going on. My feeling is once she knows someone else will be taking care of Dad, she might reconsider her decision to leave."

"She can only take Lynn for short periods of time," Peter reasoned.

"I think she will want to be with you; since you are all staying," Sammy said.

"What about you, Sammy?" Thomas asked. "Are you going to stick around?"

"I've got vacation time coming. My boss has been hounding me to take it and threatening to take it away if I don't. Besides, what would you boys do without me in a crisis like this?"

"I'm glad to hear you say that, Sammy," Thomas responded. "I'm already bored to death and wondering what the hell I'm going to do around this winter death land for a whole week."

"You mean you ran off your playmate and you are looking to replace her?" Sammy said.

"Hey! That was uncalled for. We are in mourning here. No need to make me sound like the immature fuck-up I am. You are supposed to offer comfort to those who mourn."

"I'll give you something to mourn about," she said as she whipped her leg around, rotating it at the knee as she did under the table when they needed a quick correction. They all winced at the sight. After the initial shock, their winces turned to stares of amazement. They had never seen her do this before, since it had always been carried out under the cover of the table cloth. They were impressed by her quickness and by the rapid acceleration she was able to generate. They also understood why it had hurt so much.

Noticing the impression her leg action had made on them, she decided to make the most of their intense attention. She pushed one hip forward and extended her leg, lifting her pant leg as high up as it would go, exposing as much skin as possible. In a coquettish voice she said, "My legs have still got it, don't they. You two need to call your wives. And you," pointing toward Thomas, "You need to come with me. You want a new playmate? You got one, but I own you. And just so you know, I'm not talking sex slave here. You are going to be my work horse."

"Work me, honey! Work me!"

Thomas followed Sammy out of the kitchen. Peter and John looked at each other and at the exact same time said, "I'm calling my wife." They laughed and reached for their cell phones.

Chapter 19

A Cry for Help

Fran was awake in her hotel room most of the night, thinking. A thousand thoughts, questions, and intense feelings raced through her mind. She had been desperate to shut them out, but found she was unable to exercise any control over her mind. She was most haunted by an image that kept inserting itself onto the screen of her consciousness. In this image, she saw herself naked on a bed. Her legs were spread, revealing her vagina. Her elbows were tucked into her abdomen with her hands pressing upwards, as though she was pushing someone off of her. Her face was turned to the side, in an attempt to avoid looking at the person pressing down on her. The weight on her chest crushed her, leaving her unable to breath. Throughout the night she tried to make out the body that was crushing her. Each time, before the person came into focus, the feeling of suffocation became so intense, she had to stop.

Over and over throughout the night, the unwanted image forced its way into her head and she repeated her attempt to compel her mind to reveal her unwanted lover. Each time she failed, overcome by the inability to breath. Haunted, she decided to take Marcia up on her offer to see her during the weekend. She ransacked her purse for the business card with Marcia's cell number written on the back. Marcia had given it to her in case an emergency came up over the weekend. She found it and set it on the bed, while she located her cell phone.

Fran checked the time and saw it was five in the morning. She decided it was too early to call, so she watched the clock tick off the minutes. After half an hour of clock watching, she turned on the television and looked for something to distract her. She discovered that at five thirty on a Sunday morning, infomercials are as good as it gets. She settled on some sort of food processors. An attractive and perky middle-aged woman followed a hunky male chef around the kitchen, astonished as he demonstrated the wonders of his machine.

At seven o'clock, Fran opened the phone and punched in the number. Nothing happened and the screen remained blank so she pushed buttons until she saw movement on the screen. She had stumbled on the power button. She paused until the activity stopped and settled on one image. A chimed tone informed her it was ready to use. She tapped the numbers and waited. Nothing happened. She looked at the screen and saw the number was still there, waiting to be sent. She panicked as she scanned the screen for directions on what to do next. She looked below the screen and began reading the small printings next to the buttons. She spotted the word send printed in green and pushed it.

She felt relief when she heard the varied beeps she recognized as the sound of a computer dialing a number. She waited while it rang. No one answered. After five rings, she was sent to voice mail. It beeped and she said, "Marcia, this is Fran. Could you please call me?" She was about to close the phone when she remembered she hadn't left her number. "Oh and my number is 231, 638, 57...ah...58. Thanks and sorry to bother you on a Sunday morning."

As she closed the phone, she wondered if Marcia was at church. The thought of Marcia being at church made her chuckle. She assumed everyone spent Sunday mornings at church as she had done for the last sixty years. She had never paid attention, as she had driven to church all those times, to the fact she was in a minority. Most cars were parked in

249

garages or being driven to restaurants or other pleasurable destinations, not to church as hers was.

This would be the first Sunday of her life, with the exception of a couple of sick days; she had not gone to a church service. She began to feel guilty, but changed her mind. She turned off the faucet that flowed guilt, and opened the one next to it. A feeling of grown-up pride came out of this tap. For the first time in her life, Fran was making a choice concerning church and not just following the lead of her parents or Richard. This was her decision to stay home from church today because she had more important things to do.

The phone startled her. She answered, "Marcia?"

"It is me, dear. How are you doing?"

The nurturing voice she had grown accustomed to hearing once a week struck a deep cord within her. Fran burst into tears and was unable to say anything.

"I take that to mean you aren't doing well. Where are you?"

"I'm at a motel. I left Richard." Fran burst further into tears.

"Now this is the smartest thing I've ever seen you do."

"Really? You really think so?"

"We'll have to talk about your timing, but yes, Fran. I'm proud of you. You've stood up for yourself."

"But he is dying."

"And so are you, as long as you stay there," Marcia said.

"I need to talk to you. Some stuff has come up and I can't stop thinking about it."

"Give me an hour and I'll meet you at my office. Will you be alright until then?"

"I'll be fine. I'll bring you a donut from the motel's continental breakfast." Fran stood up and looked for her purse.

"That makes me want to hurry."

"I'm kidding. I'll stop at the coffee shop and get us a coffee and a breakfast treat."

"You don't have to do that Fran. You have enough on your mind and ..."

"It will give me something to do. I'll see you there, coffee in hand." She hung up.

Chapter 20

Church Anyone?

Peter came down the stairs dressed for church. He roamed the main floor looking for recruits and found all three of his targets sitting around the breakfast table.

"Anyone up for church this morning?"

They looked at each other, taking a moment to shed the feelings of delinquency. John begged off because he had too many arrangements to worry about. Sammy passed the buck to Thomas, who rejected the idea.

"Sorry, I'm saving all the church going left in my body to get me up the stairs and through those doors for the funeral. One final visit to my house of horrors is all I got left in me."

He passed the buck back to Sammy who took it without hesitation.

"I'd be happy to go with you, if you don't mind."

"Mind? Why would I mind?"

"It might be awkward. You're married and you're a minister. You'd be showing up with this sexy woman on your arm." She touched her hair and faked primping. "They might gossip."

"It won't be a problem. They know you. You went with us almost every Sunday."

"It has been over twenty years since I've been there. I doubt anyone remembers me."

"You'd be surprised how good their memories are."

252

"Alright then, I'll get changed and meet you down here in ten minutes."

"Don't mingle too much after church. Remember, we've got plans for this afternoon," Thomas said to Sammy.

"What plans?" Peter asked.

"Thomas is taking me to his church this afternoon," Sammy replied.

"His church?" Peter had the look of a deer in the headlights.

"The brownie church," John answered.

"Ahh...but who is going to make the brownies now that Mom..."

"Sammy and I," Thomas answered. "Unless the preacher is on fire today and convinces Sammy to change her ways."

"And leave you?" Peter said.

"I was referring to our occasional habit of smoking a bit of weed together."

"I'll be rooting for the minister," Peter said.

"Here! Here!" John chimed in.

Chapter 21

The Therapist's Advice

Fran waited in the parking lot of Marcia's office for ten minutes. The smell of the cinnamon rolls and coffee filled the car and urged her toward the bonding experience for which she was yearning. Marcia arrived even more frazzled than usual. Working on a Sunday didn't appear to suit her well. Her hair was a mess (of course it always was), her makeup from the day before was worn off (what little she wore), and her wool skirt was a quarter turn off the mark so the pockets didn't line up with her hips.

She fumbled for her keys and when she gained control of them, opened the door. As they entered the office, Fran asked, "Do you want a few minutes before I come in?"

Marcia laughed. "You mean to pull myself together? I look that bad, do I?"

"No, no. I just thought..."

"You're something else, Fran Vanderhuis. Here you are in crisis and you are attempting to take care of your therapist."

Fran looked at Marcia's messy hair and was driven to check the state of her own hair doo. She wanted to look in a mirror, but didn't have access. Instead she found a tie in her purse and pulled her hair back into a ponytail. *I'm so glad I didn't cut my hair any shorter.* "It's what I do to take care of myself. I'd rather worry about others than about myself."

"That's insightful."

"I know, I know. Now you say, 'How's that working for you?' And I'm supposed to say 'not very well.' And then you say, 'So why do you keep doing it?' And I say…"

"I see we've had this conversation before."

"And we've concluded insight doesn't bring change all on its own. It has to be followed up with behavior change."

"My, you are in a foul mood this morning Fran. Did you miss your weekly dosage of church or something?"

"It seems I'm not the only one who needs a little church. I'm in crisis, what's your excuse?"

"This is me on Sunday mornings, my dear. I'm not used to exposing myself to anyone. And since you insist on taking care of me and I'm not above some moderate degree of unethical professional behavior, I'll take that coffee and cinnamon roll. I'll be much more pleasant after I've consumed your magic…"

"About my magic kitchen." Fran handed Marcia the coffee and took the cinnamon rolls out of the Styrofoam box, placing them on separate napkins on the coffee table that stood between them. "It has been working well this weekend. The boys have been getting along fine and they've been talking to me and amongst themselves."

"That's wonderful, Fran. I'm happy for you. So what made you call me?"

"Did I ever tell you about Richard's box?"

"Not that I recall. What kind of box are we talking about?"

Fran put her hands on the arms of her chair, lifted herself, and rearrange her bottom to a more comfortable position. She put the napkin with the roll on her lap, grabbed the coffee, and settled into her chair; both hands on the coffee cup which she held just below her chin.

"It's an old box his father made for him when he was a kid. But the kind of box isn't important. It is what he kept in it that has mystified our family." Fran explained the box and

255

told her about Thomas' insistence on opening it, Peter's reluctance, and her decision to have John open it.

Marcia complimented Fran, telling her she had acted as a good mother.

"Wow, coffee and a cinnamon roll do take your edge off, don't they?"

"Let's see. We've gone from denying compliments, to deflecting them, to thanking the giver for them, to insulting the one complimenting you. Somehow, this train got off on the wrong track without my noticing." Marcia got up and retrieved her pottery coffee cup. She poured the coffee from the Styrofoam cup into her own.

"You don't mind, do you?" She looked at Fran. "Coffee doesn't taste as good in these plastic cups."

Fran nodded.

"I guess you don't have the magic after all. You should try baking for you clients. It is much more effective than talking to them," Fran said.

Marcia took out a pad of paper and scribbled something on it. She signed it and handed it to Fran.

"What's this?" Fran asked.

"It is a prescription for you. Read it."

Fran looked down at it. She squinted. "Doctors and their handwriting. Let me see. 'One Sunday morning worship service.' That is funny. John says church doesn't work."

"Does he now?"

"He says it doesn't make people nicer. It makes them meaner. He says it makes people self righteous."

"Then I guess you'd better give me that prescription back."

"Oh, you'll love this one. I never told you about my brownies, did I? I've always baked these brownies for Thomas. He liked me to make them with a special kind of oregano he would provide. He always asked me to bake an extra batch to take to his friends. The boys, well actually Thomas and John, not Peter, liked them so much I started to eat them myself and feed them to Richard. Turns out; you probably already know this; the oregano was marihuana. Can you believe it? I got Richard high and didn't even know it. Oh, and it gets worse. It seems the friends Thomas took these brownies to were the same homeless people Richard was preaching to on Sunday afternoons."

Marcia and Fran laughed until their seams were about to break. "You seem to be attached to Thomas. I didn't pick up on that before."

"My affinity for Thomas is something I've just discovered."

"Tell me more."

"John and I figured it out together. Thomas has been our alter ego. He was so free with his anger and his oppositional behavior we didn't need to be angry because he was angry enough for us all. I feel bad for him though. He was the scapegoat. All he was doing was expressing what the rest of us thought and felt. I've learned to admire Thomas in a strange sort of way."

"Strange?"

"It is mixed with sadness. I admire his tenacity, but I feel sad it caused him so much suffering. He is locked in this tenacious mode and can't get out of it. He can't relax and be himself. He is driven to fight; even with his lovers."

"So what was in the box?"

A grim look came over Fran. "Pictures."

"Pictures, that's strange. Why was he hiding pictures?"

Fran remained silent.

"Were they pictures of naked women? Having sex? Pictures of naked men?"

"We all feared something like that," Fran began to talk. "Except for Thomas. He wasn't afraid, he was hoping it did. He was hoping there would be evidence to expose Richard as a hypocrite. You know, so he could destroy his reputation and justify his hatred of Richard. Peter thought it was just a diary. He didn't believe there would be anything damaging in it."

"So which one of them was right?"

"I guess both of them were, in a way."

Marcia let out a deep breath, giving away her growing impatience.

"They were pictures of his other life," Fran said.

"Other life?" Marcia leaned forward and took a sip of her coffee.

"Yes. They were separated into stacks marked by years. The kids started to lay them out in chronological order. When they were done we looked at them and we saw the story they told; a story of his other life and other family in the Dominican Republic. I told you he went there on mission trips. He had a young wife there and three kids. It was like a giant family photo album."

"I'm sorry, Fran. You must have felt devastated."

"I don't know what I feel. I have questions; questions about what he did, why he did it, how they were together. I'm afraid."

"Afraid of what?"

"Afraid his other family was better than ours. I'm afraid she loved him better than I did and that is why he chose them. I'm afraid I wasn't good enough and this other woman is proof he was right all along about me. I wasn't pretty, sexy, or interesting enough for a man like him."

"Wow! He left you holding quite the bag of shit, didn't he?"

"I guess you could say that. He left a letter."

"Did you read it?"

"It was addressed to me."

"What did it say?"

"He wants me to take care of them financially. That was all it said. He didn't explain himself. He didn't try to apologize. It's like he's above reproach and I'm supposed to do the right thing and clean up his mess; that by the way, isn't really a mess because he made it and Richard doesn't make messes."

"So, on the phone you said stuff had come up and you couldn't stop thinking about it."

Fran explained the alarming image her mind kept showing her. As she did, she looked past Marcia at the picture of the three intertwined bodies behind Marcia's chair.

"Who do you think is on top of you?" Marcia asked.

Fran shook her head as though she couldn't go there, but then changed her mind. "I can't see him, but I know it has to be Richard. No one else has ever been on top of me naked."

"Tell me how the image makes you feel."

"Did I ever tell you about the dog?"

"The dog?" Marcia tilted her head and squinted.

"Yes, the dog that peed on Richard's gravestone."

"Ahh...that dog."

"Remember how I told you it felt so gratifying to see the dog do that?"

"I do recollect you said you were quite pleased. Why do you bring that up now?"

"I don't know. It just came to me." Fran paused. "It's not so funny now. I'm angry. I wish I could pee on his grave."

"You want to piss on Richard's grave?"

"Why would I want to do that? What am I, some kind of freak?" Fran bent over and cupped her face with her hands.

"A lot of women say that is what it is like to have sex with someone who you despise. They say it feels like they are pissing on you."

Fran burst into tears. "It does." She rubbed her abdomen as though she was scrubbing something off of it. "All that sperm; all over me; inside of me; I couldn't stand it. I didn't want him to do that to me. I couldn't stop him."

Marcia fended off her desire to run to Fran's rescue, to tell her she didn't need to go on. Instead she said, "It's degrading to be pissed on, isn't it?"

"It is! I hate it! Make him stop." Fran was shaking her head while blinking her eyes. She folded at the waist and buried her face in her hands and sobbed. Marcia could hear her mumbling the words, "Piss on you Richard; piss on you."

"You want revenge, don't you?"

"I do. I want him to pay for what he did to me. Thomas and I need him to suffer."

Fran cried until she began to calm down. She was relieved when Marcia told her she could put this image away for now in order to deal with the pressing matters at hand. Fran didn't think this was possible. She thought the image was there to stay, but her mind began to obey and as they moved on to other matters, the memory faded. They began to make a plan.

Chapter 22

Child's Play

The afternoon rolled in and out of the Vanderhuis residence in a quiet manner. Peter was out of sight most of the time and when he was around the others, he made it clear he didn't want to converse. John went for a walk in the nearby woods to get away from everything and gain clarity. It didn't work, so he sat around the rest of the afternoon and caught up on all the television he had missed over the past ten years.

Thomas and Sammy made brownies. They didn't taste bad, but they crumbled when they took them out of the pan. Ray and his men felt free to complain, wondering if Thomas had fired the cook. Their criticism didn't last long. Their attention shifted from the brownies to the attractive helper Thomas had brought with him. The unsolicited attention got old for Sammy and Thomas agreed to cut the visit short. The conversation on the way home was filled with mine fields for Thomas, as Sammy attempted to unravel the matter of why this Sunday afternoon ritual was kept from her and why, in the end, Thomas chose to reveal it to John first.

The first question was easy for Thomas to answer, since the gawking and lustful looks of Ray and his men were fresh in Sammy's mind. The matter of choosing to reveal the secret to John, instead of to her, was a more delicate matter which

Thomas himself didn't understand. In the end, it was an honest confession of ignorance that brought him reprieve from the intense interrogation.

When they returned home, Thomas and Sammy joined in the Sunday afternoon boredom that had encompassed John and Peter. They all sat in front of the television and watched golf. None of them played the game, but the sunshine that warmed the air the golfer's were breathing acted as a backup to the fireplace which staved off the cold seeping through the walls of the house and did battle with the doldrums that had settled in their bones.

"I always hated Sunday afternoons," John said.

"That's because all your two-track partners were busy with church," Sammy said.

"Or feeling too religious on a Sunday afternoon to let you taint their purity before they went back for evening worship," Thomas said.

"I remember dreading the evening service. It was overkill," Peter said.

"Since when didn't you like going to church?" Thomas stretched out on the couch. He put his feet on Sammy's lap. They hung over the armrest. Sammy began to rub his long thin boney feet. He smiled at her. She squeezed his big toe and pulled it away from his foot. He squirmed and she desisted.

"The first thing I did as a minister was to delete the evening worship service from the schedule. We do small group Bible studies instead."

"That's an improvement?" Thomas asked.

"I was thinking of making myself go tonight, but I don't feel comfortable at Dad's church anymore."

"What a surprise," Thomas said. "I wonder why?"

"Give your brother a break, will you?" Sammy said. "He is trying to find some way to relate to you. I'm not sure why, but he is."

"Let's see what Mom has planned for supper," John said.

The group rose and marched to the kitchen. Dinner was a casserole which was still in the freezer. No one had bothered to read Fran's note with directions to remove it from the freezer at lunch. The result was a two hour wait, during which they played Twister for old time's sake. They twisted and turned around each other, placing their hands and feet on the appropriate color circles, discovering their flexibility had lessened with age.

"Whoever has their hand on my ass needs to remove it. There is no yellow dot there," Sammy said.

"Sorry," Thomas removed his hand.

"He was probably thinking of those panties you used to wear with the yellow smiley faces plastered all over them," Peter said.

"How did you know about those?" Thomas asked.

"I don't know. I must have seen them. Remember, it was the days of the short miniskirts," Peter said.

"You guys remember this stuff after twenty years?" Sammy said.

They both shrugged their shoulders and sheepishly looked at each other and grinned.

"My God! No wonder Victoria's Secret is making millions. I suppose you both know what color underwear I'm wearing right now?" Sammy alternated looking them both in the eyes.

"Red," they responded in chorus, giving each other a high five to celebrate their accomplishment.

"Jesus," Sammy said.

"You have been twisting and turning with those low cut jeans," John said. He was sitting this one out, spinning the color wheel. "Your thong tends to ride up..."

"Please John, not you too," Sammy said.

"Look at it this way, Sammy. It is the only thing Thomas and Peter have agreed upon all weekend."

"The color of my panties? That's infantile."

"Come to think about it, you are the one and only thing I have ever known them to agreed upon since kindergarten," John chuckled.

"I'll spin the wheel. You guys can play." Sammy yanked it from John's hands and the game resumed.

"Don't be trying to see the color of my underwear," Thomas grinned.

"That's easy. You only wear one color, black," Sammy flashed him a plastered smile while shaking her head.

"So he doesn't have to wash them," Peter said while standing on all four legs. He laughed as he toppled after Thomas pushed him.

Dinner did not meet their needs. It was a casserole they didn't recognize; one of their mother's creations she made on one of her cooking sprees. Sammy suggested they cook for themselves, since the refrigerator was full of ingredients.

"Are you insane?" Thomas said.

"What? You guys don't cook for yourselves yet? How old are you, anyway?"

"Not in Mom's kitchen. The walls would fall in," John said.

"I'm not sure the appliances would work for anyone but Eddie. I'm quite certain the spices would revolt and turn our dishes sour."

"It never even crossed my mind as an option," Peter said. "Isn't this hallowed ground? It always felt like we should take our shoes off before we came in here."

"I thought the living room was the hallowed ground," Sammy said, "with all that white your father has in there."

"That was Dad's sanctuary," Peter said.

"More like his executioner's chamber," Thomas said.

"Who did he execute?" Sammy asked.

"Us! That was where he summoned us when he decided to discipline us," Thomas said.

"And the ministers when it came time for him to fire them," John said.

"Remember how spooky that was?" Thomas fluttered his hands to the side of his head. "First he would call a secret meeting of the church council. Next thing you know the minister showed up for a private meeting with Dad and one of his lackeys. Then the ministers were gone; vanished into thin air."

"We've done a good job of defiling his space," John said. "Defiling Mom's doesn't seem right."

"A little cooking wouldn't defile your mother's kitchen," Sammy said. "It didn't stop Thomas from baking brownies with me, this afternoon."

"Yes, but look at how they turned out," John smirked. "The baking powder did revolt."

"I think it was the oregano that revolted," Peter said. "It doesn't like being lied about."

"Brownie making is a sacred activity in this kitchen," Thomas said. "From the beginning of time, women have slaved over grinding wheels; preparing the chocolate beans and the wheat berries to be used in the creation of the sacred dessert; lacing it with spiritual grass meant to enhance the souls of those who would later partake in the purification ritual..."

"Knock it off, Thomas," Peter said. "It is bad enough you manipulated Mother into producing your illegal brownies."

"You could have informed on me any time you wanted." Thomas leaned back, stretching his feet under the table, bumping John's shins.

The group fell silent. "Peter, why didn't you tell your mother?" Sammy asked.

"Why didn't you two tell her?" he pointed at Sammy; then John.

They didn't bother to answer the petty accusation.

"I thought about it." Peter leaned back, bending his knees so his feet wouldn't run into Sammy's. He put both hands behind his head. "Believe me, I thought about it. But Mother was so pleased with herself when she baked them; happy Thomas asked her for something. I couldn't bring myself to take that away from her. Brownie making was the one thing that made her feel like your mother, Thomas."

Jane came into the kitchen and announced she was leaving for the evening. She assured John he could call at any

265

time if there were problems. She hadn't been able to find an aide to cover the evening time period, so John had agreed to be in charge. She informed them there were signs Richard's organs were shutting down. The yellow color of his skin suggested his liver wasn't working well and the lack of urine being produced was a clue his kidneys were failing. "If you have anything to say to your father, you should do it soon," she admonished as she left the kitchen and headed toward the front door.

"Have you talked to Mother yet?" Peter looked at John.

"I've tried, but she hasn't picked up her phone. I did call Lynn and she told me Mom had made arrangements to stay with her tonight."

"Did you have to swat off the gossip flies?" Thomas mimicked the swatting of flies.

"Lynn seemed nice. She didn't push for information or offer me any she might have. She just told me she was expecting Mom later this evening and she would tell her I had called."

"What's happening to small town America?" Thomas laughed. "No more gossip queens?"

"I hope she is alright," Sammy said.

"I think she is," John said. "She seemed quite determined when she left."

"Determined to do what?" Peter asked.

"I don't know. I don't know if she knew."

"By the way, has anyone seen Dundee?" Thomas asked. "He seems to have found a hiding spot to his liking. The only time I see him is at meal times."

The group fell silent, denying what they knew in an attempt to spare Dundee his owner's wrath. Sammy changed the subject, suggesting they watch Desperate Housewives. Peter called it smut television, but Thomas revealed his passion for the show when he announced tonight's episode was a rerun. He suggested they turn it on even if they didn't watch it.

"This house could use a little smut television to welcome some eviler spirits."

John suggested they go out to a movie and pizza. They agreed and were out the front door before any of them remembered their father was in his room, in a coma, and couldn't be left alone. John agreed to stay behind. He sent the others off with their promise to return with the left over pizza in hand.

Chapter 23

Pillow Talk

He went into the living room and found the television had been turned on. A commercial begged viewers to hold back their trigger fingers because Desperate Housewives was coming on in five minutes. He laughed, admiring Thomas indelible fighting spirit. The amount of energy he would devote to getting the last word when it came to his father. It was no wonder his father had realized he had met his match and gave up the fight.

He was preparing to sit in his chosen chair, but stopped mid squat. He needed to see his father and realized if he let himself sit down, he would procrastinate one more day. He straightened his legs and headed for the room, soon to be his father's gateway to the afterlife.

He stopped at the door and took three deep breaths, bracing for whatever shock might confront him on the other side. As he stepped into the room, he saw his father's emaciated body buffered by a thin cotton blanket. He had to look twice to see if this was him.

John pulled up a chair, "Hi Dad."

He could muster nothing to follow these two words of greeting, so he sat in silence. He wondered why his father was still alive. Was he waiting for someone or something? Some kind of farewell? Absolution? It didn't make sense; his staying alive. No one wanted him alive. Maybe Peter, but the content of the box had put even his loyalty into question. They were done. Why wasn't his father done? Did he want to cause yet more suffering by prolonging his death? Maybe he was more conscious of his motives than he had given him credit for and was afraid of going to hell? Or maybe he didn't have control over his death. Maybe this was a fight with death and his father just wasn't capable of giving up.

Whatever the answers to these questions, one thing seemed clear to John, it wasn't fair. Death shouldn't be the sole decision of the one dying nor a third disaffected party. Those left behind should have a say as to whether it should be prolonged or ended. People shouldn't be forced to tend to a life that had caused them anguish. How cruel was that? Why should his mother be shackled and forced to face the guilt her leaving would bring? Why shouldn't Thomas just have his last word so he could get on with living? Why should he have to say goodbye, when all he wanted was for his Dad to move on and leave him be? This family deserved a new beginning.

These questions rumbled through his head.

"It's time, Dad. It's time for you to go."

He squeezed the pillow he held to his chest. It cushioned the contact his chest made with his thighs each time they met as he rocked his upper body back and forth. He repeated over and over, "It is time for you to go Dad."

At times the words came out with the force of a command. At other times they came across with the softness of a plea. Either way, their meaning was unmistakable. It was time for a death.

His cell phone rang. He released his grasp on the pillow and answered it. One of the benefits of technology is a person can screen their calls by giving the important ones a unique ring tone. This ring had a tone that identified the caller as the one person John would want to talk to at a time like this. It was the sound of a Bollywood tune Myrna fell in love with the last time they went to a movie together. She stored it in her mind and was known to burst into song and dance to it; often in the most awkward of situations.

"Hi Myrna." John leaned back in his chair.

"Hi John."

"Where are you? What is all that noise?"

"I'm at the airport; waiting for my flight to leave."

"What flight? Where are you going?"

"Your mother didn't tell you?"

"Tell me what?"

"She called me earlier today and said I needed to come to Michigan. She refused to share any reasons with me. She just said it was important I come. She said all I needed to do was get to the airport by 6:00 am. A ticket would be waiting for me. I thought you knew. Do you want me to come?"

"Of course I want you to come. I'm just shocked. I don't know what my mother is up to these days. I'm telling you, I just can't keep up with her."

"Why don't you ask her?"

"She's not here. She left."

"What do you mean, she left?"

"It is a long story, but the gist of it is she left my father. She doesn't want to take care of him any longer." As he released those words, John thought he saw a slight, but sudden jolt in his father's motionless body. He looked for after-tremors, but there were none.

He conveyed to Myrna the thoughts rumbling through his brain. He failed to sensor the rawness of his feeling, not gauging the effect his darkness might have on Myrna.

"John, you're not thinking about doing something foolish are you?"

"What do you mean, foolish?"

"You're talking like you want to end your father's life."

Taken back, he was unable to answer. He rose out of his chair and went over to the window that overlooked the back yard.

"Listen John. They are boarding the plane now and I've got to get on it. But I can't end this conversation unless you promise me you won't do anything foolish before I get there. I don't know when I will be able to call you again, but I will try. I need you to promise."

"Myrna, there is no need for this kind of drama." John looked down at his feet.

"Promise me, John. I need to hear it from you."

"I promise."

John released the pillow which was wedged between his arm and his body. He set it back on the dresser from which he had taken it. He turned and left the room, closing the door behind him.

The others returned after midnight, pizza in hand. "The place was closing, so we decided to bring the party home to you." They barged into the living room and Thomas placed the pizza on the coffee table. Sammy set the two liter of Diet Coke on the end table and went to the kitchen to get glasses.

"I would have expected you to bring home beer, not soft drinks," John said.

"Sammy and Peter didn't feel right about bringing beer into Dad's house," Thomas said. "Somehow beer is worse than wine in their eyes." Thomas leaned toward John and looked into his eyes. "God, you look awful. What the hell have you been doing while we were gone?"

"Did you check on Dad?" Peter inquired; wondering if that was why John looked so ragged and deflated.

"He's fine. It's tough to see him this way. How was the movie?" He looked at Sammy who was returning from the kitchen with four glasses full of ice."

"It was fine. Not an Oscar award winning performance, but it was entertaining enough to get our minds off everything. Have you heard from Myrna?"

"What makes you ask?" John fidgeted in his chair.

Sammy tilted her head sideways while raising both hands and rotating them so that her palms faced upwards. "Oh, I don't know."

"The answer is yes. I talked with her a little while ago. She was at the airport, waiting to get on her flight."

"Where's she headed?" Sammy asked.

"She is coming here." He saw their surprise and went on, excited to up the ante. "Get this. She got a call from Mom telling her she needed to come to Michigan."

"Did your Mother tell her why?" Sammy asked.

"She refused to give Myrna a reason; just that she needed to come."

"I'm starting to worry about your Mother. Have you heard from her?" Sammy asked.

"Not a word."

Peter announced he was going to check on Richard. The others opened the pizza box and helped themselves. The smell permeated the air. Peter breathed it in and did an about face, grabbing a piece to take with him. "Maybe this will wake him up."

"That would be ironic," Thomas said. "It's killing us with cholesterol, but it might just wake Dad up from his endless coma."

They chuckled in unison, trying to forget the killing ourselves with cholesterol part. They sat back to enjoy the pizza when they heard Peter call in distress from their father's room. They rushed to the room and found him with his ear over Richard's mouth, listening for the sound of a breath. He held Richard's wrist, attempting to find a pulse.

"He's not breathing. Someone help me start CPR."

"Hell no!" Thomas said.

The group looked at him with disbelief. "I didn't mean it that way. I meant we shouldn't start CPR because there's a no resuscitation order in place. We are supposed to let him stay dead if he dies."

"How would you know this?" Sammy asked.

"You have to sign one in order to get hospice involved. Their job isn't to keep you alive; it is to help you die. Mom would have had to sign one."

John walked over to the bed and touched Richard's face with the back side of his hand. "Thomas is right. Besides, he is already starting to get cold."

Thomas jumped back as he saw movement coming from under the bed. "What the fuck!"

Dundee began crawling out from under the bed.

"There you are. I've been looking for you. What the hell are you doing under there?"

"He's been on a death watch," John said. "I guess it's over,"

"Why the hell would he do that?" He looked at Dundee. "I thought you were on my side. You're obsessed with Peter's crotch and you're coddling my father. I'm disappointed in you."

"He is just being a dog," Sammy said. "It's not personal."

"Like hell it isn't."

"I'm calling 911," Peter said. "They'll know what to do."

"No!" Thomas yelled.

"He is dead, alright Thomas?" Peter had tears in his eyes. "You've got what you came for, haven't you? What more do you want from the man? He is dead. Now I'm calling 911."

Sammy reached over and touched Peter's hand. "I think he means you're not supposed to call 911. You are supposed to call hospice. Their people are the ones to handle these emergencies because they know about the order not to resuscitate."

"Sorry. Will you call them?" Peter handed her the phone.

"I would be happy to do that." She walked over to the dresser and found Jane's number. She counted thirty seconds before punching in each number, buying the boys the time they needed to take in this significant moment in their journey toward wholeness. *The circle of life,* she thought to herself. *Something or someone has to die, in order to give life to another.* It was an odd application of the primitive principle and yet appropriate in the peculiar circumstances in which she was immersed. Sammy was buying time; buying time in hopes she would see signs of the new life beginning.

273

Chapter 24

Shock and Awe

Jane arrived and took charge. She was firm to the point everyone knew she was in control and needed to be obeyed without questioning. Yet she was tender to the extent all involved knew she would not leave before she had bandaged their deep wounds.

It was obvious Jane and their Mom had made the necessary arrangements. Jane knew which funeral home to call and had a list of the phone calls to be made in a specific order. The ones at the top of the list were already here, so there was no rush. Just under their names, was the name of the minister of the White Lake Reformed Baptist Church. Since Fran wasn't here to receive his comfort, she asked if calling him in the morning would do. Sammy answered for them, saying morning would be fine, pointing out there were two ministers already present, both of whom were very close to the family.

John asked Jane to call Fran. He noted she hadn't returned any of his phone calls and thought she might be more apt to answer a call from Jane. Jane relayed to John and the others she had already talked to Fran and informed her of Richard's death.

"What did she say?" Sammy asked.

Jane explained Fran had remained calm. They had spoken for long while and Fran decided she would come home after the body had been removed from the house. Jane told them the funeral home had been called and would be arriving soon to remove the body. The coroner was also on his way to pronounce the death. Fran could return home in a couple of hours.

Once the question of their mother's fate was addressed, the boy's shock began to lift. It was as though things would be back to normal in an hour or so, and this was comforting. Peter left the room and went upstairs to lie in bed. Sammy took leave to the basement for her version of reprieve. Thomas and John stayed put in the kitchen.

"Well, this was convenient." Thomas tried to start a conversation in which he could relieve himself of the unexplained burden he was feeling.

"What's that supposed to mean?"

"It's not an accusation, John; just an observation. It is convenient because we are all staying for the funeral and Dad's timely death allows us to get on with this exhausting wait. What did you think I meant?"

"Nothing, it's just that..."

"Holy shit! Did you think I was insinuating that you?" Thomas was thoughtful for a moment. "You didn't, did you? I mean I wouldn't judge you, but you didn't, did you? I could understand and maybe if it was me I would...but did you?"

"Of course I didn't. Unless you can stop someone from breathing by wishing him to die...or telling him to die?"

"You told Dad to die?"

"I was expressing my frustration with him. I didn't mean it. This prolonged death was getting to me. Why couldn't he just die? It is what we all wanted. Why didn't he want that? I didn't understand why he was hanging on."

John began to load the dirty dishes into the dishwasher. Thomas pulled up a stool and sat down next to him.

"Feel free to help," John said.

"I'm good." Thomas waved him off. "Maybe he...hell, I don't know. I never did understand why the man did what he did. That's why I assumed he enjoyed making us suffer."

"I did tell him Mom had left him."

"That might have done the trick."

"I didn't tell him, but I told Myrna over the phone and he might have overheard. I thought I saw him squirm when I said it."

"There is no way of telling what he could have heard in his condition. But if he did hear you, then maybe...fuck this, John. I'm no good at this introspective second guessing bullshit. You didn't do anything wrong. You had an honest conversation with Dad that was a long time in coming. If he was hurt by it, then so be it. Honesty hurts people. That's why so few people are truthful with each other. They don't want to hurt the people they love. The end result is they end up with families like ours, detached and angry because they don't know each other. They've never had the difficult conversations they needed to have."

"You think we're detached and angry with each other?"

"How else could we have walked away from each other with such ease? I might have been the first one to leave, and the only one to shake the dust off my feet as I did, but you and Peter weren't far behind. You just weren't as honest about your leaving as I was."

"Is that why you are so blunt? You don't mind hurting the people you love?"

"That would be the simplistic assumption people would make."

John pointed to the dirty glasses on the counter behind Thomas.

"I'm more complex than that." Thomas said as he passed the glasses to John. "If you want the truth about me, I'll tell you." Thomas waited a few seconds. "I tell people my truth to avoid hearing theirs. It's a shock and awe defense. Blow them out of the water before they know what hit them. That way they won't have anything left to strike back."

276

"You are telling me you are afraid of other's truth? You are afraid it will hurt you?"

"Aren't we all? Isn't it true most people stay away from the truth because they know telling it leads to facing the bona fide reality about themselves and not just their own version of it? They know they will have to face the other person's truth about them and that will hurt. Why do you think Dad was so rigid and unyielding? Courage? I doubt that. He was like me; a coward in disguise. He put so much energy into being right because he was afraid to face the real truth about himself. Shock and awe, baby, shock and awe!"

"So you think that is why Dad left you alone after a while?"

"Damn right! He figured out my shock and awe was bigger than his, so he backed off and took another strategy."

"And what was the strategy?"

"Shrinks would call it deny and marginalize."

"And you would call it?"

"Plugging your ears."

"So your strategy for this weekend is shock and awe?"

"Believe it or not, I'm trying to change."

"Why?"

"It appears there is a lot of collateral damage connected to this strategy. When I was young, I didn't care. Let them go; good riddance. But now the sound of my front door shutting behind my relationships doesn't offer me the comfort it used to bring. It used to be like a breath of fresh air. Now, something else is slipping in before they slam it. It is called loneliness."

"I have to admit I've not seen this side of you before. I guess I've noticed a slight change in your behavior."

"I know, I know, Peter. I haven't changed much when it comes to Peter."

"Mom, Dad, the church. Must I go on?"

"I'm trying. That's all I'm saying."

"Good enough." John changed the subject back to the unfinished conversation that had jump-started this confessional. "So you think Dad was my collateral damage?"

"You weren't employing shock and awe. You were conveying a fact to your wife Dad happened to overhear. What happened in there was Dad started to stumble over his own collateral damage. He got what he had coming and decided to throw in the towel and run."

"Run to where? Heaven?" John scratched his head. "Do you know how to turn on this dishwasher?"

"Just start pushing buttons until something happens." Thomas flicked his hand.

"That's your response to technology?"

"Its how you deal with electronics when you are in doubt."

John laughed and started to push buttons. On his third try the machine made a click and the faint sound of water spraying the dishes began.

"Dad in heaven; it doesn't seem fair, does it?" Thomas said.

"Not unless God has a mind like Dad's?"

"God help me, I'm in deep shit if God thinks like Dad."

"If God agrees with Dad we're all in trouble." John opened the door under the sink and removed the bag of trash. He handed it to Thomas. "Here, take this out to the garage. And while you are at it, grab that empty pizza box and take it with you."

"Since when did I become the trash man?"

"The same day I became the dishwasher."

Thomas complied.

Chapter 25

Mom is Back in Charge

The coroner came and released the body. The funeral home loaded it onto a stretcher and put it in their van. The family watched it drive away until it was out of sight. As it slipped into the darkness, a sense of peace filled the Vanderhuis home. No one acknowledged it, but everyone experienced it. The household took a deep breath, held it for a moment, and then released it. Like an enormous lung, it contracted, and when it expanded, fresh air filled the living space.

Along with that fresh air, before the door could shut behind it, came Fran Vanderhuis; returning from her prodigal journey. Her family was waiting for her, gathered in a circle in front of the living room window. They welcomed her with an open embrace as she took the chair they had pulled up to the circle for her.

"So, tell me what happened while I was gone."

They began to talk at the same time and she stopped them. "One at a time, please. I can only listen to you one at a time. You were there when he died, John?"

"We're not sure when he died. Peter discovered he wasn't breathing after they came home from the movies. It wasn't that dramatic, Mom."

"Well good, I would hate to think your father would put you through a messy death."

"What have you been up to while you were gone?" John asked.

"Maybe tomorrow. I'm wiped out and it is late. It has been a long twenty-four hours. I think we'll all be better off with a good night's sleep before we tackle the next few days."

The group agreed and began to disperse. John followed Fran into the kitchen. "Mom, where have you been? Why didn't you call? I've been leaving you messages all day."

"I know John and I'm sorry. I had a lot of things to do and think about. I spent a great deal of time with Marcia, figuring out what to do. You know, making a plan. This, however, was unexpected. I had no idea Richard would die so soon."

"You sound disappointed."

"I'm not disappointed, just surprised. It complicates things because my plan has to be put on the fast track and some things are difficult to speed along."

Fran scanned the kitchen. "Wow, someone cleaned up."

"Thomas and I did."

"Thomas helped you?" Fran began to wipe the counter tops down.

"What is this plan you're talking about?"

"Not tonight, John. We can talk about it tomorrow, after a good night's sleep."

"It has been a rough day."

"I'm glad you got to see your father before he died. Did you have a good talk with him?"

"It was more like talking at him. I said some pretty harsh words."

"Like what?"

"Do you think a person can will another to die?"

"You told him to die?"

"It was more like telling him it was time for him to die. What? Don't look at me like that. We were ready for him to die, Mom. You know it is the truth. I just..."

"You can't will someone to die, John. You might be able to lessen their will to live, but you can't force them to die. Are you sure you weren't in there when he died?"

280

"Why do you people keep asking me that? I already told you I wasn't."

"It is just that you are acting strange. Like you have been traumatized or something."

"Guilty? Is that the word you are looking for, Mom?"

"No, it isn't. But it appears to be the one you settled on. Why would you feel guilty about your father's death? You didn't do something foolish in there, did you?"

"Like what?" John spun around clenching his fists.

"You are acting like you've done something awful; like killing your father."

"Where did that come from? Just because I was the last one to see him and – as Thomas puts it, 'he died a convenient death' – doesn't mean I suffocated him with a pillow." John sat in the stool Thomas had left in the middle of the kitchen.

"Thomas said that?"

"You know Thomas. He says what's on his mind. He has no filters for truth that is uncomfortable to others."

"That's not always a bad quality. I could have used a bit more cojones a while back. We wouldn't have been in this mess. It takes cojones to speak the truth when it is uncomfortable, but necessary."

"Necessary, Mom. That's the key word here. It isn't always necessary when Thomas does it. And Mom, cojones? Where did you get that from? Do you even know what it means?"

"Of course I do. It means testicles, you know, balls."

John turned his face and put his hands up to shield himself, as if hearing his mother use these gruff terms was more than he could stomach.

"Oh, grow up John. I'm trying to break out of thirty years of being a prissy prude. Using this language is just one way to keep the ball of change rolling."

"Who is teaching you Spanish terms for men's body parts?"

"It turns out Marcia knows Spanish. She was a Peace Corps worker in the Dominican Republic a long time ago."

"That's convenient."

281

"You mean like your father's dea..."

"Stop, Mom." John pointed his finger at Fran. "I didn't kill Dad. I just did something cruel that might have pushed him over the edge."

"And what was that?" Fran checked her cupboards to insure everything was intact.

"He overheard my telling Myrna you left him."

"And this is why you think you killed him?" Fran stopped fussing with the kitchen and looked at John. She waited for a response that didn't come. "Let me lift you off that giant hook on which you have hung yourself. If your father could hear, he already knew I had left him."

"How is that?"

"I told him before I left. You didn't kill your father with the news of my leaving him."

"Why wasn't there any warning when he stopped breathing; a beep or something?"

"Jane disconnected all that the other day. With an order to not resuscitate, there was no need for a quick warning."

"I see." John paused. "Why did you call Myrna and tell her to come?"

Fran opened the refrigerator and stared inside of it. "We're almost out of milk."

"Fine." Fran closed the door and stood before John. "I just like to be organized."

"Answer my question."

"I figured she should be here. You said the only reason she didn't come with you was because of money, so I took care of that. Besides, I want to meet her."

"You should have asked."

"You would have turned a simple matter into a huge ordeal. Besides, I know you are pleased she is coming for the funeral."

"I'm always pleased to see her, but that isn't the point. The..."

282

"John, the money is not a big deal. Your father left me more than I will ever need. It seems all those years of penny pinching have added up to a hidden fortune. Just thank me and be glad she is coming. I need to go to bed. We can talk more in the morning if you like."

"Good night, Mom."

"Good night, son."

John left the kitchen and Fran leaned back on her kitchen counter. She let out a deep sigh as she thought about the ordeal the next few days would bring. She looked at her kitchen and decided it was clean enough. She was saddened she would soon be leaving this safe place that had comforted her so well for so long. And yet, she knew. She knew it was time to leave in order to find different and healthier safe places. So she stopped admiring her kitchen and walked through the swinging doors. When she went into the living-room to turn off the light she saw it was in disarray. She sighed and left the mess behind her.

Chapter 26

Dad's Puppets

Morning came in the Vanderhuis household with an urgency that was not surprising to the persons who filled its rooms. Any sleep they forced themselves to endure was out of necessity, not desire. They awoke and rose as a choir to the rising of the sun. In Michigan this is not a sudden and dramatic happening, as the sun makes itself known in small increments, fighting to break through the thick layers of clouds. It is not the flipping of a switch, as it appears in warmer climates, but a slow cranking of a rusty dimmer switch which resists the torque of even the strongest of hands.

By nine o'clock, they all strode into the kitchen, showered and dressed for the day. The smell of warm waffles fresh off the griddle filled the air. On the counter there were bowls of fresh blueberries, strawberries, and cut up bananas. Whipped cream and warm maple syrup stood next to the bowls of fresh fruit. Fran's good silver and china displayed the food, making the counter appear like brunch at a high end restaurant.

"I take it we are still breaking the rules and eating in here this morning?" Peter took a plate and began to serve himself.

"No one has bothered to evict Dad's other family from our dinner table." Thomas said. He followed Peter's lead and placed a warm waffle on his plate. "They can have it, as far as

284

I'm concerned. I never felt like I belonged at that table anyway."

"You thought the rest of us felt we belonged there?" Peter asked.

"You had me fooled if you didn't," Thomas said. "You never looked like you were doing anything but enjoying the comfort of home and family when you were sitting there listening to Dad's bullshit."

"Just because I chose not to overdramatize every hurt feeling I experienced in order to make sure everyone was aware of my discomfort, doesn't mean I didn't feel some of the same things you did."

The family settled around the counter and began to devour breakfast.

"What are you talking about? You were his pet. You did everything he said without question. Oh! Wait. This is about your not getting to sit next to him, isn't it? You wanted John's place at his right hand, or at least Sammy's place on his left. Is that what this is about?"

"You could have had my place if you liked," John joined the fray. "I would have preferred yours, next to Mom."

"You know it didn't work that way, John," Fran said. "Your father decided where we all sat and he made sure none of us got to sit where we wanted. It was his way of keeping everything off balance. Dinner time was a staging venue where he arranged the play he was producing."

"Are you saying we were puppets in Dad's play?" Thomas asked.

"Does that surprise you, Thomas?" Fran asked.

"Well..."

"What part surprises you, Thomas? That your brothers were puppets or that you were?"

"I'm surprised you would say I was a puppet. I never did anything Dad told me to do. If he had his hand up my ass moving my body parts, it must not have been very far up there, because I didn't feel a thing."

"Why do you think you talk like that all the time?"

"Talk like what?" Thomas shrugged his shoulders, insinuating his innocence.

"As crude as possible no matter what the subject."

"I don't know. Because I like to make my point in an emphatic manner, I guess."

"I think you do it because you know it pisses, excuse me, makes your father angry. I've got to stop hanging out with Marcia so much. Next thing you know I'll be swearing in Spanish." The group gave her a puzzled look, but didn't pursue their curiosity over the comment, since they were intent on the present conversation.

"So how does that put Dad in control of me?"

"You've never understood one key aspect of this fiasco, Thomas. You see, every play needs a scapegoat. You behaved the way you did because your father disliked it. That motivated you to play your role with great passion. What you failed to realize was you were doing what your father wanted you to do. You were providing him a platter on which to load all his guilt."

"And why would he want that?"

"So he could seethe against it without hating himself. The better you played your part, the more righteous the star of the show felt. Every deluded self-righteous pretender needs a scapegoat to carry his sin for him and get it off his own back. Your father trained you to be his scapegoat and you learned to do it well."

"You believe Dad wanted me to be the way I am so he could hate me instead of himself?"

"I don't know how conscious your father was about what he did, but yes, it's what he wanted."

Thomas stood up to get another waffle and bumped his head on the edge of the cabinet which hung over the counter the family was gathered around.

"Sit," Fran said as she reached over and rubbed his head.
Thomas pulled away from her.

"You inherited your father's height." She walked over to the stove. "I'll get you another waffle, just sit and tend to that bump on your forehead."

"And what roles did these two play?" Thomas pointed at his brothers.

"You tell me."

"He needed someone to worship him, but not compete with him for his spot on the stage. That would be Peter. This would explain why Peter could never be good enough. He needed to be wounded by a son who failed to live up to his worthy calling as the star's protégé, so he could be the martyr who carried on with his laborious attempts to train his ungrateful firstborn. That would be John."

"Behold you have just heard a marvelous description of the screenplay we've all been living for all these years." Fran raised her hands and took a bow.

"What was your role, Mother?" Peter asked.

Fran walked around the counter looking over everyone's shoulders to see if they needed anything. Sammy pointed to her empty plate and mouthed it was delicious. She then signaled she wanted another waffle and Fran went to get it.

"I, my dear, was the audience. I sat and watched his play with adoring eyes and gave him a standing ovation after every act." She paused and waited for a laugh that didn't come. "That was a joke. You were supposed to at least snicker." The laugh still didn't come. "I guess it was a joke in poor taste. I didn't give him a standing ovation, but my silence let him pretend I was."

"Where did you want to sit, Mom?" John asked.

"In the kitchen. I wished I could have stayed in the kitchen so I didn't have to sit and watch it happen right before my eyes. You see, I couldn't interrupt the play. I know now I could have, but back then, I didn't think I was allowed to interrupt him. So I had to sit and watch, even though I hated the play."

They allowed her time to stop and manage her tears. Fran went on. "None of us felt like we belonged at that table and that's how he wanted it. It was his table. That's why it felt so good to eat in here yesterday morning. That's why a part of us is relieved there is another family sitting at that table."

"If you ask me, this conversation is futile." Thomas stood up. "Wishing we had done something different, doesn't change what we did. You can't excuse yourself that easily, Eddie."

"Is that what you think I'm trying to do?" Fran asked. "Excuse my actions?"

"Isn't that why you are telling us this; so we will let you off the hook?" Thomas walked over to the sink and threw his plate into it.

"I would like you to forgive me, Thomas. But I'm not trying to excuse my silence. I'm trying to explain it so you can gain a bit of understanding about what caused me to sit by and let the play go on."

"And what good will it do? You should have said something, Eddie. You should have stopped him. Don't you think I was scared? Did you ever stop to think that the reason I got in his face was I was scared to death of him? Did you ever even think to ask me about it? About the nightmares I had about him hurting me? Waking up to him suffocating me in the middle of the night? Why didn't you ask, Eddie? Why didn't you ask?"

Peter was about to intervene, but Fran motioned with her hand for him to back off. "I don't know, Thomas. I know now I should have, but I don't know why I didn't back then. Maybe I didn't want to know. Maybe I was too scared to think straight about it. I do know I should have and I'm sorry I didn't. I should have left and taken you with me."

"Like you did last night?" Thomas' sarcasm was thick.

"I suppose I deserved that. The truth is I didn't think anyone would believe me back then. You know; if I told them what your father was like. I tried once to talk to one of the church elders. I talked to Bernie Sherman."

Fran put her hand on Thomas' arm and moved him to the side of the sink so she could have access to it. She began rinsing the dishes she brought over.

288

"What did he say?" Peter asked.

"He acted shocked at first and empathetic. But when I asked him to talk to Richard about it, he changed his tune. He said every good man has a bad day here or there and I should be more understanding of the heavy load Richard carries on his shoulders."

"Why did you pick Bernie Sherman?" John asked. "He was Dad's lackey, wasn't he? I remember he was always adding an 'Amen' to punctuate all of Dad's speeches at congregational meetings; like a groupie of sorts."

"Wasn't he the guy with the big mole on the top of his bald head, and bad comb-over he thought covered it?" Sammy asked.

The family laughed. "That would be Bernie," Peter said.

"Who else was there? Fran said. "Your father built this church with people just like Bernie."

"What about the ministers?" Sammy asked.

"You mean Dad's arch enemies?" John said. "That would have gone over well with Dad. The ultimate betrayal; fraternizing with the enemy."

"I did go to the minister once." Fran's eyes were glazed over with the wetness of her tears. "I went to see Reverend Ricks. I told him a few things. He was nice. He even said he would talk to Richard."

"Did he?"

"All I know is that a few days later your father accused me of contemplating adultery with Reverend Ricks. He said if he caught me talking to him again, he would bring the matter before council. Reverend Ricks was on the chopping block less than a month later."

The door bell rang and startled everyone out of their entrenched attentiveness to Fran's storytelling. Before they could wonder who was at the door, Fran announced Reverend Vermin was the person with his finger on the bell. He was coming to meet with the family about planning the funeral. Thomas tried to excuse himself from the process, but Sammy

289

rerouted him toward the living room. He mocked the minister's name when he was introduced.

"Vermin, now that is an appropriate name for a minister. What genius thought that up?"

Reverend Vermin laughed it off by employing the old cliché, "If I had a penny for every time I've heard that one, I'd be a millionaire."

"So I'm not the only person in the world with a negative opinion of ministers? That's good to know. I thought I was all alone."

The Reverend ignored the comment and moved on. As he made his way to the living room, he glanced at the pictures on the dining room table and asked, "Who's in the pictures?"

The family turned in unison toward Fran. "Oh, those?" she said. "Those are pictures of a refugee family we are sponsoring to come to White Lake. They'll be staying here."

The family's jaws dropped to their chests – at first out of shock, but the shock soon turned to amazement at the ease with which the lies flowed from Fran's lips.

"Where are they from?" he asked.

"The Dominican Republic," she answered. "They are some of Richard's people."

"That's strange. I didn't know they were giving refugee status to Dominicans these days. I thought it was a democracy."

"Yeah, well...we're calling them economic refugees. We're hoping it will fly with immigration."

"Let me know if I can help in any way."

"You'll be first on my list. They could use jobs, if anyone in the church is hiring."

"I'll pass the word around. Will they be here in time for the funeral?"

"I'm working on it as we speak."

"That would be a nice touch. It would be concrete evidence of the wonderful work Richard did in that country."

Thomas whispered to John, "The little tramp is a pro at this game of deceit. Maybe she was bonking Ricks after all, and we didn't have a clue because she has been a pathological liar all along and we didn't know this side of her."

John dismissed Thomas with a polite smile.

"Your husband left me with a complete description of what he wanted his funeral to entail. So for the most part, my questions are all answered. There is, however, the matter of the eulogy. I need to get a feel from you of what you would like me to say about your father. I have a grasp on what he was as a professional, but I'd like to be able to describe him as a father and husband as well. It would be helpful to me if you could describe him for me in that arena. Do you have any stories I could use to illustrate what he was like with you? People like to reminisce with stories."

Thomas couldn't resist. "Excuse me Vermin, but I'm not up to date on ministerial protocol. Are ministers allowed to say the words 'fucking asshole' from the pulpit these days?"

Sammy punched him in the arm, but he felt it was well worth the satisfaction.

Stunned, Reverend Vermin turned to Fran for direction. She obliged him forthright.

"We've decided as a family to keep Richard's personal life private. You may offer all the accolades you like for his professional life and accomplishments. But as for his being a good husband and father, you do not have my permission to venture out in that area with any unsubstantiated assumptions. Please just leave it that he had a wife and three wonderful children."

"Can I at least..."

"You have my answer. Let's just leave it at that."

Thomas changed the subject. "Did you know that you are the only one?"

"I'm not quite sure what you are referring..."

"You are the only minister ever to step into this living room, whose head wasn't on the chopping block. No minister of the White Lake Reformed Baptist Church has ever stepped into this room without being summarily fired by the church council – courtesy, of course, of Dr. Richard Vanderhuis. It is quite a legacy you'll have attached to your resume."

Reverend Vermin's face contorted as his face expressed his befuddled mental state.

Fran interrupted the conversation and brought it to a quick finish. "It is a long story that Reverend Ricks – I mean Reverend Vermin – doesn't have time to hear. I believe you have what you need, don't you Reverend?"

"If you say so, then I do. Will any of you be speaking at the funeral? I know two of you are ministers. It might add a nice touch if you could say a few words. You know, to show his legacy in the church – two sons who are ministers."

John and Peter were taken aback by the question. They hadn't thought about it. Everything had been so sudden. Fran answered for them. "We'll have to get back to you on that one, Reverend. I think they need a little time to think about it."

"I know it might be a bit difficult with all the strong emotions you must be feeling. But there will be opportunity for you to speak if you decide you would like to say a few words. I would like to offer my deepest sympathy to all of you."

He turned and then remembered one more thing he needed to bring up. "Oh there is the matter of the horse-drawn carriage your husband requested to carry him from the church to the cemetery. It seems..."

"I know. It seems a bit presumptuous, but it is what he wanted. I'm working on it and I think I might be able to make it happen. If not, then we will just use the hearse."

"You'll need special permission from the city."

"I believe it is on their agenda for Tuesday night."

"My, it is true that behind every great man there is a good woman."

"Thank you Reverend Vermin. It is very kind of you to say that to me."

Fran ushered him toward the door. Thomas stopped them. "By the way, Vermin, when you get to that part of the funeral where you send my father off to the deep blue yonder; could you leave God a little leeway as to the direction he might be pointing Dad toward." He enjoyed the return of the contorted, puzzled look to the minister's face and continued. "You know, as to whether my father is headed up or down. Don't be too quick to give him a thumbs up."

Fran turned the minster around again and marched him out of the living room. He stopped at the dining room table to comment on the lovely family in the pictures. Fran humored him until he started to ask questions as to the marital state of the young woman with three kids. That prompted her to grab hold of his arm and tug him along toward the door. When they reached the door he leaned over toward Fran in a manner that signaled to her he wanted to have a private discussion.

"What is going on here, Fran?"

"What do you mean, Reverend?"

"I'm not allowed to talk about Richard's personal life? And you are tolerating that hateful behavior of your California son. I know it is a difficult time, but…"

"Look Reverend Vermin, it is a hard time for all of us and we are handling it as best we can. Families aren't always what they look like from the outside. Richard caused a lot of hurt in this family and …"

"This is not the time to address Richard's faults. I'm sure he had them. We all do. But funerals are a time to offer grace and forgiveness, not condemnation. It is the time to remember the good in him."

"I realize it isn't the right time, Reverend. I should have addressed it with Richard when he was alive, but I didn't. The result is this is the only time we have left to deal with it."

"But a public setting is not the proper place to settle your scores with him. Trust me; I've done this for a long time. You will live to regret it."

"That may well be, Vermin. Excuse me, I meant to say Reverend Vermin." She wished she had legs long enough to kick Thomas from where she was standing as she blamed him for that impolite slip of the tongue. "But I'm not asking you to

293

air our dirty laundry. I'm just asking you to be silent on the matter. I'm not judging Richard; I'm just not willing to tell any more lies about him. Pretending he was a loving father would not be good for the boys or me. People can think what they want about the silence on the matter."

Reverend Vermin conceded and excused himself, but not without one final concern. "Fran, you are not yourself, I'm concerned about you. Your behavior at the cemetery the other day..."

"I'm not changing Reverend Vermin, but I understand why you would think this. The truth is for the first time in a long while I'm being myself." She shut the door behind him and was pleased with her response. Its insight rang true to her instincts.

Chapter 27

Elaborate Funeral Plans

Fran reentered the living-room to find her family waiting for her. They were discussing the awkward visit with the minister. Peter was afraid they, meaning Thomas, had offended him. John rationalized visits with ministers are always uncomfortable.

"It's the role," he said. "The imbalance of power makes it seem like an examination."

"My parishioners don't find my visits uncomfortable, nor do they feel examined. They feel cared for in a deep way," Peter said.

Sammy, who had never been visited by a minister before, commented, "I thought it was quite pleasant. He rolled with the punches pretty well. I didn't think he was critical at all."

The rest of the family smiled at her innocence when it came to the church community's social dynamics. She had sat in the pews all those years, but somehow remained intact from the oppressive nature of the whole thing. She was a bystander – an outsider looking in through a glass that dulls the effects of the forces on the other side. Church doesn't have the same powerful effects on people who are not born into it. The preaching doesn't creep as deep into their brains when they begin listening to it at an older age. They feel like they have a choice to take it or leave it. That choice isn't available to those born into the family of God; to those who have been force fed from the time they exited their mother's womb.

Peter promised to stop by the church later in the week and patch things up. He had to assure the others that he wouldn't undo the instructions they had given the Reverend. He said he would try to explain the family's requests in a more insightful way.

"I just want a chance to communicate to him that Thomas doesn't speak for all of us." They nodded in agreement.

"We've got an hour until our appointment with the funeral director. I'd like it if you all came with me." Fran looked for responses.

"I'll tell you what, Mom. We'll all come, if you agree to drive," John said.

Fran reached back and rubbed the back of her neck.

"Come on Mother. We've never seen you drive and you could use the practice. Most families have spent a lifetime being driven around by their mothers. We have a lot of catching up to do," Peter said.

"I assure you I'm capable of driving. I've been practicing. But if you need proof or, as you put it, you need to catch up on your taxi-mothering time, I will agree to this. However, I expect no comments or back seat driving instructions; agreed?"

They agreed.

"You want to break in Puff?" Thomas asked, knowing she couldn't drive a stick shift.

"Say yes Mom. You know he won't let you near that steering wheel," John said.

"Let's leave now and Mom can drive us around town and take us to all the places she never drove us," Peter said. "You know the park, the schools, the baseball fields..."

They set off to get ready.

They met in the Cadillac. Fran walked into the garage, keys in hand. She walked around the back of the car, fiddling with her purse, opened the door, and let herself fall into the seat. Closing the door, she turned and found Sammy in the front seat, looking forward with a stern look on her face. She was wearing a bicycle helmet and her mouth was taped shut with green duct tape. Fran turned and looked behind her, finding the three boys with the same stern faces, helmets in place – except for Thomas, whose helmet wasn't big enough and sat on the top of his head – duct tape over their mouths.

Never had she felt such a need to burst out laughing, but she willed herself to maintain as serious a composure as she could muster. Without saying a word, she put the key in the ignition, turned it, put the Caddy in reverse, and backed out of the garage. She steered the car as close to Puff as she could without hitting it and enjoyed the tortured look on Thomas' face – slowing as she backed past it – noticing how the duct tape over Thomas' mouth stretched as it forced him to keep his mouth shut.

She drove down the road and for the first block everyone held their serious composure. By the second block, their bodies began to shake, as their laughter was forced to stay inside their bodies by the tape. Sammy was doubled over, her helmeted head bouncing on the dash board. Through the rear view mirror, Fran saw the boys leaning back, holding their stomachs with both hands, sniffing like panting dogs as their laughter escaped through their noses.

Still, she maintained her poise and drove on like nothing out of the ordinary was occurring. At the first intersection she slammed on her brakes and burst out laughing. Her children ripped the duct tape off of their mouths and joined her with enormous relief. They stalled at the intersection several minutes, waving the oncoming cars through the stop sign as if they had the right of way.

"Sammy! I can't believe you went along with this. It looks as if you were the ring leader," Fran said.

"I wasn't. You have to believe me. They made me sit up here because they thought if the joke didn't go well, you wouldn't be quite so mad if I was the one sitting next to you."

"You mean they thought I would be less likely to smack you than them?"

"Pretty much."

"The men in this family have a history of putting their women on the front line, don't they?" she said, looking in the rear view mirror. The family continued to laugh and stayed parked at the intersection until a car pulled up behind them and beeped its horn, refusing to go around them.

They toured the town on Fran's dime, never removing their helmets until they reached the funeral home. As they exited the car, Fran fixed their hat hair, and rubbed John's buzzed head.

They were perplexed by the arrangements their father had made for his funeral. A reasonable person would expect they shouldn't have been, since they had already heard about his request to have his casket delivered to the gravesite by a horse drawn carriage. In this day and age this request is either eccentric or self-aggrandizing. Richard never showed signs of being eccentric so that would lead even the most well meaning person to conclude that through his funeral, Richard was attempting to characterize himself in a way that would make him look important. The casket he had picked out was fit for a VIP and so was the cost. The extensive flower arrangements and the string quartet all reflected his desire to spare no expense in making his final procession down the isle of the White Lake Reformed Baptist Church and through the town a majestic occasion.

"Was Dad in his right mind when he made these arrangements?" Peter asked Fran.

"Why do you ask?"

"It seems a bit much."

"A bit much?" Thomas said. "Ostentatious would be the more accurate term."

"This isn't Dad," Peter said.

"Mr. Holt told me he did all of this ten years ago."

"It doesn't make sense," Peter paced in a small circle. "Other than that decked out Cadillac he drove, Dad was a miser who took pride in not spending his money."

"I don't know what to tell you except this is the funeral he chose."

"Can't you stop it, Mother?" Peter asked.

"I could, but I won't. I'm not covering for him any longer." Fran hugged her purse which she had placed in her lap. "This is what he chose and this is what he will get. If you think about it, it does reflect what he thought of himself and what he communicated about himself in subtle ways."

"What are you talking about?" Peter asked.

"He thought of himself as king of his little fiefdom. This is a funeral fit for a king. I'm just going to let his choice of funeral air that silly truth out in a public manner."

"And the purpose of that would be?" Peter asked.

"I don't know Peter. Maybe the truth should come out so people can move on. Maybe if we allow him to expose himself for who he was, people can make better sense of it."

"By people you mean us, don't you mother?" Peter said.

"It would include us, yes."

"But you are making a fool of him, Mother. He wasn't a fool."

Fran hushed Peter and then responded in a firm whisper.

"I'm not doing anything to make your father look like a fool. He chose this funeral, Peter. He chose to make this statement about himself while of sound mind. If you think it makes him look like a fool, then maybe you need to revise your opinion of your father. People reveal themselves through their choices."

They left the funeral home in silence. Thomas tried to resurrect the light-hearted fun from the trip to the funeral home by placing his helmet on his head again, but no one was in the mood to support him. They chose instead to ride in silence as they prepared for what appeared would be a most awkward of funerals. But then the truth is often quite awkward, whether it is revealed at opportune or inopportune times.

They stopped at the bowling alley for lunch. It was one of the few places Richard would agree to frequent if they did go out to eat. The owner offered his condolences as did the other patrons who recognized them. They were given a table off to the side for privacy's sake.

"Didn't feel like cooking, Eddie?" Thomas poured his beer into the frosty mug.

Fran shrugged her shoulders. "I guess I'm just knocked off my stride a bit. I'm sorry. I've got plans for supper though. Myrna will be joining us so I'm going to make it special."

"No need to be sorry, Eddie. This is great for old time's sake. I was just wondering."

The waitress took their order. She returned with their drinks and place settings. John stared at the young woman. When she left, he nudged Fran.

"She looks familiar." John motioned toward the waitress.

"I think that's Jim Fisher's daughter. She's pretty, isn't she?"

"Jim must have married up," Thomas said. "He was an ugly son of a bitch."

"He wasn't that ugly," Sammy said. "You just didn't like him because he bullied you."

"He didn't bully me."

"Yes he did," Sammy said. "Remember how he pulled your ponytail whenever he passed you in the hallway and called you Wuss."

Thomas shrugged it off.

"That is exactly what you did back then," Sammy said. "You shrugged your shoulders just like you did right now."

"So Mother," Peter unwrapped his silverware and placed them neatly next to his plate. "Why did you make up that elaborate lie for Reverend Vermin, about them being a refugee family? Why didn't you tell him...?"

"The truth?" Fran said.

"I don't know what you should have told him, but I was surprised you told him they were coming to live with you. You said they might be at the funeral. How are you going to explain that away when the time comes?"

"Who said it was a lie?"

"What are you talking about, Mom?" John asked.

"They are coming to White Lake and moving in – just not with me. I'm moving out."

Fran placed her purse on the floor next to her chair. None of them said a word.

"I'll explain. I've made some decisions and I should make you aware of them."

"Please do," John said.

"Your father asked me to take care of them. He didn't ask, he told me I should. I've thought about it and if that is what he wants, then that's what I'll do. It makes sense they come here, since there is no way I can help them down there, and I'm sure their prospects are not good without your father's infusion of cash."

"So why not just infuse them with a little cash a couple of times a year; like Dad must have done?" John said.

"I could, but think about it. Just the other night you agreed none of you feel like you ever belonged at our dinner table. I didn't either. So why not replace ourselves with your father's other family. While we're at it, let them take our place at church, in school, and anyplace else they care to be where we've gone before. I don't want this house and they do; at least I presume they do. I don't want to live anywhere near here and they would love it I'm sure. So why not let them have it –take it off our hands so we don't feel any responsibility to come back."

"You mean you want them to take over Dad's legacy?" Peter asked.

The waitress placed the pizza on a stand in the middle of the table. The family waited impatiently for her to leave.

"Can I get you anything else?" she said.

They waved her off.

"I couldn't have said it better. That is the term for which I've been searching the last few days. Just like they are taking over our dinner table – and by the way, none of you have bothered to take those pictures off the table so we could have it back – I want them to take over your father's legacy. Let them be his family."

"This is far out," Thomas nodded, affirming his pleasure with his Mother's somewhat twisted plan. "It would be like a total erasure."

"Get serious, Thomas!" Peter said. "What if I don't want to be erased from his legacy?"

"You would have that choice. You could still come back if you wanted."

"I'm supposed to come back and stay at a hotel and compete with Dad's new family?" Peter shook his head.

"Would you want to come back, if I wasn't here?"

"I don't know, but it would be nice to have the option."

"That isn't on the table, Peter. I'm not staying here. I don't know where I will go, but I'm not living the rest of my life under your father's shadow."

"What about the house? Are you just going to give it to them?" John asked.

"That is the plan. Of course they will have to get established so they can manage the expenses. That shouldn't be too difficult if they own it free and clear."

Fran dished out the pizza.

"Can you afford to do that?" Sammy asked.

"Your father...I mean the boy's father's miserly ways left me with more money than I will ever be able to spend. I can not only give them the house, I can set up a fund the church can administer so they can learn the language and find work so they can become self-sufficient."

"Is Richard's practice sold?"

"I signed the papers about a month ago. A young couple, both of whom are Doctors, had been practicing there for a couple of years while your father phased out. It was all arranged by your father a few years ago. You see, there is nothing holding me to this town and this house."

"How do you know they want to come?" John asked.

"To the funeral?"

"That too, but more important, to live in this country?"

"They've agreed to come to the funeral. I haven't yet broached the possibility of their moving here."

"You don't speak Spanish, Mother," Peter said. "I've heard you on the phone with them."

"It so happens that Marcia speaks Spanish. She lived in the Dominican Republic for three years as a Peace Corps volunteer, in the mountains, not far from where they live. She called them for me yesterday and served as my interpreter."

Fran wiped her mouth with the napkin.

"They have a telephone?" John asked.

"No, my understanding is a store in the town down the mountain from where they live does. Marcia left a message and we called back a few hours later and they were on the line. Interesting how primitive it all seems. I don't know what your father did in that environment. He was so helpless around our house."

"And they agreed to come?" John asked.

"After they got over their wailing."

"Wailing?"

"Yeah, you should have heard it. The woman started screaming at the top of her lungs. Quieted down a bit after we invited them to come to the funeral, but then started all over again just before we hung up."

"Aren't they required to have visas to get into the country?" John asked.

Thomas took another piece of pizza. "This is good pizza."

"They are, but Marcia knows people down there. She talked to a friend of hers at the consulate and they explained to her that it is possible to place visas on the fast track, it being to attend a relative's funeral and all. That sounds odd to be referring to them as relatives. Anyhow, they thought they could guide them through the process and make it happen."

"That would only allow them to stay for thirty days and it wouldn't give them green cards. I hope you aren't planning to have them stay in the country illegally?" Peter said.

"My understanding is if they have sponsors and promises of jobs, they can make that request while they are here. I don't know all the details. They may have to go back and then return under a different visa. But Marcia's contact said it could happen."

"I can't believe Marcia went along with this. Why would she help you throw away your life?" Peter looked at his mother.

"I didn't say she agreed with me. That isn't her job. She did understand why I wanted to do this and was willing to spend a whole day on Sunday making calls for me. She may be the professional, but it is my life and my choice."

"Did she question you at all about your mental state?" Peter asked.

"She did. She also warned I shouldn't make any rash decisions. Look, I know this decision seems like it hasn't been thought out. However, I assure you I have thought plenty about it and I'm going to do this. It feels right to me; like an escape door that will allow me to live the rest of my life unencumbered."

Fran reached for her purse and took out her wallet.

"What about Dad? People will figure it out in the end," Peter said.

"I didn't do this to your father. He did it to himself. Besides, I don't know if they will figure it out. People have always wanted to believe the best about your father. They'll convince themselves they are fruits of his mission work and will be happy to have them. White Lake Reformed Baptist Church doesn't see very many converts. This will give them an entire family."

"Now you sound like Thomas."

"Hell of a way to do mission work," Thomas said. "There is precedent for this kind of evangelism. The Spanish conquistadors were said to have impregnated hundreds of Indian women in South America with Christian babies. Our father was just a little off with his timing."

"You are having a hay day with this, aren't you?" Peter said.

"You will have to excuse me for finding this plot delicious. You couldn't write better stuff if you tried. Family replaces itself with father's bastard family and finds new lease on life. Maybe we should stage an accident and make them all believe we've died."

"Be serious, Thomas!" Peter rolled his eyes. "If you are capable of such a mature feat."

"I am. This is a plot worthy of being published. Consider the satisfaction of the reader as they experience unadulterated justice being carried out in such a Machiavellian way. Readers love it when people get what they deserve. It makes them feel safe in the world. Maybe there is a God after all. There could be no better justice than for our self-righteous father to have this as a humbling legacy. He must be rolling over in his casket. I'd like to peek in there and watch him squirm."

"Won't any of you miss this place?" Peter looked away from Thomas and toward his mother. "We can't just erase it from our memory." He looked at John. "Say something. You've been quiet this whole time."

"What is there to say? It's Mom's decision," John said. "If this is what she needs to move on and have a life, then I'm all for it."

"Don't you think she should go about things in a little more rational manner?" Peter leaned forward begging for understanding with his eyes.

"Change is a hard thing to pull off, Peter. Mom is trying to change her life after doing things the safe way for sixty years. If she feels she has to act in a radical fashion to break her patterns, then so be it. Her thinking seems rational to me, given the huge task she has given herself of remodeling her life."

"But what about Dad?"

"Alright, I'm exhausted." Fran stood. "John, you need to get to the airport to pick up Myrna. Peter, is Sandy coming with the children? I would like it if they could be here." Fran put $20 on the table as a tip for waitress.

"They are. I've been promising to take them to the circus. This soap opera might just get me out of taking them to the real thing. To answer your question, they are coming on Friday."

"It looks like we will all be together. This is going to turn out to be a wonderful week."

The group stood with Fran. Thomas picked up the money and counted it.

"Jesus, Mrs. Money Bags. This is a hell of a tip." Thomas waved the cash in the air. "First you give away the house. Now you're working on giving away the store?"

"Imagine that, us and the VanderSantos in the same house." Peter made a fist and stuck out his thumb and pointer finger, making his hand look like a gun. He pointed it at his temple and pretended to shoot. "That should make for a wonderful time of mourning. I hope Marcia is available to translate. Does she make rice and beans as well?"

They walked toward the cash register.

"What the hell are we going to do all this time? I'm bored already," Thomas said.

Fran paid the bill, thanking the waitress for the wonderful service.

Thomas leaned close to the waitress and said, "Tell your father Wuss says hi."

The waitress shrugged her shoulders and made Fran's change.

"Be careful, Mom will put you to work," John said. "She has to get this place in shape for the Spanish armada."

"You, Thomas, are going to practice being nice to this beautiful young woman." Fran winked at Sammy. "Maybe you can convince her to become an official part of this family."

"I don't know. I'm considering a Spanish woman next. It seems to have worked for Dad."

Sammy grabbed Thomas' forearm with both hands and began to twist with her hands in opposite directions. He tried to escape, but it was of no avail. After a few seconds he writhed in pain. "Uncle! Uncle!" She let go.

Thomas looked at Fran and said, "She'll have to grow up first."

Fran gave the nod and Sammy grabbed his arm and twisted even harder.

Chapter 28

A Proposal

Sammy and Thomas went for a drive. They drove around White Lake and parked Puff on the side of the road. Thomas convinced Sammy to go out on the ice with him. There were a half dozen fishing shanties a hundred feet off the shore of the lake and he wanted to explore them. The first three doors they opened revealed stoic occupants watching their fish lines dropping through the small hole in the ice. The occupants of the first shanty drank their beer and ignored the intrusion. The occupants of the second shanty told them to "fuck off." The third shanty was occupied by a lonely old fisherman who invited them in, having spotted Sammy standing behind Thomas.

Behind the next door Thomas discovered the vacancy for which he had been searching. "Voila!" he stepped aside and guided Sammy through the door by putting the palm of his hand on her lower back and pressing as she passed through. They took a seat on the camp chairs they found leaning against the side of the shanty.

"Remember how we used to come out here late at night and hang out in these shanties? It was the perfect place to smoke pot. The pot used to fill the small space so you could just breathe it in."

"It wasn't the most comfortable place to screw, though. Standing up wasn't all it's cracked up to be," Sammy said.

"Yeah, when you have to worry about stepping in that hole in the ice."

"Lying down wasn't any better. Remember when my ass slipped into the hole. God, I thought I was going to have to have my butt amputated."

"I would have still kept you on as my girlfriend."

"How gallant of you."

"Mom and Julie think we're still not over each other and …"

"Stop!"

"But…"

"Stop, Thomas! I know where you are going with this conversation. Don't get me wrong, I want to have the conversation, it's long overdue. But we are not going to have it in this old fishing shed where we got high, stripped off our clothes, and had at it. Your mother isn't the only one that needs a fresh start."

"Where would you like to have it?"

"Not here. If we are going to have this conversation, it's going to happen in an adult place. We'll go out to dinner at a nice quiet place, have a glass of wine, eat a nice meal, and talk. I don't want to keep doing the same thing we've done for thirty years, Thomas. I've got to get off that train. It goes in circles."

"That's fine with me. Go ahead and make a reservation." Thomas took a spear he found in the corner and lowered it into the hole in the ice. He pretended to spear fish.

"No, you'll pick a place I will like and make the reservation. You will drive me there in your father's Cadillac, because adults don't drive their dates around in a rusted out old bus, even if it is vintage. You will open the doors for me, pull back my chair, and push it in behind me. You will tell me to order whatever the hell I want. You will also start and carry on the conversation without my leading you."

"And let me guess…"

"No, you won't pay. We'll split the bill. I want an adult relationship, Thomas. It's time for both of us to grow up. I'm a grown woman. I don't want to carry a man around on my back."

"I get the point. I'll pick you up at eight tomorrow night?" The spear slipped out of Thomas' hand. He watched it sink out of sight.

"Good, now let's get out of this frozen igloo before the owners get back and run their spears through us."

"Spearing is illegal in Michigan."

"And you think that means they don't do it? You are not the only person in the world who believes in breaking rules, Thomas."

"Don't go bursting my bubble. I'm not ready to be ordinary."

"Change is on its way, Thomas Vanderhuis. The women in this family are fed up and have had enough of the old ways."

"Alright, Sammy Obama."

Chapter 29

Zen Restored

John's drive to the airport in Grand Rapids was disconcerting. He was ambivalent about Myrna's arrival. On the one hand, he knew he missed her a great deal and couldn't wait to look into her brown eyes and wrap his arms around her warm body. He had thought about her often over the last five days, but had expunged the thoughts from his mind and filled the space with other more pressing concerns. On the other hand, he was comfortable with her absence from this venue. It allowed him to be himself in an unencumbered way, not having to worry about what Myrna was thinking or feeling.

A part of him didn't want Myrna to know him in this setting, where his strong emotions erupted within him, making him feel the lack of control he had tolerated during his years of youth. In so many ways he had regressed to that from which he had run away. He wondered what Myna would think about him. He was afraid she would lose respect and see him as a fraud. Would she even like him? How could she, if he didn't even like himself this way?

He needed more time without her; to undo his past and master these old triggered thoughts and feelings. Perhaps if she would have waited until after the funeral he would have felt different.

Racked with guilt over his resistance to the joy of Myrna's arrival, he allowed himself to experience the pain of the whip with which he chose to lash himself. *This is the woman I love. How can I detach from her after only five days? What kind of shallow person loses touch with his passion for his lover after such a short absence? A coward; that's who lets go of his loved one in order to face his demons of old without risk of repercussions. A little man with a weak heart that fears he isn't good enough for the love he has been granted by the beautiful gracious woman, who he believes doesn't know the truth about him. Why the hell is growing up so hard to do? Why doesn't fast forward ever work? It is the damn rewind button. Its access to past scenes never goes away. Those scenes are only a button away from being front and center in your consciousness.*

As John neared the airport, he prepared to fake his love for Myrna until he felt it. He would act the part, until his feeling caught up with his thoughts. This might seem dishonest on his part, but he thought otherwise. He knew he loved Myrna. The absence of those feelings from his present consciousness was not an indication the attachment had dissolved. It was being superseded by the intense emotions seeping out of the compartments in his mind where he had hidden them years ago. Without Myrna present, he was able to set aside his feeling toward her in order to focus his full attention on the haunting feelings of the past. Now that luxury was being taken away and he was struggling to introduce all these unacquainted feelings to each other, without offending either of the parties. His two halves were going to meet and he didn't want either to feel like he had been lying to the other.

He parked the car and walked toward the entrance to the terminal. He looked at his watch and picked up the pace. He entered and spotted her running toward him, leaving her bags next to the bench where she had been sitting. John hugged her, but was anxious about the bags being left. He disengaged. "Honey, we've got to get your bags. You know how it is after 911. They don't want you to leave them unattended."

"They can have them," she said, embracing him again.

He tolerated it a while longer. "We've got to get your bags Myrna."

She obliged, taken aback by his resistance to her warmth. Within minutes they were in the warm car and traveling toward the expressway with Myrna engaged in a one way conversation. As they passed the Alpine exit, she reached over to touch his head. He hadn't buzzed it in several weeks and it was starting to grow long enough for her to feel it. She wished he would let it grow to the length it was when they met. Her hands were always touching his hair back then and he loved it. The shaven look made him look serious, untouchable.

"What's wrong? You left me five days ago with the warmest embrace you have ever given me. Today you meet me with a body made out of cardboard. Are you unhappy I'm here?"

"I'm thrilled you're here." Not a lie – just his thoughts reflecting the feelings he knew were there, but couldn't find their way to the crowded stage of his mind.

"I hear your words, but I can't sense their legitimacy."

"You know how I get when we are separated for a while."

"Out of sight, out of mind?"

"Yes; I mean no. I..."

"It's okay. I understand. Its all these clothes I'm wearing to stay warm. You can't see it's me under all these layers. You think I look like a fat bag lady. It's what it feels like to be weighed down by all of this. I'll take a cotton sun dress in the heat of India over this any day. I'll let you take them off when we get to your Mom's house. When you get down to my beautiful brown skin, your memory will come back. Can we do it at your parent's house?"

"Do what?"

"Have sex? Now I'm really worried about you, John. It's one thing for you to not hear me talking about my trip. It is quite another matter when you miss my brazen sexual proposition. What is going on?"

313

"It's nothing."

"It is something. It's hurting my feelings."

"It is this place. I feel like I've regressed thirty years and I'm back to being an adolescent in my father's house. I don't like the way it makes me feel. I don't want you to see me like this."

She knew he wanted her to rescue him, but she refused. She needed him to keep talking, so she tightened her grip on her maternal instincts to soothe and let him stew in her silence.

He did. "There are a lot of uncomfortable memories in this place I thought I had mastered. It seems my father's death has opened my Pandora's Box and I'm consumed with what happened to me thirty years ago with these people I call family. I'm overwhelmed."

"You were there, in the room, when your father died?" Myrna pulled one leg under her bottom and turned toward John.

"You know about my father's dying?"

"I called your house when you weren't there to pick me up." She nodded. "I talked to your mother."

"I wasn't there. At least, I don't think I was. I thought he was alive when I left him. Peter discovered it when they came home from the movies."

"You didn't?"

"What? Kill him? Suffocate him with a pillow? Why would you ask me that?" John slammed his palm on the steering wheel.

"You were talking pretty crazy when I called you."

"I was feeling a bit crazy, but that doesn't mean I..."

"Fine, John. I just had to ask the question. I've never seen you distraught like that before. You are usually so Zen like."

"That's what I'm talking about. This place has stolen my Zen. I'm afraid you won't love me so much when I'm Zen less."

"Zen less," Myrna smirked. "Is that even a word?"

"You get my point."

"I do, and you haven't answered my question."

"What question?"

"My brazen sexual proposition! You haven't told me if you think we can desecrate your childhood bed in your parent's home."

"What happened to you on that plane? Did you watch a Richard Gere movie or something? You always get this way when you watch his movies."

"That is an outright lie, but as a matter of fact, I sat by him on the plane and he..."

"Now who is lying?"

"It would have made a good story, though. I was bored on the long flight. I started to think about the things you do to my body. That is why I accosted you like I did at the airport. I wanted to feel your skin against mine."

"That's nice to know."

"But now that we talk..."

"What? My lack of Zen has turned you off?"

"I wanted your body when I got off the plane; the rest of you could have waited. But this cold rejection is not endearing."

"Well..."

"It was a long flight, okay. You try fantasizing about me for ten hours and see if you wouldn't be ready to jump my bones after that." Myrna untucked her leg and stared straight ahead.

"You were saying."

"Now that I have you I can see that you need me more than I need you."

"I thought I was unresponsive?"

"You were, but you don't need me for sex, you need me to get your Zen back."

"That's ridiculous!"

"Is it? Think about it. You always get your Zen from my body. I'm the source of your Zen. You come to me distraught and you leave me centered."

John considered it for a minute, but then decided it didn't matter. Even if she was right, he couldn't let her have this victory. "I don't think so."

"Very well then, let's get a hotel room and I'll prove it to you. One look at me without all these clothes and you'll be back. You will leave that hotel and the clerk will think he just saw Gandhi."

"How would he know what Gandhi looked like after having sex?"

"Now you're just being argumentative. Put your money where your mouth is."

"This is the oddest seduction in which I've ever been involved."

"You know I'm right."

"I've got a better idea. It will be dark by the time we reach White Lake. Why don't I introduce you to two-tracks?"

"Two-tracks?" She leaned over and intertwined her forearm with his, holding his hand in hers.

"They are little country paths created by trucks driving through fields often enough to form two tire tracks. High school kids use them at night to find privacy to make out and..."

"Can we leave the car running so it will stay warm?" Myrna turned up the heat and adjusted all the vents so they pointed at her.

"Trust me; you won't need any external source of heat. Our bodies will produce more than enough heat to keep the car warm. Remember, I've regressed to my adolescent days. I'm flooded with testosterone." John reached over and pointed the vent on his side of the dash back toward himself.

"Can we at least leave the overhead light on? You are going to have to see this body to get your Zen back."

"Now there's a change. The girl is supposed to want the light off. The purpose of the two-tracks is to get some privacy. You turn the lights off so no one comes looking."

"I don't think anyone is going to come looking in this weather. Besides, you always want the light on. I was just being accommodating. I need to win this bet."

"Oh, now it's a bet? How much are we wagering?"

"Winner gets to pick the next place."

"That is pretty chancy, in light of my predilection for risky sex in public places."

"I'm not worried. I'm certain I will win. Besides, your predilection for risky sex is a personal fantasy of yours."

"What are you talking about?"

"It is all talk. Even if given the chance, you would chicken out in real life."

"Hogwash!"

"Hogwash; what kind of word is that?"

"I'm telling you; I've regressed to my adolescence."

They drove toward White Lake through the back roads and when it became dark John pointed out the two-tracks. He let Myrna make the pick and they drove down it only a short distance to avoid getting stuck in the mixture of mud and snow that had been brought about by the thaw taking place that day. He stopped the car, put it in park, and turned off the engine. They talked for a short time. Myrna asked him about his two-track experiences in high school. He answered in a candid manner.

"You were a dog back then," she said as they climbed into the back seat of Richard's Cadillac. Myrna helped John undress her and then him. They devoured each other with passion. Their warmth filled the car with a moist warm air that settled on the windows, creating a sense of privacy as the full moon shone in the clear winter sky; penetrating the thin layer of fog covering the windows. They explored each other's bodies with their tongues as best they could in these cramped quarters. They were aware of how much they missed each other.

Myrna came in a long gentle way; raising her pelvis off the car seat so her legs could spread further. She held herself in that position as her body jolted with spurts of pleasure. John grasped her buttocks and pulled her toward him, helping her stay in this position that gave him such deep access to what seemed to him in the moment to be her uncensored soul. Overcome by the sight of her yearning for him to go deeper inside her, he reached the summit and let himself fall over the other side – free falling into erotic pleasure as he thrust himself in and out. Myrna mirrored his intense thrusts, absorbing the power of his jolts with her eager and receptive hips moving in concert with his. The result became a graceful dance where two bodies became one.

Spent, John let his body collapse onto Myrna's limp body, mixing their warm sweat. As their breathing slowed and lengthened, their bodies relaxed further, until it felt as though there was no distance between them. The boundaries that separated them were gone and they were one. They breathed each other in. As she exhaled, he inhaled. He exhaled, she breathed him in.

Lost in this moment, John began to hear a soft murmur. It called him back to reality. He recognized the sound. It was long and soft. It created a vibration throughout Myrna's body which made its way into his. "Hommmmmm...," Myrna's lips were closed when he looked, but it was obvious she was the source. He absorbed it, trying to ignore the inevitable. After a while, he lost his ability to control his response. The laugh began in his belly as it contracted in seizure like fashion. Myrna's stomach reacted in the same fashion, abruptly squeezing the hardness out of her. She attempted to continue with the 'hommmmm' which was broken by her laughing stomach. Their laughter spread throughout their bodies, culminating in a vociferous roar.

"It is true! You win! My Zen is back!"

"Say it! You have to say it."

"You are the source of my Zen. You center me."

"Thank you. Now let's get home to meet your family. I can't wait to tell them I made love to Gandhi on a two-track."

Chapter 30

Myrna's Introduction

"She's exquisite!" Fran said when she opened the door and discovered Myrna leaning against John, shivering from the cold. "It is so nice to have a tall woman in the family. The rest of us are so short."

"I'm glad you approve," John replied. "Wait until you get to know her."

They stepped inside the door and closed it behind them.

"I feel like I already have," Fran said. "We've had a couple of marvelous talks on the phone. We're going to get along just fine."

Peter came to the entryway but stood by silently, unable to compete with Fran's intensity.

"I think you are quite right." Myrna intertwined her arm with Fran's and walked her away from the door and further into the house. "Show me your house and tell me some stories about John. I'm getting to know a whole new side of him."

Fran introduced her to Peter who took her coat and purse.

"I would love to. What took you and John so long? I was expecting you an hour ago. Was the plane late?"

"No, John was just showing me some of his favorite sights." Myrna looked back at John and winked.

"He didn't take you on the two-tracks, did he? Those were his favorite sights, I'm told."

Their conversation was interrupted by the throwing open of the front door. Thomas burst through with Sammy close behind. "God damn it! It is cold out there."

"What are you talking about? It's Indian summer." John said.

"Who appointed you nature boy?"

"I'm just saying."

"Those fishing shanties are cold. You two should have taken a blanket," Fran said.

"How did you know where we were?" Sammy asked handing Thomas her coat.

"Lynn called and wondered if Thomas had gone crazy. She saw you walking out on the ice. I had to explain you used to sneak into the shanties when no one was watching and..."

"How did you know about that, Eddie?" Thomas threw his coat onto the small table in the entryway. Sammy came behind him and picked it up, hanging it in the coat closet along with hers.

"It is a small town, Thomas. People talk."

"You know your boys well," Myrna said, drawing everyone's attention toward the stranger in the group. "Two tracks? Fishing shanties? You kept your eyes on them."

"Oh, I don't think so. I didn't have a clue when they were growing up. But over the years people have told me what they saw and explained it to me. They got away with a lot. Richard had less of a clue than I did."

"Why is Dad's car so dirty?" Thomas pointed out the window toward the driveway.

"It's getting muddy out there," John said.

"Not enough to bathe the bottom half in mud like that." Thomas' eyes brightened. He wagged his finger at John. "You took her two tracking, didn't you? You little fucker. I take it this is your wife, Myr...Mry..."

"Myrna! Her name is Myrna," Fran said.

"You son of a gun! She hasn't been in town for twenty minutes and you..."

320

"Hi, I'm Myrna, your sister-in-law. It is a pleasure to meet you." She shook Thomas' hand and then moved on to Sammy. Having shaken Sammy's hand, she brought her eyes back to Thomas. "And since you are so boyishly curious, Thomas, the answer is yes. John took me two-tracking. I asked him to give me a good bonking in a hotel room, but he thought it more appropriate to show me his old stomping grounds." She paused a second and went on, "And the answer to your next question is also yes. It was exquisite...rather..." She placed her pointer finger on her lips and looked at John, "Zen like, don't you think John?"

"Thank God; another adult in the family!" Sammy swept Myrna away by locking arms with her and leading her toward Fran, who took Myrna's other arm. "When Sandy gets here, we'll outnumber them."

The women laughed and walked away to tour the house. Thomas looked at John with raised eyebrows. "Not bad, big brother. She is beautiful, intelligent, and best of all, a tart."

"They're right," Peter said. "When Sandy gets here they'll outnumber us. We'll have lost complete control."

"Who are you kidding?" John said. "The balance of power in this house shifted before we set foot in it four days ago. Mom is fed up with submission and she has joined the women's liberation movement. A few years late, but she is a firm believer now. You can't tell her anything."

"And now she has a posse!" Peter added.

Chapter 31

Peter Is Outed

Despite all the commotion, dinner was on time. Fried pork chops with mashed potatoes and green beans were on the menu. It was well received by the family and led to a splendid evening around the kitchen counter. The conversation centered on Myrna's history as she entertained the group with stories of her upbringing and her current life with John. The only hiccup came when Myrna asked why they weren't eating at the dinner table. "It's lovely in there and it looks so comfortable."

When the group stuttered, Myrna got the hint but struggled with how to back out of the conundrum she had created.

"We're going to use it to pick out photos for the funeral," Sammy said.

Myrna noted the table was full of pictures of Spanish people, but Sammy waved her off with a subtle shaking of the head that said, *you don't want to go there.*

That was combined with John's firm grip on her knee. "I'm sorry; I didn't know the dinner table topic was off limits. John can explain it to me later. Who wants to tell me stories about John? Let's get them all out, so he can begin to relax."

Thomas tested his new found sister-in-law to establish how hard she would push back. He teased her with an increasing level of offensiveness and discovered she was more of a natural born fighter than John. She masked her competitive instinct with her intelligent wit, which she displayed with the most courteous tone. Her slight Indian accent had a disarming affect. Much like the drawl of southern women, Myrna's accent made her sound loving and polite, even when she was cutting your legs out from under you. He was surprised John had chosen someone so unlike Fran; unlike how she used to be.

After dinner they played cards and taught Myrna how to play Euchre. Fran had learned to play when her maternal grandparents visited from the Upper Peninsula of Michigan. She had liked it so much she insisted on teaching it to her children. This began as an underground movement within the family; due to Richard's belief card-playing was a vice. But over time, when it became obvious to Richard what she was doing with the kids, for reasons unbeknownst to Fran and the boys, he decided to overlook this breaking of his rules. He rationalized it was a family tradition for Fran, and as long as they kept it within the family, it wouldn't lead to further gambling habits.

But on this day, just because they could, they decided to play for real money for the first time in family history. This was only true if playing for pennies constituted real gambling.

Myrna caught on fast and won the game. She relished her victory with a quiet fist pump and excused herself. She was tired from the long flight and needed to go to bed early. Thomas made a smart remark about her winnings, to which she responded by pushing her stack of pennies across the counter and leaving the pile in front of him.

"To what do we owe this generous act?" Thomas asked.

"I'm donating my winnings toward helping you replace that ghastly thing you call an automobile. It is sullying the front view of your mother's quaint home."

"It is a vintage automobile!" he said, wondering how she knew his weak spot.

"That is a lovely excuse, but the fact remains it is hideous. Good night." She turned to John. "Come find me when you are done talking about me with your family."

"We..." Fran was interrupted by Myrna.

"It's alright, Fran. Have at it. It is a necessary rite of passage when one joins a family. The family needs to have an opportunity to express their impressions. My family spent three hours expressing their impressions of John when they first met. Now it is your turn."

She turned and left for the bedroom. The instant she was out of the room, the group peppered John with questions and comments. Fran tried to stop them, but Thomas noted Myrna had given them permission.

"I think my life just got easier," Sammy said. "She will be helpful at these family gatherings." The family nodded in agreement. "I was proud of you, Peter."

"Proud of me? What for?"

"It's the first time your brothers have brought a woman into this house that you haven't spent time ogling her breasts."

"That isn't true!"

"I'm complimenting you Peter - on your new found ability to exercise self-control." Sammy said. "And it's not like she's flat-cheated."

Fran looked at Sammy with surprise, but when she noted Peter's minimal offense, she began to laugh. "I can't believe you talk like that to Peter."

"I'm sorry."

"Don't be. It's obvious you two have a long-standing history concerning this matter. I'm just surprised. I can't believe how much I've missed of you kids growing up."

"I'll fill you in, Fran." Sammy said.

"Please don't," Peter said. "Parents aren't supposed to know everything about their kids."

"Peter has this habit of looking down when girls make eye contact with him." Sammy ignored Peter's pleas. "It ends up he's staring at their breasts."

"He did this to you?"

"All the time!"

"That's it, I'm leaving," Peter stood up and left the room. They ignored him.

"So much so, I devised a signal to get him to look up and stop staring at my boobs."

"You call them boobs?" Fran crossed her arms, covering her chest.

"Sometimes."

"That's funny."

"He did it to John's girlfriends as well. Sometimes I would have to teach them the signal. That's if they were going to stick around for long." She glared at John.

They laughed at Peter's expense and went to bed. Thomas joined Sammy in the basement, so Peter had the upstairs to himself. Fran rationalized this would allow Peter, Sandy, and the kids to have the upstairs when they came.

John was surprised Fran was able to remove all evidence Richard had lived and died in the room in which he and Myrna were sleeping. He had taken for granted the room would be quarantined for a period, for emotional, not viral contamination. He felt no qualms when he entered the room. Myrna was asleep, so he laid next to her and fell asleep.

Chapter 32

The Frying Pan Technique

Wednesday was hump day. Plans for the funeral were finalized, including the town's council giving its permission for the casket to be carried from the church to the cemetery in a horse drawn carriage. The only stipulation was the family would be required to make arrangements for the removal of any horse excrements.

Fran met with Marcia and was encouraged by the update she received concerning the status of the VanderSantos' visas. Marcia found a great bit of humor in the family's nickname. She informed Fran that approval was almost a sure thing if they could get the money wired to the D.R. by Friday. Fran's look of surprise turned to resignation.

"You mean money for a bribe?" Fran said.

"That would be one way to put it. I prefer to call it the cost of expediting the matter."

Fran thought the matter over. She was about to respond when Marcia burst out laughing. "I'm just kidding. My friend said it was a done deal, waiting for signatures. You want this to happen, don't you? You were ready to break the law and cough up the cash."

"I do want this to happen. I feel like I'll be passing the baton or something like that."

"Like you will be getting a monkey off your back?"

"Yes. I'll get closure. Isn't that what you people call it?"

"It's an odd form of closure, but yes. You are hoping it will give you closure."

"Do you think it will work?"

"I don't know. We'll have to wait and see won't we? You had better go ahead and purchase the airline tickets."

"It's already done. I had faith in your magical abilities to make things happen."

"Good luck with that. Although... I might be more effective than God in situations like this. I'm not sure she would have been able to deliver like I did."

"She? You think God is a she?" Fran's jaw dropped.

"If there is a God, I believe she is female," Marcia said.

"Why?"

"Because women need someone up there who understands us," Marcia said. "Besides, if God created the world, she would have to be female. After all, we women are the creators." She pointed to her womb.

"It takes two." Fran thought for a while. "Maybe God is both – mixed up together."

"You mean god might have a penis and a vagina?" Marcia asked.

Fran blushed. It never occurred to her God would have one, let alone both. More surprising to her was the fact Marcia would say the words out loud. She wasn't about to speak them herself.

"That is what separates males and females, isn't it?" Marcia asked.

"Yes, but I meant God might emotionally be both a man and a woman."

"Oh, you didn't mean God might be a hermaphrodite?"

"What's that?"

"A hermaphrodite is a person who is born both a woman and a man; physically and emotionally."

"That would still mean God has a...and a..."

"Say it Fran," Marcia placed her hands on her knees and leaned forward. "Say the words penis and vagina."

"Why?" Fran pushed her lower lip outward. "I don't want to think God has either one of them."

"Why not?"

"Because they are...I don't know...dirty or something."

"I doubt that," Marcia said. "But the reason I would like to have you say the words is because sooner or later we are going to have to talk about sex and you need to be able to say the words penis and vagina in order to do that."

"Maybe when the time comes." Fran looked down and tilted her head. After a short pause she spoke again. "She did, you know."

"Who did what?"

"She answered my prayer."

"How's that?"

"Through you. God answered my prayer through you."

"Prayer!" Marcia threw up her hands."You can't really believe in it, but you can't argue anyone out of it either. There is always a rationalization to hold on to, if that is what you want."

"What? Are you mad at me for giving God the credit for your hard work?"

"Mad as hell! If a god had anything to do with making this happen, her name is Marcia." She patted herself on the back.

Fran stood up and grabbed her purse. As she headed toward the door, she turned around and proceeded to raise her hands and bow in Marcia's direction saying, "You are my goddess."

"Thank you!"

"I'll see you at the funeral. It is at two o'clock on Sunday afternoon."

"I don't recall..."

"I'm sure you will want a front row seat to witness your best client's closure ceremony. I would not want to go through this without my goddess in my corner. Besides, my family wants to meet you."

"This is the danger in playing God. Sometimes you create a monster without knowing it."

328

"I'm your monster. You are responsible. I'll see you at two on Sunday. Oh, ignore Thomas. He is sure to try and get under your skin. He dislikes therapists."

"I can handle the smart ass. It's the religious one I'm worried about. Now get out of my office before I charge you for a second session."

That afternoon Sammy recruited Myrna to help her get ready for her date with Thomas. They invited Fran to join them. Frustrated by her lack of wardrobe, they set out to the mall on a shopping spree and returned several hours later with three choices. Together the women decided which dress would work best. Once that was determined, they fussed about what to do with her hair. Sammy wanted it down, but Myrna and Fran convinced her to wear it up in a bun.

"It will thin out your face and make you look elegant," Myrna made her case. "I'll run to the florist and get some fresh flowers to put in it."

"It will show off your beautiful long neck and let your strong shoulders define the rest of your body." Fran joined with Myrna. "You'll see when it is finished. You will look thinner than you already are. Oh, and taller too."

"I'll bet my legs will stretch out and magically become long and slender, as well."

"I was just going to say that." Fran place her hand on her chest, glowing with self-satisfaction.

Myrna and Sammy looked at Fran with a mixture of surprise and admiration.

"Oh, I heard that on an Oprah show. They were doing a makeover on a homely young woman. Not that you are homely or anything. I mean…I…I'll just shut up now before I choke on my foot."

"Go on and choke on it. You are making me feel glamorous." Sammy put her arm on Fran's shoulder.

"Oh good. That's what I wanted you to feel because you are…you know…glamorous."

"Thanks, Fran."

"It feels like you are going to the prom tonight."

"I'm a bit old. Besides, I'm trying to turn this relationship into a grown-up affair."

"Prom?" Myrna looked to both of them.

Recognizing her confusion, Fran said, "A prom is a grand high school dance that juniors and seniors can attend. It takes place in the spring, just before the end of the school year. Everyone attends with a date of some sort."

"I see."

Turning to Sammy Fran said, "Isn't that what adults do in relationships; make up for past mistakes?" Fran turned back to Myrna. "In high school, Sammy and Thomas were sweethearts. Thomas refused to take her to the prom. He said it was dumb."

"It wasn't that big of a deal." Sammy scratched behind her ear.

"I could tell you wanted him to take you."

"I wanted him to want to take me. But he didn't and that was that." Sammy picked up the brush, looked in the mirror, and fussed with her hair.

"I wanted him to take you too. I even tried to convince him." Fran pulled both women toward the bed and sat down, pulling the girls down next to her.

"Why was that?" Sammy turned toward Fran and began to comb her hair.

"I thought if he took you, I might get to help you get dressed and do your hair. You know, seeing as you were over here all the time and you didn't get along with your mother very well. I thought it might be my one opportunity to have that experience with a daughter."

"I would have liked that." Sammy's eyes welled up with tears; as did Fran's.

"Well then," Myrna slapped her knees with her hands. "Prom night it is. I'll ask John to fetch me some flowers. Maybe I'll have a chat with Thomas on my way. We Indian women have ways to deal with this kind of man."

"And what is that?"

"A frying pan across the head."

The women laughed together. After a few moments Fran said, "I don't think that is an Indian tradition, my dear. I think it is a universal female instinct."

"Did you ever try it on your husband?" Myrna stood up.

"No, I was too nice for that. But my therapist suggested it might have worked a bit better than cooking him meals in it. She is not much of a believer in the power of the nice – unless you have a frying pan in one hand."

"Then it is settled. I'll ask him in a nice way before I whop him. Where might I find it?"

"It?"

"Yes, the frying pan? Which cupboard is it in?"

"Oh, the bottom cupboard to the right of the stove," Fran said.

The women laughed again and Myrna left the room.

"You don't think she is serious, do you?" Fran asked Sammy.

"I don't know, but I kind of hope she is. I like her."

At 7:30 the rest of the family sat down to a thick, savory beef stew. Sammy popped her head in and asked about Thomas' whereabouts. No one had any relevant information. They did, however, shower her with compliments over her attire. She modeled for them with repeated spins and a few provocative poses, which Myrna encouraged. The short and tight black dress, along with the high heeled dagger shoes made her look like she was all legs. She tossed her silk shawl to and fro seductively.

In the middle of the cat walk, a car horn pierced the sound of applause and whistles. Fran made her way to the kitchen window. She covered her mouth with surprise and ran over to Sammy, taking hold of her hand. "There is a limo outside."

She pulled Sammy by the hand to the living room and the rest of the family followed. They crowded around the picture window and stared at the stretched luxury car. A tuxedo sporting driver got out and walked around to the back side door. He opened it and stepped aside.

When no one appeared, the family's curiosity was stoked. They would have been concerned, except for the fact the driver stood by waiting. After thirty seconds, a tall, thin, handsome figure dressed in a gaudy purple tuxedo stepped out of the car. He lifted a bottle of champagne in one hand and two glasses in the other, as he walked toward the front door. They made him knock before Fran opened the door.

"Good evening, Mrs. Vanderhuis. I'm here to pick up Sammy."

Fran lunged toward him and embraced him in a hug.

"Please, Mrs. Vanderhuis. You are wrinkling the suit," Thomas said.

"Is he taking her disco dancing afterwards?" Peter said.

"If that's what the lady desires," Thomas said.

Sammy walked over to Thomas and he reached out his hand. She placed her hand in his. Thomas bent over to kiss her on the lips. Sammy rose onto her toes and kissed him back, bending one knee, lifting her foot off the ground.

The family fussed over them, asking a multitude of questions about the limo, where they were going for dinner, and of course, the origins of the dance ball purple tuxedo. As they prepared to leave, Fran approached Thomas and ran her hand over his hair, probing with her fingers.

"What are you doing, Eddie?" Thomas asked. "You're fucking up my ponytail."

Fran looked at Sammy who answered the question for her. "She's checking for lumps."

The women laughed, leaving the men at a loss. Fran winked at Sammy. "Guess what, Sammy. There are none. He is here of his own accord." She took a firm grasp of Thomas' pony tail and pulled him down to her level. She whispered in his ear, "Don't mess this up."

The couple walked out the door and got into the limousine, while the rest of the family watched out the window. Myrna stood next to Fran, took hold of her hand, and squeezed. "Your therapist is a wise woman. Nice, coupled with a frying pan in one hand, works quite well."

"Thanks, Myrna."

"You are welcome, Mom. But let's keep this between you and me. John doesn't like me using my match-making instincts. He says it just causes trouble."

"Does it?"

"It worked on him, didn't it?"

"And well, I might add."

Chapter 33

The Counter Proposal

Thomas took Sammy to the Arboreal – a quaint upscale dining place just south of Muskegon. She was delighted with his choice, since it mixed simplicity with elegance. The hostess brought them to a table to the side of the fireplace, with a clear view of the wintry evening. They chose a wine. Thomas had already placed an order ahead, knowing Sammy's favorite dish, Beef Wellington, needed advanced preparation. As the waitress placed a basket of breads before them, Sammy said, "I'm starved. Your mother's beef stew has been tempting me all afternoon."

"We'll have it for lunch tomorrow."

They ate their meals in a pleasant silence, interrupted for thoughtful short discussions. Sammy was pleased with how comfortable it was for her to be with Thomas. *Have we outgrown the one up-man-ship we've used to manage our relationship all these years?* Sammy realized throughout dinner how attached she was to Thomas. She wondered if he felt the same. She would have asked him, but she knew his answer wouldn't help. Her doubts would have to be removed with time – time filled with actions that offset her memories of the past.

"Thomas," she began. "It has to be different this time around. This is our last chance and we can't waste it doing the same routine we have used for the past twenty-five years."

334

"I know, but this is a good start don't you think?"

"It is a wonderful gesture on your part and I appreciate it. But it has to go further than a simple gesture."

"What do you have in mind?" Thomas wiped his mouth with his napkin, returning it to his lap when he was finished.

"I'm not moving out to Arcada; at least not right away. We've done that twice now and it doesn't work."

"So how are we going to have a relationship?" Thomas reached over and put his hand on top of hers.

"You are spending the summer in Chicago with me. This time you are leaving your comfortable nest and coming to spend some time in mine."

"Jesus Christ, Sammy..." He removed his hand from hers.

"I'm not negotiating here, Thomas." Sammy leaned forward. "This is a take it or leave it offer. I need to see you can give up for me, this time. You are coming to Chicago for the summer. There is plenty of art in the city, so you won't get bored."

"But I don't know the city and the people. Besides, I don't like big city life." Thomas took his fork and knife and began to cut off a large piece of his meat.

"Then you'll have time to miss me and think about me while I'm at work. And you'll be able to give me the attention I deserve when I come home. Besides, I know the city and it won't hurt you to be dependent on me. It will teach you to share power with me in this relationship."

He savored the tender bite of meat. "God this is good meat."

Sammy crossed her legs under the table. She raised her foot and began to rub Thomas' shin with it.

"I suppose you're right. It might do us some good. It might even do me some good to uproot myself. I've been pretty anchored for a long time now."

"And Thomas..."

"There is more?"

Sammy placed her foot behind Thomas' leg and tugged him forward. "We are going to couples counseling – preferably a sex therapist."

"Come on Sammy!" Thomas pushed himself back from the table. "Is that necessary? Look what it has done to Eddie."

Sammy put her pointer finger up to her mouth. "Shh..." She reached for his leg with her foot. "My point exactly! It has done her a great deal of good."

"She left my father!"

"Which she should have done a long time ago."

"Granted, but you aren't trying to leave me. We're trying to stay together."

"A lot of people think I should stay away from you. I'm not one of them. However, I'm not trying to stay together. I want us to grow together and become for each other what we have failed to be for all these years."

"We've been good for each other, haven't we? I mean at least some of the time?" Thomas gulped his wine.

"Drawing me naked isn't enough anymore. It never was. After talking with Julie, I figured out it wasn't me. You have been this way in all of your relationships. I want more. I don't want you to paint me; I want you to fuck me!"

Thomas put his pointer finger up to his lips. "Shh..." In a loud voice he said. "That's pretty inappropriate language for a setting like this. These people are conservative Christians. They are liable to kick us out if you keep using that kind of language."

"Fuck you, Thomas! I am taking my audience into consideration, speaking your language so you can understand."

"How would you say this in your language?" Thomas settled into his chair.

"I'd say I want you to desire me. I want you to make love to me because you are so thrilled you want to crawl inside my skin and get as close to my heart as you can be."

"I can say that." Thomas slapped the top of the table.

"I know you can say it. I also know you can mean it. My question is can you bring yourself to do it with me on a consistent basis?"

"You think a sex therapist can help us with that?" Thomas took an exaggerated gulp of his wine.

"I just know we haven't been able to do it on our own."

They finished their dinner and enjoyed the limousine ride back to White Lake, nursing a glass of wine while cuddling in the luxurious seat. As they approached White Lake, Sammy asked Thomas to tell the driver to drop them off at her mother's house. Thomas questioned her reasoning and wondered how they would get home. Sammy dismissed his questions with a promise to explain when they got there and informed him they would enjoy walking home in the cold night air.

Thomas paid the limousine driver who drove off as they made their way through the unplowed walkway toward the front door of Sammy's childhood home. Thomas went to look for the key hidden under the planter, but Sammy told him not to bother. "She hasn't locked this door for a good many years." They walked in and Sammy waved off Thomas' attempt to find the light switch. "I don't want to wake her."

"What's the point of coming here if you aren't going to wake her?"

Sammy grabbed his hand and led him through the maze of the messy house. She led him into the living room where the light from the television flittered and lit the room in an unpredictable manner. The sound was turned down so far it gave the impression someone was just watching the pictures. Sammy's mother lay sprawled out on a tilted recliner, one leg hanging over the armrest, with her head falling off the other side of the leather chair. The position pried open her robe revealing enough of her body for Thomas to see she was naked under the robe. Sammy walked over and forced the robe closed to spare both of them the unappealing sight. A bottle of whiskey sat empty, next to a half finished drink in a tall glass.

"I stopped trying to wake her up when I got into eleventh grade. Instead, I made sure I didn't wake her so I wouldn't have to deal with her drunk."

Thomas surveyed the scene in silence.

"Thomas, my mother is an alcoholic. She has been since I was a young child."

"I know. Well, I didn't know she drank like that when you were a kid, but I knew she was a drunk while we were in high school and I knew you stayed away from home because of it."

"You knew?" Sammy removed her high heels and carried them in one hand.

"Of course I knew. Everybody knew."

"Why didn't you say something? Why didn't you talk to me and try to comfort me? Didn't you realize how difficult she was for me?"

"You didn't bring it up, so I thought you didn't want to talk about it. That was how I tried to comfort you."

"By not noticing my mother was a fucked up drunk?" Sammy's jaw dropped. "Did it ever occur to you to talk to me about it? I mean, I talked to you about your father?"

"I brought my father up to you. I made it clear I needed to bitch to you about him. You never asked me for that with your mother."

"Don't get me wrong, Thomas. I'm not blaming you. I'm just trying to understand where you were coming from. I didn't bring it up and I didn't do so because I didn't want to talk about her. I needed to, but I didn't want to. I just wanted to pretend your family was mine."

"I never did understand why you wanted my family, when I was doing my best to get the hell away from them. I guess at some level, I figured your family was more fucked up than mine and that made me feel safe with you. Come to think about it, that's what made you feel safe with me as well. It was a mutual agreement. I wasn't about to judge you for your family. That would mean you wouldn't judge me for mine."

They strolled into the living room and sat down at the table.

"I want to thank you for that, Thomas. It is what I needed at the time. It was all I could handle. But I didn't bring you here just to thank you. I also brought you here because I want to tell you I need more now. I need you to not only notice my mother for who she is, I also need you to acknowledge her to me. I need you to understand what happened to me in this house."

"Why is that so important to you after all these years?"

"Because it's part of me. You can't understand me, if you don't know what my life was like when I was growing up. It was awful Thomas; watching her do this to herself, to my father, and to me every night. As a kid I thought she hated me and wanted to get away from me. I thought she got drunk because she couldn't stand me and at the same time she couldn't leave me. Her solution was to get lost in her drunken state. I couldn't understand why she didn't want to be with me. I kept asking myself, Am I that bad? Am I that awful to be with? I just couldn't figure it out, so I decided to try my luck with another family. You know, to see if they would do the same thing with me. I ..."

Thomas reached out his hands and held Sammy's. "I think I know why you brought me here."

"Why is that?" Sammy squirmed in her chair but held on to his hands.

"I think you want me to know why it is not going to work for you, to have me leaving you to smoke pot every evening."

Sammy started down the path of tears she knew would lead to her sobbing out of control. It had been her greatest fear all these years. If she let herself talk about her mother in full detail, she would plunge into a river of tears from which she would never emerge. Thomas hugged and encouraged her to go there, promising to go with her. He gave her the time she needed, before she could talk again. He wanted to speak, but he knew it was time for him to wait.

In time, she was ready. "I need you to want to be with me. When you smoke pot you leave me. I know you are going to say it is not why you do it. That if anything is true, you are trying to get away from yourself. But I feel abandoned and I probably always will, because this is what I grew up with." She pointed at her mother. "Look, I'm not a prude. I'm not saying you can't ever do it again or that I won't do it with you on occasion. But I need to know on a regular basis that you like me when you're not stoned. I need to know you don't want to get away from me. You can't prove that to me with your words. You need to prove it to me with your actions."

"Is that what the sex is about?"

"It is. I don't want you to fuck me." She smiled a tad. "Once in a while a good old fashion fucking would be in order. But on a regular basis I want you to desire me for who I am. I want you to seduce me with your presence. Your wanting to be with me is what turns me on more than anything else; even more if you are willing to see me."

"I can do that. I mean to say I want to and I am willing to give it my best effort. I'll come to Chicago. I'll go to couples counseling. I'll be with you."

"Because you want to be?"

"More than I think I've ever known."

They walked home in the cold winter night, never letting go of each other. They arrived at the darkened house and Thomas led her down to the basement, never turning on a light. He helped her out of her dress and tucked her into the bed. He kissed her good night and she fell asleep. Thomas went into the room next door and painted till dawn broke his concentration.

Sammy woke in the morning. After going to the bathroom to freshen up, she entered Thomas' painting room to turn off the light. She found him asleep, in an upright position as though he was staring at the painting on the easel before him. She sat down and snuggled up to him; wrapping her arm around his and laying her head on his shoulder. As she did,

340

she noticed what he was looking at when he fell asleep. On the easel, she saw the most beautiful painting of herself. She was clothed in the dress she had worn the night before; her hair back in a bun with the flowers Myrna had placed in her hair. The shoes were replicas, as was the makeup she had lavished on her face. She looked on amazed, wondering how he could have done this from memory. Then she saw the eyes. She didn't know why, but she could see sadness in them. There were no tears; her eyes were beautiful; but she could tell the painter knew there was sadness hidden in them.

She was going to wake him to thank him, but chose instead to disentangle herself and leave. She wanted the experience of having him show it to her so she left unnoticed, allowing him to chose the method of unveiling. As she left him sleeping on the chair staring at his painting of her with his eyes closed, she realized he had been with her. He had noticed her. And after seeing her as she was, he chose to stay up all night and paint her. She knew he had seduced her all over again.

Chapter 34

Confessions

The funeral was planned, except for the reception at the church following the funeral. Fran spent an hour on the phone helping coordinate the simple affair while the boys and Sammy played Euchre. When John saw her frustration, he asked her about it. She blamed the snags on Marilyn Voss. There was a dispute concerning the menu.

"Don't they always serve the same thing?" John laid down the high trump card, ruining Thomas' attempt to Euchre Peter and him going solo.

"Let me see," Thomas flipped John the finger. "Ham and cheese on white potato rolls, potato salad, cole slaw, pickles, olives for special occasions, and a variety of homemade square pan cakes."

"Don't forget the butter on both sides of the potato rolls," Peter shuffled the cards.

"And the German chocolate cake," John said. "That was my favorite."

"So why all the fuss, Mother?" Peter dealt the cards. "The menu is set in stone."

"Marilyn Voss is in charge and she likes to pretend to offer choices to the family of the deceased," Fran said. "When they ask for something different, she starts to explain why it would be too much work. The whole charade takes a couple of hours to work its way through the system over the phone lines. All I asked for was a little turkey to go with the ham, you know, to give healthy people that option."

"You should ask for beans and rice for our Dominican brothers and sisters," Thomas said. "I'm going alone again. I'm going to Euchre you bastards if it takes me all day."

"Excuse me." Sammy threw down her cards. "Your partner would like to play."

"Oh, trust me," Fran said. "She was hinting around about our Spanish guests – wanting to know who they were and why they were coming."

"Hearts is trump," Thomas announced.

"What did you tell her?" Peter winked at John after looking at his cards.

"The same thing I told the Vermin – I mean the Reverend Vermin." She glared at Thomas.

"That they are a refugee family?" Peter nodded for John to lay down the first card.

"That's my story and we're all sticking to it."

"I hope no one asks me," Peter said.

"Why, what will you say?" Thomas gathered the first trick.

"I don't know. I just hope no one asks me."

"It would be ironic, wouldn't it?" Thomas laid down the jack of hearts. He looked at John and Peter, pointing at the table where he expected them to lay down whatever trump they had.

"What's that?" Peter threw down the jack of diamonds in disgust. John shrugged his shoulders and tossed out a queen of spades.

"If you were the one to betray Dad's secret." Thomas looked at Peter. "It would make sense for me to be all over this one, but I'm okay with having it slip out in due time."

Thomas laid down the last three cards in his hand. They were all trump.

"I told you I would Euchre you little fuck-ups."

With a smile stretching from one of his ears to the other, Thomas changed the subject.

"I've got a surprise for everyone. Meet me in the living room."

"Not until we get our mess cleaned up!" Sammy said. "Everyone has to pitch in."

Peter picked up the cards, Sammy and John took the dishes to the sink, and Thomas left for the living room. When they finished they wandered into the living room where they found Thomas standing next to a chair draped with a white sheet. They resisted their desire to rush the show along, waiting without question, knowing Thomas was in charge of this affair and he wouldn't be rushed. Fran joined them, still carrying a kitchen towel. She tossed it over her shoulder.

"What's this all about, Thomas?" Fran said. "I've got to finish the dishes."

Thomas walked over to the chair and was about to pull off the sheet when Myrna walked in still steaming from her shower. She wore a silk robe that stuck to her naked body where she hadn't dried herself well enough. She was rubbing her head with a towel at a frantic pace.

"What's going on in here," she said.

The group became silent and the boys looked down at the ground.

"What, I'm not invited to the party?" She put one hand on her hip.

Sammy lowered her eyes toward Myrna's chest. Myrna looked down and discovered her robe had fallen open above her waist and one of her large dark nipples was exposed.

"Sorry." She closed her robe and wrapped her arms around her chest. "Didn't mean to give you all a peep show." She sat down next to John. "Let's get on with it now. My show is over." She looked at Thomas who was still standing next to the sheet draped chair. "Let's have a look at what's under that sheet."

Thomas shook his head while he gathered himself. "I don't know if this can compete with what we just saw," he said. Then he turned and with one swift long stroke he pulled the sheet off of the chair, revealing his painting of Sammy.

There was a quick gasp for air by the group, which they exhaled with a long, slow "Ahhh…"

"It is beautiful, you look gorgeous Sammy." John was the first to react.

"You have clothes on!" Peter marveled, leaving the family wondering whether he was surprised or disappointed.

"Did I miss something here?" Myrna placed one of her elbows on the armrest and leaned on it while her open palm faced upwards. "Is there a call girl career in Sammy's history of which I've been spared the knowledge?"

The family laughed. "No, nothing like that. But my goodness, Myrna; why would you jump to that conclusion?" Fran asked.

"John will attest to the fact I don't like to be left out. Sorry, just an overreaction – my personal pet peeve." She crossed her legs, intertwined her fingers, and placed them over her exposed knee.

"That's quite all right, dear. Thomas has painted nude portraits of Sammy since they met in high school. It has something to do with sex – or not having sex – I'm not sure which."

Thomas was shocked his mother knew this. "Who told you that, Eddie?" He looked at John.

"Don't look at me." John raised both of his hands in front of his face. "I'm the one in the family who keeps secrets."

"I haven't been oblivious to everything for the past forty years," Fran said. "I know some things."

"What else do you know?" Myrna uncrossed her legs and then re-crossed them in the opposite direction. She swung her foot in and out.

"Peter admired them."

"I admired what?" Peter looked at Fran.

"You admired her breasts."

"Mother!" Peter said.

"It's true." Fran looked at Myrna. "He admired her breasts. This is the first time he noticed her face. You know; with her breasts covered by the clothing," Fran finished her explanation.

"Well, she does have fantastic breasts." Myrna winked at Sammy.

"That's it! I'm out of here!" Peter stood and stomped past Fran.

Fran grabbed him by the arm. "Don't leave Peter. It is all just in fun. You were just a boy. All boys stare at women's breasts. Besides, it wasn't like Sammy kept them hidden around this house. With that itsy bitsy teeny tiny polka dotted bikini she always wore – I even caught your father staring at her a couple of times."

"Now, I'm leaving." Sammy stood to join Peter.

"Count me in, too!" the others pretended to join her.

"Stop! All of you! Sammy, you had a nice body and you didn't mind if it showed. There was nothing wrong with that. But there is a certain amount of collateral damage that comes with any decision. Your boyfriend's male family members were bound to look once in a while. But for the sake of family sanity, from now on I'll keep the rest of my knowledge of the past to myself. I promise. I just wanted to let you know I knew more than you kids suspected."

The family sat back down. "So if you knew so much about what was going on, Eddie; why didn't you do anything to stop Dad?" Thomas looked her straight in the eyes.

"Wow! I didn't see that coming." Fran squirmed.

"Is there a better time to ask the damning question we all want to ask?"

"Your timing is fine. But a little discomfort on my part is reasonable, don't you think?"

"I can give you that." Thomas sat back in his chair.

"Mom, you don't have to answer," John said. "Thomas is being self-indulgent."

"No, I do. He is not being self-indulgent; he is being honest about what he needs to know in order to forgive me."

"Thomas doesn't forgive, Mother," Peter said. "That isn't why he is asking the question."

"I think I know my sons pretty well after forty years. He is not as hard-hearted as he wants us to believe. It is a legitimate question you all have asked yourselves at one time or another; I'm sure of that."

"Fine," Peter said. "Give into him once again."

"I've thought about this question for a long time, Thomas. And before I try to answer it, I want you to know I have agonized about not stepping in between you and your father. I should have stood up and confronted him, but I didn't. I'm sorry and I will always feel like I let you down. I was the adult and you were just kids. I should have stopped him." Fran's eyes welled up with tears. Everyone, except Thomas, leaned toward her; revealing their willingness to understand before she explained. Thomas stared on with a stone cold face.

"The first part of my answer is I was afraid of your father. I don't know why, but I was. When I think back to how I felt, I don't know what I was so worried about. I mean, what was he going to do? Divorce me? Kill me? He didn't believe in either of those things. He never hit me. He didn't go after you kids physically either. I mean he spanked you, but he didn't beat you."

Sammy handed her a box of Kleenex. Fran blew her nose, honking like a goose.

She went on. "But his words were like stones that knocked the life out of me and left me unconscious. The look of rage on his face; I can still see it as if he were standing here before me. His eyes looked like those of a madman. He didn't have to hit me to make me believe he would. I don't know. I can't explain what happened to me to make me so afraid of him. The best I can come up with is it must have been a slow process, where he convinced me I was dependent on him and couldn't live without him. All I can say is I was terrified of him."

"What is the second part of your answer?" Thomas demanded to the chagrin of the others who were empathizing with Fran.

"I think I did do some things to try to minimize your father's rage toward you. You didn't see them because they were subversive. I didn't know I was doing them until Marcia pointed it out to me."

"What kind of things?" Thomas asked.

"Small things to appease his rage. I would try to please him so he wouldn't have a reason to be angry. I would spend my entire day trying to predict what he would need when he came home and made sure he had it. I jumped when he demanded something, even if I thought it was unreasonable because I didn't want him to get angry and start in on you kids. When I think back, almost everything I did was in one way or another trying to divert his rage – trying to keep the dam from bursting and drowning you kids."

"And yourself." Thomas pointed out.

"And myself." Thomas gave her a few seconds of reprieve and she used them to wipe away her tears.

"It sounds like an excuse to me." Thomas was surprised to find tears running down his own cheeks.

"It isn't meant to be an excuse. It is meant to be an explanation of my behavior that allows you to know I did love you all."

"But still..."

"I know I fucked up, Thomas!"

"Mother!" Peter said.

"I fucked up Peter. It is just a word. I'm using it because it is what I think Thomas needs to hear. It is the only language he trusts and I want him to know how sincere my anguish is. It is the best I can do. It is all I can do." Fran got up. She stepped in front of Thomas and wiped the tears off his cheeks. "I wish you didn't have so many of these locked up inside of you. Maybe now you can start to let them out. Your father never learned to do that. He insisted on keeping them inside. You don't want to make the same mistake." She walked out of the living room and into her kitchen. There was always food to be prepared.

"What is your problem?" Peter stood up and looked down on Thomas.

"I don't know. Something inside me won't allow me to let her off the hook."

John joined in the reprimand, but attempted to turn it toward a more productive end. "She was in this with us. Didn't you hear her? She was as afraid as we were, maybe more."

"Afraid of what? She was an adult. We were kids."

"She was afraid for us. She was lost in her efforts to appease him so he would let up on us."

"I don't buy that. What is so hard about making him the dinner he wanted or making sure he had a cold glass of water when he wanted it?"

"You asshole! Don't you get it? She slept with him. She had sex with him so he wouldn't take out her rejection on us!" John said.

"How do you know that?"

"I just do, alright?"

"Why didn't she say that?"

"Thomas, I don't even think she knows it yet. She and Marcia will have to get to that. Just use your common sense."

"I didn't think they had sex."

"She got pregnant, didn't she? When she was almost forty, don't you remember? Besides, every child thinks their parents don't have sex."

"God, I don't even want to think about that. I still don't know why you know so much about this. Did she tell you?"

"No! I told you! I don't think she even realizes why she did it."

"I don't buy it."

"Fine; I'll tell you how I know." John sat up in his chair and stared Thomas in the eyes. "I heard them."

"Heard them having sex?"

"Yes, I heard them having sex."

"What were you doing creeping around when Mom and Dad were having sex?"

"When I was seven or eight years old, I came downstairs to get a drink of water. I heard Mom crying. I went to their door and listened. The next night, I came down again to listen. I thought Dad was hurting her. I did that night after night, but I never heard them fight. I only heard strange noises and then when it became silent, I heard Mom crying. It took me a long time to figure it out, because I had no idea what sex was. But over the years, I learned and put two and two together."

"He humped her every night?" Thomas asked.

"I don't know Thomas. She cried every night, but I don't think it was because of sex every night. It is hard to remember those kinds of details."

Myrna wrapped her arms around John and he leaned his head into her chest and cried. She held his head.

Thomas stood by aghast. "Jesus fucking Christ, John; I had no idea. I'm surprised I'm the one who is so fucked up. It should be you."

Myrna looked at Thomas, wide-eyed with disbelief.

"It is about as close to empathy as you will get from him," Sammy said to Myrna. She softened and turned her attention back to John.

"I wanted to stop Dad. I wanted to stop him so Mom wouldn't keep crying at night. But I didn't know how. I was afraid, like Mom. So I sat there and listened to her cry, convincing myself my presence outside of her door would help."

Silence filled the room which made the sorrow more apparent to everyone. It was as though John's tears were contagious. "I'm sorry, John," Thomas fumbled his apology which gave it the genuine tone he intended to convey.

"Sorry for what?"

"I'm sorry for thinking it was just me who was suffering because of Dad. I had no idea you were hurting too."

"I guess that is how Dad planned it."

"It wouldn't have mattered," Thomas said.

"What wouldn't have mattered?" John looked up.

"If you had tried to help Eddie."

John raised an eye brow.

"Eddie didn't want to be saved back then," Thomas said. "That's what has changed. Now she does."

"Do you think he was that calculating?" John said.

"I don't know what to think most of the time. Mom thinks he had tears of his own from which he was hiding. He had it kind of rough growing up. His father was a vicious character."

"So he caused us to shed tears, too? He became his father?"

"It happens if a person doesn't find a way to short circuit the wiring they inherit."

"Maybe he was counting on his religion to make the difference," Peter said. "That would explain why he went about it in such a rigid manner."

"Well, it didn't work, did it?" Thomas enjoyed asking this question of Peter more than he should have.

John steered the train of conversation to a different track. "I don't know what to think and the man is dead so he can't help us figure it out, not that he would if he was alive. We are left with no option except to accept the fact that he was who he was toward us and toward Mom – a bastard."

"There is only one problem with that," Peter came out of his silence.

"What's that?"

"If he was a bastard, what does that make us?"

"Sons of a bastard," Thomas said.

"Yes, but do you think in the end we will become like him? He became his father."

"Only if we make the same mistake he did and expect the church to do the work of rewiring our heads," John answered. "Religion doesn't change people. Concentrated effort and attention to the truth do. I think we all become our fathers in some ways. It is our natural inclination. I expect to be fighting his nature for the rest of my life."

The family tried to play Euchre, but the energy wasn't there. They retired early. It was a sexless night in the

Vanderhuis household. John's revelation spoiled the mood in a contagious manner. Perhaps it was a tribute to their mother, a way to acknowledge her traumatic experience with sex as a wife who was out of love; or whatever one calls the opposite of being in love.

However, it wasn't that easy for John, whose mind was flooded all night with the vivid sounds he heard outside his parent's bedroom. He struggled to make sense of what he had witnessed. *Was it just casual forced sex? Is there such a thing? Was it sexual abuse? Or should I call it rape? But was it rape if Mom never said the word no?* How is a boy to know, even if he has become a man?

Chapter 35

Fran Drops the Ball

Friday didn't energize the family as they sat around and waited. With the exception of an occasional phone call for Fran concerning details about the funeral and the immigration of the VanderSantos, the house was quiet.

"We are in luck," Fran announced to the family as they sat around and watched afternoon television. "The VanderSantos are flying into Grand Rapids at the same time as Sandy and the children are arriving. We won't have to make two trips."

"That might be awkward." Peter sat up. "I'll have to prepare Sandy and the kids so they aren't disappointed if the attention isn't on them."

"I'll have to rent a twelve passenger van or something," Fran said.

"I'll stay home to make more room," Thomas offered.

"No you won't," Peter said. "You can't wait to see what your new stepfamily looks like."

"Is that what they are?" Thomas said.

"It's either that or half-family. Take your pick," Peter said.

"I was thinking." Myrna walked over to Fran and put her hand on her shoulder. "I would like to cook dinner tomorrow night. I thought you might like the night off."

The family stepped away from Myrna as though she was radioactive.

"I could stay home while the rest of you went to the airport. That way dinner would be ready when you got home. I'd fix a traditional Indian meal."

"That would be lovely," Fran said. "That is if you don't mind."

"I'd love to."

The family filled in the gap they had left between themselves and Myrna.

"Did I do something wrong?" She scanned their faces.

"No, not at all," Thomas answered. "You have, however, brought about a first in this household. You see, Eddie has never given up her kitchen before."

"That's not true!" Fran swatted him with the dish towel she had in her hand.

"Name a time," Thomas said.

Fran thought for a while. "I don't know. Sammy, didn't I ever let you cook a meal?"

"I didn't dare ask," Sammy said. "Not that I wanted to cook for this bunch. You were pretty much the owner of the kitchen."

"Well, then. I guess maybe you should cook dinner tonight, Sammy."

"I'm up for pizza," Thomas said. "Pizza and bowling, I'm bored to death."

"Pizza isn't a meal," Fran said.

"It is for the rest of America, Eddie," Thomas said. "If you are joining the rest of the world, you will have to learn to eat pizza for dinner once in a while."

"Fine, but I don't know the first thing about bowling."

"Good, Sammy won't feel so bad about all her gutter balls." Thomas braced himself for the blow which never came.

"Mark my words Fran," Sammy said with a smile on her face. "Your youngest son will be humiliated by the time this evening is over. His big ego will be the size of his small penis when he looks at the final score."

"Ouch!" Thomas cupped his crotch with both hands.

"What does the gutter have to do with bowling?" Fran asked.

"You'll see." John said. "It will make sense to you when you get there."

Pinwheels was open but empty when the Vanderhuises arrived late afternoon. They enjoyed the pizza and then took over two center lanes. They found Fran the lightest ball in Pinwheels' collection, which still was too heavy. To the family's dismay, Fran settled on the technique of rolling the ball between her legs with both hands. She arrived at this compromise after having dropped the ball both on her back and forward swings. Unable to tolerate the laughter of her children, she settled on the safe technique. The sight of her plump sixty-year-old body bending over in this manner was a little unattractive. Thomas commented it was a good thing she didn't do yoga and the group was quick to shut him down before he could get into his prepared comments about his mother's ass.

The competition heated up as the evening progressed. The family bowled, drank beer, trashed talked each other, and laughed. The more they laughed, the closer they moved toward each other; giving the impression they were a close knit family. When it was over and they were walking toward the cars, Fran marveled at the pleasure of the evening.

"That was great fun. I don't know if I've ever had that much fun before," Fran said.

The rest of the family took a deep breath of cold air and let out deep sighs of satisfaction. Fran heard them and smiled, not needing any further confirmation from her children, that her goal for this prolonged weekend gathering had surpassed her expectations.

Chapter 36

The Mistress

John and Myrna set out early Saturday morning to find the necessary ingredients for Myrna's meal. Thomas put in an order for two plates of brownies; one for this morning and another for tomorrow. He explained he wanted to invite his friends to Dad's funeral, but they were unlikely to come without the bribery of a plate of Fran's brownies. Fran toyed with him for a while; peppering him with questions, not letting on she had been briefed on the content of his oregano. In the end, she complied.

Equipped with the brownies, Sammy and Thomas went to the mission to round up Richard's old parishioners who were more than happy to agree to attend the funeral in light of the promise of another plate of brownies and an all you can eat funeral meal. On the way home, Sammy said, "You know your mother knows about the oregano."

"That's impossible. She wouldn't have agreed to make them today if she did."

"I'm telling you she knows. We told her just the other day."

"Why did you do that?"

"It wasn't me, but I think it was the right thing to do. She needed to know."

"I can't believe she still made them. That woman is turning out to be quite a surprise."

"You are not alone with that mystery. She has surprised all of us. So why is it so important to you these people be at your father's funeral?"

"I don't know." Thomas adjusted the rear view mirror. "I'm acting on emotional instinct here. I know you're thinking I'm trying to humiliate my father is some way, but I don't think that is the case. Eddie inspired me when she invited Dad's mistress and her children to the party. In some way, this is part of my making peace with him. I want to put it all out on the coffin and leave it there. I want to rid myself of my version of the truth."

"That coffin is going to be quite the dumping ground."

"Maybe we should have gotten him a double wide." They laughed and Thomas reached for Sammy's hand, which he held the rest of the way home.

They arrived home to the sight of a twelve passenger van parked in the driveway. It had a sign painted on the side which announced it was the property of the Sunrise Wesleyan Church. They were informed Rev. Vermin borrowed it so Fran wouldn't have to rent one. The plan was to take the church van and the Cadillac to the airport. Peter could pick up his family in the Cadillac and the rest could scoop up the VanderSantos in the church van. Thomas got a mild case of the hives when he thought about riding in a van designated as property of a church, but he managed to control his impulse to complain.

"It would be nice if it had tinted windows," Thomas said.

"Jesus won't trap you in the van, Thomas. He's got a bigger and better plan for your life," Peter said.

"You think he believes that horse shit?" Thomas whispered in Sammy's ear as they left the room.

"It would appear he does," Sammy answered.

They entered the living-room and Sammy motioned for Thomas to sit on the footstool. She undid his ponytail and began to braid his hair. She had enjoyed braiding his hair when they were young. It provided an intimate moment.

"It's kind of nice for Peter." Sammy said. "He believes a lot of comforting things that provide him a sense of security."

"It doesn't mean any of it is true."

"Does it matter whether or not it is true? If it works for him and there is no harm done..."

"It's a wasted life! A wasted life spent on superstition."

"Not if he enjoys his life of illusion; and he seems to be enjoying it just fine. He may be happier than you and I for all we know."

"I had no idea you were this pragmatic."

"Is that what I'm being?"

"I'll have to bring this up with our therapist – in between the talk about sex of course."

"You go right ahead. I'll bet she will be as pragmatic as I am."

"She, who said anything about going to a she?"

"Have it your way. He will be as pragmatic as me."

"Maybe we should go to a gay therapist. Then we can both have a little of what we need."

"I'll find us a therapist."

Sammy finished braiding his hair in silence.

At 1:00 the family piled into the two vehicles and headed for the airport. Rev. Vermin joined them, since he was going to accept the baton in this refugee project as soon as the funeral was over. Fran made the Reverend sit in the front seat, while John drove. She sat behind him. Sammy shoved Thomas to the back seat, in order to put as much distance as possible between him and the Reverend. She then squelched his feeble attempt to make out with her and settled into a comfortable cuddle.

It was a quiet ride except for the conversation between John and Reverend Vermin. He seemed interested in John's journeys and peppered him with questions. Upon arriving at the airport, they found the correct gate and formed a welcome line. The VanderSantos were quick to exit the plane, making their way toward the front of the pack by the time they reached the gate. The pretty little campesina made her way toward Fran in a hesitant and deferential manner. She inquired, "Frrran?" rolling her r and pronouncing the 'a' as it sounds in the word ah.

"Si! Si!" Fran exhausted her Spanish vocabulary.

"Me llamo Miguelina. Este es mi hermano Antonio." She pointed to the young man with her.

"I think hermano means brother," John said.

"It does," Reverend Vermin said.

She then turned and introduced the kids. "Este es mi hijo Juan, mi hija Mercedez, y mi chiquito Julio."

Fran shook each of their hands, prompting them to repeat their names for her as she attempted to pronounce them herself. To everyone's surprise, it was Reverend Vermin who stepped in and facilitated the conversation. He had served in Central America as a missionary for a few years and had learned the language. He had not dared reveal this to Fran, since he wasn't sure how much he would be able to recall. However, his recollection was stirred when he became the translator and he fell into a groove.

On the ride home, Reverend Vermin translated, as both sides asked each other questions in an attempt to hurry along the acquaintance process. As the ride progressed, Fran became uncomfortable with the proximity of the VanderSantos family, which became apparent in her silence. She had taken the front seat so Reverend Vermin could facilitate the conversation more effectively from the middle seat. What struck her most was the resemblance she saw between the children and Richard. Unbeknownst to herself, she had been harboring hope it was all a giant con and in reality Richard hadn't done this awful thing to her. But the uncanny resemblance left no need for genetic testing.

She wondered if she had made the wrong decision in bringing them here, but disallowed that thought in her mind. She told herself she had thought this through and decided giving up her spot to Richard's other family was the right course of action for her in this complicated resurrection she had planned for herself. However, she altered her plans for the evening in light of her strong emotional reaction to their arrival. She told Reverend Vermin they would not be having dinner with the family as she had intended, and asked him if he would make sure they got settled in the hotel and got a nice dinner at a restaurant. She also asked if he would bring them to the funeral home for a private viewing of the body, prior to the official visitation planned for 7:00.

He got the gist of Fran's emotional conundrum and agreed to take charge of the family.

John drove home and after cordial goodbyes, Reverend Vermin drove the family to the Ramada Inn, just outside of town. The family walked Fran into the house where they turned and began to interrogate her concerning her about face. She explained her reaction and they understood.

It didn't take them long to take in the aroma of spices with which Myrna's cooking had filled the air. It drew them to the kitchen where they found her hovering over the stove. They were distracted from their desirous appetite only by the sound of the Cadillac pulling into the garage. Sandy's plane had been late and Peter had stayed behind to wait for her and the kids. They all made their way toward the door leading to the garage and prepared for a hearty welcome. Soon the familiar sounds of family reuniting filled the air. The heartfelt welcomes spoken to Sandy and the dramatic expressions of surprise over how much the kids had changed, rattled throughout the room as the recent arrivals made their way into the home.

"It smells delicious in here!" Sandy flattered Myrna as they were introduced.

"Look kids, this is your aunt Myrna," Peter tried to infuse the kids with his enthusiasm. "She has made us an Indian dinner."

The kids responded in a manner which was tone deaf to their father's exuberance. "We can smell it Dad," the oldest, Robbie, said.

They hugged Myrna. She responded with a level of enthusiasm which matched theirs, in order to relieve them of the discomfort of the expectation they be zealous about meeting a stranger in which they had little interest.

Dinner was not served in the dining room. Myrna had thought to remove the pictures and set the table, but decided against that formal setting. She didn't think it was her place to make the decision to retake the dining area from the VanderSantos, but more pressing was the lack of space. She had expected the entire clan for dinner and the only way to feed that many people was to serve things potluck style. The family served themselves and found seats of their choosing.

They migrated to the living room, which in a matter of seven days had shed its formal flavor and taken on a lived in feel. Dinner was made interesting by two unrelated dynamics. Myrna was entertaining with her explanations of the food. She made it sound so exotic, that even the kids became exited about eating her creations. Second, the family took this opportunity to share their impressions of their stepfamily. This was rather problematic in light of the presence of the kids, who had not been informed of their grandfather's transgressions. Peter had prohibited it and Sandy had respected his wish.

The predominant opinion was the children's unmistakable resemblance to Richard left no doubt of their parentage. They agreed the oldest had their father's intense eyes and the girl had his nose and mouth. "She is a pretty young woman," Peter noted; causing a subtle stir in the family, since they weren't aware of which girl he was speaking. Both the mother and daughter were pretty young women. It would be, however, a major social misjudgment to acknowledge the mistress' young age and beauty in front of the spurned wife. He corrected his ambivalence and attributed his compliment to the younger.

The children were quick to ask questions. "Why would they look like Grandpa?" Peter's daughter asked. Her brother, who was old enough to have put the puzzle together tried to nudge her off her curiosity, but failed.

"No; really; I don't get it. Why is everyone saying the Dominican kids look like grandpa?"

Realizing the truth was inevitable, Peter was about to clear the matter up when his eldest interrupted him. He was bothered by his sister's precociousness and by the fact she hadn't listened to him when he had called her off, so he blurted out, "Because Grandpa was bonking her, alright!"

His father castigated him with a stare, but this was undone by his Uncle Thomas, who was proud of the boy's chutzpa. This led him to feel a kinship of sorts. "I do believe that boy is my nephew," he said.

"Yes he is," Sandy chimed in as she left the room to get seconds. "That's one more thing your brother holds against you."

Peter went on to explain the situation to his kids, but his discomfort with the touchy subject was infective and made everyone in the room feel like a disaster was about to occur. Fran stepped in. "He was my husband, Peter. I'll tell them." She explained the matter in a straight forward, although not any less awkward, way. The kids accepted the explanation with little surprise and moved on to the next subject as though nothing out of the ordinary had been reported to them.

The family finished dinner and prepared for the visitation.

Chapter 37

Wailing

They arrived at the funeral home and found the VanderSantos still there. Reverend Vermin explained the family had experienced a difficult time viewing the body and he hadn't been able to get them to leave. "Don't be alarmed, Fran. They are quite expressive in their grief," the Reverend said.

Miguelina wailed at the top of her vocal range. "Ay Dios mio! Esta muerto, mi marido esta muerto." Her brother held her, while her children clung to her as best they could. The daughter sobbed along with her, while holding the toddler in her arms.

Reverend Vermin translated, "My God! He's dead. My husband is dead." He looked concerned. "Fran is this true? Was Richard her husband?"

"It appears quite obvious, doesn't it?"

"Why in the world did you bring them here to his funeral?"

"They have a right and a need to grieve him. It's obvious they loved him a great deal." Fran found her compact mirror in her purse, opened it, and used it to check the status of her hair.

"You are going to let them live in your home?"

"I am. They can have Richard for all I care."

"Fran, I don't know…"

363

"Please don't treat me like this is my doing. This is Richard's doing not mine. We are celebrating his life and this was the life he chose to live. We'll just have to let the truth fall where it chooses to fall. Let them stay and wail if that is what they need." She put away the mirror and closed her purse.

"Are you trying to embarrass Richard from his grave?"

"If this is embarrassing to Richard, he did it to himself. He had these children, not me."

Taken aback, Reverend Vermin left the room.

The VanderSantos moved away from the casket when they saw Fran entering the room. Fran acknowledged them with a smile and led her family through a quick viewing. Each of them paused before the casket to peruse the body. Peter's youngest, Robby, strolled up to the casket, only to run off holding his nose saying, "Grandpa stinks."

When the funeral director announced it was 7:00 and opened the doors, the family moved into position as though they had done this a hundred times. They formed a line to the right of the casket so people could pass in front of them before strolling in front of Richard's body. The Hispanic contingent took up residence for the night on a couch to the left of the casket. They mourned with tears between Miguelina's intermittent wails. No one explained their presence and no one seemed to ask; at least not out loud. They simply nodded to the family and moved on.

Fran knew most of the visitors, but the children's memories had faded. They were surprised the number of people was so small. They had expected people to come out of the woodwork to pay homage to Richard. They never appeared. For the most part, it was people from the church, which had always been small, and a few people who had worked for him at his practice. Fran wondered if the word hadn't gotten out, but she was sure she had covered all the bases.

The clock rung ten and both families exited the funeral home exhausted. Fran went over to her rival and hugged her. It was not the hug one would give a rival, but instead the hug one would give a fellow sympathizer. They didn't attempt to speak to each other; they just hugged for a short moment. Then the two families went their separate ways.

The family was quick to disperse to their sleeping quarters. Only John and Fran had it in them to burn some midnight oil. They had gone to bed with the others, but when they found themselves unable to sleep, they made their way to the kitchen for a glass of warm milk. It was John who found Fran sitting in his chair in the living room, staring out the window. John sat down next to her and sensed the tears running down her cheeks in the darkness.

"What is it, Mom?" He stared out the window with her.

Fran was silent for a moment, in an attempt to let her reason catch up to her emotions. "I think they made him happy."

"Who, the VanderSantos? You think they made Dad happy?"

"Yes!"

"Why do you think that?"

"I don't know. I am just making assumptions, I guess. But what if they did, John? What if they made him happy and he became a different man for them?"

"That's unlikely, Mom. Dad was who he was."

"But what if they were the exception? What if she knew how to give him what he wanted and it brought out the best in him? I have this vision he was down there with them, happy as a lark. He was kind to those kids and acted like a father should act toward them. He was good to her and made love to her with kindness and compassion. Worst of all she responded to him and enjoyed the sex." Fran shuddered at she thought.

"Mom, don't put yourself through this," John turned toward Fran.

"What if he loved her and her kids more than he loved us?" Fran continued to stare off in the distance.

"Let's assume this was true. What difference would this make for you?"

"It would mean he was right."

365

"Right about what?"

"He was right about it all being my fault. If he could be happy with her, then it was me that made him the disgruntled human being he was."

"You and how many others?"

"What do you mean?"

"Look Mom. This wasn't just about you. If Dad was happy down there, then it would mean not only were you the problem, but us boys, the church, and the entire town of White Lake, not to mention the whole country of the United States of America, were also in the wrong. If Dad was happy down there living in the mountains, it was because they were all happy about him, even if he was a horse's ass. All Dad ever wanted was for everyone to follow his orders and be happy doing it. Maybe he found people down there who were willing to patronize him. But trust me, it wasn't because she was a better wife and they were better kids."

"I don't know," Fran began to bite her nails.

"Mom! You were angry at Dad because you felt he ruined your life. I am sure Miguelina feels like he saved her. And he probably did, financially. But that doesn't mean their relationship was a passionate romance. It was too unequal to be that."

"I suppose you are right, but I can't stop wondering if it was me. This is a cruel joke he played on us."

"It is."

"I tried to make him happy."

"I know you did."

"No, really – I mean I gave him a second chance." Fran turned toward John.

"What are you talking about?"

"I gave your father a second chance when I got pregnant when I was almost forty."

"I remember your miscarriage," John said. "Why did you try to have a baby at 35?"

"I didn't." Fran stood up and walked around. "After Thomas was born I asked the doctor to put me on the pill.

You three came out of me like ants out of a hole, not more than a year apart." She held her stomach.

John chuckled.

"The doctor was uneasy doing so without consulting your father, but he gave in. It worked like a charm for 12 years. Then, out of nowhere, I was pregnant." Fran dusted the furnishings with the Kleenex she held in her hand.

"What did Dad say?"

"At first he was silent. But after a few days he grunted, groaned, and mumbled a few unintelligible words which let me know he was pleased." Fran straightened the shade on the lamp.

"How can you see dust in the dark, Mom?"

"I can't. I just know what needs to be dusted and rearranged after cleaning this room so many times."

John motioned for her to sit down next to him.

"We both got excited; especially after the ultrasound showed it was a girl. He began paying attention to me. He talked to me; took me out to dinner. He even planned a weekend at a cottage up north. In an odd sort of way we started to like each other again."

"Did it last?"

"It did while the baby lived, but when I had the miscarriage at seven months; he walked out of the hospital and went back to his old self." Fran took a new Kleenex and dabbed at her wet eyes.

"That must have hurt."

"For the most part, I got angry at God."

"At God?" John raised his eyebrows.

"I became angry at God, because if she wanted this marriage to work, then why did she take away the one thing that seemed to make it work? That was nothing but a cruel joke."

"She? Don't tell me." John shook his head. "Marcia? Right?"

"I have let her rub off on me, haven't I?" Fran looked down and smiled. "I have to admit it feels good to call God she."

"Then by all means, call her a she. I'm sure he won't mind. But when you're blaming God, refer to her as a him." John looked up at the ceiling. "Wait, that doesn't make any sense."

"It is hard to make the switch, isn't it? You have to change your whole way of talking about God."

"It is true. It is easier to just stop talking about God." John shifted in his chair. "But back to the subject of your anger. I don't understand how the God thing works. But I do know it wasn't you."

"Thanks, John. You are a kind man. You are not your father's child." She put her hand on top of his.

"Finally! This is the moment for which I have been waiting my whole life. It is when you tell me you had a brief affair and Dad isn't my real father." They both laughed.

"I wish I could wake up tomorrow and find out he wasn't my husband. Come to think of it, that is what I'm going for in this crumbling plan of mine. I want to pretend my marriage didn't happen and he has been married to her all these years."

"I take it you don't think it is going to work?"

"I am beginning to have my doubts." Fran took a deep breath, raised her upper body, and then slumped back in her chair.

"Don't you think it is ironic it was easier for me to get angry at God than it was to get angry at your father? I mean, think about it. God could send me to hell. Your father could only give me hell on earth for a limited period of time."

"Maybe you don't believe in hell."

"Maybe that is all God is."

"What do you mean?"

"Maybe God is just something we make up to escape the reality of our lives?"

"A comfortable lie we tell ourselves?"

"Yeah, a comfortable lie we tell ourselves."

"You've been talking to me a bit too much, Mom."

"I like talking to you."

"Mom?" John paused, tilting his head to one side. "Are... you glad he's dead?"

"Of course I'm not gl..." Fran stopped herself midsentence. She sat up straight. "I guess I am." She paused. "But I feel I'm not allowed to say it out loud. I try not to feel that way, but the fact of the matter is I feel I've just been released from some sort of bondage. A whole new life just opened for me. What sadness I feel is over the last forty years I wasted on him."

"I'm happy for you, Mom."

Chapter 38

Rage

The funeral was at 12:00. The complaint through Fran's gossip vine was that 12:00 on a Sunday afternoon was inconvenient. It interrupted Sunday dinner and made for a long day in church for those who attended the evening service. Fran's instinct was to inform people Richard was an inconvenient man and one should expect no less from his funeral. She had asked Sammy's opinion of the matter. Sammy told her it was a great line and full of the truth, but perhaps an 'I'm sorry it inconveniences you' might create less drama. Fran argued she was tired of apologizing for Richard, but accepted Sammy's polite alternative. Sammy reminded her it would be the last time and that rallied Fran.

Fran drove to the church with John and Myrna. Peter and his family left early to catch the morning worship service. Richie threw a fit, seeing no one else in the household had to go to church twice on this morning. He argued that once was more than enough to please God and it should be enough to please his father. Peter scolded him while scanning the room for Thomas, who was the true culprit of his son's oppositional and defiant nature. But Thomas and Sammy had left earlier with a plate of brownies.

Julie was with them. She returned to the Vanderhuis home early morning. Sammy had called to inform her of

Richard's death. She asked Julie to return to White Lake and stay the week so she could attend the funeral. Her real mission was to convince Julie to drive home with Thomas. Sammy was afraid to have Thomas driving his contraption home alone and she wasn't able to take any more time off work.

Julie didn't agree to come to White Lake for the week, but did consent to stay in Detroit and come to the funeral on Sunday. Sammy had to pour on the guilt and offer to purchase a heated blanket that would plug into the bus' cigarette lighter, before Julie would agree to travel back to Arcada with Thomas. It helped that Julie didn't have the money for the air fare.

After accomplishing her mission, Sammy was taken aback by the strength of the attachment Thomas' women felt toward him. She was sure Julie would refuse to go along with her plan, having had such an awful experience on the trip here. But the opportunity to take care of Thomas one more time seduced Julie and she capitulated. Sammy wondered what this said about her plan to give Thomas one more try.

The three of them traveled to the heart of Muskegon to round up Richard's lost flock. Dundee, who had come back into Thomas' good graces after completing his death watch for Richard, came along to help herd the sheep. Convincing the men from the mission to stick to their Saturday commitment to attend the funeral was more difficult than Thomas expected. They were not interested in leaving their neighborhood of comfort for an unknown quantity. This, despite the Legend appearing with two gorgeous women on his arms.

Thomas devised a creative last ditch effort. He was wearing his purple tuxedo and noticed the men were quite taken with it; offering him compliments on his stylishness, even though they wondered about its appropriateness for a funeral. Thomas offered to raffle it off to one of them if they agreed to attend his father's funeral. With a unanimous consensus, they agreed and piled into the bus.

Fran was glad the family had scattered. She had grown a bit weary of the commotion created by the crowd in her house and was in need of some sanity before she faced the death that was to precede her resurrection. She was relieved John and Myrna had stayed back with her, since they seemed like the adults in the crowd.

The small sanctuary made the small crowd look larger than it was. There were several rows in the front of the sanctuary reserved for the family. It would have been plenty if Thomas hadn't chosen to seat his scruffy congregants in one of them. There must have been at least ten of them. They were dressed in ratty suits, with t-shirts underneath. They gave off a scent that White Lake Reformed Baptist Church had never before inhaled. Most of them were black, but a couple could pass for Hispanic. Several were white and one was sure to have some oriental heritage in his gene pool. Julie looked quite uncomfortable sitting in the row with them, even though Sammy had stayed with her. Fran wondered if the poor girl had been forced to ride in the back of the van with them.

Seated across the aisle in the second row were the VanderSantos. Miguelina was still in the throes of her wailings, which was quite disconcerting to the congregation. Her Spanish rants were confounding to the sheltered White Lake residents filling the pews. Imagine how they would have responded had they understood the contents of her rants. This lily white Anglo crowd had more than it could handle observing this rainbow of colors that had infiltrated their second pew. Had it not been for the hope of fertile prospects for their imagined evangelistic zeal, they might well have been tempted to ask them to leave.

Fran sat next to John and Myrna with an empty space to her right. Thomas had tried to scoot over and fill it, but Fran waved him off. He gave her a perplexed stare which Fran ignored, putting a hymn book between them to make it clear no one was to sit there. What she didn't let on was the space was being reserved for Marcia. Fran didn't expect her to show up. She knew it was too much to expect of her therapist and realized her brazen manipulations as she left the office would have little persuasive effect on Marcia. She also knew Marcia was even more averse to church than Thomas, let alone the front pew of a conservative congregation. So although she didn't harbor a penny's worth of hope Marcia might show up, she wanted the space empty so she could pretend Marcia was sitting next to her and holding her hand in a comforting manner. This would make it easier for her to hear Marcia's soothing voice talking her through this eminent crisis.

Just prior to the processional, the family gathered in Reverend Vermin's office for a short prayer. Thomas tried to escape in order to join his pack, but Fran coaxed him back. He was experiencing some serious anxiety being trapped in his former prison sanctuary. Sitting in Reverend Vermin's office, Thomas couldn't help but remember the long hours he spent tolerating long judgmental sermons targeting every aspect of his personality. He was mindful of how anxious church made him feel and how alone he was as a recluse in the back pew. He remembered that back then, he found relief by cracking silly jokes with whoever might have joined him in the rear end of the congregation. For the most part, this would be Sammy, but upon occasion a fellow disgruntled teen's parents would let them keep Thomas company in the heckler's pew. This was the reason he yearned to join his pack as soon as he could. He figured they would make a good audience for his jokes, seeing they weren't versed in church etiquette.

The prayer was quick and the funeral director's instructions for the family processional were concise. The straggling viewers were rushed past the casket and into the sanctuary so the casket could be closed and fastened. The family was paraded out of the pastor's office and stopped to watch the casket get locked down. They shared a sense of closure they felt when it was shut and locked. He was gone and would not be back. They had doubted before, but seeing the lockdown made the realization sink a bit deeper into their consciousness. Thomas yearned to walk over to the casket and retighten the clamps.

The casket was rolled into the sanctuary and Reverend Vermin led the family to fall in behind it. When they reached the front pew, Reverend Vermin stepped aside to watch the casket placed in the center of the sanctuary, while the family filed into the front pews.

Richard's favorite hymns were sung. They inspired Peter, while stirring up uncomfortable emotions for John and Thomas. Neither of them was ready for Amazing Grace, when it came to their father. Fran was stoic during the hymns; unable to bring herself to join the choir. Myrna was quite confounded by the whole affair. She found herself unable to place the experience in any existing category of prior experiences. This was her first visit to a Christian ritual. She was not sure what to make of it and John was in no shape to walk her through it. So, she waded through her perplexity on her own. Sammy just enjoyed it as she always had. It was a place to hang with her boyfriend, Thomas.

Reverend Vermin stuck to the script Fran had provided him. His eulogy focused on his professional and ecclesiastic accomplishments. He was tempted to use the VanderSantos and Thomas' pack as evidence of his generosity on a personal level, but sensed it would bring too much curiosity to a can of worms. Instead he opened up the microphone to anyone who wished to speak. A number of people came forward with stories of their experiences dealing with Richard. They were all reflective of how grand he presented himself in public.

Miguelina stood up with her brother and tried to speak. Her brother comforted her and filled in the blanks. No one in the congregation except for Reverend Vermin knew what she was saying and he wasn't about to translate. There was one other person who knew enough Spanish to pick up on the clues that solved the mystery. It turns out Ray, the true leader of Thomas' pack who had kept the memory of the legend alive, had lived with a Columbian woman for a few years. He picked up the ability to understand it, even though he couldn't speak it. He understood it best when it was being directed at him in shrieks and wails. He had not done a good job of nurturing in that particular relationship so shrieks and wails were a familiar association for him when it came to Spanish women.

Once he caught on to the Days of Our Lives element of the plot, he was desperate to share his understanding. He leaned forward and tilted his head into Thomas' ear. He proceeded to whisper at a volume audible to those around them. "She is your father's fucking whore?"

Thomas acknowledged the truth of the statement in as low a key as possible. He didn't want Ray to feel the need to prove the veracity of his information and cause a further scene. At the same time, he waved him off; hoping Ray would comprehend the inappropriateness of his timing and desist.

He did desist with the family, but felt the need to spread the word to the rest of the pack. He turned to the men on each of his sides and repeated his claim. In turn they turned to the next man and did the same. One by one they began to shake their heads from side to side with a mixture of disgust and amazement as they got the news. In the end, when the entire row was informed, their heads moved from side to side with the synchronicity reserved for dance groups, as they expressed their sympathy for those in the pew in front of them.

Reverend Vermin spotted their head movement and assumed they were referring to his message. The only problem was he couldn't tell if it was a nod of agreement or not. He wanted to believe it was a vote of confidence, but in his mind heads shaking from side to side reflected a negative reaction. He interpreted their sympathy for the family as a judgment of shame on his sermon and looked past them, encumbered by a slight loss of poise.

The last man in the row received the news and spoke a return message into the ear of the man who had informed him of the predicament. The return message was this, "No wonder this family likes the brownies." The message reached the original source who nodded in agreement. Feeling great empathy for the Vanderhuis family, the men dug into their pockets and pulled out broken pieces of the brownies they had wrapped in napkins and stuffed in their pockets. Going into the Lord's House high was crossing a line for them, so they had agreed to save their reward for the ride to the cemetery. They each leaned forward and offered their manna to the family member sitting in front of them.

Not knowing what else to do, the Vanderhuises accepted the gifts with as little fanfare as possible, so as not to attract unwarranted attention. The men then leaned back with deep satisfaction at the generosity this church had brought out in them. Embarrassed, the Vanderhuises slid the napkins into their pockets for safe keeping. Thomas felt free to eat his, wondering why he hadn't thought of this trick thirty years ago. It would have made his penance in the back row much more tolerable.

Reverend Vermin's sermon centered on a verse which described the feet of those who spread the good news of the gospel as beautiful. He began by describing people's disregard for their feet. They are often dirty and beat up from doing the back-breaking work of carrying their owners around. He proceeded to point toward his feet which he described as disfigured by bunions. The congregation gasped for a moment; afraid he was about to remove his shoes and socks to illustrate his point. He was known for getting a bit carried away in his zeal to provide concrete evidence to back up his points – visual aids of any sort.

Their fears were dissuaded as he went on without disrobing his feet. He explained this disregard for our feet led people in general to feel their feet were the ugliest part of their body. He pointed out that washing someone else's feet was an ancient Christian ritual which was meant to teach humility. A person must be humble to touch another's feet. Shaking someone's hands takes nothing away from us, but washing their feet? That is a different matter. He then brought his sermon full circle by driving home the point that from the Gospel's point of view, even the feet of those who spread the

Gospel of Jesus Christ were beautiful and precious. Richard, he concluded, had 'grace full' feet. That pun made him feel like he hit a home-run. The congregation, on the other hand, was lost in their disgust over the image of bunion deformed feet.

The service was concluded with an invitation for people to join the family for a light meal, followed by a processional behind the horse drawn carriage to the cemetery for the internment. They were informed Richard's soul would then be committed into the hands of God and his body buried so it could return to the dust until that day when God came to collect the dust and return Richard's body to him fully renewed. They responded with a loud "Amen" and exited the sanctuary after the families, both the official and unofficial members, were excused.

The meal took on a jolly feel. In part this was because the members of White Lake Reformed Baptist Church believed funerals should be a celebration of the person's life and their good fate to be in the presence of God. However, the hilarity of Thomas' pack was at least in part, responsible for setting the light mood. To the amusement of the crowd, they devoured the food and laughed with gusto at each other's jokes. Most important of all, they distracted the crowd from Miguelina's wailings which had become disturbing by this time.

The meal was concluded and the funeral director began to organize the processional. He asked for the pall bearers to step forward. Fran was aghast when she realized she hadn't planned that detail. She told her three boys to stand up and then looked around the room for three more draftees. She recruited Antonio and Juan for the other side and Reverend Vermin volunteered to be the sixth man. They followed the casket as it was rolled toward the front door of the church. When they exited the building, the men took hold of the casket, walked it down the stairs, carried it a short distance to where the carriage was parked, and slid it inside. They were careful, afraid of breaking the glass that made up the sides of the carriage.

A few cars lined up behind the carriage. Some suggested they should walk. Fran nixed that suggestion at its inception, stating it was too cold. In actuality, she was concerned about the kind of impression the sight of this motley crew might make on the rest of the town. Besides, walking would delay things and she was ready for this to be over, so her new life could begin.

A large white horse pulled the casket bearing carriage out of the parking lot and onto the road. A single police car was waiting in the street with its lights flashing. It would serve as an escort for the unique processional. It was indeed a sight to behold – Dr. Richard Vanderhuis' legacy on wheels. Behind his casket was his Cadillac, carrying his wife, his eldest son, and his exotic Indian daughter-in-law. Second in line was John's rental car, filled with Peter and his family. Third in line was the twelve passenger church van Fran had borrowed for her husband's mistress' family. Antonio was driving. Miguelina's window was open, despite the cold, so her spontaneous wails could be heard by those the procession passed.

Taking up the rear of the family's portion of the parade was Puff. Thomas was driving. Crowded into the passenger seat were his ex – now present – girlfriend and his present – soon to be ex girlfriend. Neither of them wanted to ride in the back of the bus which was filled with Thomas' pack. The windows were down in this vehicle as well. Julie had opened the front window to allow fresh air to circulate and do battle with the odor coming from the back seat passengers. She looked at Sammy and wondered if the bus would be habitable after this for the trip back to Arcada. Dundee was bad enough, but this was quite intolerable.

Dundee was busy in the back taking turns smelling the men's crotches. They didn't seem to mind, so he squeezed his way through the crowd making his rounds. Except for Ray, they took to Dundee and anointed him their mascot. Thomas explained his name and they renamed him the Crocodile Man's dog. Ray, however, had not had good luck with dogs in

378

his life. He had several scars to prove it. When Dundee approached him, he panicked and pulled out a plastic fork he had pocketed at the church. He held it out in front of him, threatening the Crocodile Man's Dog. The pack laughed and proceeded to hold him down so the Crocodile Man's Dog could sniff his junk. The van shook visibly back and forth as they rough housed in the rear. Crocodile Man's Dog finished his business with Ray and moved on.

The men began to lament they had given away their brownies to the grieving family. They had looked forward to partaking of them during this part of the journey. Tiring of their whining, Julie reached under the driver's seat and pulled out what remained of Thomas' stash. She tossed it toward the back of the bus. Once the men realized the contents of the zip lock bag, they cheered her with a loud "for she's a jolly good fella." She waved her hand in acknowledgement and they responded with applause and cat calls. The bus filled with smoke which drifted out of Puff's front windows, mixing with the cold air and dissipating into the wind, like holy incense.

As the makeshift parade drove through the town's main drag, Fran was struck by the lack of attention the event attracted. In her mind, this was a colossal event for the town of White Lake. Dr. Richard Vanderhuis, its long time family doctor and influential citizen, had died. She expected the town to take note and stop to pay its respect. The opposite was true. Life went on as normal for the town residents; as if they had not noticed what was happening to them. The small church sanctuary had not busted at the seams, as she had expected. Only the members of White Lake Reformed Baptist Church were there and even some of them were missing – no doubt home watching the football game. The procession of cars behind the horse drawn carriage was minimal, many of those present at the funeral choosing not to brave the cold. She noticed one little red headed boy point out the horse to his mother as they were forced to wait for the processional before they could cross the street. She was surprised when the mother brushed him off in her visible disgust over having to wait until it passed.

As she observed the lack of attention the processional received as it made its way to the cemetery, it dawned on her that all these years she was mistaken about Richard's place in the world around her. She had experienced him as this enormous personality at the center of everything happening in her sphere of life. She assumed he wielded the same influence everywhere he went.

But Richard had died and White Lake had not noticed. There was no dance of freedom around the dictator's casket. Nor was there a throng of people lining the streets to say goodbye to a fallen hero. Life in White Lake went on as though nothing had changed.

Richard's power and influence had all been in her head. His fiefdom ended at the parking lot of the White Lake Reformed Baptist Church. He had convinced her of his own grandiosity; perhaps because he was so convinced of it himself. She had fallen for it and bent over in submission; believing there was no life for her and her children beyond his reach.

She squirmed with shame, as in retrospect, she realized how foolish she had been. She could have been free years ago, but she didn't know it. She had missed the gate to freedom that lay open just beyond their front door. Richard had scrambled her brain, rewiring it to his liking, blinding her to her own power. She wondered if he laughed to himself each day as he left, knowing she could follow suit, but wouldn't because he was in control.

Fran burst into tears as they neared the cemetery. Her tears were not sorrow, they were rage. For the first time in her long marriage to Richard, she seethed with hatred toward him. She had felt inklings of hatred on various occasions throughout the past year, but held it at bay; sensing it was wrong to hate your spouse no matter what he had done. But today, on this last ride behind Richard before he was locked in the ground for good, she owned it. She raged in the core of her being, as she smashed her fists into the door of Richard's Cadillac, sobbing. John and Myrna turned around in shock. They thought she was about to open the door and jump out. Reverend Vermin reached over to comfort her by putting his hand on her shoulder and telling her Richard was in a better place.

In her core she screamed *I hope he is in hell!* But it only came out in the form of tearful sobs. She felt powerless and hated herself for it. Richard was dead, and yet here she sat crying her eyes out, unable to speak. She wanted those in the car to know they were tears of hate and not sadness, but she couldn't communicate. Tears were all she could muster. The words were lost inside of her and could not find the gate to freedom. She felt as if she was suffocating, choking on the words stuck in her throat. She willed herself to calm down. She remembered John talking about deep breathing, and how it calms the body, so she employed the technique. She lengthened each breath and as she did, she came to a resting peace. She regained control of her breath and with that came access to her words.

She stopped them before they reached her audience's ears. She realized voicing her hatred was not necessary in this setting. What was important was that she own her feelings. She didn't need others to join her in order to know they were real. It was her hatred and it was real, whether or not the world agreed with her. She let them believe her tears were driven by sadness; allowing them to comfort her according to their incorrect diagnosis. She gave herself permission to translate their words into language that soothed her. She heard them say, *It's okay to be angry with him. It is only natural you would hate someone who betrayed you in this manner. You will get over this infernal fire that rages inside you. It will be okay when you start your new life.* She looked up, and for a short moment, saw Marcia's face on Reverend Vermin's body. She was assured she had heard them correctly.

The committal was short because of the bitter cold. Everyone wanted to lower Richard's body into the cold earth and get back to their warm houses. Miguelina's wails were muffled because her vocal cords had given out. Several of Thomas' friends took over from her, imitating her sounds of grief as best they could. It was unclear to those around them whether they were offering empathy or mocking her.

After the casket was lowered into the ground, the family walked past the hole, picking up handfuls of the cold dirt and tossing them onto the lowered casket. Peter had to drag Robbie away with two hands full of dirt as he cried, "I want to fill the hole."

Chapter 39

Fran's Offer

The Vanderhuises arrived home and Fran went to her kitchen to prepare supper. The VanderSantos were invited to come, so she could explain her generous offer. Reverend Vermin promised to come following the evening worship service and serve as a translator. The others fell into various seats around the house, too exhausted to offer Fran a helping hand.

An hour later, Thomas came home with Sammy and Julie, after dropping his pack off at the mission and raffling off his purple suit. He walked into the house in his underwear, since he was unwilling to exchange clothes with the winner of the raffle. The girls were sure he would die of hypothermia in the heatless van, but he survived. Dundee sat on his lap the entire drive home, providing some of the needed heat. The family members who saw him come in were too tired to ask the relevant questions. Not even Fran, who offered him a cup of coffee when he came into the kitchen shivering in his skivvies, requested an explanation.

The VanderSantos arrived around five. No one was sure how they had gotten to know their way around town, but were prevented from asking the question due to the language barrier. Fran gave them a tour of the house, using her creative side to make up a slang version of sign language. She wasn't sure how much they understood, but they seemed interested in the house, stopping to admire different things, talking to each other with perplexed intonations.

Dinner was served and they were ushered into the dining room. Fran had cleared the table of their photographs and after placing card tables at each end of it, managed to squeeze in seating for the adults. The kids (foreign and native) were given instructions to take their plates into the kitchen and sit around the counter on the stools.

Richie whined, "What are we supposed to say to them?"

"Just smile a lot. Now get in there and pretend to be a gracious host," Peter said.

Richie grumbled as he led his Hispanic counterparts into the kitchen.

Dinner at the adult table was quiet. The VanderSantos complimented Fran on her casserole with a repetitive, "Muy bueno." Fran tried to remember the Spanish word for thank you, but drew a blank. She settled for nodding her head and responding with the English version. They were all relieved Miguelina's wails had subsided.

After the table had been cleared and the kitchen cleaned, Reverend Vermin arrived. He came out of the cold looking exhausted. Fran offered him supper, but he declined.

"Got a little long winded this evening, Vermin?" Thomas said.

"The congregation was in a mood to sing this evening. I didn't have the heart to cut it short. They kept coming up with more personal requests for hymns."

"I've got to hand it to you, Vermin. You've impressed me this weekend. You've been a good sport about all this commotion we've created," Thomas said.

"I'll take that as a compliment and add it to my minister profile. 'They say I'm a good sport.' That will land me a job at a mega church."

Those who spoke English laughed down the level of stress a notch or two. Reverend Vermin got right to it. He explained Fran's proposal to Miguelina.

She was stunned. "Ella quiere que nos mudemos aqui, en esta casa? Y ella va a pagar?"

"Si," Reverend Vermin said.

"Porque?"

"She wants to know why you are doing this."

Fran thought for a moment. "Tell her Richard would have wanted it that way."

"Ella dice que Ricardo hubiese querido esto."

"Y ella, donde va a vivir?"

"She wants to know where you will live."

"Tell her I don't know, but I won't be around here."

"Ella dice que no sabe, pero no se va a quedar aqui."

A discussion ensued between Miquelina and Antonio. The back and forth became heated. The daughter became annoyed with Miguelina, rolling her eyes and stomping her feet. Miguelina cut it off and said, "Digale gracias, pero no queremos vivir aqui."

Reverend Vermin gave her a moment to rethink her response. When no alternative was forthcoming, he translated "She says thank you, but they don't want to live here."

Fran was surprised. She had been so sure of her plan she hadn't prepared for a rejection on the part of the VanderSantos. "Can you find out why?"

Reverend Vermin had a long conversation with Miguelina. When he felt confident he understood, he turned to Fran and said, "It appears she is quite happy where she lives. Richard built her a nice home and several others she rents to tourists. He also established a small colmado, which is an unsophisticated version of a convenience store. Her brother runs it with the help of the kids. All this makes an adequate income for her. I'm not sure, but I think he left her a small slush fund as well. She says Richard loved it there and would want them to stay. Did you know he built a church there and served as the minister? Baptized babies and all."

Fran searched for her next move. "Please ask them if there is anything I can do for them."

Reverend Vermin translated Miguelina's response. "She says you have been generous in allowing them to attend the funeral and paying for the expenses. The only thing she might need is help with the children's education, once they are ready to study at the university. She says Richard was determined they receive a good education."

"Tell her I would be happy to make arrangements to help them finance their education."

Thomas noted the daughter was perturbed and said, "It looks like she would like to stay Eddie. Maybe you could take Mercedez under your wing."

Miguelina stepped in front of her daughter and looked Thomas in the eyes. "Ella se va con migo; no se queda."

"No le hagas caso, Miguelina," Reverend Vermin said. "El es un pendejo."

The VanderSantos chuckled as they grinned at each other.

"What did you say to her?" Thomas asked.

"I told her to ignore you because you are a buffoon."

The family laughed; as did Thomas; as did the VanderSantos.

"I take it that is the Christian word for asshole?" Thomas asked.

"You would be correct; or should I say Reverend Vermin is correct," Peter said.

Mercedes' eyes brightened. "No, no!" She waved her pointer finger back and forth. "Moder fokeerr, Moder fokeerr."

The family turned and grasped.

"Maldito turistas!" Miguelina turned to her daughter. "Ya callate. No seas sin verguensa."

"What do turistas have to do with this?" Thomas said.

"I'm sure she blames them for teaching her daughter such things," Reverend Vermin said.

"Well I'll be damned. So you think I'm a mother fucker," Thomas said. "You're alright, Vermin, I'm growing to like you."

"I'll add that to my resume as well; buffoons like me."

Thomas roared. He leaned torward Sammy and said. "I guess you are stuck spending eternity in that extra plot at the Vanderhuis gravesite."

"Over your dead body."

"Kinky, I might like that."

Sammy pushed him off of as he attempted to kiss her.

Reverend Vermin took the VanderSantos back to their hotel and made arrangements to take them to the airport the next day. The family dispersed to their rooms to pack. Fran laid on her bed, contemplating her next move in her new life.

Chapter 40

Hopes for the Future

Fran was up early to make breakfast for everyone before they left. She was unsettled and coped by creating a veritable feast of breakfast foods to send her family off in a grand way. One by one they trickled in and sat down at the dining room table. When all were present, John asked the question to which they were all eager to know the answer. "What are you going to do now, Mom?"

"Well," she began. "I talked with Reverend Vermin last night over the phone. He was concerned and called to check on me. He told me there is a missionary family coming home on furlough this week and they are in need of a home for six months. They have four kids and this place would be great for them. He also explained he has dreamed of having the church sponsor refugee families; real refugee families. He said this house would be a great place to house them until they got on their feet."

"What did you say to him?" John asked.

"I told him I thought both of those ideas would be great options and to go ahead and make the arrangements."

"Where will you go, Eddie?"

"I talked to your women last night. By the way, you've got two right now, Thomas. We made a plan."

The boys looked at their partners, wondering how they had escaped them unnoticed.

"Don't look so surprised, boys. The men in this family have long been known to sleep through the loudest of thunderstorms. We chatted in my room and here is what we decided. Sammy invited me to spend the next several weeks with her in Chicago. I'll stay here the rest of the week, or perhaps at Lynn's house. There are a lot of loose ends with which I need to deal. Sammy volunteered to take the train back on the weekend and accompany me to her house. She says she will show me the town. I've always wanted to go there and see the windy city. We are going to see the museums, take in a couple of shows, and taste all the good food."

She turned to Peter. "Then I thought I would visit you and Sandy for a while, Peter. I've never gotten to know my grandkids and Sandy said she would love it if I could come down for a while. Thomas, I hear you are going to spend the summer in Chicago. Sammy and I thought I could camp out at your place for the summer. Sammy says it is beautiful there. I hope you don't mind, but Sammy says it doesn't matter if you do."

She turned to John. "Myrna invited me to come live with you in the fall, John. She says the house is set up with in-law's quarters, since sooner or later her parents will come to live with you, as is the tradition in her culture. She said she could use some help in her work. I could work as much as I wanted or not."

"I would love that, Mom, but you realize..."

"I know how you live is less convenient than what I am accustomed. But I'm not as fragile as you think. I can take it."

"What about Marcia?" Myrna asked. "You seem quite attached to her."

"I haven't figured that out yet. I think I can talk to her over the phone if I feel the need."

"I've heard some therapists do therapy with instant messaging. You can do that from anywhere in the world," Sammy said.

"I'll suggest it to her at my two hour session with her later this morning."

"Aren't you terrified?" John asked. "I mean you have lived in this house and this town for so long. I would think you would be frightened at the prospect of leaving it all behind."

"I'm trying not to think about it because I don't want to change my mind. I just know I need to get away from all of this if I'm going to make a new life for myself. If I let myself dwell on it for too long, I don't know if I will be able to do it. Part of me wants to leave for Chicago today, with Sammy."

Thomas cleared his throat, drawing the group's attention. "Eddie, about you coming to my place? I'm not sure that is such a good idea."

"Why is that?" Fran asked.

Peter answered before Thomas could phrase together a response. "He is backing out mother. He doesn't want you there in case he needs to escape from Chicago."

"Is that true?" Fran inquired.

"For once the asshole is right." Thomas couldn't bring himself to look at Sammy. "I'm not backing out; I just want to be able to come home if I need to."

"Thomas, this is Sammy we are talking about. You aren't going to need to come home."

"You know what I'm like. I'm not long-term relationship oriented and I doubt a relationship counselor is going to be able to fix that. I want to try, but I need a backup plan."

The group turned to Sammy, expecting her to be broken-hearted. She was unfazed. "Thomas, I'm not going to break if this doesn't work. I know it might not. All I'm asking is we give it a good try. You can have your backup plan if you need it. All I need is for you to try."

"Just because I'm there doesn't mean you can't come home. I won't get in your way."

"For all I know, when I get back from Chicago you'll be living it up with a couple of surfer dudes servicing your sexual needs," Thomas said. "You will have redecorated the whole thing into contemporary Midwestern."

Fran blushed. "Don't be ridiculous, Thomas. I won't touch your things. And as for the surfer dudes; I would never do something like that. I don't know if I will ever go near another man. I'd have to see Marcia for another ten years if I was going to go there."

"Don't be too sure of that, Mom. Myrna has a couple of possible suitors lined up for you. She believes she has the gift of Cupid."

"I prefer to refer to my gift as the gift of the goddess of love. I'm sure there is such a goddess in India somewhere. They have one for everything," Myrna said.

"She does," Fran said. "She turned Thomas around, didn't she? She persuaded him to get the limo and everything."

"Yeah, Fran is right. She does have the gift." Sammy said. "It is called a frying pan over the head."

"You knew about that and you let her come after me?" Thomas acted aghast. "She was threatening to cause me permanent brain damage."

"I would have too," Myrna said, "if you hadn't listened and did what I said."

Sandy's eyes brightened with excitement. She turned to Peter and said, "You know that older gentleman? What's his name, Peter? You know, he recently lost his wife? You officiated at her funeral. He is the nicest man; quite dapper as well. Come on Peter, what's his name?"

Peter thought for a while, "You mean Ted; Ted Teller?"

"Yeah, that's the one. He would be perfect for your mom! I'm serious Fran."

"I don't think so Sandy," Peter said.

"Why not? He is a nice handsome man."

"He is one of our most conservative members."

"So what? Your mother would fit right in with him."

"Have you not noticed what has gone on in this house over the last week? With Dad gone, the house has gone ape liberal. Mom is swearing, lying to the minister, and taking advice from an atheist counselor. I'm not sure she is Ted's type anymore."

"Oh that's ridiculous. Ted could stand to loosen up a bit. He is a drag on your congregation. I'll introduce you to him when you visit, Fran. Maybe he will have phone sex with you while you're traveling the world." Sandy flashed Peter a sarcastic, accusatory stare and then smiled as though she was quite pleased with herself for outwitting her husband.

Peter ignored her. "I think Mother should look for a boyfriend in Thomas' neck of the woods. They are two peas in a pod these days. One of Thomas' surfer dudes is more up her alley than Tom Teller."

"Stop it right now! All of you! I told you I'm not interested in landing a man. I've just gotten rid of the one I had and I'm relieved."

"Hell, Mom," Thomas said. "In Arcada you can take up with another woman and no one would notice."

"And why would I want to do that?"

"Oh, I don't know. Maybe because the man in your life didn't work out so well and celibacy isn't a very good alternative.

Julie and Sammy clinked their glasses to toast Thomas' celibacy comment.

"You are all terrible," Fran said. "I've raised a family of reprobates. No wonder your father up and died. He didn't want to have to face his offspring."

"It sounds like you have a plan worked out, Eddie," Thomas said.

"I guess I do; not that it will turn out anything like I envision, but it is a plan."

"We're happy for you, Mom," John said.

"I am happy for myself. I'm happy for all of you as well. I never would have predicted this weekend would have turned out this way."

"Here! Here!" Thomas raised his glass of orange juice to prompt a toast. Everyone responded by raising their glasses toward the center of the table. "Do you have any champagne, Mother? For an occasion like this we should be drinking Mimosas."

"As a matter of fact..." Julie got out of her chair and made her way to the pantry, returning with the bottle of champagne she had seen earlier in the week while searching for the wine. Thomas popped the cork and foam sprayed across the table. He poured the champagne over the orange juice in the adult's glasses and tried to slip some into the kid's glasses. They had grown bored and found places to squeeze in with the adults. Sandy caught his eye and stared him off.

He raised his glass and was about to speak, but was interrupted by a disgruntled moan from Dundee, who was resting his snout on the corner of the table. He was upset over not having been served champagne. Thomas filled his glass to the brim and then raised his glass one final time.

"Here is to surviving this dinner table!"

"Here! Here!" the group cheered.

"And to meeting at new dinner tables!" Fran toasted.

"Yeah!" some of the family agreed.

And the Vanderhuis family laughed. They laughed so hard their eyes began to produce tears. Tears of happiness joined with tear of sadness. For in their lives, the two had always been inseparable – as is the case in every family that tries to love.

Epilogue

Thirty years later, on a cool but sunny October day, the Vanderhuis family gathered in a circle on the sands of Duck Lake Channel Beach to follow the wishes of their mother upon her death. She asked her ashes be mixed forever with the grains of sand. She explained this place had provided her and her children with a safe playground, full of memories that forever informed them life could be good. In the center of the human circle stood the urn which contained her remains – a beautiful bronze vase, stamped with imprints of doves hovering in the air. No one seemed in a hurry to empty it. They were content to mingle around it until the time seemed right.

Fran was in death as she was in life – convenient. She had died the day after her 90th birthday celebration, while her children and their families were in Michigan for the festive celebration. Her heart failed in the middle of the night. They stayed on a few days to participate in the modest ritual she had outlined for them. She was to be cremated and then dispersed on the beach by her family and the few friends that were still alive.

Fran left written instructions for her funeral in which she foresaw her children's reactions and responded to each. She told Peter not to worry it might be illegal to scatter human ashes on a public beach where children played. They should make plans to apologize after the fact if necessary; blaming the insufferable state of mind grief brings upon stricken families. She explained to John she did not want her ashes separated and carried by her children to their respective homelands. Although she had enjoyed her time with each of them in their chosen venues of life, the organic nature of their essential connection was grounded in this place and on this beach. She chided Thomas for acting as though he didn't care about the matter; still pretending the beaches of the west coast were disconnected from the sands of Michigan. She told him one of the main reasons she chose the white sands of Duck Lake Channel Beach was so Thomas would think about her every time he set foot on one of those surfer crowded replacement playgrounds, to which he was so attached. "After all," she wrote, "he was the one who shared her mesmerized relationship with beaches."

As for Sammy; she thanked her for understanding her last will and testament; offering her the best wishes in her attempt to coordinate the boys' reactions to her last request. "You are," she wrote, "a much better daughter than I could have ever hoped to give birth to myself."

Fran had fought hard to make it to her 90th year. Her goal had been to extend her new life forty years by making it to her 100th birthday. It seemed only fair she enjoy her second life for as long as she suffered the first. She reasoned that 100 would give her 40 years of happiness to match the 40 she had spent with Richard. But when it became apparent enjoying life past 90 was going to be difficult, she reframed her perspective (as Marcia had taught her), rationalizing the first 20 years of her life were happy in the midst of her family of origin – meaning 90 years would balance the scales of justice in favor of her happiness.

The family hadn't expected this event to take place back in Michigan, much less in White Lake. Upon the death of their father their mother left town, vowing never to return. Her certainty was convincing. She had carried out her plan to the letter. She visited Sammy in Chicago for several weeks and then drove down to Florida to acquaint herself with the grandchildren. She proceeded to spend the summer in Thomas' home in Arcada; leaving, upon Thomas' return to spend a year in India with John and Myrna.

Her visit with Sammy was healing for Fran because it was downright fun. They wandered through Chicago doing whatever Fran desired. Sammy kept whispering in her adopted mother's ear, "It is about you now, Fran – just about you." Sammy pushed Fran only once. It was a rather dull day for both of them so she insisted Fran accompany her to the bar and do a couple of shots. "It works wonders if you save it for days like today." Fran was reluctant but acquiesced. They met a group of Sammy's girlfriends at a hot spot in the middle of city.

The women let their hair down for a girls' night out, while Fran watched from the sidelines. She marveled at the freedom these women possessed to celebrate themselves in such a candid manner. She would never have allowed herself to attract so much attention. After a while, she joined them in a restrained manner; downing several shots to their cheers of approval. The alcohol loosened her tongue and Fran was moved to tell her story to the young women who listened with great curiosity. They were supportive, but Fran didn't notice. Instead she listened to herself as though she were a third party, marveling at the sense of release she felt as she made her life public for the first, and perhaps last, time.

Her visit to Peter's home was ambiguous. She couldn't put her finger on why, but she felt uncomfortable. Perhaps it was because they were a family with established rituals which she, as a guest, disrupted while Sammy's single lifestyle was accommodating to guests. She tried hard to accomplish the purpose of her visit, which was to get acquainted with her grandkids. The unforeseen problem was the grandkids weren't interested in their grandmother and Fran herself found them mind-numbing.

It made her wonder what kind of mother she had been to the boys, since she seemed to possess a complete lack of desire to nurture her grandkids. She asked the boys if they remembered her nurturing them when they were young, but they didn't recall much of their earlier years. Sammy, who would have remembered, wasn't around in those early years so Fran was forced to consult with Marcia on the matter to see what they could piece together. Marcia dismissed the concern, stating evidence from the present to establish Fran was a nurturing person. The issue was that at this stage of her life, Fran was seeking to nurture herself. Kids are by nature vacuum cleaners of nurturing; giving very little back in return. After hearing Marcia's description of kids, Fran wondered if Marcia had kids of her own. She hoped she hadn't for the sake of the kids. She said a short prayer for them, just in case God's wisdom had lapsed and he/she had opened Marcia's womb.

What became clear to Fran was her discomfort at Peter's house was at least in part, due to their robust involvement in the church. Everything they did revolved in some way around church activities. This, in and of itself, shouldn't have made her uncomfortable, since it resembled the rhythm of her and Richard's lifestyle. But then again, that is why it made her feel ill at ease. She was trying to get away from the church's sphere of influence and Peter and Sandy were basking in the glory at the center of it all. So Fran spent two months forcing herself to engage with a social realm of grandchildren and Christian folks from whom she wished she could get away.

Her time at Thomas' place was rich, but lonely after he left. He was there with her the first couple of weeks and that time was precious to her. She forced herself on him and he didn't insist in his attempts to get away from her. She basked in the light of his status as an artist and a professor; smiling with pride whenever anyone identified her as his mother. She spent hours looking at his art and asking him questions about its meaning. He was surprised by her interest and her ability to process the awkward themes of his work. Even the graphic sexual nature of some of his pieces stirred her curiosity and drove her to enlightening discussions with him.

After he departed for Chicago, she was left to herself and she found the solitude of Arcada both excruciating and insightful. It was excruciating because the silence led her to a more mindful awareness of the sadness she felt about the life

397

she had lived. In the silence of his apartment and her walks in woods, she couldn't hide from the sorrow of regret which filled her soul. Tears carved a slow crooked path between the wrinkles under her eyes.

But the silence which forced her to own her feelings also allowed her to see her path to freedom, as she became more aware of who she was and how she felt. The knowledge of her sadness revealed the content of what she hoped for in the future and allowed her to begin to put together a plan to live out her dreams. She envisioned herself as strong and independent; a woman with a purpose of her own. She imagined herself surrounded by people who were interested in her; a man with whom she could engage.

She did travel to the beach for a day in order to experience the part of this country that caught Thomas' heart. She smiled when she saw the young men playing in the surf, remembering Thomas' harassing comment concerning her hooking up with one of them. It made her pause for a while and wonder what her life would have been like if she had met and married someone carefree like them; as opposed to meeting Richard and getting caught up in his twisted seriousness. *I would have done well as a surfer girl,* she thought to herself. *I would have fit in well with this lifestyle. I could have traded Duck Creek Channel Beach for this and been happy in this freedom loving place.*

At the end of summer, Fran headed for the unfamiliar country where John had made his home. She was excited to participate in new and strange experiences. The experience titillated her as she had hoped it would; allowing her to lose herself in the learning experience, while her soul cleansed itself of that which had been decaying within her. She stayed with them for a year, helping Myrna with her schools. The language was slow to come, but she managed to communicate well enough to accomplish what she wanted. Her time with John consisted of learning the practice of yoga. He was happy to teach her and she found its calming effect soothing to her apprehensive spirit.

But after a year, she decided it was time to get out of their hair and she returned to the United States. To everyone's surprise, she returned to the state of Michigan – to White Lake. Time and distance had washed away the despair this town had brought and she began to miss her roots. Or as she put it, "I'm going to take back the life Richard stole from me."

Reverend Vermin's refugee ministry was going well. Two families cohabited in the Vanderhuis residence. Regardless, Fran had no intension of living there. She relieved Reverend Vermin's apprehension when she offered to donate the house to the church. She decided to shake things up in her new life by purchasing a condo across the lake in Montague, White Lakes' rival city. A rivalry played out in every high school sporting encounter.

As for going to church, Fran tried to return to Reverend Vermin's fold, but found the environment oppressive with its rigidity. At Marcia's suggestion, not that Marcia had ever attended the church, but had encountered several clients who spoke well of the place, Fran immigrated in to the Unitarian Congregation in Muskegon. There her soul found a home that let it fly as she needed it to soar. She found a few kindred spirits with whom she could share her life and in an attempt to replace boredom with meaning and purpose, she threw herself into the work of the congregation.

It worked for Fran, distracting her from tedious things with the promise of purpose. But not as effectively as the men who came into her life over her last thirty years. Through sheer force of will she confronted the faceless figure in her memories that pressed down his weight on her body. She squeezing him out from between her legs, and shoved him out of her bed. This reclaiming of her body freed her to welcome others into her personal space, others who would come by invitation only, faces displayed and known to her. She improvised and found that placing her weight on them allowed her the sense of security she needed in order to be comfortable with such intimacy. From this position she could still breathe and maintain enough control to know she could stop and leave at a moment's notice.

There were two men that met her precondition that required they stand on their own two feet and not lean on her. Both her lovers were generous and loving toward her. She loved them both, but refused to marry either of them. She outlived them. The relationships were as discrete as possible, but in a small town nothing is ever discrete, even from a rival town across the lake. But Fran didn't care about the talk. In fact, she relished it to a small degree, as it allowed her concrete evidence she had escaped her old life and had begun anew. She chose to share this small devious part of herself with Thomas, who relished this side of her with increasing respect. She kept it from Peter, whose wife's infidelity had left him broken hearted and more committed than ever to the sexual boundaries Richard had preached. She was open about it with John, who was happy to see her living her life as she saw fit.

As the Vanderhuis family gathered around Fran's dust filled urn, they realized they were not the same family that had played on this beach as children, so they made good hearted attempts to reacquaint themselves with each other. John still loved Myrna and continued to believe he was married to a woman with the body of a goddess; even though her curves had widened her body and wrinkles had weathered her face. "We've wrinkled, thickened, and grayed together," he would say to her. "It's a thing of beauty." Her response was, "Some of us more than others."

John continued to write books that interested him, but did little to tickle the fancy of the populous. Myrna had not stopped working to build new and better schools for the children of her country. Her pace slowed, but her heart for the children of India grew stronger.

Shortly after Richard's death, Carrie came to visit as she had promised John on the airplane. Carrie and Myrna bonded the instant they met, so Carrie stayed on to help Myrna in her work. She bunked with Fran for the year Fran spent at John and Myrna's, leading to a lasting friendship which resulted in another adopted daughter for Fran. Carrie would visit her in Montague whenever she visited her parents in Michigan.

Shortly after Fran's departure from India, Carrie fell in love with a cousin of Myrna's. They married and settled in as neighbors to Myrna and John. Carrie and John remained theological nemeses, staying up late into the night arguing about the relevance of religion and the existence of God. Myrna and her cousin sat back and watched as they sipped wine. At some point they would look at each other and smile, relieved their upbringing left them free of this baggage their spouses carried on their backs.

Following the theological discussion, the couples retreated to their homes. Myrna helped John rediscover his Zen. Carrie made use of her husband to prove she was no longer uncomfortable with her sexuality (or as she would say, her horniness), even while she held on to her moral beliefs.

Myrna and John never had any children of their own. Instead they adopted four orphans Myrna met while doing her work. She located two for Carrie as well. John and Myrna didn't share why they hadn't had any children of their own. Some guessed it was because they couldn't, while others said it was because, for whatever reason, they had no desire. They never spoke of it because they didn't want to diminish their relationships with the children they did have and considered to be their own.

As for Thomas and Sammy; their summer in Chicago went well. The sex therapy improved their performance in the bedroom, the living room, the dining room, Sammy's office, and the park bench hidden behind the overgrown bushes. Finding new venues was one of the pieces of advice the therapist offered that made sense to Thomas. They worked on the relationship as well, trying to squeeze a bit more mutuality and empathy from Thomas. He was successful when he focused his attention on the effort, but as soon as he turned his attention away in the slightest degree, he slipped back into his old selfish patterns. He made it through the summer living Sammy's way which was more than anyone expected of him; including Sammy.

He returned to Arcada at the beginning of the academic year, only to be surprised by a phone call informing him of his greatest accomplishment of this summer of love. Sammy gave him, in actuality she shouted it at him as though he had committed an intentional crime against her, the disturbing news he had made her pregnant against her will.

Dumbfounded, his response was, "How did that happen? It must have been that damn park bench. I was nervous about getting caught."

"What the hell kind of a response is that, Thomas?" Sammy said. "Nerves don't circumvent a condom nor do they alter hormones."

"What the hell do you want me to say?"

"Try telling me you love me."

"You know I do."

"But that doesn't mean you want to have a baby with me, right?"

"I think that question is a bit irrelevant at this point. Unless you are thinking about..."

Sammy cut him off. "Don't you dare go there!"

"Mom will be thrilled. She'll be ecstatic to have a grand-baby that comes from someone other than Peter; even better a grand-baby that comes from you; her favorite daughter."

Sammy moved to Arcada after the baby was born. They tried living together, but discovered having their own places worked better for all of them. So they built a creative duplex and settled next to each other. Their daughter, Izzy, short for Isabel, had a large bedroom from which she could access both houses. Another door provided access to both houses through the enclosed pool patio. Dundee, actually Dundee III, had free roam of both homes through both portals.

Although Sammy and Thomas never married, they stayed monogamous lovers, accessing each other through the common back entrance when the desire was aroused – or when Thomas desired to paint her naked body, whose wrinkles he used to give her beauty the depth he had come to see.

Julie stayed friends with Sammy, visiting her several times a year. The visits always began with a short penance session for Thomas, where the women blamed him for the ills of all men. It seems Julie wasn't done picking selfish men. Her only consolation was she never married any of them; exiting her relationships with the same huff with which she left Thomas behind. Thomas was always glad to see her. He joked he did better with two girlfriends in his life. Sammy continued to possess karate kid feet.

The family didn't know what to call Sammy and Thomas' relationship until Richie overheard his father Peter complaining about the arrangement. "I think people call it friends with benefits, Dad. Ask Grandma. I think she has a friendship like Uncle Thomas and Aunt Sammy."

"You don't know what kind of relationship your Grandmother has with her boyfriend." Peter attempted denial to protect himself and for the sake of his children.

"You might not know, Dad. But the rest of the world does. And, might I add, no one cares."

"I should have never let you meet your Uncle Thomas. Big mistake on my part."

"What are you talking about? He is my favorite uncle. He helped get me into Humboldt – into their art program. I loved taking his classes. Besides, he has Aunt Sammy and she's a hottie, even at 60."

"Like I said; it was a big mistake on my part."

"Mom thinks he is cool; well she says he can be an ass sometimes, but Aunt Sammy makes up for him."

"Your Mom doesn't know him as well as I do."

"Mom says you have to get over yourself. He is your brother."

"Well, your mother seems to believe in friends with benefits as well, so it doesn't surprise me she would take that tone."

"Move on Dad, will you. Just move on."

Moving on hadn't been easy for Peter. Five years after his father died, Sandy had asked him for a divorce after meeting someone else. They had become detached from each other and Sandy wanted more. She attempted to draw Peter back toward her, but he was engrossed in his work at the church. He begged her not to leave and she acquiesced for a while. Unfortunately, she only acquiesced long enough to slip into an affair with her devotee, leaving Peter and the children devastated. The children adjusted, but Peter flailed. He resigned as minister of his church, only to begin again somewhere else, where grace would be more available to him. For the sake of the children he softened toward Sandy, allowing his resentment to flare up only upon rare occasions.

It would have been easier on him if Sandy could have given him good reason for her departure, something he could hang his hat on in order to be at peace with the whole matter. She tried, but found none of her reasons were good enough for him. Her last and perhaps most honest explanation to Peter was rooted in his trip to Michigan for the weekend that ended in his father's death. "I wanted to have phone sex with you, Peter. I wasn't joking. You blew me off, no matter how much I tried."

"But you were joking."

"Only because you wouldn't take me serious, and that is the story of our relationship."

Realizing there wasn't a good enough reason for Peter, she desisted and just took the blame upon herself, agreeing she was troubled.

Peter tried to accept that, but understood it was only true in part. He knew deep down he had always made her uncomfortable around him, as though she wasn't good enough, which he also did to his children, which his father had done to him while sitting at the dinner table where he always felt as though he didn't belong. He knew he wasn't his father; but he had come to realize he was a kinder version of him. The question he had was whether or not this softer version of his father was an improvement; or an even more twisted version of the same? He didn't know. All he could do was try and soften his opinions, in hope that his judgments would follow suit. But how does a person live with such compromise? Can a person feel good about choosing relationship over righteousness? Or more aptly put, does a righteous warrior always end up alone – on a cross – like Jesus?

The Vanderhuis family snuggled closer to each other, surrounding Fran's urn in an attempt to stay warm and console each other. A tall, thin woman approached the family, struggling to keep her balance in the wind and sand. She was dressed in tights, covered by a disheveled flowered dress that flapped in the wind, causing the gaudy strands of beads she wore to bounce on her flat, boney chest. She held the beads down with her right hand and with her left she pushed back her short tousled grey hair to keep it out of her eyes.

"This must be the Vanderhuis family gathering," she said when she reached the group.

They looked up; surprised she was there to see them.

"That would be us," Thomas spoke up. "Who might you be?"

"My name is Marcia," she said. "I was a friend of your mother's."

The group stared at her with a blank look.

"A friend my ass," Thomas said. "You're her therapist; the one that helped Eddie dump our asshole of a father. Job well done. You must be a hell of a shrink, because you managed to help her turn her life around 180 degrees."

"Still with the ponytail; it suites you even at this age," Marcia said. "You're Mother said I would like you. I had my doubts, but maybe she was right."

Sammy jumped up and shook Marcia's hand. "Hi, I'm Sammy."

"You're the polka dotted bikini who set the house on fire, aren't you?" Marcia said.

Sammy's face turned red. "Fran said that about me?"

"Sorry, I couldn't resist. You still look like you could wear that bikini. Fran was always jealous of your figure. I don't know why, since she had a perfectly fine one herself. But enough of that, my instructions were to avoid giving away any secrets that could get your mother in trouble."

"Eddie asked you to come here?" Peter said.

The group made room and Marcia took a seat in the sand. The group wondered how she was going to crunch her old body into a seated position on the ground. She began in a controlled manner, but halfway down she just let herself fall.

"A couple of you will have to get me up from here. As to your question, the answer is yes. She insisted I come. She could be a pushy broad. Not too many people can make this old lady do anything she doesn't want to do. I never did figure out how she let your father push her around for forty years." She shuffled her bottom in the sand in an attempt to find a more comfortable position. "She wanted me to come to the church for the funeral service. I told her there was no way in hell that was going to happen. Churches creep me out."

"I'll vouch for that," Thomas said.

"Your mother's solution was to skip the church service and go straight to this beach where she wanted her ashes to be scattered."

"Why did she want you to come?" John asked.

"I'm not certain. She said she wanted me to meet you. We've discussed you for so long I feel like part of this family."

"This family will do that to you," Sammy said.

"She wanted me to make sure you all knew how much she loved you, but I'm sure you know that by now."

"That's odd," Peter said. "Why would she send a total stranger to tell us she loved us?"

"I don't know. The sense I got was your mother wanted to take care of us."

"Us?" Peter said.

"Your mother was a caregiver at heart. She took care of everyone, if they let her. I think she wanted me to step in and take her place with you. She worried about you and she couldn't help herself from trying to help me find the family she insisted I needed."

"She gave you us?" Thomas said. "What a cruel joke."

"Not in your mother's eyes, Thomas." Marcia scanned the family with her eyes, while she extended her hands with her palms up. "She wanted to give me her most precious possession. That's a hell of a gift."

A long silence made way for the tears that filled everyone's eyes.

"It's getting late," Peter said. He was about to pick up the urn to move things along before people started to experience the symptoms of frostbite, when Sammy inquired about John and the grandkids whereabouts. Everyone looked around and were surprised they had been able to slip away unnoticed. They turned in circles, scanning the shoreline and the foot of the dunes, but found it barren as it usually is at this time of the year.

It was Sammy who heard them first, waving their hands and yelling at the top of their voices while they jumped up and down hoping to catch the rest of the family's attention. "Look, up there, on the top of that dune." She pointed the group in the right direction.

"What are they saying?" Peter asked.

"I think they are saying 'this is for Grandma Fran' or something like that." Sammy replied. "Okay!" she waved in order to acknowledge they had been heard.

The kids, led by John, hoisted themselves into the headstand position in honor of their Grandma Fran, while Dundee III ran circles around them. Fran had loved the headstand more than any other yoga position John had taught her. She had worked hard for over a year to master it and had held that position daily for five minutes until her body would no longer cooperate.

When John asked her why she loved it so much, she replied, "When you came home for the weekend on which your father died, I saw you standing on your head. You looked ridiculous, but you also looked at peace and satisfied. I decided then and there that this was going to be my one thing."

"Your one thing?"

"You remember, don't you? Marcia told me I had to pick one thing to do different on that weekend in order to start a chain reaction. I decided standing on my head was going to be mine. If you want a new life, you have to be willing to turn yourself upside down. So I have done it every day since you taught me."

"But Marcia said you were supposed to do something different on that weekend."

"I did. I made up my mind I was going to get you to teach me to do what you were doing, and that was enough to spark things in me, don't you think?"

"I can't argue with that, Mom. You did turn things upside down on that weekend."

The family looked up and marveled at the sight. John stood straight and steady in the middle. Fran's great grandchildren wobbled on both sides of him. Later, when he was asked how he had managed to get them to cooperate and learn to stand on their heads, he replied, "I tried to get them to do it for Mom, but they weren't buying it. You know, Mom wasn't all that endearing to the kids. So I resorted to manipulation. I told them they would be pansies for life if they didn't do this. If an old granny can do it, and they can't, then shame on them."

"It worked?" Thomas asked.

"You saw them."

One by one the kids began to fall over and tumble down the dune. At first the adults were worried, but when they heard the laughter of the falling children and saw that when they managed to come to a stop, they threw themselves forward so they could continue to roll down the dune, they relaxed and laughed with them. At the bottom, they gathered and began to chant. "Uncle John, Grandpa, Dad, Uncle John, Grandpa, Dad..."

Thomas took several steps forward and yelled at the top of his voice, "Do it for Mom!"

With that John let himself fall forward, but instead of curling up into a ball and rolling down the dune, he let himself collapse on his back into the sand. At sixty-five, rolling down a dune could cause serious damage. Instead he stood up and began walking down the dune. The kid's kept egging him on, calling him a pansy, and so half way down the dune he began to jog the rest of the way, allowing himself to fall into the welcoming group of children and be mobbed and tackled once he arrived at the bottom.

Once things calmed down, they returned to the circle surrounding Fran's urn. One by one they took turns recalling memories of her. John spoke of the long talks they shared in private. Peter spoke of how she had loved this beach so much and the fun they had playing here as a family. Thomas reminisced of the oregano laced brownies she never stopped making for him. And Sammy; Sammy just cried while she spoke to Fran. "I hope you know what a great mother you were to me. I hope you believed me when I told you. I need you to know that, Fran; Mom."

Sammy did the honors and spread the ashes. First she had the great grandkids dig a hole as deep as they could. She proceeded to pour the ashes into the hole from a shoulder high position, letting the wind blow most of them away to be mixed with the sand forever. The kids that were down wind, scampered to get out of the way of the blowing ashes. Diana, Peter's six year old granddaughter, was not quick enough and breathed in the dust. She spat, while brushing off her tongue. "Shit!" she said. "I think I just ate grandma."

The family looked for Peter's response. He wanted to say, 'One weekend in a house with you Thomas, and she is cussing like a barmaid.' But he held himself in check. He forced himself to forget about the expletive and joined the group in laughing with his granddaughter.

Sammy then closed the urn and the kids filled in the hole.

Everyone went home except for the sons and their wives. Thomas retrieved a cooler he had stashed in the dunes and began to offer everyone a beer. They popped the lids and raised their bottles to the center where they touched.

"Just a minute; everyone hold on." Peter went to the cooler and picked out another beer. He walked over to the place where Fran's ashes had been buried, popped the lid, and bent over, placing the bottle of beer in the sand above Fran. He came back to the circle and said, "Mom would want to be included in this."

They watched in silence as Dundee III sauntered over to the bottle of beer and lingered to investigate. He circled the beer bottle as his nose perused the sand.

"Call off your hound." Peter starred at Thomas.

"Would you rather he sniffs your crotch?"

Dundee III circled faster, shaking with excitement.

"For God's sake, Thomas. He is going to pee on Mom's grave," Peter said.

"He loved Eddie. It is his way of expressing his devotion to her; putting his mark on her."

"Well I don't like it." Peter stood.

Dundee III stopped, dropped to the ground, and curled up into a ball. He looked at the mourners, laid down his head in the sand, and let out a sigh, blowing the sand away from his brown nostrils.

"Satisfied?"

Peter sat down and starred at the sand.

"You know why she picked this place, don't you?" Thomas asked.

"She liked this place because it holds good memories for her." John said.

"True, but there is more to it."

"Alright, let's hear it." Peter said.

"This was the one place Dad would never set foot. You remember the one time he came here looking for us."

John laughed. "He was dressed in a suit and didn't even take off his shoes. He looked like a black man in China."

"He didn't know what to do. You could tell he knew he had made a mistake and just wanted to leave," Peter said.

"It was the only time I ever saw Mom with the upper hand." John said. "I think she chose this place because she wanted to be far away from him – maybe even safe from him."

"Maybe we should all be buried here," Peter said.

"Maybe so; with Mom," John said.

"She would like that," Sammy said. "And so would I."

"I take that to be your formal rejection of the extra plot next to Dad?" John said.

"I'm making it official," Sammy said.

They laughed and finished their beers.

About the Artist

Professional Artist Christi Dreese was born and raised in West Michigan and has been involved in the arts since she was a child. She spent summers as a young girl on her father's boat coasting along Lake Michigan. It was there she grew to love the calm waters, sunsets, and relaxed atmosphere. Many of her oil paintings are inspired by the Lake Michigan coastline.

Along with Christi's passion for the lakeshore, she has found abstract to be a great emotional release and different creative process from her impressionistic landscapes. Every work of art is inspired by her thoughts and feelings.

Christi received her Bachelor of Art degree at Aquinas College in Grand Rapids, emphasizing in painting, and also attained a business administration major.

Christi's love for the arts, lakeshore and personal growth continues to inspire her to create new works of art and have purpose in life.   www.dreesefineart.com

About the Author

Stephen Nauta's experience of 18 years as a missionary's kid in the Dominican Republic (the land of cuentos), 12 years working as a social worker amongst youth with troubled histories, 10 years telling stories from the pulpit of a conservative protestant church, and 8 years as a psychotherapist collaborating with clients in the rewriting of their personal histories has left him brimming with stories of the human saga. Sitting at the Wrong Dinner Table is one of these tales.

Stephen lives, works, and writes at Isabel's House in Spring Lake, Michigan.

Stephen Nauta at Duck Lake Channel.

Steve's Future Book Projects

Self-Help

PARALLEL CO-PARENTING

An innovative approach to parenting for divorced couples who find it difficult, if not impossible, to be in the same room with each other.

Children's Books

"HELP, THERE'S A MONSTER IN MY HEAD"

The story about a young girl's struggle to overcome anxiety.

STUMPY GRUMPY

A children's book about the healing power of gratitude.

STREAMER THE DREAMER

The story about a young boy's friendship with his imagination.

Next Novel

SECOND PLACE

A promising athlete makes a surprising move when he gives
away his gold medal to his Chinese rival. His decision is met
with a barrage of hostility. He is forced to go into hiding.
There he attracts a dubious band of groupies that aide him in
his quest to understand his intuitive decision to quit his
enviable life.

For more information about these books,
please visit stephennauta.com or
isabelshouseupstairs.com.